GRAND CENTRAL
PUBLISHING

LARGE
PRINT

Anthem

A Novel

Noah Hawley

GRAND CENTRAL
PUBLISHING
LARGE PRINT

Cover design ay Alex Merto
Cover photos © Getty Images
Cover copyright © 2022 by Hachette Book Group, Inc.

Grand Central Publishing
Hachette Book Group
1290 Avenue of the Americas, New York, NY 10104
grandcentralpublishing.com
twitter.com/grandcentralpub

First edition: January 2022

Grand Central Publishing is a division of Hachette Book Group, Inc. The Grand Central Publishing name and logo is a trademark of Hachette Book Group, Inc.

The publisher is not responsible for websites (or their content) that are not owned by the publisher.

The Hachette Speakers Bureau provides a wide range of authors for speaking events. To find out more, go to www.hachettespeakersbureau.com or call (866) 376-6591.

Print book interior design by Sean Ford

Library of Congress Cataloging-in-Publication Data

Names: Hawley, Noah, author.
Title: Anthem : a novel / Noah Hawley.
Description: New York : Grand Central Publishing, 2022.
Identifiers: LCCN 2021033391 | ISBN 9781538711514 (hardcover) | ISBN 9781538710234 | ISBN 9781538711507 (ebook)
Classification: LCC PS3558.A8234 A83 2022 | DDC 813/.54—dc23

LC record available at https://lccn.loc.gov/2021033391

ISBNs: 9781538711514 (hardcover), 9781538711507 (ebook), 9781538710234 (large print)

Printed in the United States of America

LSC-C

Printing 1, 2021

For Guinevere and Lev. Do your best please.

Author's Note

This book contains math. Not calculus or trigonometry—no dense columns of equations—but numbers arranged in order, divided or multiplied, added or subtracted. You will find the odd fraction, the occasional % or $. The math in question is employed—like all symbols in this book—to convey ideas. For example: A century is made up of 100 years. A year is made up of 365 days. There are 24 hours in a day. We use these numbers (24 x 365 x 100) to measure human history. And yet few of the bipedal animals we call human beings live for 100 years. Statistically, the life span for an average male living in the United States of America is 72.4 years. The average American female lives 76.6 years. In Congo, men can expect to live to 55.7. In China the typical woman will make it to 66.3. This is the math of our existence.

At the time of this writing, I, the author, am 53

years old, which means I was born in 1967, a little over half a century ago. A half century before my birth was the year 1917.

½ century + ½ century = 1 century.

That is an objective measure of time. But time is subjective, which is why, as I age, the year 1917 seems more and more like ancient history. A long, long time ago: before the treaty of Versailles and the end of the first World War, before Influenza killed 22 million people worldwide, before prohibition, before the Great Depression and the Dust Bowl, before big band and swing music, before the Second World War and the Korean War, before the birth of rock and roll and the British Invasion, before Elvis, before the Cold War and the Kennedy Assassination, before Levittown and the rise of the middle class, before a chicken in every pot, before mechanization, before television, before penicillin.

53 + 53 = a different era, in other words.

Logic would dictate, then, that the year 1967 must—to most non-53-year-old human beings to-day—also feel like ancient history. Before *peace with honor* ended the Vietnam War, before the Summer of Love and the Manson murders, before Watergate, before the Great Recession of the 1970s, before the Reagan revolution and trickle-down economics, before the personal computer and the internet, before the first George Bush presidency and the second, before globalization, before the ATM, before the Clinton impeachment and the Obama presidency, before the cell phone, the tablet, before Siri and Alexa, before the global financial crash, before the gig economy, before the resurgence of nationalism, before the 45th president, before COVID-19, before Apple, before Google, before Amazon.

Before most things we consider to be modern. In summation—

1967 = ancient history.

Realizing this makes your author feel old, old, old. Or, as his mother might say—

Boo phooey.

The phrase *boo phooey* comes from a children's book the author's mother used to read to him in his youth. The book was called *The Thing in Dolores' Piano*. It was the story of young Dolores who played the piano so terribly that the *Do* note came out and begged her to stop. When she wouldn't, the *Do* note locked the keyboard.

Dolores couldn't play a single note.

But Dolores was eight and refused to surrender to the will of others. She followed the *Do* note back inside the piano, moving from room to room, encountering all the other notes (*fa, so, la, ti*), demanding they release her piano to her so she could play. Each note refused. Dolores felt an unfamiliar emotion; despair. It was a feeling she rejected, as any strong-willed child would. Inside a pitch-black room, Dolores discovered something. A note so monstrous the other notes had locked it away. *Aha*, thought Dolores, who knew an advantage when she saw one. She threatened to let the monster out unless the other notes unlocked her keyboard, unless they surrendered to her will. The monster was horrible. The monster was terrifying. The other notes had no choice but to concede. They unlocked the piano. Dolores had won. She returned to the outside world and resumed her assault on music itself.

At which point a chorus of voices rose from the piano. They shouted as one. And what they shouted was—

Boo phooey.

By which they meant, *We don't like the way this story has ended. You were a bad sport and a bully. You forced your will on us, and we don't think that's right.* By which they meant, *Life is unfair.*

The author's son says this a lot. He too is eight. *That's not fair*, he says. By which he means, *I didn't get what I wanted.* Or, *My sister got to do something that I didn't.* This idea of fairness exists nowhere else in the animal kingdom. The dinosaurs went extinct, and none of them said *boo phooey.*

The last dodo passed from the face of the Earth, and none of them said *boo phooey*. All around us, the honeybees are fading from existence, the frogs are vanishing. Neither species gives their fate a bitter thought.

Imminent danger they understand. *Mortality* is beyond them.

We discuss their lives and deaths in terms of numbers. Three thousand African elephants remain in the wild, two hundred snow leopards. Each death is an act of subtraction. Each birth an act of addition.

Be fruitful and multiply, God told Moses.

Divide and conquer, said the generals.

You do the math.

Now, your author understands that math is not why readers read novels. He asks your indulgence and your patience and promises that there is more to this story than numbers. There is drama. There is catharsis. Everywhere you look in this book, you will find people. People in need. People who want what you want—to feel safe, to be loved, to do unto others as they would have others do unto them. Each of their deaths is an act of subtraction.

This is their story. And if you don't like it, your author encourages you to put the book down and shout—

Boo phooey.

Anyone who can make you believe absurdities can make you commit atrocities.

—Voltaire

"I had my hand on a metal base-ball bat, just in case," said Nate, twelve. "'Cause I was going to go down fighting if I was going to go down."

—*New York Times*, May 9, 2019

Anthem

Before

The Nadirs

There they are, America's future. Alone at first, then all together.

PS29, Brooklyn. The hushed reverence of boredom commonly known as a children's recital. It's 6:00 p.m. on a Thursday. The elementary school auditorium is like a chapel, a nondenominational holy space where adults congregate to worship the promise of their young. Piano, piano, dance troupe, Mozart violin screech, inappropriately suggestive pop ballad, ginger magician. It's April 2009, and the stock market is spiraling. Parents sit on folding chairs, trying to shake off the muffled outrage of their commute long enough to experience the emotional transcendence of *actually being present*, while at the same time recording young Sasha or Liam or Nicole's musical efforts onto a digital medium, never to be seen again. Beside them, older siblings slump, locked in the broad Kabuki of their tedium. Peppered through the crowd, clots of younger siblings fidget and whine, feet dangling, caught in the witching hour of their bedtime. They are two kinds of difficult—jittery from hurried car snacks or slumped in butter noodle lethargy.

The stock market fell 325 points today. It will fall 325 more tomorrow. You can smell the panic in the air.

Judge Margot Nadir sits fourth row center with her second husband, Remy. There is a sculpted plastic infant carrier on the seat next to him. Inside, their ten-month-old son is sleeping, for now, chirping his somnolent baby nonsense. That constant runner of gasps and clucks, what the judge and her husband have come to realize for young Hadrian are simply the sounds of being alive.

Judge Nadir. It is a term of address she is still getting used to, having been appointed to the federal bench late last year following a high-profile career as an assistant US attorney in lower Manhattan. Now—instead of battling traffic every morning in sneakers, her dress shoes stuffed inside her tote— she dons the robes at Cadman Plaza, *hear ye, hear ye,* the newest distinguished justice of the US District Court for the Eastern District—having been transported from their apartment in Brooklyn Heights in an official black car.

After years of advocating a position, her opinions

are now recorded as law. She has become *the Decider*. It is a power they joke about at home— Remy reminding her she's only called *your honor* at work. *At home*, he says, *we make decisions together*. And she smiles and says *of course*, because she wants him to feel heard. They are still in the honeymoon phase of their marriage. Twenty-two months. Thirty if you add in the courtship. Long enough to cohabitate and have a baby but not long enough to learn all the tier-one secrets.

It is the second marriage for her, the first for him. Remy arrived with a record collection. She came with a six-year-old daughter.

Onstage the curtain flutters, nervous third and fourth graders peering out through the gap. Judge Nadir unfolds the paper program handed to her on the way in by a young girl in a wheelchair. She scans the list of names, finds her daughter, Story, who turned nine on Saturday. She's listed first of twelve. A wave of relief passes over the judge. Maybe they can slip out before the medley from *Phantom of the Opera* and make it home in time for some kind of decent meal. The judge has an opinion to finish tonight, and she doesn't want to be up until all hours writing.

The People v. Gary Fey. Tax evasion and money laundering. It's what people with money do these days. Invent a latticework of shell companies and funnel their millions offshore. Divorce among the rich has become a matter of international intrigue.

Remy reaches over and squeezes her hand.

"Good day?" he says.

"You know—" she says, meaning there's too much to say about the weight of the world in this place, at this time.

He nods, takes a lollipop from his pocket, unwraps it. Remy has a low blood sugar affliction—not diabetes but diabetes adjacent. Rather than seek medical supervision, he has devised a self-care plan that seems sketchy at best, something people on the internet swear by. Margot doesn't like it, but part of marriage is looking the other way when your spouse engages in patterns of questionable behavior, so as to *accept the other person for who he is.*

They came separately, she and Remy—Margot from the courthouse and he from home, giving himself time to stop for a much-needed cup of coffee. Before leaving the apartment on Pineapple Street, he did the OCD pat—wallet, keys, phone—and then, slinging his semi-masculine baby bag over his shoulder, he stepped out into the early-fall chill, lugging Hadrian's rear-facing car seat and snapping it into the Nordic stroller, hearing that satisfying mechanical *clatch.*

Together they headed out past the playground

and the promenade, working their way south on Henry. Remy waited for the light at Atlantic Avenue, even as others jaywalked, aware that he is a Black man pushing a $1200 stroller in an affluent white neighborhood. Light-skinned, but still— a Black man on foot in the Heights.

The baby, on the other hand, was dark skinned enough at birth to have given Remy pause. A wild thought went through his head in the hospital nursery—*did my wife have an affair with a Black guy?*—before realizing that the Black guy was, in fact, *him* and that his son's coloring must have been a recessive gene passed down from his mother's side. At that moment, a seed of worry was planted inside him, a worry unfamiliar to white parents. Because, though there is a Black man in the White House these days, it doesn't make his son safe. The signs read HOPE, after all. Not EXPECT or DEMAND. As if the promise of a better world could still be discussed only in the language of dreams.

In the auditorium, Remy pulls the blanket up over the baby and tucks it into the corners of the space-age pod. He is still getting used to this. To being a husband, a father, a stepfather, still getting used to being a federal judge's spouse, a position that arrived with background checks and routine threat briefings. If you asked him what he does, he would say he is a writer, working on a book about

William F. Buckley, father of modern conserva-
tism. But the truth is, he is a stay-at-home dad with
a writing problem.

They belong to the party of Lincoln, he and
Margot. She a Stanford grad and he a product of
George Washington University, raised by a union
plumber and a registered nurse, both believers in
the struggle, supporters of a safety net. And yet
something about the community he grew up in felt
aggrieved and self-pitying, this constant lamenting
about how *the man was keeping a brother down*.
Remy wanted his street to be safer, his classmates
to be more respectful. Opportunity, wealth, pres-
tige, these were his ideals. He rejected the burden
of history he was told he had to shoulder, replacing
it with the mythos of personal achievement. Today
Remy believes that his success is a product of individual effort. He made good choices. He worked
hard. Everything else is just an excuse.

In the center aisle, a family of three arrives late,
sidestepping the row to their seats. Remy plays
pickup basketball with the husband a couple of
times a week, and they nod to each other the
way men do. The crowd is at fever pitch now,
a white noise of voices—child sopranos laughing
and sharing screens, investment banker father's
whiskey-sweating through their shirts, engaged in
a   denial-anger-bargaining-depression-acceptance

spiral with their cell phones, the younger kids running and playing, deaf to the worry on their parents' faces.

The lights flash, signaling the event is about to get underway. People move to take their seats. A group of unvaccinated third graders clamber down the aisle to join their renegade families. They are biologically unprepared for mumps or measles, chicken pox or rubella, but anecdotally free from the whispered threat of autism.

Everybody has a theory, Judge Nadir has come to believe. A conviction, dogged and tenacious, which they refuse to surrender. This is the American way. We have home remedies we swear by, superstitions we will not renounce. We are optimists or pessimists, trusting or suspicious. We confirm our theories online. The internet, invented to "democratize information," has turned out, instead, to be a tool of self-affirmation. Whether you believe you're suffering from chronic fatigue syndrome or that 9/11 was an inside job, the World Wide Web exists to tell you you're right.

You are always right.

It is making the laws harder to enforce, Margot has noticed. Lately she has found an increasing number of defendants who refuse even to recognize the authority of the court. They talk about the Fourteenth Amendment, about the facade of the federal government. *What qualifies judges and lawyers to say what's legal and illegal, what's right and wrong?* Like some kind of Kafka meets Abbott and Costello routine. *Every American*, they write in their self-defended briefs, *is an institution, a judge capable of deciding for themselves what path to follow, what truth to believe.*

Which, while existentially true, is not how society works. And certainly not how the American judicial system—with its tiers of law enforcement, lawyers, judges, prisons, and parole officers—was designed to function.

The curtain opens. Miss Cindy comes out onstage, smiling nervously. She thanks them for coming and shills the bake sale upcoming.

"Just a reminder," she says, "that there's no school next Thursday or Friday for parent-teacher conferences."

A collective groan rises from the crowd—the involuntary sound of adults who have neglected something critical, in this case scheduling childcare for unprotected workdays. Before Miss Cindy's even finished, smartphones have appeared, screens lighting up, messages of desperation sent into the void.

"And now please welcome Story Burr-Nadir."

And then Miss Cindy is gone and young Story steps out onto the stage.

There she stands, willowy and blond, with her impossible blue eyes and effortless human grace. Looking at her, Margot realizes she's holding her breath. A nine-year-old girl is a weightless butter- fly—hair brushed imperfectly, adult teeth still too big for the mouth—and yet possessing a rare, fleeting beauty, like a newborn colt, legs comically long, but walking immediately, miraculously. So many critical systems are still forming for girls of this age, the paper-thin wings of their identity. Story is on the small side, just eyes and a smile. She is a hater of dresses, freckles beginning to emerge from beneath the down of her skin. Her blond hair will turn brown one day, surrendering to genetics, but for now she wears a golden mane, her bangs blunt cut with construction scissors to a length (short) that still makes her mother cringe.

She steps into the light. It's clear from the micro- phone and piano accompaniment that she will be singing, but the song isn't listed in the program. Nor, Margot realizes, does she know exactly what her daughter has chosen. There was talk of a recent pop ballad, then talk of an old folk number, but in all the hurry of the day-to-day, mother and daugh- ter disconnected on this one critical issue. Like a Halloween costume unmade.

And yet here she is, about to sing.

Watching her, Margot experiences a moment of

dislocation, a sudden vertigo of distance, as if her nine-year-old daughter has unexpectedly become a stranger—an individual with a mind of her own, a life of her own (her own theories). And then the accompanist plays middle C and Story begins to sing.

"O say can you see, by the dawn's early light?"

Silence. And then—like a wildfire—as it becomes clear that Story Burr-Nadir is, in fact, singing the national anthem, parents spring to their feet. Military veterans and sports fans first, but the ascension spreads—most rising with legitimate patriotism, but some from a sense of obligation. Some even with resentment—*I just sat down*. Others with irony—*patriotism is so Midwestern*.

"—what so proudly we hailed, at the twilight's last gleaming."

Judge Nadir stands as if lifted. She stands the way the hair on the back of her neck stands, raised by a sudden wind of superstition—superstition in its purest, Old Testament form, a hallowed wave of *rightness*. As if this moment—in which her daughter has decided to give voice to the war-torn hopes of a new nation—combined with the surprise of hearing her sing it for the first time, has created a synchronicity of deep spiritual meaning. It is not a voluntary feeling. Not an intellectual choice. The judge spends her days sitting on a dais before an American flag. She herself is an American institution—*Her Honor*—steeped in the power and history of symbols.

"*—whose broad stripes and bright stars—*"

Later, they will eat ice cream on the promenade and watch construction crews on the night shift prepare the waterfront for the parks to come. They will laugh about Clive and his overweight Michael Jackson impersonation, and *wasn't Hannah's voice pretty*. As he bounces Hadrian in his arms, Remy will reenact the way Malcolm kept pulling up his pants. It is the first warm night of April. Families from all over the neighborhood are out on the streets. The traffic on the BQE has quieted. They eat mint chocolate chip and raspberry sorbet with rainbow sprinkles. Margot can't stop talking about how proud she is, how surprised she was.

"Did you see everybody standing?" she says.

"They had to stand, Mom," says Story. "It's the national anthem."

Margot meets her husband's eye and smiles. He smiles back, feeling both restless and content. *Content* because the idea of America when absorbed through imagery or idealistic song brings an almost overwhelming sense of identity, of belonging. A swell of national wonder. And *restless* because feelings are not facts, and the desire to belong, to *be* something, doesn't make that dream come true.

Hope.

From the promenade they can see the Statue of Liberty and the Empire State Building. They can see kids on scooters and kids on bikes. They can hear the happiness of boys on swings, vaulting up into the twilight, their feet kicking—*higher, higher.* It is the hour after dinner, when all the nannies have gone home for the night, when families cleave together with the illusion of permanence. A parent will always be a parent. A child will always be a child. Like a warm breeze that brings with it the feeling that happiness is a temperature.

Everything is all right. *Mommy's here.*

You don't have to worry. *Daddy's got you.*

As if time itself wasn't devouring every second, propelling the young toward old age and the elderly toward death. As if the parents themselves weren't once children, clinging to their own parents' legs. And their parents weren't toddlers themselves a few decades before. As if any moment could last forever, caught in midair, like a single note trembling without beginning or end, like

the home of the—

brave.

Book 1

Slow Violence

Now

The summer our children began to kill themselves was the hottest in history. Around the globe, the mercury soared. We argued about this, of course, on news networks and in op-eds, talking heads from both sides—their likenesses beamed to gas station flat-screens and airplane seatbacks—debating the definition of *heat*, of *history*, some arguing that the very idea of measuring temperature itself was a liberal ploy. Meanwhile, tornadoes plowed furrows through Midwestern cities, and sales of mobile air conditioners sparked riots in cities like Oslo and Reykjavík. This is who we had become by then, people who gathered in the rain, arguing over whether or not they were getting wet.

No one can say with certainty whose child was the first to go. Suicide, while tragic, has never been exactly rare among teenagers and young adults. We tend to think of it as a local phenomenon—

house by house, community by community. A playground peppered with stunned faces, school flags lowered to half-mast. Like any variation on death, we measure it in tears. Mothers and fathers hollowed out by grief, oblivious to the horns of other motorists as they idle at crosswalks long past green. Counselors brought in to minister to the existential heartbreak of friends and loved ones. *Why would they do that? Why couldn't I stop them? What else could we have done?* All the fundamental questions of human existence born from a solitary, self-annihilating act.

And something else. Fear.

Suicide, you see, is an idea. And like any idea, it can spread from person to person to person. Anyone who has ever stood at a great height and felt the impulse to jump recognizes the draw. And what is adolescence if not a great height from which we are all expected to jump? A precipice of hormones and doubt, of alienation and longing. No longer a child. Not yet grown. Trapped in the pain of becoming.

But what if you could make the pain stop?

What if the answer was not to endure the transition and all its adjacent misery but to end it?

After all, what lies at the end of adolescence if not the future? And as one pundit said on CNN recently, *The future isn't what it used to be.*

We had surrounded ourselves with technological miracles, but all they did was show us how primitive the human meat between our ears still was. Our problems had become Stone Age once more. Superstition, tribalism, et cetera.

All.

A single spark can start an inferno. Or it can flare harmlessly, like a firefly.

The difference is oxygen, kindling, and luck.

And the oxygen in this case was the contagiousness of ideas, the awful *stickiness* of self-murder that most of us failed to understand in that critical first wave. We were living in the age of the meme, after all. Children pledging themselves to Slender Man, leading their classmates into the mossy woods, kitchen knives in hand.

O

The Carpenters of Madison, Wisconsin, were the ones that people noticed first. On May 15, young Brad Carpenter, sixteen, fashioned a noose from an extension cord and hanged himself in the attic of the three-story Edwardian his parents had renovated six years earlier. His mother found him dangling, a stack of his underwear, laundered and folded, in her hands. Two days later, Todd Billings, seventeen, captain of the ski team, put a plastic bag over his head at the exact moment that Tim O'Malley, fifteen, mathlete, sliced a vein, then another, bleeding out into the bathroom sink. All were firstborn sons. Each drove a hand-me-down car. Todd died with his braces on. Brad's last regret was that he wouldn't live to see his acne clear up.

Each had written somewhere near the scene of their death the symbol *A11*.

What did it mean? Why those numbers, that letter?

In the next eight days, three more teenagers in Madison would die by their own hand—concern rising to panic among parents in the area. Wisconsin residents took to watching their children while they slept. They suggested that younger kids potty with the door open. Three counties over, the homecoming queen swallowed a bottle of pills, washing them down with vodka and Red Bull. At the southwestern tip of the state, five girls on the swim team made a suicide pact and jumped from the city hall clocktower.

CNN took notice. The *New York Times* published an exposé. Mental health professionals held hurriedly scheduled town halls, answering questions from corralled teenagers and their parents. People took to crossing themselves whenever their children left the room. Twitter and Facebook put headers on their homepages, listing phone numbers you could call. But still, we thought of suicide as a local phenomenon, even as we admitted that technology may have increased its reach.

In Travis County, Texas, Nadine Ort came home from work and found her sixteen-year-old daughter with a garbage bag over her head. The next morning Nadine's hair had turned from gray to white. Around the country, strangers held each other in public, crying until they were numb.

Delaware was next. Hawaii. On May 21 there was a cluster of twenty-five in Nebraska. A week later, forty-three teenagers killed themselves across the state of Missouri. If there were an emoji for this growing crisis, it would be the openmouthed scream. Newspapers filled with photographs of parents falling to their knees, their lips spread in an impossible O. All that nail-biting work, the investment of time, love, money. The sheer willpower it took to keep our children from suffocating in their cribs, from running into traffic, all those nights felting costumes for the school play, the hours spent driving them to playdates, hosting sleepovers, all the tears, the fights, pushing them to do their homework, the extracurriculars, soccer Saturdays, the onset of adolescent hormones, voices changing, hair growing on private areas, taking and retaking SAT prep courses, all the bullies and broken hearts. All of it wiped away with little more than a gesture.

Those of us yet untouched saw footage of their windy funerals and held our kids closer. We felt their foreheads and asked if they were feeling okay. We smelled their breath and looked at their eyes under bright lights. Was it drugs? Were they sad? Hopeless? They shrugged us off—teenagers to the end—and said they were fine. Some, though, broke down crying, racked with nerves, tired of fighting, drawn toward the ledge of some dark mystery— like sailors caught in a whirlpool, sucked down into the depths.

We held them and wept, fear building in our hearts.

Things were picking up speed.

In the next few weeks, when the trend had become first national, then global, we scoured the internet for theories. We read the news and analyses, as if our children's lives depended on it, which, of course, they did. We hushed our spouses on the way to supermarkets, turning up the radio whenever we heard the words *cry for help*. We read articles about the terrible costs of cyberbullying, about the perils of sexting. But these were but trees in a forest we couldn't yet see.

A11. What could it mean? Why did it keep appearing in suicide notes, scrawled on walls, written on bathroom mirrors in blood?

Three of the president's cabinet secretaries lost a

child in early June. And just like that, the national number reached one thousand kids a day. Movie stars recorded PSAs. High school classrooms took on a visible tension. Op-eds were written—*Is this the end?* It was, of course, just a few years earlier that the COVID-19 plague had swept the planet, locking us in our homes, dooming the elderly and the infirm to panicked suffocation, spurring the almost-civil war, the flashpoint of a brewing culture clash, where the word *mask* became an invocation or an insult.

Now we had to wonder, had the "Lost Year," that endless lockdown our children endured, had long-term mental health effects—all that computer schooling, the chronic fear of falling behind academically, socially, the endless months of heightened anxiety and uncertainty? But there was no way to know for sure, enmeshed as those factors were with "Stop the Steal" and the Big Lie, which had turned the country into a nation with two presidents—one legitimate and the other not—where QAnon shamans peeled back the layers of an invisible, untraceable fraud and patriots beat police officers with flagpoles. Our histories had been revised recently to highlight the stories of all Americans. Now they were being revised again in state houses across the country, angry crowds roiling at school board hearings, demanding a more patriotic curriculum. And so new textbooks were issued decreeing that accusations of racism were now themselves racist. This was who we had become, a nation of symbolic acts, where what "we" believed and what "they" believed were not just contrary, but opposite. Up is down; black is white. This final fracture of reality had given birth to an existential riddle: What skills must our children master to survive in a world where reality itself is polarized? Had this impossible struggle driven them mad?

Is that what A11 was supposed to mean?

Whatever the cause, we were reeling from a new plague now, a plague of surrender. A plague of fatigue. Conversation in public places stopped when teenagers arrived. No one knew what to say to their own children, let alone the children of others.

On May 25, finals began on college campuses around the country. Aggressive new policies were instituted. Harvard and Yale insisted on nightly inspections of all dorms, administrators looking for pills, blades, anything that could be used to aid in self-extermination. And yet each morning dozens more bodies were discovered. By the twenty-seventh, universities across the country closed, parents flying in on red-eyes, racing cross-country in Volvos to rescue their young.

Each child is precious, unique, but once the

phenomenon became widespread, their deaths became a statistic. We began to think of our children as a collective. To talk about them as a *generation,* desperate for some kind of lightning-strike insight. They *were* less connected, we told ourselves, to each other, to us, while conversely being more connected to the constant flow of mis-information that had become our society. Today's teenagers were having sex later. They were going out less, spending less time with their friends—less *physical* time—while staying connected to them electronically close to twenty-four hours a day. Was this a lingering vestige of the pandemic, or had some kind of deep fear of their fellow man settled in their bones, robbing them of the desire to touch? Was that the problem, a chronic sense of dislocation, a fatal remove, or something more immediate, a hidden trigger we couldn't see? We turned to our priests for answers, to our rabbis and imams, to statisticians and social scientists. They told us that rates of depression and anxiety dis-orders had been on the rise for years. Why were we just noticing now?

And yet to say that any of this was the cause of their deaths was speculation at best. A fumble in the dark. A way to comprehend the incomprehen-sible. Some said it was God's will, others the work of his counterpart who resides deep in the fiery pit.

Liberals pointed to elevated environmental toxins, to algae blooms in the Atlantic, to leaching plastics, even as the talking heads of right-wing media denied that suicide was a problem. They saw it as a false flag operation—even as their own children began to eat the gun, in a loop of cause and effect that would seem ironic if it weren't so tragic.

In the end all that mattered was that we were their parents.

It was our job to keep them safe, to make them happy, to keep them alive.

In June the phenomenon expanded. Young adults up to age twenty-five were declared *at risk*. Children as young as twelve. Parents took their kids' phones and tablets and smashed them with hammers. They canceled their social media accounts. Televisions were moved to the garage, newspaper subscriptions canceled. If this were a wildfire, we would starve it of oxygen, instituting blackout conditions. Still the death rate climbed, crossing oceans. Europe was first, then Russia and China. Financial markets nosedived. In July, Major League Baseball canceled the rest of the season.

With a virus, you could inoculate. You could isolate. You could watch for physical symptoms. But this—this was something heretofore unseen in human existence. An act of collective surrender. It felt to many of us as if the species itself was giving up. We took to sleeping in bed with our grown children, watching their chests rise and fall, listening for their breath, as if they were babies once more.

Help us, we prayed in the midnight silence. But to who? And why did no one answer?

The Olivers

Later, people would say that it was just like Claire to leave an essay in the wake of her death by pharmaceutical overdose entitled *Notes on the name "Claire"* in the place of a traditional suicide note. She had always been that person, smarter than you, a bit world-weary, like a character out of a Salinger short story. Her wit had bite. Her eyes held a knowing sadness. She had a way of talking to her father that resembled the slumped disappointment a PhD professor shows the worst student in her class. To properly transcribe their conversations, one would need to include a parenthetical *sigh* before each of her responses.

To wit—

Ty Oliver, father: "Claire, you understand we have rules in this house for a reason, yes? It's not just whim."

Claire Oliver, daughter: *(sigh)* "I understand that

the family unit is a body politic, like any social collective. And that within its infrastructure, there is a power base—i.e., you—whose sole ambition is both to retain your power at any cost and to *legitimize* said power in the minds of those who must adhere to it. To wit, you pressuring me to acknowledge your right to rule over me."

"Claire, dammit—"

Her father said these two words so often that Claire's younger brother, Simon, upon learning to speak, believed this was her name—*Claire Dammit*—and addressed her as such for months, much to the horror of his parents. Claire, however, was delighted and insisted well into his teenage years that Simon address her this way.

"Claire, dammit," her father continued, "can you just have the same conversation I'm having— for once? Which is that you, as my daughter and a seventeen-year-old sleeping under my roof, that when I say *Be home by midnight,* you say, *Yes, sir.*"

A kind of delight spread across Claire's face. Her sigh this time was more one of pleasure at having been proven right.

(*sigh*) "Sir, is it?"

"Claire—"

(*sigh*) "No, I get it. Alarmed by the tenuousness of your authority, you've increased your strongman tactics to try to intimidate me into falling in line. FYI, Daddio—that's not how a democracy works."

"A family is not a democracy."

(*sigh*) "My point exactly."

Her relationship with her mother was less Clarence Darrow versus William Jennings Bryan, and more Road Runner versus Wile E. Coyote, in that her mother was always trying to *recapture* Claire, to *domesticate her* into being her little girl once more, often physically—thus reenforcing her own delusion that Claire had once upon a time been naive and trusting, when what she had been from the moment she could crawl was independent, suspicious, aloof.

In the Oliver household, this was what passed for love.

"Trust me, kiddo," Claire would tell Simon whenever he would come into her room and lie on her bull's-eye rug reading his comic books, "you're better off taking the blue pill and staying in the Matrix. The minute you see through this whole mommy-daddy bullshit, your life is officially fucked. Pardon my French."

Later, when the truth began to come out about their parents, about what her father *did* for a living, not just a CEO, but a pusher, when details emerged about the internal emails he'd sent, the way he'd instructed the advertising and marketing division of Rise Pharmaceutical to encourage doctors to prescribe more pain pills at higher doses, even *after* the proven risk of addiction was clearly understood—that is to say before the stories appeared in newspapers, but while the journalists were digging around, asking questions—when their father started drinking earlier in the evening, coming home in a clear gin sweat, agitated, looking for a fight, that is, when their mother upped her dosage of Prozac and fell prey to fits of nervous knitting—Claire would sit outside her father's study and eavesdrop on his panicked phone calls.

"Old Ty is shitting the proverbial brick, *maintenant*," she'd tell Simon, then fourteen. And yet, though she herself knew the truth about the family business, she remained tight-lipped in front of Simon, aware perhaps that naivete was the most precious gift she could give him, the ability to complete his childhood with the belief intact that his parents were good and trustworthy people.

It's possible a similar motive was at play in the formation of her final words, a desire to protect Simon from the spectrum of what she understood to be her family's, and her own, terminal pathology. And yet the act itself—as tragic and *permanent* as it was—was still rich with irony. This too, her friends would later say, was classic Claire. For the way Claire chose to take her own life—a suicide that predated the global surge of adolescent self-murder by nine months—was to surreptitiously collect hundreds of oxycodone sample packs from her father's office over a period of weeks and then off herself in her parents' palatial, second-story bathroom. It was the first weekend of summer. Ty and Patty Oliver were in the Hamptons with young Simon. Horse shows and white parties, the Ogilveys and the Dunkirks, and the Nichols helicoptering in from the Cape. Claire begged off going, stating she had a hot date with the "starting lineup of the New York Knicks" and didn't think she'd be able to walk properly "for some time afterward." She watched them load their weekend valises into the town car for the drive to the heliport, given a hearty wave as they drove off. The last thing Simon saw, as he turned to wave back, was her wink.

You and me, kiddo.

He still sees the wink every time he closes his eyes.

O

Photographs of the scene, taken three days later, after her mother's frantic 911 call, showed the following:

The entirety of her parents' two-hundred-square-foot marble bathroom had been covered with small foil packets of oxycodone. They were glued in meticulous rows to the walls and ceiling, to the floor, the door, even the venetian glass mirror (leaving only a four-by-four square of exposed glass at her father's exact eye level, so that were he to stand in front of the mirror he would see himself framed against an art installation of his own culpability, his dead daughter visible slumped over in the red velvet chair she had dragged from her room onto the white bathroom tile, like a still from a Kubrick film).

She wore all white, our Claire, a satiny rope looped around her waist and tied in a bow at the back of the red chair. This was both gift wrapping and a practical means of keeping herself from tumbling to the floor as she lost consciousness. On her head sat a white tiara, pulling her hair back from her face and giving her corpse a *sad princess* air. The foil packets were white as well, a red *O* emblazoned in their center, so that the effect in the room was of hundreds of red *O*s staring in judgment at Claire's father, who stood in the doorway, slump-shouldered in abject human defeat, unable to look away from the precious life he'd made who had finally and for all time had the last word.

What she couldn't have counted on or predicted

was that it would be Simon who found her, as historically their parents' master suite was strictly *verboten* to the children. *On penalty of death.* But their mother had had a headache on the helicopter ride back to Manhattan, and upon entering the house, she had asked Simon to *be a dear* and run to her bathroom and *get Mommy's special pills.* Which he'd done immediately, a fourteen-year-old boy whose mind was still deep inside the twelve-hundred-page Chinese science fiction tome he'd been devouring on his iPhone since they'd left for Southhampton.

He took the stairs two at a time and opened the door to his parents' wing with trepidation, part of him worrying this whole thing was a trick and that his father would spring from the shadows, yelling, *What did we tell you about going into our room!* So, later Simon would have no memory of the state of the bedroom—was the bed made? Were there clothes thrown across the divan? His first real memory was of the bathroom door, how taped to it, dead center, was a small foil packet with a red *O* printed on it. It was a symbol he recognized vaguely without context, but he was moving quickly and didn't even slow, worried that if he took too long his mother would yell out from the bottom of the stairs, her cutting annoyance ringing through the house. And so, without pausing to examine the packet, he pushed open the bathroom door.

His sister sat slumped in the center of the room, a marionette in white with her strings cut. The absurdity of the tiara cleaved her black hair, so that it fell in a waterfall *around* her face, which was ducked from sight, as if in a deep bow. She had vomited in her lap at some point before her death, and the smell—thirteen hours old—filled the room. All around her, dozens of red eyes glared down on Simon, unblinking, like the eyes of the damned. A sound rose inside the room, a kind of keening air-raid siren of grief that bounced off all the hard surfaces of the palatial bathroom— a sound that Simon would later understand came from him—and shot back through Simon's body into the master suite like a sonic weapon.

Tucked into his sister's shirt pocket, folded like a pocket square, was a handwritten note on mono-grammed correspondence stock.

It read as follows:

Notes on the name Claire
or
What are we to do with this life we're given?

The kay *sound in modern phonetic speech remains the harshest of all consonants, both guttural and expressive. One could argue that all the best curse words begin with* kay*—Cunt,*

Kike, Cocksucker, *to name just a few. At the same time,* kay *is known to be the* funniest *hard consonant, a favorite of comedians from Mel Brooks to Larry David.*

As Neil Simon wrote in his play The Sunshine Boys:

> *Fifty-seven years in this business, you learn a few things. You know what words are funny and which words are not funny. Alka Seltzer is funny. You say "Alka Seltzer" you get a laugh…Words with "k" in them are funny. Casey Stengel, that's a funny name. Robert Taylor is not funny. Cupcake is funny. Tomato is not funny. Cookie is funny. Cucumber is funny. Car keys. Cleveland…Cleveland is funny. Maryland is not funny. Then, there's chicken. Chicken is funny. Pickle is funny. Cab is funny. Cockroach is funny—not if you get 'em, only if you say 'em.*

A 2015 study by the University of Alberta concluded that the effectiveness of verbal humor can be explained by whether or not the words used seem rude. Perhaps this is why the name Claire *has always felt like both an insult and the punchline to a joke.*

TAXONOMY

Claire is a skinny girl's name, some rigid blonde with pronounced cheekbones. It's the name of the girl in your elementary algebra class who always gets an A, the name of the girl whose mother paid kids to go to her daughter's birthday parties. You know Claire. She wears pearls and scallop-collared shirts. Her teeth are very white and extremely straight. At the same time, she has the kind of dark arm hair that comes from an eating disorder. Claire listens only to happy songs, so as to stave off the bottomless despair hidden deep within her psyche. What you don't know is that 87 percent of girls named Claire keep a ruler by their beds and wake multiple times in the night to measure the distance from the edge of the blanket to the box spring.

Fact: No one in history has ever said the words oh, Claire, fuck me, Claire, *in the heat of libidinal passion. And yet, once grown, Claire has fantasies of dating a boy whose penis is so large it can only be called a cock.*

She is afraid to buy a vibrator and similarly terrified of pudding.

Claire is the girl in your PE class who had the heaviest period. She played field hockey.

She had bangs. Claire sleeps in a flannel nightgown, even in summer. Her favorite candies are those colored sugar buttons that come on strips of waxed paper, because they are the only casual sweet arranged in perfectly symmetrical order.

Claire has always been too afraid to make a joke, because what if no one laughs?

Claire is the name of that woman in HR whose name no one can remember. It is the name of a female sitcom president who is incapable of connecting with the workingman. There are no poets named Claire. *Similarly, no woman has ever chosen* Claire *as her stripper name.*

There are no cats, dogs, ferrets, or parakeets named Claire. Human beings who transition from male to female never name themselves Claire, because—of all the female appellations—it is the most male. As proof one need only to look to the éclair, *the world's most phallic pastry (cock shaped and cream filled).*

Claire is the nickname you give that annoying girl in study hall, who lines her pencils up in perpendicular rows and won't stop asking what you got for number six on the final. It's the name your parents give you when they were hoping for a boy, and still—fingers crossed— think you could grow up to become one. It's what they name you when the position in the family they're looking to fill is that of rule follower, *of* daddy's little girl, *of* mommy's perfect darling. *Dammit, Claire, they say, whenever you show signs of independent thought. Dammit.*

Claire has always been a disappointment.

In summation, why go out the window, when you can use the door?

Later, alligators,

The girl formerly known as Claire.

PS. In heaven, all the angels are named Claire. They smile at you with kind eyes, wiping the tears from your cheeks, and say with music in their mouths, What took you so long?

Simon

Of all the mysteries of the universe—*what is the nature of time? Is there sentient life on other planets?*—the one we may never solve is the mystery of other people. *Why do we make the choices we make? How much of our identity is biology and how much is choice?* Simon Oliver considers these questions often as he is hyperventilating into a paper bag. There is something about sucking in his own carbon dioxide—light-headed, nose filled with the earthy brown essence of *sack*, ears fixed on the expansive paper crackle, as the receptacle for all his anxiety becomes a lung, ballooning and emptying—that bends his thought to the meaning of existence. *What is the value of this absurd slog?*

Then, as his breathing slows, as his oxygen-starved brain unclenches, he surrenders thought entirely, a wave of euphoric exhaustion crashing over him.

He has the meds, sure. Sertraline, Propofol, Effexor. But the bag is solid. The bag is trustworthy. The bag is an emergency brake, glass to smash in case of disaster—the world's simplest stress reliever, forcing his outtake to become intake, a simple biofeedback loop. So he keeps it packed in his pocket during daylight hours, folded under his pillow at night. It's his EpiPen, his defibrillator. Always the same bag. Its sameness is key. The bag has been with him for months now, since before Float, before the ever-tightening noose of adolescence that led to the panic attack and the private plane to a suburb of Chicago, where he has only vague memories of his check-in to the Float Anxiety Abatement Center. Otherwise known as "the great hold button." Finish high school? Hold. Go to college? Hold. Find a girlfriend? Hold. Inherit the world? Hold, hold, hold.

Instead he does equine therapy and strikes yoga poses. He plants seeds and picks vegetables in the garden. They have plushies and squeezies and weighted blankets and heated stuffies that smell like lavender, which you pop in the microwave. Objects of infant comfort, which is what they have become, babies once more, pampered and inconsolable.

Float is a self-sustaining community, empowering its charges with a sense of earth, of tactile action and reaction. *Being a teenager is already so abstract*, Lemon Holbrook, the founder of Float, believes. It is through grounded physical task and spiritual expansion that modern adolescents can be given the skills they need to handle the uncertainty and terror of today's world. Does it work? Simon can't say for sure, but he does feel less like a fingernail on a chalkboard most days. That is, until he thinks about going back out there, about his eight-hundred-square-foot bedroom on the top floor of a New York brownstone, about the elite prep school and the ever-escalating pressure to succeed. Until he thinks about the headlines and the lawsuits. About how his last name has become synonymous with greed, with addiction, with death.

Until he thinks about Claire.

He is fifteen years old. It's been ten months since he found her in his parents' bathroom. Ten months of going through the motions—school, hobbies, friends—insulated inside the ether of the rich, while outside the palace walls, the line between fact and fiction continued to soften. Out there, in the land they called *Main Street,* the God King still ruled. Even as the Kingdom of *Wall Street* prospered, as the wealthy bought third and fourth homes, as boats became yachts and yachts became islands, mythical creatures were born anew in the forested loam outside of lofty cities, warlocks and sorcerers rutting in dark places, trolls and goblins poisoning the rivers of reason. They bloomed under shadowy roots, like toadstools, hidden from sight. As newspaper editors in the land of plenty assigned missives on the return of the EPA— *protecting the land and the sea once more!*—orcs and ogres tunneled deep into underground chatrooms and Parler groups, biding their time. They knew what Obi-Wan knew—that by striking them down, we had only made them more powerful. And so, even as we saw the return of what university professors referred to as *normality*, it was only a simulation. A smiley face hiding the sickness underneath.

All the while the divide between reality and fantasy grew, but which was which?

Sometimes Simon wonders if it is his own kingdom that is living in a dream. The Kingdom of Wall Street, where educated men and women believe that if the residents of Main Street just had all the *facts,* they would see the world as we do. The delusion that science and reason are real, and, more important, that they *matter*. Perhaps this is the true definition of insanity. Not belief in an all-powerful God who created the universe in six days, not the unwavering superstition of a conspiratorial citizenry. No. Perhaps the Enlightenment itself was a psychotic break. The belief that all things could be measured. Maybe Galileo was the lunatic, Einstein.

In the Kingdom of Wall Street, a fourteen-year-old boy turned fifteen. His father took him to Switzerland to ski. All evidence of Claire had been removed from their home, her room converted to a gift wrapping station and decorated for the holidays. Her photos were drawered. Her name was verboten, as if her very existence before was a humiliation to her parents that must never be mentioned. Simon, too, was expected to hold his tongue, to banish her from his thoughts, the older sister who had held him in the night when he was afraid, who had taught him pig latin so they could share their own language.

One night in the living room at the ski lodge he found a book filled with facts. Not about Wall Street or Main Street, but about the Earth. Simon stayed up late reading.

This is what he learned:

1. The extra heat from all the carbon dioxide we've put into our atmosphere in the last one hundred years through the burning of fossil fuels is equivalent to four hundred thousand Hiroshima-size bombs exploding every day.

2. Combined it would create a column of solid carbon eighty-two feet in circumference that would rise all the way to the moon.
3. By 2050 the ocean will contain more plastic than fish by weight.
4. Endocrine disruptors in said plastics, shampoos, cosmetics, pesticides, canned foods, and ATM receipts have caused sperm counts to drop and women to suffer declining egg quality and more miscarriages.
5. In certain Chinese cities, the air is so thick with pollution that officials have installed giant video screens to show the sun rise.
6. In 2020 the weight of "human-made mass"—everything we've built and accumulated from cars to buildings to hairbrushes—exceeded the weight of biomass on the planet for the first time.
7. For example, there are nine gigatons of plastic on Earth and four gigatons of animals.
8. Eighty years from now the world's oceans will be so hot they will stop producing oxygen. Considering that two-thirds of all oxygen in our atmosphere is produced by phytoplankton in our oceans, this will signal the end of all life on Earth.

The end
of
all
life.

In the beginning there was Claire's death. Now, here in black-and-white, was the death of everyone and everything else. The Ur death. The death of a planet. And with it Simon's own death, suffocating on a molten, boiling ball of misery.

Did grown-ups know this? Had they read this book? Surely the whole planet was uniting to address the issue and undo the damage. Wall Street and Main Street were settling their differences to join forces against the death of all living things. And yet, back in New York, Simon wasn't so sure. He watched as his parents replaced his sister with clothes and technology, with the false comfort of *things*. As they continued to deny both her death and her life, even in the face of all evidence. And like a plant without water, Simon began to wither and die. The stress of keeping up appearances, of *pretending*, settled in his bones, and a great anxiety was born. He became The Boy Who Has Panic Attacks, terrified of everything, paralyzed by doubt. Life for him was a microphone left too close to a speaker, high tones rising, his posture stuck in constant cringe, anticipating the feedback screech.

One day Simon stopped getting out of bed. His parents sent him here, to the Spa of Ultimate Indulgence, in Wall Street's neighboring kingdom, *the Land of Self-Help*.

In the cafeteria he grabs a tray and a plate and studies the options. A saffron risotto, some kind of grilled fish. Snap peas are in season. Simon picked some himself just this morning, pushing his hand through leafy vines to find the green pods within. The dining hall is an atrium connected to a set of sliding glass garage doors, creating the illusion of a modern Italian villa.

He finds a seat at a courtyard table next to Louise. She's fifteen, Black, with no eyebrows. Her race makes her a rarity at Float, where the clientele resembles a string of pearls formed in tight spaces under intense pressure. So too does her moderate economic status, which sets her apart from Simon and all the other wan sufferers of affluenza whose summer-home-parents send care packages filled with French face creams and exotic vitamin supplements.

As Simon sits, she is holding a snap pea pod up to the light, studying the peas inside.

"I picked that," says Simon, "probably."

Louise lays it carefully back on the plate, all the pods aligned at a right angle from the carrot sticks. She wipes her silverware clean with her napkin.

Order is priority number one for her, immaculacy. Her plate is a kind of culinary Mondrian.

"What do you think all the normal kids are doing right now?" she asks him.

"Moving their thumbs."

He pokes at his food, trying not to think too much about what will happen inside his body when he eats. The fluids excreted, the masticated morsels shrugging their way down into his filthy inner core.

"I miss my phone," says Louise. "Sometimes I worry that selfies are what made me real."

She holds her right hand up, mimics holding a self-facing phone. With the other hand she primps her hair, making pouty movie-star lips into the nothing. How much easier it is to pretend to be something you're not. Recently Louise has gravitated to a clot of Southeast Asian girls who dorm on the south side of campus, doctors' daughters who, like her, have assimilated into a culture that demands skinny arms and big boobs, light skin and boy hips. They speak in code about the pressures they feel to be "pretty," to be "sexy," to fit in. They are a closet full of clothes, all trying to become a clean white shirt. And the impossibility of this has miswired their brains.

"It's the behavior point," Simon tells her. "The moment technology stops being a tool and becomes instinctual. The toothbrush, for example. That first cigarette of the day. Language. I'm saying actions we take without thinking. Wake up, check your phone. Irrational, involuntary motion. Just watch the first weekers, clammy, jittery. It's not anxiety. It's withdrawal."

He takes a cautious mouthful of fish, trying not to think about microplastics.

"Upper East Side?" Louise asks him.

"West Village," he tells her. "The pink building, used to belong to Julian Schnabel."

"Ooh, rich boy."

"Financially," he says. "Morally we all seem a bit bankrupt."

She reaches up to pull a hair from her eyebrow but discovers she's pulled them all already, giving her the look of an abstract artist's rendition of a person. It's a gesture she makes a hundred times a day. Sometimes, when her eyebrows are thick, she puts Scotch tape on them to remind herself to leave them alone.

"San Francisco," she says about herself. "Just outside. Renters."

She makes a face—*forgive me.* It is instinctual, this need to apologize for her life, to round herself up to an acceptable number.

"My grandma took out a loan to send me here," she says. "When she dropped me off and saw the horses, she asked if she could stay."

"Depression?" asks Simon.

"Something," says Louise, then turns and makes the selfie gesture again, as if capturing the moment. Simon notices she's bitten her nails all the way to the quick.

"Let's just say I like the feel of a good pair of crafting scissors on my supple Black thighs," she tells Simon, opening her legs suggestively. Slowly she draws up her skirt. On the inside of her thighs, near her panty line, Simon sees the scars. Old rail lines for trains no longer in use.

Louise meets his eye seductively.

"Wanna feel 'em?"

Simon blushes. She is a few months younger than him, but light-years ahead. It is a performance, of course, a way to draw attention and approval without having to expose the real Louise inside. This is what they all do here at Float, thinks Simon, hide in plain sight.

A voice calls out.

"Louise!"

Louise sighs, pulls her skirt down with a face like, *Spoilsport*, then turns and waves a hand in the counselor's direction.

"Sorry."

Simon sees the counselor staring at them. He waves as if to say, *She did it. Not me.* Unconsciously, he fingers the paper bag in his pocket.

He has the impulse to show her the map of the compound he drew his first night here, marking the emergency exits and location of the smoke alarms. Every day he walks the exit route, memorizing the number of steps, in case he has to escape in a blackout during heavy smoke conditions. Before he'd even sat down, his eyes had found the door nearest to his seat, his mind measuring the distance.

It's June. Around the country the suicide epidemic has already begun. There are whispers inside the facility. A noticeable bump in night terrors. A slight uptick in patients with suicidal ideation. A feeling of hopelessness in group sessions. *The horses felt it before we did,* Simon will realize later, watching them whinny and shy away from patients, *as if the smell of death was already on us*. After midnight, residents hear what sounds like screams coming from the stables, waking them from their sedation. *Is this the rapture, the trumpets of St. Paul?* But when the sound comes again, it's clear they're just the neighs of agitated equines.

"It's so boring here," says Louise. She takes the short straw from her orange juice, pretends to light it like a cigarette. She is the queen of exhausted pantomime, her eyes weary, the eyes of a sixty-year-old woman. What have they seen, those eyes, to wear her young soul out?

"I drank all my mouthwash last night," she tells him. "Lefty Pete said it might give a buzz, but he's full of shit. All I got was the runs."

She is a party girl, fifteen going on forty. Simon knows her type, though those girls never paid him much attention. He is skinny and tall and looks younger than his age, like someone took a ten-year-old and stretched him out because they thought it was funny.

She pokes at her food for a moment, then pushes the plate away. If asked what she's anxious about, Louise would say "Three things. *Everything. Nothing. Myself.*" If pressed, she would turn the question around on you, because though she's desperate for attention, the one thing she really doesn't like to discuss is herself.

"Are you a good kisser?" she asks.

"Medium," he tells her. "But that's not in the cards for us."

"Says you."

"I think we're just gonna be friends."

"Boring."

"You say that because you've never had a friend before."

"I've had friends."

"A *real* friend."

"And what's that? A *real* friend."

"Someone you can trust."

She thinks about that, then looks at him with a challenge in her eyes.

"That's a big word."

"Stapler is bigger. Minivan."

She makes a face.

"Be honest. You'd spend real American money for a blowjob."

"Nope. Scout's honor."

She leans forward.

"I'm really good at them," she says softly, licking her lips.

"I'm sure you are."

"But you're not interested."

"Sorry."

"Because—"

"You're not my type."

"You like blondes?"

"I like boys."

A beat; then she raises a hairless eyebrow. "I'm flat chested. You could pretend."

He puts his hand on hers. "Louise," he says.

She lifts her eyes to his, but this time the look is cautious, scared. "What?"

"Trust me."

O

A week later Simon meets the Prophet. He'd gone to bed late that night—working through all the checklists for his nighttime ritual took time— and was awakened an hour later by the sound of hushed voices in the hall, footsteps. Simon had always been a light sleeper. He felt no disorientation, sitting up, reaching for the light. The voices came again, moving down the hall. Under the door he sees the hallway overheads come on. He sits up slowly, goes to the window. It's dark outside, maybe 1:00 a.m. There is an ambulance in the driveway. Its back doors are open, lit by an interior bulb. Simon turns and goes to his door. He turns the handle slowly, pulls the door open just enough to see out into the hall.

Two paramedics are wheeling a gurney out of the room next to his. There is a body on it with a sheet pulled over its face. It's the new kid, Jeremy something. He moved in on Monday. A ginger someone shot in the face with a freckle gun. Simon watches as the orderlies rolled him down the hall and onto the elevator. Then a male counselor comes out of Jeremy's room and sees Simon.

"Go back to bed."

"Was that—what's his name—Jeremy?"

"Kevin," says the counselor. "I'm afraid there's been an accident."

"An accident."

"Go back to bed. We'll talk about this tomorrow."

The counselor hurries off after the paramedics. Simon watches him turn the corner and disappear. From behind him he hears a voice.

"There are no accidents."

Simon turns. A boy is standing in a doorway down the hall. He has long hair—not Jesus long, but to his shoulders—and glasses. He is eating a Twizzler.

"You're saying—what are you saying?" Simon asks.

"It's all part of the plan."

"Whose plan?"

The boy waves the Twizzler at him, smiles. "That," he says, "is the million-dollar question."

And he turns back into his room and closes the door.

O

Before his sister killed herself, Simon thought his father was a doctor the way his pediatrician was a doctor. He pictured a medical office with a waiting room filled with sniffling children and grouchy adults. In his mind, Dad wore a white lab coat and carried a stethoscope, maybe a joke tie. But, of course, Simon's father never wore joke ties. He wore three-thousand-dollar suits and nine-hundred-dollar shoes. They had a view of the Hudson and a terraced roof, and every morning his father would eat a soft-boiled egg—what he had learned to call *a soldier* from his time at Oxford—and then he would put on his suit jacket and climb into the back of a private town car, ready for the drive to the office in a skyscraper on Fifty-Seventh Street, because Ty Oliver was, of course, the CEO of Rise Pharmaceuticals, a multinational conglomerate started by his grandfather in 1901.

To this fact, Simon, of course, was blind. He was a fourteen-year-old boy, insulated from controversy. Nor did he know at that age that Rise Pharmaceuticals was the single largest manufacturer of prescription opioids on the planet. And prescription opioids were one of the most addictive drugs ever created in a laboratory.

Boo phooey.

A factory worker in Pittsburgh goes to the doctor for his trick knee and comes out with a bottle of pills. Six months later, he has sold all his furniture and is buying pills in ones and twos from the back of a used Toyota. Or an Olympic skier has ankle surgery. She's put on bed rest for two weeks. She takes the pills cautiously at first, trying to stay ahead of the pain. But after a while she finds that the time-release mechanism isn't delivering the dose she needs, so she crushes the pill up and snorts it. And the rush she feels is like nothing a sentient animal could ever experience in the wild.

Scientists have proven that if you put a lab rat in a cage and give it one button to push for food and another for a dose of an opiate, the rat will push the opiate button every time, even as it wastes away. The only thing more addictive than painkillers is money, which, it turns out, can be made in astonishing amounts from the sale—legal and illegal—of prescription opiates.

So when Simon's father put on his suit jacket in the morning and rubbed his son's head, he wasn't going to a cramped basement medical office to check for strep or test people's reflexes. He was going to the top of a glass and steel office tower to look for ever more profitable ways to turn pain into $.

Don't get me wrong. Ty Oliver was already a multimillionaire before the pandemic. Back then he was worth a mere $922,000,000 (nine hundred and twenty-two million). Twelve months into the pandemic, his net worth had risen to $4,000,000,000 (four billion). This is what a year of staying home did to people—exacerbated their pain, their need for escape. And Ty Oliver was there to sell them a solution.

For him and the thirty-six other newly minted billionaires, whose collective wealth grew from a combined $2,950,000,000,000 (2.95 trillion) to $4,000,000,000,000 (four trillion). The pandemic was great for business.

Here are some other numbers that Simon learned in the year before he checked himself into an adolescent center for anxiety:

> There are more than forty-one million opioid users on Planet Earth.
> Three hundred thousand of them die each year from an opioid overdose.
> Claire killed herself by swallowing eighty-six pills.
> She was one of two hundred plus Americans who died that day from overdosing on pills Simon's family created and sold. This was before the suicide epidemic began. Just another Tuesday.
> Math, it turns out, has its own morality.

O

Simon sees the Prophet again in group therapy on Monday. They sit in a circle out on the west patio, shaded from the early-summer sun. The moderator leads off with an announcement. Kevin Foster had passed away in his sleep over the weekend. She asks them how they feel about that.

"When you say *in his sleep*," says Greta Moracin, sixteen, "can you be more specific?"

Greta is a slight blond waif, probably anorexic, definitely ADHD.

"What do you want?" asks Ashton Hunt, thirteen, the youngest among them. "The gory details? Like did he swallow his tongue or aspirate on his own throw-up?"

"Nobody swallowed their tongue," says the moderator in a reassuring voice. "What we know is that death is simply part of life. It's all part of the great cycle."

Simon sits under the trellis next to Cookie Yamamoto, a seventeen-year-old depressive who likes to draw on herself with a ballpoint pen. In Japanese culture, social anxiety is called "*taijin kyofusho*," which means the fear of offending or embarrassing *someone else*. How liberating it must be, thinks Simon, not to endure the Western terror of awkward self-humiliation, with its endless, obsessive, narcissistic myopathy.

He doesn't tend to say much in group, focusing mainly on his breathing. Today he is also studying the Prophet out of the corner of his eye.

"Death is *the end* of life," says Betsy, chewing her cuticles.

"You know what else death is the end of?" says Ashton. "Worry."

They think about that, thirteen teenagers who spend their days and nights trapped in a vortex of constant agita. Information from the outside world is suppressed here. There is no internet, no phones. Contacts must be listed and approved to reduce the possibility of confrontation or triggering. This means none of the children in Simon's group have seen the news in weeks. They don't realize that Kevin is just another grain of sand in an hourglass, slowly draining away, or that death is a virus now, ravaging the world's young.

Simon looks at the moderator, who clears her throat gently and bangs a small bronze gong to get their attention. The group goes silent, listening to the reverberations.

It is then that the Prophet speaks.

"Modern America," he says, "has some of the highest rates of depression, anxiety, and loneliness in human history. This isn't my opinion. It's statistical. Things are worst in the cities, and among the wealthy. Which is the opposite of what you would think."

"And why is that?" Simon hears himself asking.

The Prophet turns and looks at him. He is fourteen years old. The rumor is he comes from Wisconsin, that he grew up on a farm that went under during the financial collapse. Others say he was born on the four corners between New Mexico, Arizona,

Nevada, and Colorado, delivered under a full moon in the back of a Nissan Pathfinder. But these are just rumors.

"The !Kung people of the Kalahari Desert," he says, "work as little as twelve hours a week. Everything they do, they do together; hunting, gathering, the great washing of clothes. Every resource they have is shared. Food, water, shelter. The biggest sin you can commit in the !Kung culture is to be selfish. Interestingly, they have the lowest rate of mental illness in the known world. Is it because they have no personal belongings or time to themselves? No word for *I*? It's hard to say. But what we know is that the pursuit of personal property shifts a person's focus from the group to one's self—shifting the words in one's head from *ours* to *mine*. This is for the worse, as evidenced by the fact that today you can live your whole life encountering mostly strangers, surrounded by luxury and yet completely alone."

"What does any of that have to do with Kevin killing himself?" asks Ashton.

"Now, hold on a sec, Ash," says the moderator. "Nobody said anything about Kevin killing himself."

Everyone ignores her. They are interested in what the Prophet has to say.

"Self-determination theory," he intones calmly,

as if the moderator had never spoken, "states that human beings need three basic things in order to feel content. Number one, they need to feel competent at what they do. Number two, they need to feel authentic in their lives, and number three, they need to feel connected to others. Is there anyone here who feels they can check all three of those boxes?"

None of them raise their hands. There is a pause. Then the moderator's hand shoots up.

"You know what else matters?" she says. "*Trying*. It matters that we're here and that we're *trying* to feel good. Does anyone else want to share something with the group? Betsy?"

Betsy shrugs. She is drawing a noose on her leg in blue, ballpoint ink.

"The thing to understand about groups," the Prophet says, "is that cooperating with others triggers high levels of oxytocin in the human brain. Sharing, banding together. All lead to feelings of trust and bonding among men and increases the instinct to breastfeed among women. We literally *feel* better when we're working together."

"That's great," says the moderator. "Thank you for that, Paul. See, kids? It's important we work together."

Simon chews some loose skin from his lip. Now he knows the Prophet's name. *Paul.*

"I asked you not to call me that," says the Prophet mildly.

"Sorry. I forgot," says the moderator. "What would you like to be called?"

The Prophet takes a moment, then says—

"I don't want to be called anything. I'm not here for me. I'm here for you. It's the only way the future will be any different from the present or the past. We need to forget ourselves and focus on each other."

He turns to Greta.

"Did you know," he says, "that when a country goes to war, suicide rates plummet? In Paris, during World War Two, the psychiatric hospitals emptied out. Bombs falling from the sky and people had never felt better. See, when we have a common cause, we feel better about ourselves. Charles Fritz has suggested that modern society— with its urbanization and alienation—has disrupted critical social bonds between people. But disaster forces us back into a more organic and ancestral way of relating to each other. War, famine, flood. A blackout in Manhattan, blizzards. When these things happen, neighbors come out of their homes. They hand out bottled water. Restaurants serve up the food they have for free, rather than let it go to waste. And yet what is this world our parents are giving us, if not a disaster? A problem we can't solve. That's why we're so anxious. That's why we're all here. And that's why Kevin killed himself."

With that, he leans back in his chair and closes his eyes.

The moderator gives a nervous chuckle.

"Okay," she says. "I think that's all we have time for today. Just know that Cindy and I will have expanded office hours this week, in case any of you want to come in for a little chat. Those of you with equestrian therapy, go ahead and walk on over to the stables."

She stands encouragingly, as if to say, *Get out there and seize the day.*

The children rise from their seats with collective apathy. The sun is just cresting the roof of the center, and for a moment, as he stands, Simon is blinded by the light. He lowers his head and blinks away the sunspots inside his eyelids. When he looks up, the Prophet is standing in front of him, hands folded in front of his waist, face serene.

"Walk with me," he tells Simon, then turns and heads into the gardens.

Simon looks around to make sure the Prophet was actually addressing him and him alone, but all the other kids are already loping off toward their next scheduled activity. Simon himself has exposure therapy in ten minutes, but he doesn't hesitate. Picking up his notebook, he hurries after the boy who doesn't want to be called Paul.

O

They walk through the rose garden to the aviary. Headmistress often says she finds birds to be the wisest of animals, and she encourages the clients to spend time watching them and listening to their distinctive cries. As they walk, Simon counts backward from one hundred. The Prophet walks beside him, hands clasped behind his back.

85, 84, 83.

The closer Simon gets to the number fifty, the more anxious he becomes, so he puts his hand in his pocket and rubs the paper bag folded inside, knowing it's there if he reaches zero without a break in the silence.

He thinks of the Belt of Uninhabitability that will soon replace the Middle East, India, and most of China. A corridor of the planet emptied of humanity by heat and endless weather. Seventy million, eighty million, one hundred million. Where will they go? Who will take them in?

Claire has always been too afraid to make a joke, because what if no one laughs?

"I had a vision," the Prophet says just as Simon's brain reaches twenty-six.

They walk in silence a moment longer. Simon wonders if he should ask, *What vision?* But the more he thinks about it, the more paralyzed his mouth becomes.

"About you," says the Prophet. "They come to me late at night, when everything is quiet. That's when I hear it the clearest."

"Hear what?" Simon manages.

"The hum. They say two percent of the population can hear it, but I've never met another. Think of the lowest frequency sound wave you can imagine, then lower the pitch by two-thirds. It's a feeling, more than a sound honestly, like putting your ear to the train tracks as the train is coming. Some people think it's generated by power lines or buried gas mains. I've even heard a theory that the sound is produced by tectonic motion under the ocean floor. But I think what I'm hearing is the voice of God."

He stops and studies a green parrot, sitting on the branch of an elm tree.

"At first I asked myself—*why would God talk to me? I'm not special.* But then I thought—*why not me?* Maybe that's the point. What is history if not a mass grave filled with the bodies of followers of Special Men? Maybe averageness and blandness is what we need right now. Anonymity. Follow the words, not the person."

Simon keeps his eyes on the parrot, but his focus is on the Prophet. He wants the boy to get to the part of the story that contains his Simon-related vision, but he is too afraid to ask.

"Is your name really Paul?" he finally asks, a question he hadn't planned and one that immediately caused an anxiety spike.

Claire has always been a disappointment.

But the Prophet merely shrugs.

"I'm not important enough to name. You can call me *boy* if you like, or *old what's his name.* A redneck outside a Dairy Queen called me a *fucking faggot* once, but I don't think it was a form of identification, as much as an expression of contempt. Lastly, I didn't ask you to walk with me to talk about myself. We're here to talk about you."

"Me."

"Yes. God spoke of you to me."

"God did."

"Yes. He told me about Claire."

Simon feels a low unease rise in his gut. There are no last names used at the facility. How does the Prophet know who Simon is?

"You carry a heavy burden. We all do. But God wants you to know that her death was not in vain. She was the first, but she will not be the last."

"The first what?"

"Martyr."

Simon blinks.

"What else did he say—God?"

"He said you were there, at the museum, when the pill bottles fell from the sky."

Simon turns and looks at the Prophet. He is a tall kid, underweight. There is a sadness in his eyes. How could he know that? Does he know about the red paint they threw in Simon's mother's face outside the Waldorf Astoria? Simon's heart is racing.

"What's your damage?" he asks. "All this holy man bullshit. What are you covering?"

"I'm sorry if I upset you," says the Prophet. "Many things that God says to me are upsetting. Extinction. This is what we talk of most. What happens to a species when you destroy its natural habitat, when you corrupt its essential nature and purpose—when you take its biological instincts and mandates and use them for a different purpose? You confuse our higher and lower functions, harnessing our drives and motivating us down an unnatural path, one in which human beings are reprogrammed to covet products and ignore reality."

Simon feels his face flush. Despite his best efforts to resist, the words stir something in him. The prophet licks his palm and smooths a cowlick.

"There is evidence corroborated in multiple countries that suggests if a man or woman has not had intercourse by age twenty-five, there is a reasonable chance he or she will remain a virgin at least until age forty-five. My point is, look around, you have a population of adolescents, who in any other decade would be fucking their brains out, but instead, we're on TikTok."

"You said God spoke to you about me," says Simon. "What did he say?"

"He said the sins of the father must be made right by the son. He told me to tell you that it's hard to be useful and sad. Also, *remember the red eyes*. Does this mean something to you?"

Simon feels something in his hand and looks down. Without realizing, he has taken the paper bag out of his pocket.

"No one here has a phone," he says, "so I think— TikTok—your theory kind of falls apart. We're in recovery."

"Have you ever heard of a dry drunk?" the Prophet replies. "The identity remains, even though the behavior has stopped. In the case of our screens, we're not to blame. They designed these addiction machines in cheerful spaces with napping rooms and personalized yoga mats. At first they were just another way to get human beings to spend money, to buy commodities. But then the shift happened."

"What shift?"

"We *became* the commodity. Our data. This is the secret of modern life. We went from being citizens to consumers, and now to commodities. Our personality profiles, our social and financial history, our likes and dislikes, all used to accurately predict future behavior. How will we vote? Will we take to the streets or roll over? The data knows all, which is why today our data is more valuable than our bodies. How does it make you feel to know that, Simon Oliver? That your value to the world resides in your thumbs? The buttons they push. God is unhappy. You should know that. He created us to love each other, to be the miracle, not to swipe right. And it forces one to ask—at what point does the human animal move so far from its biological mandate that it begins to fail?"

He puts his hand on Simon's shoulder.

"I'm talking about extinction. This is really why Kevin killed himself. Because somewhere deep inside he knew. We're trapped. All of us. The future is a problem that can't be solved. A one one."

"What?"

"A one one."

"That doesn't mean anything."

"It means everything. Just not to you. Not yet."

He looks Simon in the eye.

"It meant something to Claire."

Simon blinks. In his mind he sees plastic bottles

in prescription orange raining from the circular balconies of the Guggenheim. They fell in slow motion, a biblical plague. Except the real plague, he knew, was the drug inside—a miracle of time-release engineering. Oblivion in pill form. Seventy-six billion pills shipped in seven years.

And Claire. Beautiful Claire. Queen of the dead girls.

"Don't talk about her."

"I'm sorry. These aren't my words. They're His."

"Look," says Simon, "I don't know what you want from me. I'm fifteen. None of this is my fault."

"And yet you feel guilty."

In summation, why go out the window, when you can use the door?

Simon is hyperventilating now. He turns away, pulling the paper bag from his pocket and lifting it to his mouth. He breathes into it—in, out—recirculating his own air. There are spots in his field of vision, stars. Gently, the Prophet puts a hand on Simon's back, helps him over to a wooden bench. On it, a bronze plaque reads SERENITY IS THE DIVINE ART OF BEING PASSIVE.

Simon sits there, bent over, head between his knees, losing his shit, while the Prophet speaks to him in soothing tones.

"There are two great motivators," he says. "Love,

and fear. Of these, fear is the easiest to manufacture in others. Fear provides the quickest path to a visceral response. We know this at our primordial core. Scared animals defend themselves. Fight or flight. So now let's talk about history. American history. *Our* history. In the 1990s politicians began to harness the power of fear to create a different kind of America. A nation of perpetual fear—fear of crime, fear of race, fear of government. Then came the Twin Towers and the never-ending War on Terror. They warned us that everything we believed in and everyone we loved was in constant danger. Fundamentalist Islamic terrorism. Mexican rapists. Rental vans plowing through crowds in European cities. Active shooters. Autism from a doctor's needle. In 2016 that fear brought us the God King and his troll army, the great plague and the fear of literal death."

He holds up one fist.

"Wear a mask!"

Then the other fist.

"Liberate Michigan! You remember. And so Us against Them became the world. But the more fear is used to motivate people, the more afraid they will become, the more fear will come to define their lives."

The Prophet gets down on the ground and looks into Simon's eyes. He is a wavering form, a ghost of carbon dioxide and light.

"Those frightened people were our parents," he tells Simon. "And rather than raising us, their children, from a place of love, they raised us in fear. Doesn't it stand to reason that their fear would shape the adults we become? Anxious, plagued by a constant sense that something, *everything,* is wrong. Their fear has crippled us, and our inability to function only feeds our anxiety. We are failing at life. So now all we are is failure."

The Prophet leans back and rests his face in the dappled sun.

"Doesn't that sound like your life?" he says.

Simon's breathing is normal now—a recycled calm coursing through his oxygen-starved blood. He lowers the bag.

"I don't understand."

"I'm saying the world you think is real is a lie. Liberal, conservative, the so-called Culture War. It's a delusion. The end result of fear over love. And worse, our parents are training us to pick a side. But it's all bullshit."

Simon breathes into the paper bag, but his heart rate is de-escalating, his breaths becoming deeper, longer. The Prophet takes off his glasses, exhales on the lenses, and wipes them with his shirt.

"Listen to me, Simon," he says. "The world they're offering us is a lie. Do you know how I know?"

"How?" says Simon, his mouth dry. The words come out like a croak.

The Prophet returns his glasses to his face, and the effect is to magnify his already big blue eyes. He blinks at the return to vision and leans forward.

"Because we're still dying."

Simon lowers the paper bag. The colors of the world seem brighter now, the air fresher.

"What did God say?" he asks. "About me."

"That he has a mission for you. That you will be instrumental in building our new utopia."

"Our new—"

"Utopia. See, this is the message he has told me to spread. The adults are lost. We, their children, are starting over."

On July 12, the president makes a statement from the Oval Office. He sits behind the Resolute Desk, hands clasped, expression somber.

"My fellow Americans," he says, "I speak to you now at a moment of true peril for our nation. Not just the physical borders that define us, the physical makeup of this great land, but for us as a people. Our children are dying. They are taking their lives in numbers never before seen in the history of the planet."

A pause as he rubs his eyes, looking tired. We know from news reports that he has slept very little since this crisis started. Visits with grieving parents. Phone calls with local officials. Round tables with physical and mental health professionals. He has pounded more than one table, demanding answers.

Now he sets his jaw, shaking off his personal feelings.

"Many of my aides," he says, "asked me not to make this statement tonight, but I'm not just your president. I am also a father, and as a father I feel I must speak. You should know that your government is doing everything it can to understand and disrupt this phenomenon. As of this morning I have declared a state of emergency and have tasked FEMA with responding to this crisis as they would a hurricane or other act of God, for what else can you call this, if not a cataclysmic human event? Their first order of business will be to open and operate clinics around the country. I have also signed an executive order drafting all medical and psychiatric professionals to form a new corps of first responders and asked them to suspend their private practices to work instead for the good of all Americans, no matter the cost. If this is some kind of new virus or infection, we will diagnose it and find the cure.

"But there is only so much we can do. Your children are not the property of the United States government. They are yours. And though we can support you in your efforts to raise them, to care for them, to keep them alive, we cannot do it for you. So I beseech you, my fellow Americans, let us come together now—whatever our differences—and face this crisis, the way we have faced all great crises in our past. With heart, with dignity, with strength.

"And to you, our troubled youth, let me say this: We see you. We hear you. Nothing is more important than your safety. And to my own children, now ten and twelve, let me just say, Nathan, Rebecca, Daddy loves you. Mommy loves you. America loves you."

The president pauses, his eyes welling. For a moment he chews his lower lip, getting his feelings under control. And then he nods and addresses the camera once more.

"It has been my great honor to be your president these last two years. There is no country on Earth as blessed or as commanding as this great nation. Let us come together now to meet this challenge, to save our children from darkness, so that they may one day enjoy the freedoms and opportunities that we enjoy. So that they may experience all the hope and promise of which our democracy is capable. So that they may one day lead us into the future.

"God bless you and may God bless the United States of America."

The Conklins

What is a wanted child? Some women know from a young age that they want to be mothers. They spend hours picking out names, imagining their daughters and sons. Some men dream of starting a family as soon as they're old enough to vote. They yearn for a feeling of purpose, of completeness. And then there are the others, the accidental parents, the *late-night-hookup* parents, the *condom-broke* parents, the *verge-of-breakup* parents. How many heroes of history came into the world this way? How many geniuses? How many great composers, mathematicians, poets, philosophers? Wanting a child is not a litmus test for having a child. Louise Conklin—she of the imaginary selfies and the missing eyebrows—figured that out at an early age.

She was born in a public hospital in Freemont, California, to a teenage mother, with no father listed on the birth certificate. They lived with

Louise's grandmother for a few years, then a series of her mom's dud boyfriends. There was Jerome, the long-distance trucker who sang country music, and Ray, who kept a Monster Energy drink on his bedside table to guzzle when he woke and spent twelve hours a day playing *Call of Duty* while wearing a headset. Then it was back to Grandma's in a suburb outside San Francisco. She'd bought a fixer-upper in the sixties in a neighborhood that had been mostly Black but had since gentrified, leaving Grandma the only dark face on a street filled with Teslas and boxy modern remodels. Her new neighbors were friendly, smiling and waving, proud of themselves for living in a neighborhood this diverse.

Grandma had one of those cushy government jobs, sorting mail for the post office, and Louise would ride the yellow bus to school every day, her clothes clean and pressed. Mom was mostly MIA in those years, descending without warning, smoking Pall Malls, her teeth loosening, fingers drumming on the kitchen table. Louise would find her passed out on the sofa upon her latchkey return from school, one shoe still on. What felt like an hour would unfold with Louise standing in the front doorway, backpack on, staring at her snoring form.

Stay or go?

And yet where would she go? This was the only home she had. So, as quietly as possible, Louise—nine, ten, eleven—would pad into her bedroom and close the door, vibrating. But remaining in her room wasn't an option. Whenever Louise stayed in one place too long, the feeling would build inside her. The piranhas in her belly. The colored spots at the corner of her vision. *Do something. Clean. Organize.* It was her ritual. She was a straightener, a mopper, a duster of bookshelves. The alternative, inaction, was the same as nonexistence. So she would change into her cleaning clothes, psyching herself up in the mirror. *You can do this. You are invulnerable.* And then she'd open her door and get to work.

Everything.

Nothing.

Herself.

If you boiled her anxiety down, it came to these three things.

1. Everything meaning everything. The world. Six thousand years of human history, following one hundred and ninety-four million years of pure animal survival, in which the strong dominated the weak. Where tribes became kingdoms and kingdoms became democracies—*civilized*—and yet, under the

surface, tribal allegiances remained. Who had power and who suffered from it. Who got rich and who stayed poor. Everything meaning everything you couldn't say out loud about discrimination and inequality, about the way the world worked—not to lift people like you up but to keep you down.

2. Nothing meaning the absence of tangible threats—no gun to her head, no knife to her throat—and yet what is poverty if not a threat? What is being called *that word* or followed down the street by packs of boys if not a threat? Nothing meaning the dread that builds in your heart every morning and every night as you relive the insults of the day and agitate over what the next one will bring. Will you be dismissed? Will you be assaulted? Will you be killed?

3. Herself, meaning—well, just look at her— the girl her own mother didn't want, flat chested and weird. The latchkey kid whose best friends were cleaning products, who used to bite her own tongue until it bled. She was like a child who had been made in a lab to provoke the hostility of privileged men.

And so she cleaned.

It was the same routine every day, starting in

her grandma's bathroom. She would organize the cupboards, scrubbing the sink basin. She used tile spray on the grout, mildew spray on the shower curtain. She scrubbed the toilet with bleach, using the wire brush, then washing the brush under scalding water in the tub. They lived in a two-bedroom clapboard house near the commuter line, trains rattling the glassware fifty-four times a day. Grandma had lived there for twenty-two years, first with Grandpa—who died at forty-eight in an industrial accident at the printing plant—then as a single mother. And now as a single grandmother, raising a twelve-year-old girl with a cleaning fixation.

"I can see myself in the toaster," Grandma would say with amazement some mornings. "Did you do that?"

Louise would shrug. She didn't like to talk about her need to clean. But every day after school she'd snap on the yellow gloves and get to work. It didn't matter that the house hadn't had time to get dirty since yesterday's clean. Louise knew that even if you couldn't see the dirt, it was there.

This is what would keep her from becoming a needle drug user ultimately, when she began to self-medicate her anxiety at the age of fourteen, the idea of that dirty spike going into her arm. Sharing a joint or a pipe was similarly untenable, all those germs and viruses passed back and forth. Booze and pills. That would be her route. A way to numb the cranial itch. Of course, all that started a couple of years later, in eighth grade. Gabby Macintosh stole some Valium from her mother's vanity, and Hart Overman smuggled a fifth of watered-down vodka from his uncle's shop. It was the third Tuesday in September 2022. They were in the rec room of Gabby's house, Louise the only one with any melanin in her skin. She and Hart were drinking from the bottle, but Louise got herself a glass from the kitchen, poured herself a finger.

"Hey," Gabby told her, "take this first."

So Louise put the yellow Valium on her tongue, washed it down with the burn of vodka. She was hoping for oblivion but would settle for a dream. That was the first time she ever felt free. The first time the constant hum of anxiety disappeared. A fucking miracle, and so simple. One pill, one drink.

$1+1 = peace$.

That afternoon she skipped the cleaning. Her grandma came home to an empty house, Louise wandering home an hour later with a mouth full of Lifesavers.

"And is that when it started?" her therapist asks. It's fifteen months later. They are sitting on a screened-in porch at the Float Anxiety Reduction Center. "This fixation on sex and sexuality?"

Louise drops the Crocs from her feet, crosses her legs. She is sitting on the wooden porch swing. Incense burns in a tray on the table beside her. There is a cool afternoon breeze blowing in from the east, and she can hear the bleat of the lambs and goats from the animal enclosure next door.

"Can't get to Carnegie Hall without practice," she says.

"Meaning?"

"Meaning if you want to be the best at something, you gotta work for it."

The therapist makes a note. He is in his mid-forties with an island of brown hair in the center of his forehead, which he combs back like a bridge to connect with the rest of his receding hairline.

"And what does that mean to you, being *the best* at sex?"

Louise leans back, the swing moving with her, and rolls her eyes to the roof. Sex is part of her currency, her exoticness here and at home, the stereotype of the sensual Black woman. It's a role she adopted without realizing, drawn by the allure of approval, the gravitational pull of being wanted. But at night she slid crafting scissors across her skin in places only teenage treasure seekers would see them—a warning carved into the rock outside a sacred cave—for you cannot take something sacred without leaving pain and suffering behind.

Because, of course, there is a fourth thing that makes Louise anxious, a foundational fear that dwarfs all the others, a traumatizing experience that led to her breakdown and her escape to this picturesque suburban facility her grandmother can't afford.

And that fear's name is the Wizard.

"It's, God, it's a joke, dude," she tells the therapist. "Lighten up."

He makes another note.

"I feel like we've made a lot of progress recently," he says.

"Great."

"Would you agree?"

"Would I agree we've made a lot of progress? I don't know. What is that? Progress, when it comes to me, you know, not losing my fucking mind?"

"Well—you seem more relaxed."

"That's pharmaceutical."

"Are you sure?"

Louise sighs. She doesn't like looking straight at things. She's a peripheral person. Like how a boy doesn't have to ask for head, you just know he wants it. Even *this* guy. Therapy Man. She sees the way he writes down her stories, the way he licks the end of his pencil before jotting down the gory details—not literally, but with his mind. He acts cool and detached, but Louise knows if she dropped to her knees right in the middle of the session, he wouldn't put up much of a fight.

"Often," the therapist says, "promiscuity at a young age is brought on by abuse. What do you think about that statement?"

"I think I'm the one with the questions and you're supposed to be Mr. Answer Man."

He clicked his pen once, twice. *Click-click.*

"You're fifteen, Louise. And if you're telling the truth, you've had sexual encounters with a dozen boys."

"Don't forget the girls, dude. If she's got the sway, I'll munch a well-groomed carpet any day."

Her therapist takes off his glasses, wipes the lenses with a cloth.

"Are you trying to shock me?"

"I could give a shit. I'm just being factual."

"And how," he said then, "do you think your race plays into all of this?"

She stares at him. "For real?"

He nods, comfortable in his professional detachment.

"Fine," she says. "Lemme ask you this: You think anxiety is a personal problem? You're anxious. I'm anxious."

He draws himself up, an expert thrilled to pontificate his expertise.

"Anxiety," he says, "is a psychological affliction."

"No," she tells him. "It's a *we* problem. *We're* anxious—Black people, brown people, women. Anxious about discrimination. About violence. About our bodies and their physical health. About being seen—really seen—which I'm thinking, Steve, is not a problem you have."

"Because I'm white."

She raises her eyebrows. *Duh.*

He wipes his glasses, a pained expression on his face.

"It hurts," he says, "that you would judge me on the color of my skin."

She stares at him.

"Seriously?"

She watches as he puts his glasses back on.

"Was there racism against Black people in the past?" he says. "Yes. No one's denying that, but I think we can all agree it's rare now. Individual cases, sure, but—"

She stares at him. He trails off, not wanting to get *political*. He's done a lot of reading on the subject, however. How the Civil Rights Act was a success, followed by affirmative action, and now there's equality. Baseline equality. *I mean, sure*, he thinks, *people are struggling—Black people, white people, everyone—times are tough, but it's important we teach our kids the truth, not a bunch of liberal talking points.*

Imagine, he thinks, *teaching innocent white children that they're guilty of racism from the moment they're born?*

But this isn't his therapy session. It's hers, so he holds out his right palm, inviting her to talk.

"O—kay," says Louise, making a mental note to keep her real feelings to herself from now on.

He smiles.

"And hey," he says, "we feel how we feel. That's your experience of the world, and I want to honor that."

For some reason his smile—empty of meaning—reminds her of He Who Must Not be Named. This is the story her therapist really wants to hear, but no way she's gonna tell it. The Wizard and the Troll. The guardian at the gate and the mansion on the hill. He'd take one listen and write *make believe artist* in his little book. But what is a tall tale if not a portrait of some larger truth?

You like to party? Because this is a party house.

Bowls of pills. All the vodka you could drink.

But first you had to get by the Troll.

Instead, Louise lists all her favorite cleaning products—Borax for scouring, 409 for light degreasing. She talks about the strengths and weaknesses of push brooms. She even talks about her mother on the sofa, one shoe on, the other foot

filthy, like she'd hobbled through some muddy
field to get here.

"And what would you say her biggest problem
was?" the therapist asks.

Louise chews her lips. She doesn't want to talk
about this, any of this. She wants to talk about how,
all around campus, kids are disappearing, how
the ambulances have taken to showing up without
lights or sirens, sneaking in through the dark gates
at night, and in the morning all that's left is empty
rooms and sage. Ten kids in the last month, the
cafeteria lines getting shorter. But instead, she says
nothing, because what would be the point? No one
here ever gives you a straight answer.

"She was a drug addict," says Louise.

"Is that what bothers you? The drug use? I know
from our sessions that you've experimented quite
heavily yourself."

Louise sips her tea. "Fine. You wanna know
what her biggest problem was? Me."

Click-Click

O

The Troll's name was Evan, but Louise didn't learn that until the Wizard named him. Outside the ivy walls, the Troll pushed the button, talked into the box. *Yeah, it's me,* he said. *I got one.* The gate opened. The Troll pulled into an enormous cobblestone circle in front of a mansion bigger than anything Louise had ever seen.

The Wizard was waiting, gate clicker in his hand, wearing jeans and a polo shirt. He was sixty going on forty-five, chiseled, polished, like a man who tans, who has a personal trainer and a personal shopper, a man who gets his slate-gray hair trimmed every week, who does yoga and eats only organic fruits and vegetables. Like a man who Gets What He Wants Always, who surrounds himself with acolytes and yes-men.

Like a billionaire. Which is what he was.

"Ice maker's on the fritz, Evan-baby," he said. "Be a doll and pick some up at the local you know."

He handed the kid—Evan was what, nineteen, twenty?—a handful of hundred-dollar bills, like how much did he think ice cost? Ten pounds of frozen water? But Louise noticed. Shit must have been seven hundred dollars, as in *keep the change.* And given the size of the estate—fuck *house,* this was a palace with acreage, and *in* San Francisco—seven hundred dollars was monkey dick to this guy.

Evan said *no problem-o*, and jumped back in the Mercedes convertible.

"Be bad," he told Louise, and pulled out of the circle and back down the long driveway.

Louise was wearing white shorts and a sleeveless button-down. It was late summer, but the first chill of fall was in the air. She had her backpack with her, because Evan said it was critical that Louise's outfit scream *schoolgirl.* Inside was her Intro to Algebra book, her journal, and some colored pencils. Plus Purell in three different delivery vehicles (spray, lotion, and roll-on).

She looked over at the Wizard, who stood just outside the lamplight, like a vampire.

"Give us a spin, kitty-cat," he said. "Let the Wizard take a lookie-loo."

Louise turned self-consciously. She thought about her grandmother sorting mail at the post office, about her mother out there somewhere, lost in America, about the father she didn't know. Maybe this was him. Crazier things had happened.

"Meow," said the Wizard, his eye hidden behind a pair of two-thousand-dollar sunglasses. He invited her back to the pool to meet the others.

They walked up the grand stairs and through the foyer. Louise could feel the front door recede behind her, as if she were standing still and the exit were running. Ahead of her, the Wizard disappeared through a door. Louise hurried to keep up but stopped short in the doorway. The room was black with scripted white writing on the wall. *Moloko Plus*, she read. *Moloko Synthemesc. Moloko Vellocet.* Lining the rectangular wall were six life-size alabaster mannequins, all kneeling on pedestals, giant white bouffants on their heads. But they weren't just women. They were fountains. A thin white liquid spouted from their nipples into a milky moat below.

The lighting was low, everything white glowing against the dark walls.

At the far end of the room, Louise saw, four men dressed all in white, wearing black bowler hats. They sat on a white bench and stared at her from under heavy eyelids, motionless.

She froze.

Where is the Wizard? What am I supposed to do?

The tinkle of six fountains filled the air. Behind it was a light classical score, uplifting, familiar. A little bit of the Ludwig V.

Tentatively, Louise entered the room and moved toward the men—*why don't they move? Is this a gauntlet? Am I the show?* But when she got closer, Louise saw they weren't men but silicon replicas. Statues. Which was somehow creepier. She stopped. Behind her, suddenly, she felt a man's breath on her neck.

"You like milk, kitty-cat?" the Wizard whispered in her ear. "A little bit of the chocolate meow-meow."

Louise turned and took a step back, her foot sinking into the floor's channel moat with a splash.

"I'm—" she said. But the Wizard just smiled from behind his sunglassed eyes.

"Wanna see a trick?"

He raised his right hand and pointed at the four replicas.

"Let there be light."

Louise turned. Ahead of her, the black wall

seemed to split, revealing a bright light, which filled the room, blinding her, as two of the seated statues swung out to the left, the other two to the right. It took Louise, her right foot submerged, soaked to the ankle, a moment to realize that what she was looking at was the outdoors, an enormous white terraced patio. She followed the Wizard outside. And it was there that Louise understood the sheer size of the estate, its vast terraced gardens, its startling view of the San Francisco skyline, and, directly below her, an enormous swimming pool, around which sat a dozen young girls, just like her. A man in a dark suit moved among them, carrying a white pitcher, from which he filled their elevated wineglasses with milk.

"Look," Louise will tell the therapist, sitting across from him on the screened-in porch, "you wanna talk about Mommy left me, or Daddy wasn't there, that's cool. I got no problem with the deep dive into why Weezy likes to clean the bathroom three times a day, but we're not pals, and I don't owe you anything."

The therapist clicks his pen a few times. "It's not what you owe me," he says. "It's what you owe yourself."

Louise smiles, not because it's funny, but because he's acting like words matter, like being clever matters, like he can fix it all if she'll just pick away the scab and let it bleed. But what if all your blood is gone? What if a vampire took it in the night and replaced it with something milky, something white?

"Why did Kevin kill himself?" she says. "Any of them? All."

"Did you know him?"

"I saw him. He was here. We're all here."

Click-click went the pen.

"Why do you think he killed himself?"

"Because he didn't want to live anymore."

"That simple?"

"That simple."

Click-click.

"It's interesting, I think," he says, "that when I asked if you'd had experience with abuse, you brought up suicide. Is there an implicit threat? Dig too deep and I'll kill myself?"

Louise sighs. There are cobwebs in the top corners of the porch, and it takes all her willpower not to climb up and wipe them off.

"Does anybody ever clean out here?" she asks.

He looks behind him, sees where she's looking and at what.

"Does that bother you?"

"Everything bothers me," she says. "People don't do what they're supposed to do, and no one tells the truth about anything."

Click-click.

"What are they supposed to do?"

She looks up at him from under her brows.

"The real question," she says, "is what *aren't* they supposed to do, and who's doing it?"

"Meaning?"

"Meaning, you know, figure it out."

"I'm gonna need a little more—"

"I'm saying sometimes the city is full of rats, and you call the Pied Piper, but instead of killing the rats, he steals your kids. I'm saying what does the Bible say about a trusted man who will rise one day, tricking people with signs and wonders?"

Click-click.

"You consider yourself religious?"

"I've been to church, but that's not the point. The point is people say they love something, but really what they love is *using* it."

"You feel used?"

She smiles again, this time bright with a kind of giddy rage. "It's not a feeling."

"What is it?"

Louise takes a Tootsie Pop from her pocket, peels off the wrapper. She slips it into her mouth. "It's the facts of fucking life, kitty-cat."

O

She sees Simon at dinner, sitting alone on a bench outside. He is sitting alone in front of an empty plate. It's been three weeks since the Prophet told Simon that God has a plan for him. Three weeks of questions, of paper bag interludes and restless leg syndrome. In that time Simon has asked a thousand questions of the *what where why how* variety. The Prophet doesn't answer them all. He tells Simon, *I know only what God tells me.* Each time, Simon's anxiety spikes, and the doctors up his dosage of Klonopin, which makes him tired all the time and muddies his mind.

Then the dreams begin.

At first all he sees is a house with a red door sitting on a quiet street. An empty street. No people. No animals. No birds. No life of any kind. For many nights this is all there is. The street. The house. The door. And a sound, like scratching fingernails. He wakes sweating, dread in his gut. The next night he finds himself in a fluorescent kitchen. The walls are sweating. There is a bubbling pot on the stove. The room has no doors, no windows, the air so cold he can see his breath. And there is a smell, like a sour cabbage abattoir.

What's in the pot?

At night, while he slumbers, the ambulances arrive, sirens off, flashing lights strobing the walls of the children's rooms. The outside world is stalking them. Its sickness. But in their bucolic retreat, all they know is whatever happened to Kevin is going around—shoelace nooses, broken-glass wrists, or pills stored, hidden and gorged upon. Some nights it feels like the whole fire department arrives, trying to smother the problem with overwhelming force. But every morning, group therapy gets a little emptier, until afternoon check-in arrives, new clients flocking to the center each day, their parents hoping against hope that institutionalizing their offspring will ward off the suicidal ideation of the outside world, never realizing that a psychiatric treatment facility is a prison for experts—experts in self-sabotage, experts in starvation, experts in knot tying and pill taking, in sharp object management and plastic bag suffocation.

And experts talk. They share techniques, until your child too is an expert in falling apart.

Inside the cafeteria, all the other kids are lined up with their trays, trying to decide between chicken and salmon. But Simon seems to be here by accident, as if he had been wandering, lost in thought, and simply felt the pull of collective destination. Louise sits down next to him.

"Are the choices that grim?"

He looks over, his eyes focusing.

"What?"

"The meal. There's only so much organic faro a growing boy can eat and all that."

"No," says Simon. "It's not—"

He sighs, trying to find the right words in his drug-induced haze, then settles on the simple truth.

"My sister killed herself."

Louise flushes. The intimacy she's used to is physical, not emotional.

"Shit. When?"

"Last year."

He leans closer, glances around to make sure no one can hear.

"She was the first," he tells her. "But now it's everywhere. The Prophet told me."

"What do you mean everywhere?" asks Louise, even though deep down she knows. Didn't her friend Gabby kill herself last month, taping the vacuum cleaner hose to the exhaust pipe of her parents' BMW? And hasn't Louise's grandma been extra nice to her since then, calling every night just to "make sure she's okay." *Her* grandmother, who never missed an opportunity to tell Louise that emotional distress was a luxury only white kids could afford?

"Kids are hanging themselves in Delaware," Simon tells her. "In Oregon they're eating their parents' guns. In Mississippi they're drinking drain cleaner. And other places. Japan, Israel, Russia. It's everywhere and it's kids."

A tingle starts at the base of Louise's spine. "How many?"

But Simon doesn't answer. He chews his tongue, trying to think. "Did you know the Prophet's name is Paul?" he asks.

"No shit? I would have thought Ezekiel or Boaz. Something biblical."

Simon nods. "He says this is how it ends. Us. The human race. Unless—"

"Unless what?"

Simon jabs his hand through his hair, then rubs his head vigorously. The effect is of a normal scientist going suddenly mad. "Unless we escape from the castle, find Samson, and listen to his story."

"His story?"

"The Prophet says utopia is out there," Simon tells her. "That we can stop this if we find it. Start over."

"Utopia."

Simon nods. To Louise it sounds crazy, but she washes her hands five hundred and nineteen times a day, so who is she to talk?

"And how do we do that, find utopia?"

Simon turns to look at her. "We have to fight the Wizard."

And suddenly Louise can't breathe.

She sees her mother's filthy left foot.
Hears the sounds of fountains.
Her heart racing.
Do you like milk, kitty-cat?
Darkness closing in.
"Are you okay?" Simon asks.
But Louise has already fainted.

Book 2

Megalophobia

Theories

There was no shortage of theories. Those who believed in original sin saw our children's suicides as a sign of secular corrosion. They blamed the war on Christmas, the separation of church and state. Gun control advocates saw our children's suicides as a form of PTSD. They called them the Mass Murder Generation, raised on active-shooter drills. Hadn't our sons and daughters come of age, after all, to the headlines "Eleven dead in a Virginia middle school," "Thirteen gunned down at Denver High"? Hadn't they awoken each morning to see gun control laws debated but never passed, policies introduced but never ratified. Change, they were told, was too difficult. And so gunfire echoed through their cafeterias, our fear skyrocketed, and to combat that fear we bought more guns.

To try to better understand our new reality, we gorged ourselves on podcasts, parroting their complex theories of human behavior. Status anxiety, we were told, not financial self-interest had motivated the rise of the God King. Perceived loss of standing had torn our country apart. The fear of losing ground to those beneath us. As proof, experts pointed to the drained public pools of the 1950s, where white suburbanites had physically drained and paved over their beautiful, newly built public pools rather than share them with Black families. Rather than elevate those they perceived as lower status to their own level. Deep down, it seemed, many Americans were convinced that a gain for others was a loss for themselves.

For our children this status anxiety manifested in the language of pornography. The word *cuckold* entered the mainstream lexicon. First relegated to XXX sites, the slang insult quickly infiltrated our politics, becoming a favorite burn for internet trolls. To be a cuck or cuckold was to be emasculated to the point of negation. A cuck, we were told, was a man who stood by helplessly while another man, usually a Black man, had intercourse with his wife. To be a cuck, we read in *New York Times* op-eds, was to be the weakest of the weak. Our children knew this already, however, because 84 percent of boys and 54 percent of girls in our children's generation had watched some form of online pornography before their eighteenth birthday. From stepmother porn and gonzo clips they learned that sex is a performance. They absorbed the lingo—*BBW, BBC, DVDA*. They talked about scarfing and veggie porn. The internet taught our daughters that sex is aggressive and that women like pain and humiliation and taught our sons that the worst thing one could be was cuckolded. And yet the antithesis of the cuck, it turned out, was not the man whose wife was faithful. It was the man who screwed other men's wives, who cuckolded *them*. Weakest or strongest, the smartphones told our children, there is no middle ground. If you are not dominating others, then you are being dominated. Had this cold, zero-sum ideology driven them to despair?

We had originally thought the internet would be the new town square, giving everyone a voice and making even the most excluded among us feel comfortable. Instead, it became a war zone, turning the most comfortable of us into the most uncomfortable. Every day we were given new phrases and appellations to learn—cis-gender, nonbinary—and sanctioned when we used them incorrectly, or didn't use them at all.

Age-old norms and codes about race and gender

were being rewritten day after day, and we struggled to keep up, the fear of all this change creating a backlash of bathroom bans and teen sport brawls. Our children were adaptable—children always are. They felt liberated even not to have to conform to the rigid castes of jock and nerd and beauty queen. But our adult brains had been wired to see the world the old way, and we either struggled to adapt or raged against the ask, fighting to put our sons and daughters back into the boxes that made sense. Had this rejection of who they wanted to be in favor of who we felt comfortable parenting flipped a switch?

Most had been born under the financial uncertainty of the global economic collapse in 2008, only to spend their first critical teenage months imprisoned at home, "distance learning," while their parents day drank and communed with their screens, trying to maintain some sense of momentum in their children's lives. The economy collapsed again. Depression spiked feelings of apathy and dislocation.

How ironic that the spread of the vaccine that "liberated" them from their endless quarantine also sent them back into the shooting range that was high school and middle school and elementary.

Remember Folkdale High. Remember Crosby Middle. Remember Altamonte University.

Was this it? we wondered. *Were our children simply killing themselves before someone else did?*

We blamed ourselves, of course. Had we neglected them? Smothered them? Were we tiger moms or elephant moms or dolphin moms? Helicopter parents or lawn mower parents or attachment parents?

Was it our politics? Our endless bickering? *Please tell us. What is the answer?* we asked ourselves. *What did we miss?* But maybe the answer was so obvious we were looking right through it the whole time.

Maybe it was us. Maybe humanity itself was the problem.

When you think about it, the numbers of our existence are crushing. We have grown so used to the historic weight of our collective past, with its pogroms and purges, its fossil fuel anguish and genocidal wars, that we forget what it feels like to learn about them for the first time. A child is born. He or she asks their parents, *What is this world I am entering*? And before they're old enough to drive or drink or vote, they have learned about slavery and the holocaust. They've learned about colonization, voter suppression, and civil war.

We cook them waffles and send them to school, their mittens clipped to their sleeves, so they can learn that, between 1525 and 1866, 12,500,000

Africans were hunted, captured, and shipped to America to be slaves.

Twenty-six percent of them were children.

Now eat your vegetables.

We drive them to playdates and buy them smartphones, installing software so we can monitor their Snapchats and TikTok accounts for inappropriate content, then show them how 6,000,000 Jews were killed in concentration camps during World War Two—1,320,000 of them executed in just three months.

How was school today? we ask when we pick them up. *Did you make any new friends?*

We carpool to birthday parties, acting like homelessness is a normal part of the social order, like mentally ill people yelling at cars in the crosswalks was something we'd accepted, something they would just need to learn to live with.

We assault them with facts—577,000 Syrians killed in a civil war that created 5,600,000 refugees and displaced 6,200,000 people. Meanwhile, in China, the government has rounded up more than 1,000,000 Uighurs and forced them into "reeducation camps." We tell them to memorize these "facts" in case there's a test, as if the math of human mass murder is the same as the volume of a sphere. As if the past is a bloodless lesson they can absorb and file away, just like the Smoot-Hawley Tariff Act.

We act, in other words, like hatred, intolerance, and violence are normal. *Now be a good boy*, we tell them. *Be a good girl. Don't have a nervous breakdown. Don't self-medicate with alcohol or drugs. Don't call us hypocrites or reject our moral authority. Don't think about ending it all before you grow up to become hypocrites like us. We are your parents, your elders, and we know what's best.*

Thinking about it now, in hindsight, we could do worse than to ask—is this what drove our otherwise sane children to suicide?

The Nadirs

There are two major political parties in America. I would write their names here, but the words themselves cause otherwise good-mannered people to curse and spit on the ground, so instead let's use names that are more onomatopoetic—that means names derived from the sounds each party makes. To wit, let's call one party the Party of Truth and the other the Party of Lies. But here's the catch. Members of each party believe their party is the Party of Truth and that their adversaries belong to the Party of Lies.

For example, right now the Party of Truth is in power.

Before that the Party of Truth was in power.

(Except it was the other party.)

You can see how this is going to go.

For short, let's call one side Truthers and the other side Liars.

Which is which depends on you.

Margot grew up in the Party of Truth, back when it was called something else. Her father was a Truther and his father before him. The truths they believed were bootstrap truths, fiscal truths, truths about patriotism and free markets. Remy also grew up in the Party of Truth, except his parents' party believed truths about hope and equality, about safety nets and personal sacrifice. In college Remy came to believe his parents' truths were fantasies. There would never be equality for the masses, he realized. In the real world, there could only ever be personal achievement. So he switched from the Party of Truth to the Party of Truth.

And yet it's hard to dispute that in the last few years, the truths themselves have gotten murkier. For instance, it used to be the Party of Truth that believed in reducing the national debt. But somewhere around 2016, they abandoned that truth in favor of the Truth of Massive Tax Cuts. As a result, the Other Party of Truth became the Party for Reduced National Debt. Which means that now, for Remy and Margot's side, reduced national debt has become a lie, fought for by the Party of Lies.

Try to keep up.

Margot herself uses a different analogy. She looks at her party as a Bar and the other party as a Restaurant. This makes her a Drinker, and the other party's members Cooks. The Cooks claim they want to serve food to as many people as possible. They act like all they want is a big, warm forever feast, a giant Norman Rockwell melting-pot-Thanksgiving, but the truth is what they really want is to tell their patrons where to sit and their suppliers how to farm.

Rules. Snobbery. Guilt. These are the dishes they serve.

In the Cooks' restaurant, new diners are made to pay the bill for old meals because historical debts can never be repaid. In the Cooks' restaurant, those with more are punished and those with less are praised. See, the Cooks believe that the rich should give their seats up to the poor, often forgoing their own meals entirely, so that those who didn't call ahead, who didn't make a reservation, who can't afford to order an entrée or dessert, should get the all-you-can-eat buffet, free of charge, until the very function of a restaurant—to feed customers in exchange for money—has been repurposed and the people who have the most eat the least.

A Bar, on the other hand, is a place for adults to drink, adults who—because they're adults—can make their own decisions about what to order and how much to consume. The Bar Margot belongs to used to be a Cigar Bar, where well-educated Christian family men and their wives drank brandy and discussed tax shelters and exporting American freedom to the tropics. But then, a few years ago, the Bar changed management. It became a Sports Bar! Now, the only thing the Drinkers inside care about is winning. And their enemy is everyone outside. The more drinks they have, the more damage they want to do, until their reason for living is not just to beat the other teams but to destroy them.

Sure, there's still a small backroom where Drinkers who believe in moderation can sit, but the tone of the place has changed. In the main room, the customer is always right, and so the drinks keep getting bigger and stronger. Fights break out, but if the Bartenders try to cut people off, a mob forms and threatens to destroy the Bar, so they apologize and pour another round.

In the old days, Drinkers used to choose leaders who believed in small government and free enterprise. These days the leaders that get the most votes are the entertainers, the emotionalists. They buy round after round, telling the sad Drinkers that the world is a sad place and the angry Drinkers that the world is out to get them. *Only in the Bar are you safe. Only your fellow Drinkers deserve a say. What do the Cooks know about suffering? All they do is eat their Sunday dinners and judge.*

Now, personally, Margot is a moderate. She will have one or two drinks maximum. And she tends to believe that others should do the same. The problem is, her Bar has been taken over by the drunks. And though she doesn't believe in drinking to excess, she thinks the moment you start making rules about who can drink and how much, you turn adults into children.

And Judge Margot Burr-Nadir is not a child.

O

Then one day she is in Texas, like a tall tale, a twist you never saw coming.

It is the Year of the Rabbit, another collection of Q1s through Q4s, days to work and bills to pay. Late April specifically. The days in Austin have just started to get Texas hot. Armpit weather. Ninety-eight in the shade.

There is a rental car driving into the city from the airport. A blue Ford going fifty-five in the far-right lane. Margot is in the passenger seat. Remy is driving. Hadrian, twelve now impossibly, with a size nine shoe, sits in back. They are headed to visit Story, now twenty-two (*also impossible*), an adult by any measure. She moved to Austin two years back for law school, though it may be she has dropped out. Margot isn't clear. A few weeks ago, phone calls became text messages and then text messages became Facebook posts, and since then communications have mostly ceased.

It is still the early days of the wave. In Wisconsin, Brad Carpenter is already dead. As are Todd Billings and Tim O'Malley, plus the girls at the Wisconsin border. There are clusters in Oregon and Alabama, but no clear sense yet that larger events are afoot.

In back, young Hadrian listens to an audiobook on wireless headphones. Harry Potter, maybe? Remy isn't sure. He always means to police the device better than he does.

"She knows we're coming, right?" he asks as he scans the road signs.

"She should," says Margot. "We planned this trip over Christmas. And I left a bunch of messages."

Remy nods. He likes to think that he and Story have a good relationship, but the reality is *who knows?* She was always close to her dad, and Remy is the extra wheel, though he tries to be straight with her, a shoulder to lean on, an impartial ear in times of struggle. He looks back on that period of his life—Hadrian's first five years, a new marriage, trying to launch a writing career—as a blur. A triage of constant crises, bob and weave. In the end, he thinks what most parents think.

I did the best I could.

In the passenger seat, Margot is reading

evidentiary briefs on a bank robbery case. In Flatbush not too long ago, a man made a startling discovery. Anything written in the juice of a lemon is invisible to the naked eye. If this so-called invisible ink could make words disappear, the defendant thought, what else could it vanish? Three days later the man walked into a bank with lemon juice smeared all over his face. He smiled at the security cameras. He felt so confident his face was invisible that he drove across town and robbed a second bank. Later, when the police arrested him using CCTV footage of his face, he cried out in confusion and misery, "But I wore the juice!"

Oh, people, thinks Margot. We know so little and talk so much. Cooks and Drinkers alike. We animals called human beings, who move through life with such conviction, such sureness. So many opinions. Such confidence that our beliefs and ideas are right. So certain are we that the decisions we are making are clear and reasoned that we reject all evidence to the contrary. The Lemon Juice Bandit was the victim of his brain. We are all victims of our brains. They tell us to do things and we do them. They tell us to believe things and we believe them. They hide our blind spots from us. All the while we believe we are making choices. This is the best trick our brains play on us. They tell us we are rational, decision-making machines, when really we are obeying machines, hardwired by DNA.

Margot's phone rings. She checks the number. Unlisted. Normally she wouldn't answer, but it could be Story.

"Judge Nadir."

Remy doesn't hear what's said on the other line, but suddenly Margot goes pale.

"Everything okay?" he asks.

She doesn't respond, just chews her bottom lip, mind racing. Because what the voice on the other end of the phone said was—

"Please hold for the President of the United States."

Outside, the landscape wears its summer coat. Spanish moss on the trees, rain-green grass. They pass new subdivisions on Riverside, the city growing like a weed, sprawling farther and farther from its center. Margot sits speechless in the passenger seat.

"Judge Nadir."

"Yes, sir."

"Is this a bad time?"

"No, sir. Not at all."

"You sound like you're on the move."

"I'm in Texas, sir."

"From Texas?"

"No, sir. I'm from Michigan originally. My daughter's in law school here."

"Okay, good. Good. Well, I'll make it quick. Hasn't been announced yet, but Judge Baker's gonna retire."

What Margot hears is the blood roaring in her ears. She didn't vote for this president. He is a Cook and she is a Drinker, so how can he be calling her right now with this news? With the offer the call implies?

"He says he's done," says the president, "and I believe him. And so that means I got a seat on the Supreme Court opening up."

Margot turns and looks at her husband. He is trying to keep his eyes on the road, but it's so clear there's something happening, he keeps turning to look at her.

What? he mouths.

She shakes her head, unable to speak.

"You there, Marjorie?"

"It's Margot, sir."

"Ah, shit. I'm an asshole. But they wrote it down wrong."

"That's okay, sir. I can be Marjorie if it gets me on the court."

He laughs, and she feels a thrill of triumph. Sometimes it's just that simple. You can have all the qualifications in the world, be a paper-lock, but at the end of the day organizations still run on human connection, the feeling of *I like this guy.*

"Touché," he says. "And look, I know you're not the obvious choice for a president of my persuasion, but I'm pushing for unity here, trying to reach across the damn aisle, build a bridge, and all that, so, look. The first step is you come in and meet. When can you get here?"

"Here?"

"To DC. That's where I live. It's a white house on Pennsylvania Avenue. Can't miss it."

"Yes, sir. I deserve that."

"Thing is, time is of the essence, as they say. Nobody in this town can keep a secret worth a damn, and when the news breaks I want to be ready with a solution."

"Is tomorrow okay?" Margot asks. "I flew all this way. I feel like I should at least see my daughter's face."

There's a pause. Margot worries she's blown it.

"I got seven people shaking their heads at me here," says the president. "But that's fine with me. I got daughters myself, younger, but still—if they lived in a different state, well, I'd wanna visit all the time. Go ahead and grab a bite and then catch a flight later tonight. We can meet in the morning. Chuck here'll reach out in a few minutes to work out the details."

"Thank you, sir. And should I go ahead and assume I'm not the only judge you're meeting on this?"

"Yeah, that's a fair assumption. But it's a short list, and you're at the top. So wear your good shoes."

"I will. Thank you, sir."

"Don't thank me yet. Impress me."

She swallows. The world racing toward her is in Technicolor.

"I'll try."

She pushes *end*. The silence that follows lasts a thousand years.

"Babe?" says Remy.

Margot keeps her eyes forward. There is a pickup truck with a bumper sticker. She focuses on that, because if she turns and looks at her husband or her son, she's going to start to cry.

"I'm going to be on the Supreme Court," she says.

O

Remy has his own theory of politics. In his mind the two parties can be broken down into Swimmers and Surfers. The Swimmers are the party of FDR and Obama. The Surfers are the party of Reagan. The Swimmers move in packs through the ocean of history, pulled along by the current. They feel connected to the water, buoyed by their progress, but also vulnerable to the undertow and crushing waves. The Surfers ride on top of the water, choosing their own path. In their minds they are birds, not fish, creatures of the wind. Their progress is not driven by the ocean but by their own muscles and will.

Remy is a Surfer, because who doesn't want to fly?

Over the last decade, as Judge Burr-Nadir has grown in stature in Surfing circles, Remy too has been busy. His first book on William F. Buckley was respected but not successful. His next, an analysis of why the Party of Swimmers doesn't actually serve the interest of Black Americans, gained him a recurring slot on *Fox & Friends*, and entrée into the high-profile world of conservative punditry. One speech he made on the show in 2015 has been viewed on YouTube more than sixteen million times. In it Remy says:

"I don't want to wear four hundred years of history chained to my ankle. It's time to let go of the past. I am not a slave. My parents are from Trinidad. They were never slaves, and their parents weren't either. Blacks in America want a clean slate. But the [Swimmer] Party refuses to free us from the chains of slavery, the chains of civil rights. They like us shackled to all the old grievances, because it helps them win elections."

At this point he took something from his pocket.

"You remember that movie *The Matrix*? Laurence Fishburne makes a speech about what the machines are using people for. Well, it's the same with liberals. Blacks, immigrants, people of color—this is all we are to them."

He holds up a nine-volt battery.

"We empower them. They use us for our votes, and what do we get in return—tell me? Eight years of Clinton, eight years of Obama—are we better educated? Are our neighborhoods safer? No. They use our power to fuel their own interests, and they do it by keeping us down on the plantation."

The battery metaphor got him invited to meet top leaders of the Surfer Party in Washington and VIP tickets to high-profile events in New York and Los Angeles. *See*, thought Remy, *this is what I'm talking about. Every man has the ability to invent their own future. Black, white, brown, it makes no difference. Just say no to the party of grievance, the party of reparations. Ride the wave. Don't let the undertow of yesterday's problems pull you down.*

But as the invitations from elevated white circles increased, Remy found himself decidedly unwelcome in places he used to love. They took the kids out of public school—where all those Swimmer parents now gave him the evil eye—and moved out of Brooklyn to a six-bedroom Colonial in West-chester. Here, while Hadrian went to an elite prep school, Remy wrote a weekly column and another book and regularly took the town car ride down the Major Deegan to film segments for Fox News, Fox Business, Bloomberg, CNN, you name it.

By the time the God King came into office, Remy had become conservative royalty. A Black man "who told the truth": social welfare programs *oppressed* people of color; affirmative action had accomplished what it was designed for, and now must end. *Praise the Lord*, the races now had equality in the eyes of the law. If only the Swimmer Party could achieve equality in their own minds, could leave the current of dependency, the current of grievance, the current of inadequacy.

And yet, at the same time, starting in 2016, something shifted under his feet, for what was the God King if not the Emperor of Grievances? The wave Remy thought he was surfing—a sunny-day wave of self-reliance and free will—became a storm surge of outrage and injury. Remy started to worry that Surfers like him had lost control of their wave, or maybe that feeling of control had been an illusion all along, the way a bird isn't in control of the wind. He tried to turn, to stand up for the values he had preached, but more and more he found himself shouting into the storm. In 2017, 2018, Remy watched other sunny-day Surfers denounce this new culture of grievance and saw how in an instant they were pulled from their boards and drowned. And so Remy had a choice to make—speak up and vanish into the cold depths, or convert and live. Either way, the wave was surfing him now, and they were headed for the rocks.

And so he changed his battery speech to a speech about liberal elites sucking the blood from the common man, a speech about moral corruption, about exploitation. He pledged allegiance to the God King, impeached but never removed, indicted but never convicted. What could explain his miracle ascent, his Teflon bouyancy, if not magic? In short, Remy did what he had to do to survive. Or not just survive, but to prosper, for he had grown accustomed to the perks of punditry, the book contracts and Twitter followers. He liked standing out in a crowd, and so he said what he had to say and did what he had to do, but make no mistake, the undertow had him and it was pulling him down.

O

They reach the address Story gave them in sixteen minutes, following the calm commands of the GPS docent to the letter—even the ones she has to repeat because everyone in the car is screaming.

Good news is like oxygen filling your lungs. You become light-headed, enraptured. You feel you might just live forever. Unless, of course, you are one of those people who has the strong impulse to hide under the bed—which is the feeling that strikes Margot after the initial wave of adrenaline has worn off. She hears her mother's voice, like a scared rabbit, her mother who liked to point out you're never more vulnerable than in a moment of celebration.

What will it be? Margot wonders. *Car accident? Maybe my flight to DC will crash.*

But at the red light she smiles when Remy squeezes her shoulder. Smiles when her son leans up from the backseat to hug her. At that moment she realizes she's been waiting for the phone call for forty years, that she's never wanted anything in this life as much as she wants to be a justice on the highest court in the land. And that terrifies her. As do the dizzying political ramifications of being a well-known Drinker, nominated by a Cook. *A unity play*, he called it, and that works for her just fine, being an old-school moderate who can still remember functioning government. But will she be seen as a traitor by her own party, or celebrated as a Trojan horse?

"*In three hundred feet, turn right,*" says the GPS docent.

"Do we have to move?" Hadrian asks.

"Let's not—get ahead of things," she says. "It's just an interview."

"He said there was a list?" Remy asks. "There's usually a list."

"You know this how?"

"Books. Newspapers."

"There is a list," she confirms. "But not a long one and he said I'm on the top."

It hits her. "Shit," she says. "Flights." She takes out her phone, brings up the browser.

"You book your own?" Remy asks. She searches for flights, Austin to DC, enters today's date.

"I don't know. He said the chief of staff would call me."

"Chuck Malcolm is gonna call you?"

"You say that like I didn't just talk to the president."

"Right. That's—I'm an idiot."

She touches his hand, offers a smile. "You're not an idiot. It's just—we're off the map now."

"In two hundred feet, turn left. Your destination will be on the right."

She thinks about telling her daughter—*will she scream?*—thinks about the moment she'll meet the president, that first step into the Oval Office— *what will she wear?* The thought paralyzes her. She hasn't brought a *meet the president* outfit.

Would Story go shopping with her? Is there even a store in town that sells pantsuits?

As her mind races, her life separates itself from time, miles passing without impact. Nothing her body experiences physically—the temperature in the car, the landscape passing outside, the sound of the radio—imprints itself on her memory, and therefore it's as if the journey itself never happens. For twenty minutes, Margot exists in a state of internal debate, lost in the blast zone of a dream come true.

What Margot's mother, were she alive, would have warned her to consider is that the other shoe may have already dropped.

Beside her, Remy focuses on the road. Where Margot's mind is sharp, his thoughts are scattered. It's all for nothing, he thinks, if he drives up on the curb right now and kills someone. The roads in Texas have a central turn lane, and on direction from the GPS docent, he signals and slows, pulling over. His hands are tingling again. They have been, off and on, for a few weeks, and he's been dropping things—silverware, pens. But absent-mindedly, in moments when his brain was focused on something else—so he chalked it up to the collateral damage of living a life of the mind. But at his physical last month he mentioned it—numbness in his hands, being a bit of a butterfingers.

The doctor checked his eyes and asked him to grip his hand and squeeze.

Remy did, or tried, because his hands didn't seem to be as strong as they used to be.

"Is that all you got?" the doctor asked. His name was Mike Esby, and he and Remy had become friendly over the last few years, after their social circles merged when Hadrian started prep school with Mike's son.

"Just a little off right now," Remy told him. "I had the flu last month. Hard to get out of bed."

"Yeah, Jeremy had that," Mike tells him. "It was going around the school."

The doctor sent Remy for an MRI, looking for a tumor or a spinal disk pressing on the nerve. When that came back negative, he ordered blood tests and an electromyogram, a test Remy had never heard of that involved a technician inserting an electric needle through the skin into various muscles. It was as enjoyable as it sounds and made him feel jumpy for hours afterward.

Then, yesterday, when he was on the treadmill, Mike's office called and asked him to come in. Remy showered and took a cab into the city. He was a forty-six-year-old man with no history of health problems, and an optimist to boot, so he wasn't worried. While he waited for the doctor, he read an article in a travel magazine about Vietnam that made him want to go, and he took a picture of it with his phone to help himself remember. Then the nurse called him in.

"ALS," Mike said, when Remy was seated across from him, and for a moment Remy thought he was talking about baseball.

"Is it the playoffs already?"

"What?"

"No," said Remy, a cold sweat breaking out suddenly on his back. "What are *you* talking about."

"I'm saying the tests came back—and I ran a few of them just to be sure—and, well, there's no easy way of saying it, but you've got ALS."

"And I'm saying what is that?" Remy's tone is more aggressive than he intended, but he's worried that his inability to understand the acronym may be part of the condition, like he's now medically unable to speak English.

"Sorry," Mike says. "Amyotrophic lateral sclerosis. You may know it as Lou Gehrig's disease."

The words hit his brain but didn't penetrate.

"Didn't he die of that?" Remy asks.

"Yes," says Mike. "He did."

Remy's heart began to race. "But—"

"There are drugs," Mike told him, "that can slow the progression. But there's no meaningful treatment. I'm sorry, Remy. There's no easy way to say this. You have an aggressive neurological disorder that is going to take over your life, and you need to prepare yourself for that. Does Margot know you're here?"

But Remy wasn't listening anymore.

O

You have arrived at your destination.

He pulls over on a quiet, tree-lined street. The internet has told him that the loss of muscle control in his hands will worsen and spread. The muscles in his body are literally wasting away, deprived of nourishment. One day in the not-too-distant future he will lose the ability to walk, then speak, then eat, then breathe. And then he will be dead.

He shuts off the car. Beside him, Margot is still buzzing.

"Six three one. This is the place."

They get out. The sound of cicadas hits them along with the heat, as if the temperature itself is a life-form. They are on the east side of town—east and west separated by highway 35, a north/south artery commonly known as the NAFTA superhighway. The area used to be predominately Black, but the last ten years have seen the blooming creep of gentrification. first the artists, then the restaurants, then the strollers, housing prices rising, driving out the existing community. In some ways it is the history of the United States played in perpetuity as a meme. The manifest destiny of wealth to spread and absorb. The word "reclamation."

Story and her boyfriend—Felix?—moved into a sublet on Holly Street near an artisanal restaurant that used to be a Laundromat. It's a small white clapboard house that needs a paint job. The lawn, Remy notices, has surrendered to the heat and lies sickly yellow beside the cracked concrete walk. The house has been squeezed between two adjoining homes, one a modern remodel, the other a dilapidated Craftsman with a FOR SALE sign by the curb.

"We could buy that one," says Hadrian, already taller than his mother at twelve.

"She'd love that," says Margot, wishing she'd thought to bring a gift or a bottle of wine. *Do you bring alcohol to your adult children?* she wonders. *Is that a thing?*

They approach the house. The shades are drawn. There are lights on inside.

"You told her we were coming?" Remy asks for the third time since they landed.

"Again, yes," says Margot, a hint of annoyance coming into her voice. "I texted, but I didn't hear back."

Remy knocks. The front lawn is sunlit and hot, and they stand sweating, waiting for the kids to answer.

"You—"

"She knows," says Margot. "Maybe we should have gone to the hotel first."

Hadrian goes to the living room window, peers in.

"Hadrian," says Remy.

"I'm just looking."

"This is Texas. Black men shouldn't look in people's windows in Texas."

"He's twelve," says Margot.

"You don't think they shoot twelve-year-olds here?"

Margot checks her watch. In her head she's already heading to the airport to fly to DC. She steps past Remy, tries the door. It's unlocked.

"Mistake," says Remy.

"I've got to pee," Margot tells him.

She steps inside. There is no entryway. The front door opens into the living room. The decorations are a mix of post-college IKEA assemblage, his and hers. Margot recognizes a few heirlooms— Grandma's trunk, covered with a linen doily, Story's childhood armoire. Several black-and-white photos in cheap frames line the walls—*the boyfriend's work?* On her way to the bathroom, Margot passes two suitcases and a leather overnight bag but doesn't notice them. Why would you?

Remy and Hadrian enter behind her in time to see the bathroom door closing. Even though it's his stepdaughter's house, Remy feels nervous at the trespass. He closes the front door quickly. Inside, the air-conditioning is on. The coolness is welcome, but with it comes a smell—a subtle sourness, like milk that has turned. He looks over at Hadrian, but the boy has his phone out already. So Remy follows the smell to the kitchen door, opens it.

The smell is stronger inside. Remy can see that the kitchen table has been set for dinner. Plates full of food, forks half-buried. Pots sit on the stove, dishes in the sink. But it's the chairs that get his attention, both set at forty-five-degree angles from the table, frozen as if in mid-move. The story they tell is one of simultaneity, a mirror dance, chairs slid back in harmony and abandoned at once.

Remy examines the table. Chicken and potatoes, maybe. A potpie. There is a bowl in the center of the table, wrapped in a dish towel. Remy looks inside, recoils. It looks like rice at first, but the rice is moving.

How long does it take for maggots to grow? he wonders. *Three days? A week?*

"Babe?"

He turns. Margot is standing in the doorway.

"They're not home," he says.

"I know."

"They haven't been in a few days."

"What's that smell?"

Remy is trying to process what it means. A spontaneous getaway? Late for an outing. *We'll do the dishes later.* A medical emergency—*we should call the hospitals,* he thinks.

Margot sees the maggots. "Oh my God."

He takes her arm, leads her back into the living room. "When did you talk to her?"

"Thursday?"

"On the phone?"

"She texted."

Hadrian calls out from the sofa, eyes still on his mobile screen. "What's that smell?"

"Dishes," says Remy.

Margot thinks about the exchange with Story. Thursday was *US v Valice,* a federal racketeering case. And then administrative meetings. She texted Story from the elevator.

Excited to see you.

An hour went by and then a response.

Who?

Very funny, she wrote. Did you pick a restaurant yet? I can have Barbara make a reservation.

She waited for a response, but nothing came. Then, as she put her phone in her robe pocket, it buzzed. She pulled out the phone, looked at it.

Ha ha ha.

What did that mean? She texted back, but got no

reply. For some reason she thought about the silliness from her daughter's youth. Thirteen, fourteen, fifteen. This obsession with skinniness, the oversize sweatshirts hiding weight loss, dinners unfinished, lunches uneaten, and then the realization that Story was literally starving herself to death.

Where did my daughter go? she wondered, sitting in the waiting room at the doctor's office, *the girl who stood on that stage and sang with such bright innocence?* And then she saw the number on the scale and nearly fainted.

"The police," she says. "We should call the police."

As if on cue, her phone rings. The number is unlisted. She answers.

"Judge Nadir, this is Chuck Malcolm. Is this a good time?"

"It's—I'm not sure. We're in Austin visiting my daughter, but she's not here. And there are dishes on the table and bags packed in the living room. And I haven't talked to her in five days."

"You're worried."

"Yes."

"She lives alone?"

"No, with her boyfriend. But he's gone too. I don't have his number."

She breathes, mind racing. "There are maggots."

A pause on the other end of the line. "I've just

sent Randy to call the Justice Department. Someone from the FBI field office in Austin should be there within the hour."

Relief, warm and overflowing, fills her. "Thank you."

"Given the circumstances, should I put your flight on hold?"

She looks at Remy, who has been listening. He shakes his head, mouths, *Go.*

"I don't know," she says.

"I understand, and no one will fault you if you think you should wait until you know what happened to your daughter, but this thing is moving. And there's no pause button I can hit. So—"

Remy squeezes her shoulder. "Go," he says. "I'll find her."

She nods, her eyes watering of their own accord, looks to her son.

"We got this," he says.

She nods. "No," she says, "I'm still coming. Just tell me where and when."

"Give me your daughter's address. Someone from the field office will take you to the airfield."

"The airfield."

"It's important we keep things quiet for now. The press knows the justice is thinking about retiring. They'll be watching the airports."

"What time is the flight?"

"Whatever time you show up. The plane's en route."

"Oh," she says. "I don't have—I need something to wear to meet the president. I don't have—I packed for barbecue."

"I can do that for you. I'll have someone reach out to your office."

"Thank you—I—you're kind."

"Well, thanks, but the fact is—you're my choice, and I want you to win. So not a complete altruist."

"Fair enough."

"But, Margot?"

"Yes," she hears herself say.

"I'll be praying for you and your family."

She hangs up. "I need some water," she says, "or to sit down."

Remy goes into the kitchen, gets her a glass, fills it from the tap. When he comes back, she's gone. Hadrian points.

"Bedroom."

Remy doesn't know where that is exactly, but he moves down the hall, finds her standing in a south-facing room that looks into a fenced backyard. Margot is going through the dresser.

"Her underwear is gone."

She closes the top drawer, goes to the closet. Inside are mostly bare hangers.

She remembers rushing her daughter to the

hospital that day, her vitals all over the map, electrolytes nonexistent, suffering from severe dehydration. An hour later Story was on a feeding tube, her hands strapped down so she couldn't struggle. A void. Where her child had been there was now a void.

That was the beginning of a journey that lasted five years, what Margot now calls *the silliness*, because calling it what it really was is to admit how close she'd come to failure as a parent. To death.

"So she packed all her clothes," says Margot, "but then why leave her bags in the house?"

"Did you check if her car is here?"

Margot's eyes widen. She pushes past him, moves down the hall and out the front door. Story drives a blue Camry, a hand-me-down from her uncle. Margot searches the street but doesn't see it. Remy follows her out onto the lawn, still carrying the glass of water.

"Tell me the boyfriend's name again?"

"Felix," she says. "Moor. I think. The last name."

"I saw a desk. I'll go through it, but it's all phones anymore."

"The FBI will know."

Neither of them states the obvious; which is that all around the country children are disappearing permanently. That the next step for them is to call the hospital or a morgue. Instinctually they agree

to think of this crisis in terms of solvability. Gone
X number of hours, last seen headed in Y direction. A mystery. What they're facing is a mystery,
nothing more.

Remy feels weak in the knees suddenly. The heat
maybe. He's not used to this much humidity. He
reaches out and leans against a pecan tree. Margot
notices.

"Are you okay?" she asks.

"I'm fine. It's just—a lot."

She nods.

"Promise me you'll find her," she says.

"I'll find her," he says as a black sedan pulls
up to the curb, parks. A man climbs out of the
passenger seat. A woman from the driver's, both
in suits. The FBI, as promised, has arrived.

That July the forests of Alaska caught fire. Black smoke ringed the Pacific Northwest like a smoldering halo. Bigfoot sightings in the Rocky Mountains rose by 58 percent. In a six-day period, more than ten million people watched a YouTube video of a lumbering giant moving furtively between evergreens outside Boulder, Colorado. Still the suicides rose. Funeral homes couldn't keep up with demand. Around the country people woke hearing footsteps that had no source, strange knocking sounds in the walls. Rooms, normally heated evenly, developed unexplained pockets of cold air.

Massachusetts, West Virginia, Utah.

Google searches for "ghosts" and "apparitions" rose nationally by 352 percent. Experts wrote it off to delusions of grief, but the phenomenon was not restricted to homes that had suffered a loss.

Wyoming, Oregon, Texas.

Evangelical preachers claimed these were signs of the rapture, as laid out in the Book of Revelation. The Four Horsemen of the Apocalypse were on the move. But still the stock market rose. Plastic goods from China steamed across the Pacific on their way to the rec rooms of the Midwest. Starbucks' website introduced a countdown clock—not to the end of the world, but to the return of the Pumpkin Spice Latte.

In the words of Antonio Gramsci: "The crisis consists precisely in the fact that the old is dying and the new cannot be born; in this interregnum a great variety of morbid symptoms appear."

Broke divorcées and soldiers on leave who rode the Greyhound line from Weehawken to Pittsburgh began posting Instagram photos of a tall white man in Revolutionary War garb who claimed to be Alexander Hamilton. He sat always in the same seat by the window across from the rear doors with a faraway look in his eyes. Riders who engaged him in conversation described him as "confused" and said he would repeatedly ask them what year it was and tell them he was trying to get home to his Eliza. At Montecito, in Virginia, tourists wandering the grounds of Thomas Jefferson's estate reported sighting an old man with a billowing collar and velvet pants who seemed to hover several inches above the floor. No one could get a clear photo, but an audio recording surfaced in June of the apparition, who seemed to be reciting passages from the Liberty Papers.

In Saudi Arabia the temperature reached one hundred and forty degrees.

At night, Abe Lincoln could be seen wandering down the center divider of I-55 between Peoria and Springfield, stovepipe hat in hand. Tears ran down his cheeks, glimmering in the oncoming headlights.

At the Senate confirmation hearings for Judge Margot Nadir, viewers noticed a ghost seated directly behind the judge. It was the third day of testimony. After the lunch recess, when the judge took her seat once more, you can clearly see a young woman seated directly behind the judge, wearing a white dress. The young woman is pale, her blond hair pulled back into a loose ponytail. She wears oversize black sunglasses, her head bowed. On the dais, the committee chairman gavels the hearing back into session. He welcomes the judge back and jokes he hopes her lunch was more relaxing than the grilling she's taken all morning. The judge smiles politely and leans over to pour herself a glass of water. As she moves, the young woman behind her lifts her chin and appears to look directly into the camera. Judge Nadir's body blocks the young woman from the camera for 1.5 seconds.

When she sits back, the young woman is gone, replaced by a middle-aged man with a goatee.

Twitter erupts. Video clips are posted by the thousands. Frame-by-frame analysis and animated GIFs. 1) The judge leaned over. 2) The young woman looked up. But when the judge settled back in her seat, 3) the young woman was gone. Was it a special effect? Was the entire hearing a computer-generated simulation caught in a glitch? Every pixel was inspected thoroughly and then in-spected again. Internet researchers dug up photos of Judge Nadir's daughter—missing now for four-plus weeks—and post them side by side with grainy blowups of the mystery woman. The meaning is clear. Story Nadir, twenty-four, is dead, and this is her ghost. Twitter parses each element of the image for hidden meaning—the white dress, the dark glasses. Why appear in that specific moment— after lunch on the third day? Why vanish?

The anomaly causes such a stir that an hour later the chairman is forced to recess for the day. Leav-ing the chamber, Judge Nadir appears stunned— as if she has somehow crossed over to another di-mension, one in which Bigfoot is real, and Einstein never divined the Theory of Relativity. Flashbulbs capture her surprise. Back at her hotel, Margot reviews the footage with her husband—their son, Hadrian, plugged into a handheld video game in the next room. Remy rewinds the clip several times, playing it in slow motion. What does it mean? Where had the young woman come from and where did she go? She is blond, like their daughter, but the sunglasses make it hard to see her features. Sitting there, Margot is convinced there has to be a rational explanation. This is the kind of brain she has. It believes in rational thought and scientific explanation.

Next to her, Remy feels a headache coming on. His brain is more superstitious, always hoping for a miracle. When he reaches to pause the video, he realizes foolishly that his left hand hasn't responded. He looks down—puzzled—to see the hand flat in his lap like the hand of a stranger.

Still the bodies fell. In state after state 911 was overwhelmed with frantic calls, twenty-four hours a day. Connecticut, Nebraska, Hawaii. *My son is dead. There are demons in the wall.*

The signs were everywhere, it seemed. What it meant depended on which god you worshipped. The God of Denial, the God of Revenge, the God of Beauty, Prosperity, Youth. All shared the same name—*God will lift you up. God will strike you down!*—but it wasn't possible that White Supremacist Jesus and Civil Rights Jesus were the same person, that *splash a pregnant woman with blood* Jesus and *turn the other cheek* Jesus were even the same species of deity.

We had returned to the age of polytheism without realizing it. Which God we worshipped depended on which tribe we belonged to, which wish we prayed granted. Even Reason had become a God to millions over the last century—an omnipotent being of pure science, worshipped by lettered liberals in the organic produce aisles of their local Whole Foods. And Whole Foods Jesus knows there's no such thing as ghosts.

Firm in this conviction, pundits on MSNBC dismissed the Nadir footage as doctored, or offered rational explanations for what appeared to be a miracle—the young woman must have slipped away in an instant, giving up her seat to the goateed man and moving low across the room, unseen. And yet that night even Rachel Maddow woke with ice in her heart. For weeks after she felt the chill. Objects in her house seemed to move at random, left in one room and discovered the next morning in another. Doggedly she continued to deny all possibility of the fantastical.

Montana, New Mexico, Rhode Island.

We choose our reality, you see, just as we choose our god. And the man who believes in ghosts and demons can no more accept Stephen Hawking's empire of reason than Stephen Hawking could retire to the land of werewolves.

Quest

At night he dreams of Claire. Claire before her anti-Claire screed. Before the red eyes and blouse vomit. Her dark bedroom, moon through the blinds. A poster on the wall. The painting. *Her* painting. Simon was there the night Claire saw it for the first time at the Guggenheim, the night of the gala, the night the pill bottles rained down upon the rotunda, society patrons looking up, stunned, like turkeys in the rain—Oxycodone smart bombs, tumbling end over end—then covering their hair and running for cover.

Murderer, was chanted from the spiral above.

Profiteer.

Earlier, during the perfunctory handshakes, the copious cocktails, Claire, terminally bored, had wandered away from the clot of gray-haired men and their trophy wives, from bespectacled lawyers in bow ties and society matrons in their gowns with the diaphanous sleeves that cloak their flabby arms. Simon followed her up the circle ramp instinctually, like a satellite compelled by gravity. On the lower levels they scanned the rectangles of the permanent collection. *Painting* rectangle, *photo* rectangle. Art. Foot after foot, Claire frowned her disdain.

"Hack," she said. "Pretender."

Modern.

Abstract.

Fauvist.

Cubist.

Boring.

And then halfway up the ramp she stopped. Simon, still looking at a Mondrian he thought was maybe not *so* bad, bumped into her.

"Sorry," he said reflexively, but Claire said nothing. She'd been hypnotized.

Simon stepped out from behind her. He read the plaque.

A Boy Defending a Baby from an Eagle, by Frederic Leighton, 1851.

Simon looked at his sister's face. Her lips were parted, the tip of her tongue fixed between her teeth, her pupils the size of saucers. He'd never seen her so still. He turned to the painting.

It was as described. A baby, cherubic, asleep on a white blanket, thumb in mouth, lying on a grassy slope. A huge brown eagle hovered over it, wings extended, frozen in mid-flap, the baby's diaper in one talon, pulled up to reveal a snowy hip. But the eagle's attention was elsewhere, its head turned. Because here, to the rescue, was a boy no older than eight, dressed in a kind of soldier's jacket, his left hand raised before his face, defending against the eagle's other claw. In the boy's right hand, frozen in mid-swing, was a hooked scythe, a wall of wheat at the child's back, as if the weapon itself symbolized a kind of harvest.

But there was more.

On the grass, incongruously, before the baby was an amphora of wine and a still life of food— a picnic clearly set by adults. Where were they now, these adults: mother, father? Adults who may have lain in *this very spot* not that long ago, drinking their wine, peeling their grapes, flirting, laughing, surrendering to their animal passions. Making babies. Adults who had become parents as thoughtlessly as one falls to the ground. And yet where were they when they were needed most, when the very lives of their children depended on them? Nowhere to be seen, represented in their absence by the wine of their irresponsibility, the picnic of their neglect, leaving the children to fend for themselves.

Claire stared at that painting as the museum

filled with donors, with artists and politicians, with philanthropists and pop stars. She stared at it as champagne corks popped, as whiskey sours were shaken and poured. And Simon, standing at her right hip, stared at her. What was she seeing there in the colorful smudges? This was no abstract appreciation, no academic respect. Something personal was happening in the space between his sister and this one-hundred-and-fifty-year-old painting. Around them the lights dimmed and rose, a sign that the presentation was about to begin. Simon tugged at Claire's sleeve. He was thirteen years old and consumed by fear, fear that they were doing something wrong, fear that they should have stayed with their parents, that their mother would be mad or their father would be disappointed, fear that they were *missing something critical.*

It was the story of his life, this inability to be where he was. To live in the moment.

"Come on," he said. "It's starting."

But Claire shook her head. "You go."

Simon swallowed hard. He felt responsible for Claire. Claire who was always wandering off, always talking back, Claire who couldn't just be nice and do what she was told.

"Claire," he said.

But she was done talking, and they stayed that way until their mother came to drag them downstairs, lips pursed, pinching their arms a little too hard, smelling of scotch and fear.

O

It's midnight when the Prophet comes to get him. Simon is sitting on the edge of his bed, his bag already packed. He is like an old woman with a doctor's appointment, up and dressed at 4:30 a.m., anxious he will sleep through the alarm, worrying their route. What if they're stopped? What if the guards are mad? What if they tell the doctors and the doctors call his parents? Simon Oliver, jailbreak artist, outlaw. The thought makes him shiver. It is a fantasy both rich and terrifying. To wantonly cast off the rules of society. To say fuck it. Fuck it all.

Could he do it and survive? Or would a bolt of lightning strike him just for asking the question? Sitting on his bed—*he has made his fucking bed*—he fingers the paper bag in his pocket, focuses on his breathing. Deep in. Slow out.

Don't think about how many private planes you've been on, how many gallons of jet fuel were burned to move four spoiled, selfish people around the globe. Think about what you personally can do to free yourself from the paralysis of this knowledge, the survivor's guilt of being rich and white and male with your whole life ahead of you.

Redemption. Ever since the Prophet said the word, it's all Simon can think about.

The dorm is soundless at this time of night, just the hum of his own jittery blood roaring in his ears, so the crackle of car tires on the gravel outside is like a scream. As headlights hit the wall of his room, Simon freezes. Another ambulance maybe, here for the latest escapee. The paper bag in his pocket crinkles when he stands, crosses to the window, looks out.

As he does, he tries not to think about how in China they call it the *airpocalypse*. How in India the simple act of breathing outdoors is equal to smoking two packs of cigarettes a day. Pollution has been linked with increased mental illness in children and dementia in adults. But sure, let's all just keep pretending that nothing's wrong.

There is a van outside, something out of the 1970s. Airbrushed on the driver's side is a painting of a mythic warrior, wielding a battle-axe, facing a horde of demons—a buxom woman in a chain-mail bikini at his side. Smoke emanates from the open driver's window. Smoke that, through the partially open window, smells of skunky rec rooms and shag carpeting.

Is this our getaway car? he wonders. *Or did someone order a pizza?*

There is a sharp knock behind Simon. He turns.

The Prophet is there with Louise. She is wearing short shorts and has a Hello Kitty backpack on her back. The Prophet holds nothing, of course, as if, being an elevated being, he requires none of the ephemera the rest of us cling to—clean clothes, a toothbrush, time.

"Fly, you fool," says Louise.

Simon grabs his knapsack, struggles it onto his shoulder. Looking at them, it's clear he over-packed, but there's no time to adjust, for the Prophet has turned and is already on the move. Louise claps her hands, delighted to throw off the shackles of "progress," to take all her newfound maturity and coping devices and torch them on a pyre. She dances off, skipping down the hall with little effort to be quiet.

"How are we...?" whispers Simon, hurrying to catch up. "What's our exit route? There are two guards at the front desk until three. And this one nurse, the old guy with the limp, he's on rounds until five."

But they ignore him. Ahead, the Prophet opens the door to the back stairs.

"Wait," says Simon, following them into the stairwell. "They keep...The back doors have alarms."

The Prophet descends one flight, giving no indication he's heard or that he cares. Behind him,

Louise appears to be singing to herself, sound-tracking their escape.

So you're a tough guy

Like it really rough guy

Simon, hurrying to keep up, makes the turn to the ground floor. He would tell you, if you asked him, that there is a dead zone the size of Florida in the Arabian Sea. A dead zone so big it may include the entire Gulf of Oman. Trillions of gallons of H_2O with no O.

Bye-bye, dolphins. Bye-bye, mollusks. Bye-bye, whales.

On the landing, he sees the Prophet standing at the back door, talking to the night janitor, who is holding the door open at his back, alarm disabled. The janitor is a small Mexican man, grizzled, in his sixties. His head is bowed. The Prophet lifts his right hand and places his palm on the man's head, as if offering a benediction. Simon looks at Louise, who lifts her eyebrows, bemused, as if to say, *Here we go.* And then they are outside, breathing the warm summer air, the wind in the evergreens. Ahead of them, the van is waiting, side door open, the painted warrior with his axe slid back toward the taillights, erasing his enemy. Viewed from the ground, the buxom wench at his side seems to glow.

"Whose van is that?" Simon asks, but no one

answers, and he watches Louise jump inside, her short shorts riding up as she enters like a trick pen that goes from burlesque to nude when you write with it.

"Hey, handsome," he hears her say to the driver— still just a glowing joint in the front seat, a plume of smoke exhaled.

The Prophet stops at the side door, turns to Simon, as if he has known all along that the final step toward freedom will be the hardest.

"This is your journey," he says.

"You say that, but where—"

The Prophet shakes his head. "Where is just a place. What matters is the path. And this is yours."

He points to the dark mouth of the seventies van. Inside all Simon can see is the pinpoint glow, passed backward, and the flicker of Louise's face as she inhales.

Simon grits his teeth, eyelids fluttering. He thinks of how the probability of simultaneous crop failure in the biggest grain-growing regions once we reach four more degrees rises to 86 percent.

He knows he worries too much, knows he needs to leap first and look later, but it's hard. Every unplanned step feels like death. Every sentence in his brain ends with a question mark. All noise, no signal. But what good is living if the life you lead is brittle and dead?

Behind him he hears voices. Lights go on inside the building.

Adults.

Then, like a bell, he hears Claire's voice: *When in doubt, charge!*

He forces his feet to move, surging into the van. And then the door slides closed and the driver floors it, spraying gravel. Louise whoops. Simon's heart is racing. He worries he will pass out, his right hand clutching the paper bag in his pocket. His eyes find the Prophet, who sits on a cooler smiling, his back to the oncoming road.

"Welcome to the rest of your life," he says.

Then a hand reaches back from the driver's seat.

"Duane Yamamoto," says a deep voice. "Wilkomen to das Valkyrie."

Simon looks up, meets Duane's brown eyes in the rearview mirror. He is biracial handsome, half Japanese, half Black, nineteen years old, a dark-skinned teen with curly black hair. The hand he offers Simon is attached to a muscular arm, un-encumbered by a sleeve of any kind. Instead, the T-shirt he wears has been cut off at the shoulders. There is a tattoo of a broadsword on his forearm.

Duane smiles into the mirror. "I'll take you all the way," he says.

And just like that, Simon falls in love.

The Troll

Behold the human condition refined to its clearest form. All our unsolvable dilemmas, our tribal wars, our polarization, all our impossible moral equations can now be reduced to a single jpeg.

This is the sword *and* the shield, the culmination of centuries of struggle, of empires rising and falling. Sticks and stones. The fig leaf and the fall. Language invented. Warfare, politics. Magic begat medicine. Science begat technology. Technology begat the internet, which begat the cell phone, which begat the text bubble, and then—and only then—was the entirety of human yearning and misery focused like a laser into three simple letters. Two letters really, the *l* as racket and backstop, and the *o* as a ball forever bouncing between the two. An endless circle of mirth. Whatever you care about. Whatever offends you. Whatever morals or ethics or decency you hold dear.

l o fucking l.

Evan Himelman has spent his whole life looking for those letters. A way to bat it all away—every gripe and grievance, history's epic feuds, the bills his generation was supposed to pay for the sins of their fathers and mothers. Genocide, poverty, racism, misogyny, climate apocalypse, blah, blah, blah. Like walking into the middle of a fistfight you didn't start but are somehow expected to finish. The smothering weight of moral expectation. (((Jesus))) said *Do unto others as you would have them do unto you*, but they arrest you for fingerbanging strangers, so...

Listen, if you flog yourself the way all those libtard social justice warriors demand, if you let them clamp on the ball-and-chain of responsibility that nobody asked for, then every white boy in

America is a slave trader. It's enough to make you turn on the gas oven and put your (((head))) inside. Because who on Earth can read all the millions of words written by the world's wisest men and women, epic treatises and manifestos, meticulously laying out every nuance of every position. History and alternative history. Christianity, Judaism, Islam, Richard fucking Dawkins. When all along the answer has been right in front of us.

Genocide? *lol*

Racism? *lol*

Some Arab toddler facedown on a Greek beach?

Like the Joker used to say: Why so serious?

The Troll grew up Evan Bryan Himelman in Santa Monica, California. Land of fruits and nuts. That liberal Hollywood melting pot, where the Summer of Love never ended. It just bought a Tesla. Where liberalism was a birthright. Where your parents put a silver spoon and a copy of Obama's first Democratic Convention speech in your crib. Phil and Linda Himelman. They recycled. They composted. They jogged. The Troll grew up in the back of a Volvo listening to Terry Gross. But he was a cuckoo in another bird's nest. His radio heroes were Joe Rogan and Howard Stern. He rejected the fundamental principles. Give me the red pill or give me death.

In the beginning, he fought toe-to-toe. He made Reasoned Arguments. He joined the debate club. But then he found those three magic letters, and his true purpose in life came to him, like the sun through the clouds. He was a farmer of Liberal Tears, a trigger for social justice warriors, a nemesis to the woke.

14,88

BTFO

ICE puts Mexican kids in cages?

Some frat boy calls you a fat cunt?

Hands up. Don't shoot?

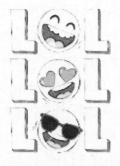

All hail KEK, the God of Chaos and Darkness. Like the bumper sticker says, *Life's a bitch and then you die.* So why not have as much fun as you can and then die in a hail of bullets? Fast cars, good drugs, underage pussy. Wash it all down with a nice tall glass of shut up juice, seasoned with liberal outrage. If you're not part of the problem, you're part of the solution, which, nobody wants that.

And then he met the Wizard, and the true purpose of his life became clear.

O

O

In the beginning, for Louise, the Troll was words on a screen. Somebody's friend had a friend who could score weed or booze or pills or whatever. Or maybe it was a guy Davy worked with at the copy center whose older brother served with a guy in Iraq. The truth was, it didn't matter and they didn't care. They just wanted the high, and this was the handle they found through the magic of social networking. Gabby said Hart should ping him. Hart said Gabby should do it. In the end it was Louise, never afraid of a little hard work, who entered the digits into WhatsApp.

She wrote:

—Said the fish to the hook, feed me your worm. Said the hook to the fish, put me in your mouth. And she did. And was hooked.

She waited two days. Then a ping.

—What else will she put in her mouth? he wonders.

It came at night, after Grandma had gone to bed. Louise was in the middle of her lotion routine. First a heavy cream for her hands and feet, then a milder blend for arms and legs. Dry skin made her cringe, calluses and blisters, and with all the cleaning supplies she used—even with the yellow gloves—her skin needed constant care. It was a kind of vicious cycle, the first obsession drying her out, the second obsession greasing her up.

Ping, went the phone. And something in Louise jumped like a dog for a ball.

She sat on the windowsill, illuminated by the digital blue glow.

—What else will she put in her mouth? he wonders.

She wiped the moisturizer from her hands, but before she could type a reply, another ping.

—A big black cock? A jew schvantz? A Mexican prick?

Louise stared at the screen, uncertain. Then another ping.

—LOL
She typed.
—Who is this?
A beat.
—My name is Yon Yonson. I work in Wisconsin.
I work in a lumbermill there.

Louise sat and looked out the window, trying
to figure out if she had something to lose. Her
grandma always said *it's the journey, not the
destination*, but then she worked in the post office,
sorting mail to places she never went.

—I'm Louise, she wrote.
—No names, came the reply.
—Can we meet?
—Meet or Meat?
. . .
—You wouldn't like me, typed Louise, I weigh
as much as a house.
—You like it in the living room or round back
through the kitchen door?
She sent him the shit emoji.
—Spicy.
—You know what they say about spicy food,
she typed.
—What's that?
—You think it's hot going in . . .

O

The next day he pinged her during her history class.

—Happy Holocaust Day!

She flushed, slid her phone back into her desk. She felt it buzz again through the tip of her pencil.

—Are you in art class? If the teacher asks you your favorite painting, tell him it's anything we stole from the cold dead hands of the jews. LOL.

She hid the phone beneath her desk, typed—

—You're one sick puppy.

Her phone buzzed almost immediately.

—Are you on your period?

—Why? You like it bloody?

Why did she write that? What did it even mean? The closest she'd come to sex at that point was sharing Dennis Cunningham's chewing gum in 6th grade. She glanced down at her phone, but it was dark. For a moment she worried she'd offended him, if that was even possible. She thought about telling Gabby and Hart that she'd blown their connection to the nirvana pipeline. Why were her hands so dry? They felt like paper.

Before she could think better of it, she typed—

—Well, you hooked me. Are you gonna reel me in?

A moment later, just as the class bell rang, her phone pinged again.

—Gamestop. 4pm.

And just like that, she was in.

Simon

Louise, it quickly becomes clear, is also in love with Duane. Or at least heavily in lust. Almost before they're out of the driveway and fishtailing onto the main street, she levers herself into the front, crossing her legs in the passenger seat.

"What's your story, kitty-cat?" she says.

"It's not complex," Duane tells her. "I can sum it up with this haiku: *My friend Barry died. My father used to beat me. Now I must lift weights.*"

"Deep," she says, touching his arm and taking another hit off the joint.

"Oh," says Duane, "before I forget. No politics in the Valkyrie."

"Because …"

"Because there are no politics," he says. "What people call politics. There's thoughts and there's feelings. So we live true in my ride. We call things for what they are."

Louise puts her feet on the dashboard, stretches her toes. "I'm gonna need you to unpack that a little, Romeo," she says.

Duane hits his turn signal, changes lanes. "So, divorce, right? Say you're a kid and your parents get divorced. They show you that this thing called family, with all the rules and responsibilities is bullshit. Don't trust it. Can't rely on it. So then when you grow up, you think people are gonna be, whatever, pro-establishment? No. Look around. I guarantee you that 99 percent of so-called *abolish the government* types are just getting back at Mommy and Daddy for their broken home. So we don't talk politics in my ride. We keep it real."

Simon doesn't want to think about family right now, his or anybody else's, because when he does, all he hears—from that undermining voice in his head—is disappointment.

"How do you know *the Pr...*," he says, then flushes. "I mean, Paul?"

Duane takes his joint back, changes lanes without signaling. "We're brothers of the chan, spelunkers of the secrets caves, diviners of the cosmic mystery."

"What does that mean?" Simon asks.

The Prophet takes out a handkerchief, wipes his brow. "Can we agree," he says, "that if God exists, he exists everywhere?"

"Or *she*," says Louise.

"Or she," says the Prophet. "The key is figuring out what messages are him. And what's just noise. Have you heard of Jerusalem syndrome?"

Simon shakes his head.

"Jerusalem syndrome is where some people who go to Israel suddenly decide they're Jesus."

"Come on," says Louise.

"It's true. I'm the second coming incarnate, says the dentist from Weehawken or the plumber from Stockholm. So the danger's clear. All of us want to feel special, touched. Some of us are just crazy. But I'll tell you a secret."

He studies them, making sure they're listening.

"God doesn't talk to grown-ups. Only children. Because children are still magic."

Oncoming headlights blind Simon for a moment. He closes his eyes, thinks of Claire tied to a chair, dead. Did God talk to her? Simon for one has never heard a word from the guy. But he *wants* to believe that the world is a magical place, that somewhere someone cares about him.

"We met online is what he's trying to tell you," says Duane, changing lanes.

"So you're nerds," says Louise, pretending to take a selfie of herself with Duane. She purses her lips, leans toward the dashboard, framing Duane behind her.

"If by nerds you mean men of intelligence," says Duane, "of passion, explorers, warriors. Then *hai*. The blanket of ignorance must be pulled back."

"Ooh," says Louise, "and what's under the blanket? Or should I say—how big is it? In inches?"

Simon turns and looks out the window, a spike of jealousy piercing him. Like all his love stories, this one is destined to be one-sided. How could any creature on Earth compete with Louise's adorable, crystalline, waifish appeal? The Prophet leans over, opens the cooler. He offers Simon a juice box.

"How does it feel?" he asks. "Freedom."

Simon takes the box—Cranapple—and shrugs. "Like I'm being eaten by ants."

He strips the straw from the box, removes the plastic.

"Ants meaning uncertainty," he clarifies. "I mean, who's gonna give us our meds? I'm on a lot of shit just to manage. How are we gonna—"

The Prophet watches Simon poke the straw ineffectually at his juice box for a minute, then he takes it, slips the straw through the foil the first time, hands it back.

"Forget your ills," he says. "This is the beginning. Your beginning. If we know this, we know that we are moving toward what we call the middle. From there we will find the end. So you see, there is no uncertainty. Not in life. We all know our final destination. Death."

Simon frowns. That's not better. "You said—I came because you said I could *fix things*."

Redemption.

The Prophet sips from his juice box. "How do we save ourselves?" he asks. "By saving others."

"I know. But how? Who?"

The Prophet rubbed his temples. He'd been raised on a farm outside Lincoln, Nebraska, surrounded by corn. His best friend was a tree stump his uncles used for target practice.

"Has Louise brought up the story of the Pied Piper?" he says. "How first he took the rats, then the children?"

Simon nods.

"People act like the story is about the Piper, the evils of a man who steals children. But it's about adults. The corruption of adults. This *delusion* that they can get whatever they want for free. That they can lie needlessly, promise anything, and then cheat the consequences. This is the delusion of power. The belief that power erases the need for honesty. That power in and of itself is a fact that supersedes all other facts. And what is the price they pay, our elders for stiffing the Piper? Their future. Because what is the future, if not children?"

"So...," says Simon.

"We are going to save the children, Simon, not from the Piper, but from the arrogance of power. The certainty that the grown should control the young."

Simon sighs. It's all so vague.

"But...," says Louise. "From the Piper, too, though, right? 'Cause guys with flutes are creepy."

"Definitely," says Duane.

The Prophet studies Simon. He can tell his words haven't lessened Simon's doubts.

"Louise," he says. "Tell Simon about the Wizard."

In the front Louise freezes.

"That's...," she says. "Do I have to?"

A long pause.

"We are, all of us, here for a reason," the Prophet tells her, implying *This is yours*. So Louise—who was feeling so good, so high and free and weightless, exhales raggedly and begins.

"Okay. So I don't know his name, but the Wizard is, like, a billionaire from a, whatever, hedge fund or energy fracking or something. And he likes young girls. And he has a mansion in San Francisco and, like, a compound in Texas, and maybe an apartment in Paris, and his own island, I think. And he has this kid in San Francisco, the Troll, a teenager, who finds him young pussy. And I mean young, thirteen, fourteen, fifteen. Plus, like, a whole team around the world who serves him up these girls. Feeds them to him—one, two, three a day."

"And you know this how?" the Prophet asks.

Louise is silent. "You know how," she says.

For a long time the van is quiet. Simon watches the streetlights pass. They have left the wealthy suburbs, snaking into the urban outskirts. Sherwin-Williams Paints, Arby's, Ross Dress for Less. The buildings are closer together now, older-model cars parked at the curb. The traffic picks up. Concrete and steel. They are inside the city limits—streetlights and sidewalks. Nightlife.

Welcome to McDonald's. May I take your order?

In the distance there is the flashing of blue and red lights. Police activity.

For a moment Simon worries that this is the dragnet, closing in. That he has become public enemy number one, and the cops—when they stop the van—will shoot to kill. But he shakes it off. Float is a private facility, one his parents checked him into voluntarily. Plus, cops are not his father's style. No, when dad finds out Simon has run away, he will call Gabe Lin, his head of private security, and Gabe will track them down.

"So is that where we're going?" Simon asks. "San Francisco?"

Louise looks at Duane's phone, mounted to the dashboard by a remote arm. Google Maps is open, broadcasting the blue line of their future.

"The magic device says Missouri."

Simon is about to ask, *What's in Missouri?*
when he sees a clown standing under a street-
light. Or more accurately, he sees a bald man in
a clown costume, his face painted white, his nose
red, exaggerated black lines painted over his eyes.
You know, a clown. Except this clown has a thick
mustache and he is smoking a cigarette. Plus the
costume is filthy, streaked, and the clown has an
AR-15 strapped across his chest, its long black
barrel pointed down. A clown with a rifle. But it's
his eyes. How his eyes are on the van, watching
as it passes. So much so that Simon feels like the
clown is staring straight at him.

A filthy, mustached, middle-aged clown with an
assault rifle looking at Simon.

And then they are past him. Simon turns to look
through the back windows.

"Did you see that?" he asks.

"What?" the Prophet asks.

"It was a—clown. With a gun."

The Prophet glances to the front of the van, his
eyes meeting Duane's in the rearview. Something
passes between them, a flash of fear, as if deep
down somewhere they're not surprised, that they
were afraid this might happen. But it's too soon.

Too soon.

"Did he see you?"

Simon shrugs, shakes his head, worried that if

he says *yes*, it will make the clown real. Not that he knows why that would be bad. But something inside tells him to say no.

"What's in Missouri?" he asks.

"Shit," says Duane, braking hard. The van slows, stops. They are at a crosswalk, traffic light a solid green overhead. Ahead of them a large crowd moves across the intersection. A river of people with no beginning and no end. They hold signs and banners—lit from the front by a distant orange glow, flickering. And from behind, a counter light, flashing blue and red. Smoke drifts through the intersection.

Save Our Children.

A father in a blue Izod climbs a lamppost. He is calling, *Scarlett? Scarlett?* A group of mothers walk past below, weeping, but whether from emotion or tear gas it's impossible to discern.

Simon and the others sit for a moment, watching thousands of human beings move silently through darkness. The primal scream of parents wailing for their young. Are they marching to protect their children or bring them back? Not for the first time, Simon wonders if this whole escape has been a dream. He rubs his eyes, then, lowering his hands, catches movement to his left. He turns. Clowns move past the van. Dozens of them. Men in their thirties and forties, some with beer bellies and beards, some rail thin with amphetamine eyes. They wear flak jackets over striped blouses and balloon pants, their mouths obscured by painted masks, grinning ceaselessly into the darkness. Some wear night-vision goggles and carry automatic weapons. Others are in Hawaiian shirts, their red noses obscene.

"Duane," says the Prophet.

"I see them," says Duane. "Hold on."

He shifts the van into reverse, begins inching backward, hoping not to draw the clowns' attention.

"Nobody move," he whispers.

Slowly they reverse. Simon stares out his window, hypnotized by the spectacle. The clowns close on the crowd, swaggering. And then the clown with the mustache is there, walking beside the van, his AR-15 up. His eyes find Simon's. He smiles, lifts his left hand to his face, holding his index finger to his lips. *Ssshh.*

Simon raises his crumpled paper bag—unaware that he's even removed it from his pocket—the only weapon he has against a world that wants to destroy him. He presses it over his mouth as the van clears the clowns, speeding up, the world moving past them in reverse, headlights illuminating the clown army. Then a protester notices the armed clowns, screams. Others turn. The men in big shoes raise their weapons. Through ragged, paper bag breaths, Simon sees a question cross Louise's face—lit by the headlight bounce—the heady, giddy horror of *what's going to happen next?* And then the headlights pan right off the crowd as Duane turns the wheel, spinning the van and quick-shifting into drive, his foot on the floor now, racing away from the kindling and the spark.

O

They reach St. Louis around 4:00 a.m. This is where the twitches hit, the dental buzz of nerves beginning to creep back into their skulls. It's been eight hours since their last pill. Sertraline, olanzapine, diazepam. Simon feels it the worst, a hollow throb behind the eyes, but Louise isn't far behind. She rolls down the window, sticks her bare feet into the wind, her pulse fluttering. She can't get the image of those clowns out of her head, the silent coordination as they raised their rifles.

Simon lies on his back on the metal floor, feeling every bump and pothole. The initial rush of escape has worn off. For the first time in months, he feels something other than dread. He feels excitement. He is free.

Outside St. Clair, the hard rock station switches over to talk, and they hear the familiar sounds of the God King, his nasal New York bluster, coming to them from an undisclosed location, a rasp on the wind. Is it live? A replay? Who can say for sure. Inside the city limits you can forget that he's out there, twenty-four hours a day, transmitting his every thought. You forget that in the country-side and suburbs his voice is the soundtrack of people's lives.

"...an omelet and the breakfast sausage, right? I love breakfast sausage. We know this. And they bring it, a little coffee, a little orange juice—and lemme just—Florida orange juice, okay? We grew up with this. The pinnacle. The best of the best. And at my club, no expenses spared—it's like you died and went to heaven, seriously—but they bring the omelet and so far I'm happy. Nice size, good color, with, like, a little spinach and cheese—and I got my Diet Coke. First one of the day, chilled, a little ice—not like if the other party had their way. We'd all be drinking broccoli juice, or, listen to this, kale? You ever have kale? It's like eating a vacuum cleaner bag—but I'm lookin' at the—and did you see what this guy did this morning? The Pretender. The Imposter. Our poor country. This guy in the White House, like those old commercials—I've fallen and I can't get up—remember those commercials? I used to love those commercials. But hey, it's your money, folks, tax payer cabbage—and he's using it to—he's got trucks on the southern border—these big powerful trucks—and they're pulling down the wall. Our big, beautiful—and I see this, and I think, what kind of sick puppy—but then what are you gonna do? They're—they've got grudges, like, up the wazoo. They hate me. Boy do they hate me. But the omelet comes and the sausage—can I just tell you—the size of my pinkie, okay? Or smaller, 'cause I got pretty big hands—but there's maybe two of them. And I go—I say—what the heck is this? And the waiter, from like Ecuador, he says, *ees sausage, señor.* Probably came over in the trunk of somebody's car—never seen a sausage before in his life—this is what we're dealing with, folks. First they steal the election. Then they take our breakfast sausage."

Duane reaches over and changes the station, and they listen to Charlie Daniels for a while, "*The Devil Went Down to Georgia,*" and for the next two hours nobody says a word.

O

They drive through the night and stop around noon the next day at a campground near Springfield, Missouri. Bleary from the road, they tumble from the van, squinting into the steamy daylight. It is already ninety-five degrees in the shade, thunder-storms promised for the evening. Simon has fallen into a fitful sleep. He wakes as Duane pulls off the main road onto a winding country road and sits up to find a landscape thick with kudzu, lined with campsites and RVs. Dust rises from their tires.

Louise rolls her window down, letting in a loud insect thrum. This is her first time in what people on NPR call *rural America*. The woods are filled with tents and lean-tos. Makeshift laundry lines have been strung from the trees like spiderwebs. Corduroys, blouses, underwear, socks. They pass a Subaru station wagon surrounded by bookshelves, an elderly man seated in their center reading aloud to a group of children.

"Where are we?" Simon asks.

"More important," says Louise, "did those clowns murder, like, a thousand people back there? Is anybody else freaking out?"

Simon feels his stomach turn. For some reason he thinks of an old woman standing at the stove in her kitchen. He watches as they drive deeper into the park. There are vehicles everywhere, campers and bicycles, people's living rooms set up right there in the open under plastic tarps. Somewhere a radio is playing loudly—a sonorous voice broadcasting a conspiratorial tone.

"...trust the plan—we know this. Do your research, and remember—you are the news now."

Megalophobia is defined as the fear of large
objects.

What is this place? Simon wonders. *A music
festival? Are they refugees?*

Are there refugees in Missouri?

His short-term meds are all the way gone now,
a hot tingle returning to his thumbs. Anxiety,
the devil's tickle torture. *There is a small-town
pharmacy,* his brain whispers, *in a rust-belt river
bend that ordered more than 5,700,000 pills between 2005 and 2011. Three hundred and eighty
people live in that town. In 2008 alone, the pharmacy received 5,264 pills for every man, woman,
and child.*

He shuts his eyes, tries to squeeze the balls back
into his head.

Stupid brain! Why won't it stop whispering?

There used to be a place called Central America.

There used to be a place called Sudan.

There used to be a place called the Mekong Delta.

But now there is just the oven.

Hyperobjects are what we call concepts or phenomena that are too large to grasp with the human
mind. A planet without ice. A forest without trees.
An ocean without life.

In the woods, someone has constructed an out-

door shower from buckets and junk lumber. Simon
watches as men and women wait in line holding
towels and toothbrushes. Ahead of them an all-
terrain vehicle moves between people's campsites
collecting trash.

"If it helps," says Duane, "pretend you're at
Burning Man."

They park next to a massive RV with its own
satellite dish, the owner grilling sausages on a
hibachi at the edge of a bramble, while his wife
sets a folding table for lunch with a plastic cover
and metal plates. The smell of cooking meat makes
Louise growl.

"We'll sleep here one night and then head south,"
says the Prophet. "There's someone I need to see."

"Here?" says Louise.

"I gotta drop a deuce," says Duane, wandering off.
Simon watches him go, heart beating fast. Just the
idea of touching his beautiful face makes Simon feel
faint. He looks around at the citizens of this shopping cart farm. Nomads on beach cruisers. Gypsies
of the dented can emporiums and Walmart discount clubs. He watches children chase one another
with secondhand Nerf guns and scavenged sticks.
Somewhere in the forest echo Tom Petty sings
about an American girl raised on promises. The
idea of sleeping on the ground has always horrified
Simon, of walking barefoot, of eating Hormel from

a can and going to sleep with dirt in your mouth. But, then, he grew up in a mansion. His family's version of camping was to fly commercial.

"How long did I sleep?" he wants to know. "Did the world end?"

"That's the thing about the world," says the Prophet. "It never ends. The Roman Empire fell, not in a day, but for four hundred years."

The retiree at the grill smiles and waves them over.

"Howdy, strangers," he says, "I'm Norm, and this is my better half, Glenda. Good to have some new blood around here."

Louise, who will talk to anyone, anywhere, doesn't need a more formal invitation. She crosses over into their camp and sits herself down on a folding chair.

"What's for lunch?" she asks.

"Got some beef franks on the grill and vegetable for the missus. She gave up on animals after that second round a' colon cancer."

Louise mimes lighting a cigarette and exhaling.

"I'm Louise and this is Simon, and that's Paul. We're from St. Louis, just out for a roam in this great land of ours, which—you wouldn't happen to have a spare beer or two for some weary travelers looking to celebrate their newfound freedom?"

Glenda studies them. "How old are you?"

"Old enough to survive a drunken father with fists for hugs," says Louise, "and a mother who fell asleep with a needle in her arm and never woke up."

Louise sticks out her bottom lip and widens her eyes. Lying is easy for her.

"For Chrissake, woman," says Norm, "give the girl a Miller Light."

Simon stands awkwardly, not sure what to do with his hands.

There used to be a place called India.

There used to be a place called Africa.

"Simon?" says Louise, and when he looks up, everyone is staring at him. It's clear this isn't the first time Louise has said his name.

"What?" he says.

"I said grab a chair. The Goodwins have invited us to lunch."

Simon finds an aluminum folding chair, tries to figure out how to unfold it. He has never been in a campsite before. It is a foreign country filled with strange customs. When Duane comes back, he finds them all sitting around the card table eating Ball Park franks and drinking light beer.

"Wow," he says, "what did I miss?"

"This is our savior, Duane," says Louise, "driver of the mythic Ram van, and broad swordsman extraordinaire."

"Peace," says Duane as Norm pulls over a cooler for him to sit on.

"Have a seat," he says, cracking a fresh can and holding it out. Duane takes it with a smile.

"Right on," he says, dropping onto the cooler.

Watching from his high tech folding chair, Simon feels both real and unreal at the same time. This time yesterday he was in group therapy in a fifteen-hundred-dollar-a-night facility, sleeping on Egyptian cotton sheets and eating sea bass. The city he's from is made of glass and steel, town cars and NPR. People drink kombucha and do CrossFit. They *summer* places and go to white parties.

Duane reaches out and rubs the side of Norm and Glenda's bus. There is a name stenciled on the lacquer, *The Diplomat.*

"That's quite a ride," he says.

"She's a beaut, all right," says Norm. "Gas mileage is a turd, but no price too steep for freedom. Am I right?"

The kids look at him. It's the kind of thing grown-ups say, combining mundane in-jokes about household budgets with vague aphorisms inspired by go-for-broke hail Mary monologues in sentimental entertainment. Bumper sticker catchphrases filled with nostalgia for a world that never existed. A morality of symbols. Flags and flyovers. Mom and apple pie. The cemeteries of Normandy and

WWJD? At that moment there is a shift in the elders. Mister and missus exchange a look. Norm puts down his beer koozie, leans forward.

"What," he says, "do y'all know about Q?"

O

Later, Simon and Louise wander the periphery. They are dazed after two hours of Norm and Glenda proselytizing the insidious cabal of the Deep State and the stolen election. Witch hunts and secret socialists.

"Where we go one we go all," they said, their mouths full of supermarket meat and relish.

Louise kicks an empty beer can. They are in a scrubby field, upwind of the porta-potties.

"So, the Wizard," says Simon.

Louise stiffens. They walk for a while in silence. Then she takes Simon's hand, holds it. "Are you my boyfriend?"

"I told you. I don't—"

Louise sighs. "Whatever. It's not about—sex. I don't think I ever really want to have sex again, honestly. It's what you said. Trust."

He nods. "Trust," he said.

She smiles, squeezes his hand. "People talk about evil," she says, "but what does it mean? Dracula? The holocaust? I don't know. I'm not good at what things mean. All I know is it's cold and senseless. Evil. Like there's no *sense* to it, if you think about what an animal should be, a human animal. The reason we exist. 'Cause, shit—I don't know—what are we here to do? Feed ourselves, make babies? Warm things. Family, society. And that's good, what we call good. You know, do unto others, et cetera. So, what's evil?"

"Fucking children?" says Simon.

A long pause. Then Louise nods.

"It's cold, right? Not love or hate, we're not talking about passion or genocide, you know, but the *planning* for it, the science of it—so many gas chambers operating so many hours a day. So many teenage girls found where, for what price? How you hook them by saying 'two hundred bucks for a massage'—a *massage*, like a brand name that's been focus tested to sound harmless and clean, versus what it is, which is *I want to rape under-age girls*. It's all so—calculated. Fake smiles, fake tears. Cynical, you know. A lie pretending to be the truth, like, I don't know—the big bad wolf dressed up as grandma. Meanwhile, *good luck on your first day at school, kids!*"

"LOL," says Simon.

"Exactly. Fucking LOL—ha ha ha rape. Ha ha ha hate crimes. It's such a boy thing, pretending nothing matters, everything's a joke."

Simon frowns. "I don't do that."

"You're gay."

"So?"

Louise shakes her head. They're getting off track. They pass a clot of teenagers with mountain bikes doing tricks in a rocky grove. Simon feels her fingers tighten, remembers how Claire used to hold his hand so tight. She'd tell him that if an eagle were trying to steal him away, she'd kill that raptor dead.

Believe.

"So the Wizard is what, then?" asks Simon.

"He's the wolf. And he's in the shadows, watching and waiting. He sees the grown-ups getting so distracted they forget to watch the children, and he slips in and feeds, smiling his crooked smile—*the better to eat you with, my dear*. Then he boils us and skins us alive. Or I don't know. Do I have to keep talking about this?"

Simon shakes his head. "The Pied Piper," he says. She nods.

They reach a dirt road. On the other side they see rows of orange cones. Work trucks are parked in loose clots. Men in reflective vests erect large white tents, filling a sprawling field, sweating in the midday sun. Simon sees a woman with a clipboard watching the men work.

"What is this?" he asks her.

The woman turns. "That's optometry. Those'll be dentists. To the west is where you'll find your internists and pediatricians, and this year we've actually got an orthopedic surgeon. Which is so helpful, 'cause too many people these days have a problem with their hips or knees."

"I don't understand," says Louise.

"Medicine," the woman says. "Since most of the rural hospitals closed, people drive a hundred, two hundred miles just to see a dentist, except who can afford a dentist? So we go around the country and set up these clinics, try to get people straightened out."

"For money."

"God no," she says. "This is—we're not for profit. Started in the nineties to help third world countries, you know. Sending doctors to Indonesia and the Amazon rain forest. But now—well, there's just too much need here."

"Is that why all the people?" asks Louise, looking back at the campground.

The woman shrugs. "It's kinda the chicken and the egg. Used to be folks would drive to us and sleep in their cars, waiting in line. But now, well, the lines are home. So we come to them."

Simon nods, watching the men work. They are building a hospital like you set up a circus. A tent for the elephants. A tent for the clowns.

The thought of clowns makes Simon shudder.

Most of Vietnam will be underwater by 2050, as well as parts of China and Thailand.

He grits his teeth, his neck muscles tensing.

There used to be a country called Australia.

There used to be a country called Norway.

In the distance he sees the Prophet, standing under a willow tree, talking to a teenage boy, maybe sixteen, tall and wiry, wearing a leather duster despite the heat. As he watches, the Prophet points back toward the campsite. The kid in the duster shakes his head, points up the road. They argue for a moment, then the Prophet nods and the kid in the duster walks to the road. The Prophet follows.

Simon nudges Louise. She says goodbye to the woman with the clipboard, and they set off after them. It occurs to Simon to give Paul his privacy, but Simon's anxiety won't let him. There's an idea in the back of his head that wherever the Prophet is going, he is going there to talk about Simon.

They follow the pair through some low trees. There is a clearing on the far side. The kids they saw doing mountain bike tricks are assembled in a loose circle. The Prophet stands in the center with Duster and Duane.

Simon grabs Louise's hand, pulls her into the shadows behind a tree.

"Is this it?" she asks. "Are we gonna make out?"

"Sshh."

Simon leans through the gap, trying to hear. Most of the kids are in board shorts and T-shirts, some of them vaping. Duane is showing his sword tattoo, flexing his forearm. Another kid is jumping his bike on its back tire nearby, making small clouds of dirt with each hop.

"I know," says Duster, "but nothing ever changes. So maybe forget saving the world and just blow some shit up."

"Each step is a step," says the Prophet.

"What the fuck does that mean?"

"It means of course things change. But slowly. One step at a time. This is what God says."

Duster spits into the dirt. "We don't believe in God."

"*Their* god. I'm talking about ours."

"We get a god?"

"We get *the* God. And he is mighty and righteous and pissed."

Duster lights a cigarette, blows a smoke ring. "So on this quest you need what?" he asks.

"The right things in the right order. The Babe in Arms, the Burning Witch, the Last Stand."

The Last Stand? thinks Simon, then feels a hand clamp down on the back of his neck. One of the crew has returned from the porta-potty and discovered Simon and Louise eavesdropping. He shoves them into the clearing.

"Spies," he calls.

Simon shrugs himself loose. The sun is high overhead, and he's sweating in the small of his back.

"Friendlies," says Louise, then freezes. The skate punks and BMXers have all pulled pistols and knives. They're aiming them at Simon and Louise. Duster holds an honest-to-God six-shooter that was holstered on his hip like a cowboy.

The Prophet waves them off. "Namaste," he says. "We're on the same side. Chill your aggression."

They lower their weapons reluctantly. To pull a gun and not use it feels like going to a dance and leaving before the music starts.

"These are my friends," says the Prophet. "Simon and Louise."

"I'm a pacifist," Simon tells them.

"Fuck pacifism," says Duster. "I was at Parkland. I know the truth."

"What truth?" says Louise, aware, always aware, that hers is the only black face in the group, and this group has guns.

"The only way to stop a bad man with a gun is a kid with a gun."

He holsters his gun, spits in the dirt.

"Randall Flagg," he says, offering his hand. "The Dark Man, the Walking Dude."

"Isn't that a character from a Stephen King story?" Simon asks.

"What do you mean *story?*" Duster asks.

Simon frowns. "You know—a story," he says. "A made-up story."

Randall Flagg exhales a plume of smoke. "No," he says. "That shit happened."

"The world ended and the devil took over Las Vegas."

Flagg nods.

"Then how are we here today?" Simon asks.

"Look," says Randall Flagg. "It's a fictional world, dude. Why can't I be a fictional character?"

For the life of him, Simon can't think of a reason.

Randall Flagg looks around.

"We should get inside. A lotta boogaloos at this rodeo."

They start walking, flanked by the others.

"Boogaloos?" asks Simon.

"The Hawaiian-shirt crowd, fighters of the coming race war, also known as the Big Igloo or the Big Luau. You remember Capitol Hill—all those jokers with body armor, live streaming anarchy."

"Clowns?" Simon asks.

"Sure," says Flagg. "Clown World is real. Those are some serious barracudas. We get two notches for each clown we take out."

"Seriously?"

Flagg pulls back his duster to show his six-shooter.

"This shit ain't theoretical, Mr. Ivy League."

"I'm fifteen."

"What can I say? I'm a time traveler from the future back with your 401(k) millions and your house keys in Greenwich fucking Connecticut."

Simon's thumbs are tingling. He fingers the paper bag in his pocket.

They reach a tented enclosure—tarps hung in a rough rectangle next to a corral of dirt bikes. Inside are camping mats, a cooktop, and a battered cooler. Randall is the last one in, casting around the woods for spies before closing the curtains. Inside, Louise finds a small battery-powered hand fan and holds it up to her face, blades spinning.

"Mercy," she says.

Flagg crosses to the cooler. It's full of ice water and chocolate milks. He reaches deep, pulls out a ziplock bag. Inside is an old flip phone. He hands the bag to the Prophet.

"I found your guy, Javier. Wasn't easy. His number's in the phone. It's good for one call. Then torch that shit or SWAT teams are gonna rain down on you like hellfire."

The Prophet unzips the wet bag, takes out the phone. "Four three two," he says, reading the area code on the number. "Where's that?"

"West Texas, Daddy," says a heavyset Chicano kid with a wispy mustache, wearing a Heinz ketchup T-shirt.

"Don't call until you're close," says Flagg, opening a cold chocolate milk. "I don't know how much time you'll have."

The Prophet puts the phone in his pocket. "And you'll take us?" he says.

Flagg punches the tiny straw into the milk carton. "For ten thousand."

"Dollars?" says Louise.

"We take Bitcoin," says a girl they call Katniss, her black hair pinched in pigtails.

The Prophet puts his hand on Simon's back. "He's good for it," he says.

Simon turns. "Me?"

The Prophet meets his eye. "No one ever said redemption was free."

Goblins

Gabe Lin is a big believer in advertising. *Announce yourself to the world*, he tells people. *Declare the man you want to be, and the world will see that man*. He started his own private security force twelve months after making detective at Manhattan Vice. Chutzpah, some called it, but he knew the truth. That thought is action. If you visualize something, if you claim it without hesitation, then it is yours. That was when he got his first personalized license plate. It had come to him in a dream one night, the car, the plate, all of it, after he watched *The Dark Knight* at the local AMC.

A black Dodge Charger with a red racing stripe, the windows tinted as dark as the law allowed. Darker even. What good is being a cop, after all, if you can't bend the rules a bit?

Goblin, that's what he would call himself, and

that's what he would call his firm. Picture the license plate—black text on a yellow backing.

G0BL1N.

The rig was so badass that when it all came together, Gabe found himself grinning for weeks, even in the middle of a standard perp beat down. Nightstick out, Collins would dopesmack Gabe in the back of the head and say, *What the fuck are you grinning at?* And Gabe would turn on him, screw up his face and say—

Why—so—serious?

—the way Heath Ledger said it in the movie. Guttural, possessed. Like a crazy person.

Goblin Security Consultants. He had cards printed the next week. Forget Kinkos. Gabe spent the money to do it right, finding some boho chick with a letterpress and having that shit *embossed*. Ten years later he is right where he wants to be: on top of the world. Goblin Security is a global concern with offices in London, Jakarta, Rome. They provide body men for Fortune 100 CEOs, Hollywood celebrities, you name it. All because of Big Client One (BC1), as Gabe calls Ty Oliver, CEO of Rise Pharmaceutical. The first fat cat to take a chance on an arrogant New York City cop with a dream. And that shit Gabe Lin never took for granted. For the first five years he went above and beyond, available twenty-four hours a day. He brought in extra guys, paid them out of his own pocket, recruited handsome young killers straight out of Special Forces. They wore slim-fitted suits with stretch, kept their hair regulation length, even stuck to a stringent skin-care regimen. The key word was *aspirational*. See, Gabe intuited what other firms hadn't yet figured out—that personal wealth and the luxury class were going to skyrocket and that the wealthy would shop for security firms the way they shopped for handbags or yachts.

As a fashion accessory.

He could tell the first time Ty rolled into Davos with the goblins at his side that the other CEOs felt suddenly poorer. They looked at their stocky body men with their rubber earwigs and black Kmart athleisure shoes and saw the profound lack of style that signaled you were on your way out. Whereas Ty, with his advance team of Benetton models all wearing the latest in lightweight tactile fabrics, biceps straining against the weave, with their futuristic communications gear and ceramic handguns seemed like the Wrath of fucking Khan. A pre-vision of the gleaming Star Trek future. It was all uphill from there. Cutting-edge. Gabe was the first to recruit all-female teams—former softball MVPs, WNBA pros, and ex-helicopter pilots who walked the line between grace and power.

Feministas, he called them. His warrior princesses.

Three years after Gabe printed those first business cards, Goblin Securities went from two clients to fifteen. Eighteen months later they opened their first overseas office. On Sundays Gabe would go to his Long Island mega-church and throw his hands in the air. *Praise Jesus*, he'd sing, *for investment yields dividend, for praise gets you that raise*. The money he donated helped build a Chick-fil-A in the lobby and fund Bible study groups for a decade. Forget the Old Testament with its dour preachers and afterlife rewards. This was the Gospel of Earthly Rewards. All prosperity, no waiting.

And all of it, thanks to BC1. So when Mr. Oliver calls Gabe at 3:00 a.m. on Saturday night and says his son is missing, escaped from his rehab resort in suburban Chicago, Gabe is pedal to the metal in eight minutes flat, running red lights, gunning for the Fifty-Ninth Street bridge, his personal license plate a flashing ultraviolet rectangle.

The G0BL1N is on the move.

O

By 8:00 a.m. on Sunday morning, Gabe Lin and his recon team are on the premises in suburban Illinois—walking the halls of Float

Anxiety Abatement Center, past stunned teens and twentysomethings practicing their yoga poses and watercoloring horses in the Meadow of Contentment. He talks to Jacob Wells, the administrator, while Aragorn and Legolas check out the kid's room. This was another genius move on Gabe's part, his code name system. All his operatives got the names of heroes from famous fantasy stories—*The Lord of the Rings*, *Game of Thrones*, Shannara, Xanth. Hell, he even had a kid called Morpheus, another called Neo, and a chick named Trinity. *Be larger than life*. That's what he told his crews. For a few months he tried christening some Marvel superheroes, but wouldn't you know, after they did Super Bowl security for Bob Iger, Disney served him with a cease and desist.

Gabe himself is the Goblin King. Forget that the guy in *The Hobbit* is like a twelve-foot-tall Elephant-Man-looking motherfucker with a suppurating neck goiter. The name is badass, and Gabe has it engraved on the barrel of his Glock.

It's a muggy Midwest morning. Wells is the turquoise necklace type, a curly-haired elf with small, soft hands. Gabe, six foot four, steps in too close for a handshake and squeezes hard. This is his strategy with non-clients. Dominate.

"The three of them left together, we think," says

Wells. "Sometime after midnight, as you can see from the security footage I sent you."

Gabe reviewed the footage on his drive in. Simon—the target—fled the premises with one female (slight, androgynous) and one male (tall, reedy, bespectacled), both in their teens. Gabe calls them *the corrupters*. When he asked Mr. Oliver how he wanted them handled, BC1 said *quietly,* which means Gabe can do just about whatever the fuck he wants to them, as long as it doesn't come back on the client.

"What about his accomplices?" Gabe asks. "Louise Conklin and Paul Fisher?"

"Well," frowns the administrator, "I wouldn't call them accomplices. All our charges are here voluntarily, so they're free to leave the premises whenever they'd like."

"Fine," says Gabe. "His friends. What can you tell me about his friends? Their backgrounds?"

Gabe, of course, has done his own research. His information network is CIA level. He knows that Louise is basically a vagrant from the East Bay and that Paul is an Okie who grew up on a farm. Nobodies, in other words. What he's looking for is color, a sense of where to start looking.

"Both Paul and Louise came to us to help them address a certain underlying feeling of inadequacy.

Both were making tremendous progress before they left, as was Simon."

"Mr. Oliver."

"Excuse me?"

"You will refer to my client as Mr. Oliver."

Wells frowned again. "I'm sorry. I thought you were here on behalf of the father, not, uh, young Mr. Oliver."

Gabe picks a black fleck off Wells's desktop, flicks it away.

"For over a decade I've been charged with the well-being of the Oliver family. That makes Simon my client, and seeing as how his net worth is that of a small country and how his family is building you three new buildings next year, my feeling is he deserves to be called *mister*. Last I checked, a fifteen-year-old king is still *your majesty.*"

Wells forces a smile. "Of course. My apologies. Well, as I said, Mr. Oliver was making great strides toward self-soothing and impulse control management. That's why it saddens me that he chose to check himself out."

"You had a string of suicides here in the last month."

"Yes. That's—unfortunate—but I suppose you could say we're no different from the rest of the world. It's an abomination really. Such a tragedy, this loss of faith in our future."

Gabe rolled his eyes. What psycho-babble bull-shit. *Loss of faith in the future.* Suicide is weakness killing strength, and good riddance. *You show me a kid who had it worse than me and I'll buy you a fucking pony,* Gabe thinks. *Kids kicking the shit out of me every day, calling me slant-eyes and ching-chong chink. Mother dies in a factory fire. Dad drops dead of cancer after twenty years breathing dry-cleaning chemicals. Sister raped and murdered at community college. And did I surrender? Fuck no. I fought back. I made the world pay its bill. End of story.*

"Did Simon seem suicidal?" he asks.

"Simon? No. Nor did the others. As I said—"

"They were making great progress. I wrote that down. What about a getaway car?"

"I'm sorry?"

"Well, they didn't just walk out. The security camera shows them going out the back door, but apparently you didn't think to put cameras on the back entrance, so I can't tell who picked them up."

"George—"

"The janitor."

"Night custodian."

Jesus, thinks Gabe, *how PC can you be? The guy mops up rich girl bulimia while you sleep.* But he nods.

"George said it was some kind of van," says Wells.

"Old? New?"

"He didn't specify. But he did say there was a painting on the side. Some kind of muscular warrior in battle. Is that helpful?"

Gabe rubs his eyes. *The kids fled in a Frazetta van? Like it's 1981?* This whole thing was turning into some kind of sick joke.

"Make? Model?"

Wells shrugs. "I have every faith that when you find him, Simon will be healthy. Perhaps he's just blowing off steam. It's not uncommon for adolescents upon whom we put such pressure to succeed."

Gabe stands. If he has to listen to this guy another minute, he's gonna put him in a choke hold.

"We'll be in touch," he says.

The Goblin King reconnoiters with Aragorn and Legolas in the parking lot. Their wheel man, Gandalf, is parked at the curb in a rented black Suburban, engine running.

"The client took his underwear," says Legolas, "a few pairs of pants, some shirts. He left his heavy coat behind, so heading south maybe."

Aragorn flips his iPad so Gabe can see. On it he's got photos of Louise and the Prophet's rooms.

"Girl took everything basically, except a few

paperbacks from the library. The other kid, the male, not sure he took anything. His closet has everything ironed and hanging. Three button-down shirts. Three pairs of pants. All the same."

Aragorn produces a small Bible from his pack. "He left this behind, by the bed."

Aragorn hands the Bible to Gabe, who opens it. The book is like a madman's brain inside. On every page, written in the margin in tiny red print, are notes, arguments, even pictures. Gabe hands the Bible back to him.

"Get this to the Chicago office. I want a full scan and analysis by sundown."

Aragorn walks off to call it in. A messenger will be here on motorbike in ten minutes. Gabe climbs into the Suburban. He puts up a hand to stop Legolas from following.

"Liaise with the local cops. I want traffic cameras, banks, everything. Get eyes on this fantasy van; map out a search grid. If they give you shit, bypass to the FBI. A lot of people in this town owe me a lot of favors."

He leaves them there, working their devices. It's important to put some distance between yourself and the help, so they don't get too familiar. *That's part of what's wrong with the youth of today,* Gabe thinks. *Too much familiarity. Too many expectations. Entitlement. No wonder they're knocking themselves off in record numbers. Mommy and Daddy cut up their fucking string beans for eighteen years and then send them off to college, where suddenly they have to do their own work and nothing's handed to them.*

Indulgence makes us soft. But Gabe Lin isn't soft, and his goblins certainly aren't soft. They're killers who hunt at night. Meat eaters who ninja-train day in, day out. Gotta live up to the code name.

We'll run this kid to ground, thinks Gabe. *One day, two max.*

Margot

She has dinner her first night in Washington with the president's chief of staff, Chuck Malcolm, and Jay Bryant from the Liberty Society. She's wearing a black dress bought for her by Malcolm's assistant. It needs to be taken in under the arms, and it hits her right above the knees, but she pairs it with a scarf and blows out her hair, determined to power through. They eat at a French bistro on K Street, in a dark corner away from other diners. Margot has known Jay Bryant since her law school days. He is a genteel sixty-five-year-old man committed to what he calls *God's work*, systematically converting the judicial branch of the American government to a body of conservative will. Margot first met him in 1996, through her Constitution Law professor at Notre Dame, one of a dozen conservative teachers across the nation who kept an eye out for promising young students. And Margot, who came from loyal Reaganite stock, who believed that America was God's country, who had been captain of her debate club and valedictorian at Yale, might as well have been built in a Liberty lab.

Chuck Malcolm is the last one there, rumpled and soup stained. He is on two calls at once, an iPhone to one ear, a Samsung Galaxy to the other.

"No, you tell him—no, I'm talking to Rene— I said—what? Rene, God damn it just—call me after dinner."

He hangs up both phones, drops them into sagging jacket pockets, sits as Margot stands, hand outstretched.

"What?" he says, confused, then stands again, his manners catching up to him. "Sorry, my brains are in my other pants."

He shakes her hand, hi-fives Jay. They sit.

"First off," says Malcolm, "how's your daughter? Did they find her?"

"No, sir. Not yet. Remy, my husband, talked to the FBI, which *thank you again*. He gave a description and as clear a picture as he could of her routine, her boyfriend."

She puts an exasperated smile on her face. "She's probably just—at Coachella or camping or something. You know, twentysomethings these days."

"Do you think," says Jay, "with what's happening right now—the unfortunateness, that—I mean, she's a bit out of the demographic, so that's—I won't say good, but—"

He stops talking, aware how he must sound. Margot picks up her menu. Suicide. They're talking about suicide. It's not how she wanted the evening to start.

"Are we eating or drinking?"

The two men relax, freed from the burden of unpleasant thought.

"Try the confit," says Malcolm. "And a glass of the Pinot. Are you a drinker?"

Margot smiles. Both she and Jay are Drinkers, and she's beginning to suspect Chuck Malcolm is a Drinker pretending to be a Cook.

"Even Jesus drank wine," she says, closing her menu.

Malcolm waves the waiter over, orders for all of them.

"Bring us two bottles of the pinot and then fuck off except to clear the plates," he says.

After he's gone, Malcolm exhales. He's slept three hours in two days.

"Here's the deal," he says, "this is heady stuff, I'm sure. History of the nation. Highest court in the land. You want it. I want you to get it. Blah, blah. So let me lay things out for you. This president, my boss, is a moderate, and he's tried to govern as a moderate. Hell, he's even got a secretary of defense

from your side. I got picked for chief of staff because I did time running campaigns for evangelical
figures in the Bible Belt. That's his motto. He's the
Compromise President, and he believes we're in a
war for the soul of the nation. And that the only way
to win the war is to relearn the art of cooperation.
To focus on our similarities, not our differences.
But what is the war for a human soul, and who
do you fight against? The devil. And we all know
there can be no compromises with the devil."

"Amen," says Jay.

"It's a fight to the death," says Malcolm. "So
we've sold you to our president as an agent of compromise. Just look at your family, for Chrissake.
It's a goddamn rainbow coalition. You're young.
You're attractive. You're warm. And on paper you
don't look like a zealot."

"I'm not a zealot."

"That's good," says Jay. "Say that."

Malcolm's iPhone beeps. He ignores it, leans
forward.

"When you sit down with the president tomorrow,
tell him you want to heal the wounds of the nation,
that you will lead this divided court toward unity.
And you will, but it'll be *our* unity. An alignment
of the like-minded, a conversion of the non-
believers, until this country gets back to its proper
destiny as a God-fearing Christian nation."

For some reason Margot thinks of her daughter at nine, standing on a stage in Brooklyn singing our national anthem, and how the whole room rose to its feet.

"I'm not an originalist," she says.

"We know," says Jay. "That's fine. Your rulings for the last ten years have all been well reasoned, your opinions sound. It's clear your heart's in the right place."

"I won't make any quid pro quos," says Margot.

"No one wants that," says Jay. "Just be who you are. But, you know, remember that a lot of time and money has been invested in your education, your advancement, your career. You've been groomed for this moment, Margot. By me and Bruce and dozens of right-thinking Americans willing to put their money where their mouth is. We all believe in you, but you need to understand that you're a piece of a puzzle that's bigger than all of us. You believe that, right?"

"I believe God has a plan for this world, and we are here to do his will, yessir. I truly do."

"That's good," says Jay, "but with this president it's best—he's Christian, but with a small *c*, if you know what I mean."

"Yes, sir."

Malcolm rubs his eyes. "We're going to win this

war," he says. "We have to. But we can't do it without you. Do you understand?"

Margot nods. She knows that her whole life has led her to this moment. Every choice she's made. Every ideal she's fought for. Every compromise. "I won't let you down," she tells them.

The wine arrives. The waiter starts the opening presentation, but Malcolm shoos him away. He massacres the cork, places the bottle between his knees and muscles it open, spilling red wine on his pants. He pours them each a full glass.

"Cheers," says Margot, and they clink glasses and drink. Malcolm lowers his glass, looks at Margot like she's the turkey on Thanksgiving.

"Fucking A," he says.

O

The next few days are a blur. Margot tours the Russell Senate offices, shaking hands. She meets Drinkers and Cooks alike. From their faces, she can tell she is a Cook's worst nightmare. A conservative judge married to a Black man with a mixed-race son. Margot charms them as best she can, saying only that she will rule on every case based on its merits, not on a prescribed set of beliefs.

The Drinkers are suspicious too, trying to figure

out the angle. A Cook nominated a Drinker. Is the Drinker not a real Drinker, or is the Cook not a real Cook? The idea of true bipartisanship never occurs to them.

On Friday she sits with the junior senator from Idaho, Kurt LaRue. He is a wiry man in his forties with a black comb-over, swept from left to right. LaRue was raised in a Christian community outside Devil's Elbow. He is a building contractor turned land developer, who won his Senate race last year by just under one hundred votes. Before she's even in the room, he grabs her hand warmly, two male aides standing in the background. They look like Bible study missionaries, just out of high school.

"An honor," he says.

"Thank you, Senator."

She sits. LaRue is across from her, sipping a Diet Coke. He is a Drinker who doesn't drink, wearing a brown mudslide of a suit, tie loose at the collar. When he finishes his Diet Coke, an aide automatically brings him another.

"Big days," he says. "Critical days."

She nods.

"Praise the Lord and pass the ammunition." He smiles.

"I'm sorry?"

"That's what my daddy always said. He was a preacher in our Samsonite community."

"I'm not familiar with the Samsonites."

"Fine people," he says, "honorable people, committed to the idea that Eve, made from Adam's rib, existed as an instrument of his will. But that man must be ever vigilant, lest the female of the species sap him of his life force."

"You're talking about the story of Samson and Delilah."

"That's it exactly," he says, smiling. "A good man, a pious man seduced and betrayed by a fallen woman."

He raises his glass and sips the last trace of his Diet Coke loudly, rattles his glass. An aide brings him another refill.

"You were raised in the Church of Christ," he says, wiping his sweaty brow with a pocket handkerchief.

"I was. My family is quite devout."

"Praise be."

He takes a long sip. "And your husband is—"

"He's from Georgia originally, raised Baptist."

LaRue's office is narrow, with a desk and two guest chairs. There's a small round table by the door. The other senators' offices Margot has visited have been busy places, overwhelmed by paperwork and briefing books, but LaRue's office is clutter free, empty of both work product and personality. No documents, no books on the shelves.

"Well," says LaRue, leaning forward, "I'm so happy you came to see me today. Because I know we speak the same language. That we see the truth they try so hard to hide. This world may look like the world we grew up in."

He holds up his glass. "This glass may feel like just a regular glass. And in some ways it is, the way the *Titanic* was still a boat, even when it was sinking, but when you connect the dots, when you really understand what's going on, you know the truth. We are locked in an uphill battle against the forces of evil. Forces that attacked and undermined our former president, hallowed be his name. Forces that have infiltrated the highest level of our finest institutions. I pray on it every night. There's a storm coming, Your Honor. It may already be here. Certainly, I can hear the hooves approaching. The pale rider. You understand? January sixth was just the beginning. Our government cannot save us. Our courts cannot save us. Only He can save us. Wouldn't you agree?"

Margot nods. She has a cousin back in Michigan who holds court at family reunions about Satan's plot against a Christian America, about the duplicity of powerful elites. On some level it's nothing new. The Bar has always had Drinkers like LaRue, perched at the curve, talking about the end of the world, but their section is bigger now. The hooch they drink is addictive and cheap, and they pour from their own bottles for anyone who's curious. Margot tells herself they mean well, men like LaRue, that they're just afraid of powers greater than themselves, state powers, cultural forces, Hollywood elites and other profane agents of Satan, sent to seduce our youth. Their words are just words, after all, and aren't our words protected by a blessed document?

Don't we all have a right to our own opinion?

That's her theory anyway.

"Senator," she says, "I do believe that we are here for a reason, all of us. That we do not get to choose the role we will play in His plan. All we can do is try to live according to His principles, for the betterment of all mankind."

LaRue closes his eyes and sits back. There is a smile on his face, his hands raised in a triangle to his chest. One of his aides steps forward.

"The senator will pray on what you said," he says, indicating that Margot should leave.

She calls Remy on her break, questioning him on every detail. He tells her the FBI has traced Story's cell phone to a trash can at a gas station on Interstate 10, a hundred miles west of him.

"Looks like it was dumped sometime in the last few days," Remy tells her. Hadrian is playing with his Nintendo Switch on one of the twin beds in their hotel room. They're in downtown Austin at the Four Seasons, looking out at the Colorado River. Remy is tired today. His right leg is twitching. Earlier Hadrian asked his father if he was mad at him.

"Not at all," said Remy.

"Well, you look mad."

So Remy looked in the mirror and the kid was right. His face at rest was a scowl. He took a deep breath, forced a smile onto his face, but it looked wrong. Crooked.

Not yet, he thought. *I need more time.*

There is a feeling that comes over a body when it realizes it's dying. A feeling that has nothing to do with one's brain. When Hadrian is asleep, Remy finds himself sitting on the bed, sweating, even though there is a sixty-degree difference between the temperature inside the room and outside the building.

On the phone he tells Margot that he thinks Story has left Austin. Maybe he and Hadrian should fly to DC so they can be together.

"I'll stay if you want," he says, "but I'm not sure what I'm doing here except harassing people, and, well, given where you are right now, your people can harass the FBI better than me."

So Margot agrees, and the next morning her

husband and son arrive at the hotel on Pennsylvania Avenue. The relief she feels seeing them overwhelms her, the sense that her real allies have finally arrived. She hugs Remy tight. He puts his arms around her.

"I missed you," he says. "How are you holding up?"

She lets him go, looks around the lobby. "Are you...?" She leans in. "Have you been drinking?"

"What? No."

"Well, you're"—she lowers her voice—"you're slurring a little. Your words."

Remy puts his hand over his mouth, as if to check his tongue physically. "I'm—no. I'm just tired, I guess."

And then Hadrian pulls at his mother's arm, and she turns.

"Mom," he says, "did you meet the president?"

"I sure did. He's taller than I thought."

"Like LeBron?"

"Not that tall," she says, "and I doubt he can jump." She checks her watch. "Why don't you guys get up to the room and settle in. I've got a practice session with the team, but there's a dinner later with a few senators and members of the president's staff. Sound good?"

Hadrian nods.

"Don't just play your game, okay? Get out and see the capital. It's—well, honestly, it takes your breath away."

Hadrian hugs her.

"I know," she says, hugging him back. "I miss her, too. But she's okay. I promise."

"How do you know?"

"Because God is watching, okay?" She squeezes Remy's hand. "And he wants only good things for us."

O

Later, after the dinner and all the toasts, Margot and Remy lie in bed. Hadrian is in the adjoining room watching a movie. He's at that age where his parents literally can't stay awake later than him, so now Hadrian is the one turning off their television and tucking them in.

"What's he watching in there?" Margot asks. They are still in their clothes, lying on top of the covers.

"He's been on a horror movie binge," Remy tells her. "He started with haunted houses and then slashers, and then I showed him *Alien*."

"That's awful," she says. "All the gore and violence."

"He likes it. Besides, it's normal for kids his age

to wanna scare themselves. It's part of establishing their independence."

"And what book is that in?"

Remy pulls his wife on top of him, tickles her. "I'm a good father," he says. "Say it. Say I'm a good father."

She laughs, kisses him, softens. "You're a great father."

Later, they lie together under the covers with the lights out. It's after eleven, but they can still see the flickering light of Hadrian's iPad under the door and hear the occasional screech of horror movie violins. Margot looks out the window at the glowing tower of the Washington Monument.

"Do you remember when Story sang the national anthem?" she says, then—"Oh, shit. I'm sorry. Were you asleep?"

He rolls onto his side, facing her.

"No, I was just—that was at the house on Pineapple Street, right? And she was what—ten?"

"Nine. I don't know why, it just popped into my head last night. Seeing her up there."

"Right, wow. I haven't—everybody stood up, right?"

Margot nods.

Remy's eyes well up with tears. He tries to speak, but there is a catch in his throat. "I'm sorry," he says after a moment, his voice shaking.

Margot sits up. She puts her hand on his chest. "It's okay," she says. "We'll find her."

Remy nods, trying to fight back the feeling. "I'm not—" he says, but then can't continue.

She holds him, pets him. The truth of what he has to say is bigger than he can conceive. His own death. The abandonment of his wife, his children. His mental and physical decline. How he will soon become a burden, a dependent, staining their otherwise perfect lives.

He knows that when he tells her, she will want to withdraw her name from the court's selection process, that the combination of his news and Story's disappearance will feel like a sign, and she will quit on her dream at the very moment when she is closest to reaching it. And he can't let that happen. He can't let his weakness be what crushes her rise. So he nods and holds her and cries, and lets her think that his heartbreak is for someone else.

Simon

They drive all night and through the next day, stopping for gas outside Plano, then again near Midland. Flagg and Katniss ride lead, looking for trouble, dirt bike engines whining at speed. Cyclops brings up the rear. His bike has chopper handlebars, and he leans against the backrest, nodding in time to music only he can hear. For long stretches of time the Prophet sits staring at the flip phone in its ziplock bag. Up front, Duane plays an array of CDs, mostly eighties metal—Dio, Slayer, Ratt. He recounts epic tales of video game levels mastered, as if he himself were a demon slayer or a starship pilot. He drives with one arm out the window, feeling the breeze, even at highway speeds, making the inside of the van a kind of rock-and-roll tornado.

'Twas in the darkest depths of Mordor
I met a girl so fair

Float Anxiety Abatement Center seems like a different life. Driving the empty miles, Simon feels like what he is—an immigrant in a new land.

Texas. We're in Texas. He sees lawn signs for the God King, his face Photoshopped on the Terminator's body with the words "I'll be back," a promise or a threat, depending on whether you watch that movie and root for the machines. They pass exotic game ranches and billboards for Christ. Nine out of ten towns look abandoned, junked cars surrounding run-down homes, western store fronts long empty, but the churches remain. Faith. This is the Kingdom of Main Street.

Though the language spoken here appears to be the same, the meaning of each word can be vastly different. What they mean when they say *freedom.* What they mean when they say *equal.* What they mean when they say *fair.* They sing the same anthem in this America as they sing in Simon's, quote the same Constitution, but the words feel like contronyms: words that mean both one thing and its opposite. As in *to cleave,* defined as both to *split apart* and to *join together.*

The Kingdom of Main Street.

Lying on an Indian blanket on the metal floor, Simon slips into slumber.

And dreams he's flying.

Below him the ocean sparkles. There is a fog

bank ahead of him, a wall of snowy white. It reaches out and pulls him in. Blindness takes him. He can smell the salt air. Waves form below him. He can hear them crash against the shore ahead. And in the dream he feels no anxiety, no fear. His mind is blank. Dew bathes his face. He dips and soars.

On the tip of his tongue are the names of the angels.

Semanglaf, who helps the pregnant. Shateiel, the angel of silence, Abathar Muzania, the weigher of souls.

In the depths below something stirs.

And then he is over a beach and entering a city, moving through palm trees and low-slung concrete homes. But where are the people? The streets are empty. No pedestrians. No cars. He flies through the canyon of buildings, heading east—white wall, red door—but then the canyon becomes a hallway. White wall, red door. A dark and narrow corridor. Ahead is a door, half-open. The sounds of cooking from inside. He moves toward it, drawn in by a woman's voice.

Protect me, O Dumah, angel of dreams.

Watch over me, feared Azrael, forever writing names in the Book of the Dead.

She is standing at the stove, her white hair cut to the shoulder, her back to the door, dressed in black, her frame skeletal. She is stirring a giant pot with a wooden spoon and humming a tuneless tune.

It is Israefel who will blow the horn on Judgment Day.

How does he know this? Or that it is the angel Forneus, who seeds love inside the hearts of mortal enemies.

Now Simon is in the kitchen, and there is a meaty humidity to the room and that Slavic cabbage stench. It's possible that Simon is not in his body. That he is not *physically* there in the kitchen, for when he looks down he has no limbs, no body. He comes close enough to see the hairs on the back of the woman's neck rise. Close enough to see what's in the pot.

It's hands. Human hands. Dozens of them, stewing in a febrile broth.

They are small hands, one could even say *child-size.*

The woman turns. Her eyes are filled with teeth.

Simon wakes in the van to find the Prophet sitting over him. Behind him is the glow of the setting sun.

"He's talking to you," says the boy formerly known as Paul.

"Who?"

"God."

Simon shakes his head. His mouth tastes woolly.

"Who is Uriel?" he asks, unclear of where the name has come from, just that it is in his mouth.

"Some say he is a cherub or a seraph, but most believe he is an archangel. When the ten plagues descended on Egypt he was known as the Angel of Death. It was he who wrestled Jacob, he who told Noah of the coming flood. Did you see him?"

Simon thinks of the woman stirring her pot of hands, shakes his head. "No. It's just the—withdrawal. Must be. All the pills."

"You still miss them," says the Prophet. "Klonopin, Zoloft, Adderall."

Simon rubs his eyes. "I never took Adderall. That's for kids with ADHD."

The Prophet takes a Twizzler from his shirt pocket, takes a bite. "The feeling though," he says. "That medicated distance. The artificial quiet."

Simon looks out the window. The sun has set, but the horizon is still aglow. They are thirty miles from Fort Stockton. Scrubland and asphalt, pump jacks nodding in the gathering darkness. Three pills in the morning. Two at night. Day after day, year after year? Does he miss them? Is he the same person without them? And if he isn't, which Simon is the real Simon? The medicated one or the raw boy?

"People talk about freedom," says the Prophet, "but how can we be free when we are sicker and

poorer and more afraid than we've ever been? Free
to do what? What about freedom from poverty,
freedom from health care debt, freedom from the
drugs we have to take to numb the pain of all the
freedom we don't have?"

They come around a curve and the buttes become
a silhouette. Simon closes his eyes.

"Who is Javier?" he asks.

The Prophet offers him a Twizzler, but Simon
shakes his head.

"Did you know that two-thirds of Americans
believe that angels and demons are active in the
world?" asks the Prophet.

Simon yawns. "That seems high," he says.

"Meanwhile," the Prophet says, "only one-third
of us are certain that global warming is real and
caused by CO_2 emissions. One-third is also the
number of human beings who believe that our
earliest ancestors were not apes, but other humans.
So much for the theory of evolution."

He smiles. "Not the same third, I'd imagine."

"What about you?" Simon asks. "Do you believe
that angels and demons are real?"

"I believe that suffering makes us long for
meaning but it also pisses people off. They feel
wronged. Never have so many claimed to be victim
to so much. And what does the Bible tell us? In
times of strife, we can be saints or we can become

martyrs. Turn the other cheek or pick up the sword. Which—you tell me—does this feel like, the Age of the Saint or the Age of the Martyr?"

"What's the, you know, difference?"

"Martyrs believe their suffering makes them holy. That sacrifices made in this life will gain them reward in the afterlife. They get romantic when they talk about dying for a cause. *His name was Duncan. Her name was Ashli. His name was Timothy McVeigh.* This is the difference between the martyr and the saint. Sainthood requires self-lessness. One cannot aspire to sainthood, because the very desire to be a saint is in and of itself unsaintly. But people are angry. They feel abused. And so we go back to a God of wrath, a God who smites his enemies, who pulls down walls and kills the unbeliever."

He returns his glasses to his face. "As it is writ-ten—Saint Oswald of Worcester died on his knees washing the feet of twelve poor men. Saint Ida of Toggenburg was accused of adultery and thrown from the castle window by her husband, but angels saved her and she became a nun."

"He threw her out the window?" asks Simon.

"A martyr dies for a cause, in other words, thus the phrase *to martyr oneself*. There is no similar phrase for saints."

Simon thinks about this.

In heaven all the angels are named Claire. They smile at you with kind eyes, wiping the tears from your cheeks, and say with music in their mouths, What took you so long?

"You ask if I believe," says the Prophet, returning to his original text. "What I believe is irrelevant. In the last year, belief in Bigfoot rose from eleven percent to twenty-five percent. Here's another figure: thirty percent of Americans believe that aliens have visited Earth in the not-too-distant past."

"I don't care about that," says Simon. "I want to know what *you* think."

The Prophet nods. He turns to look out the window and is silent for some time.

"I believe the world lives on the edge between magic and science," he says finally. "And that it tips back and forth, depending on what we believe."

"So because more people believe in Bigfoot, then Bigfoot is more—real?"

The Prophet finishes his Twizzler, takes out the flip phone. "In the original Greek, the term *apocalypse* is translated as *an unveiling*. It describes a moment in time when something long hidden is finally revealed."

Simon thinks about that, how it's interesting and all, but also a diversion.

The Prophet studies his face. "Javier," he says,

"is the key to the Wizard's castle. Our way in. To rescue the dragon and start our exodus."

"Rescue the dragon," Simon says.

The Prophet nods.

"And exodus to where?" says Simon, feeling like he's taking a quiz. "Utopia?"

"Yes. First we find the boy who is not lost."

The Prophet slips the phone from the ziplock bag. He presses number one on the speed dial. Seven musical notes chirp from the speaker as it connects. Hearing them, Duane asks, "Is this it?" turning his head. "Are we doing it?"

Next to him Louise is still asleep, her feet up on the dash.

On the radio Black Sabbath sings.

Close the city and tell the people that some-
   thing's coming to call
Death and darkness are rushing forward to
   take a bite from the wall, oh

As the phone rings, Simon leans forward, staring into the worn fabric of Duane's bucket seat back.

Then a click.

"You've reached the Fort Stockton Walmart," says a voice. "We are currently closed. We will be open again at nine a.m. tomorrow. Please visit us then."

There is a beep, as if inviting them to leave a message, but no directory is offered—no *for Javier press one.* The Prophet hangs up, lost in thought. In the front seat, Louise stirs, sits up. She can feel the tension in the van.

"What?" she says. "Did something happen?"

Duane checks the rearview, changes lanes. "The Prophet dialed the number."

"And?"

"And it's a Walmart," says Simon.

"And?"

"And it's closed," says Duane.

Louise squints into the headlights of an on-coming semi. "Wait. What's the number supposed to do?"

"Javier," says Duane. "It's supposed to be his number."

"So he works at Walmart. Duh. What's the issue?"

"They're closed."

"Not, like, forever," she says. "So we go in the morning."

The Prophet stirs, shakes his head. He snaps the phone in half, throws the pieces out the window one at a time.

"No," he says, "Randall said once we call, we won't have much time."

Simon looks out the back window. He sees

Cyclops riding his dirt bike, lit red by the taillights.

"Time before what?" he asks.

"Before they find us. Before they find Javier."

"Wait," says Louise. "Who's *they*?"

The Prophet doesn't answer.

Louise smacks Duane's arm. "Dude, who's *they*?"

Duane frowns. "Them," he says. "The forces of
darkness."

Simon blinks. In his mind he hears, *Two-thirds
of Americans believe that angels and demons are
active in the world.* His thumbs start to itch. What
does he believe? God? The devil? No. He has
always been more of an agnostic. A scientific
method acolyte—theory, experiment, proof. But
that was before the experiment he calls his life
landed him in an anxiety center with no shoelaces,
before the children of the world began to murder
themselves. Even now he wants to be rational, but
nothing in his life makes sense. He is a fifteen-
year-old boy from a wealthy family with a dead
sister and parents so corrupt they believe the only
point in life is to make and spend small pieces of
paper, even though every dollar they make seems
to be killing someone. *Angels and demons.*

*By the year 2100 half of all species on Earth will
be extinct.*

Just Do it.

Fifteen percent of greenhouse gas emissions caused by humans are due to deforestation.

Think Different.

He lives in a world where clear evidence the human race will go extinct is met with government ambivalence and consumer tie-ins. Maybe this insistence on rationality *is* the problem. His problem. Facts, logic, science. Wanting things to make sense. Wanting things to happen for a reason.

Maybe if he just let go and went with his feelings, this monster inside of him would go away.

In heaven, all the angels are named Claire. They smile at you with kind eyes, wiping the tears from your cheeks, and say with music in their mouths, What took you so long?

"I'm gonna need something more than *forces of darkness*," says Louise, turning down the radio. Simon looks at her, so thin, no eyebrows. He considers telling her not to bother. That the details are irrelevant. Life is a joke. And as Neil Simon used to say, explaining a joke never makes it funnier.

"People in power fight to stay in power," says the Prophet. "This is the nature of power. You've been to the Wizard's parties. You know his circle."

Louise nods. She does. For a panicked moment her only thought is to run.

"Moguls," says the Prophet, "heads of state.

They take what they want. They erase anything that annoys them."

"And we're about to annoy the shit outta them," says Duane.

The Prophet looks at Simon, who's been quiet so far.

"What do you think?"

Simon shrugs. He's already done the hardest part. He got in the van. He broke the cycle of paralysis. Now it's just inertia, momentum.

"We go to Walmart," he says.

Louise frowns. "And if Javier isn't there?"

The Prophet straightened his glasses. "Then God will show us a sign."

O

They reach the Fort Stockton Walmart just after 11:00 p.m. Flagg calls on his walkie-talkie and tells Duane to hang back. He and Katniss snake into the parking lot, killing their headlights. They circle the dark box store on low idle, wary of an ambush.

In the last forty years more than half of the world's vertebrates have died.

Simon sits in the back of the van next to Louise. The sound of their breathing feels too loud for the space. The engine is running, lights off. The Prophet squats on the floor with his back to the wall, eyes closed. Perhaps he is communing with his Lord. Beside him, Simon feels Louise take his hand in the dark, squeeze. But when he looks down, both her hands are in her lap.

A chill runs through him.

Claire?

Up front, Duane's walkie-talkie crackles.

"All clear," says Flagg.

Duane slips the van in gear, coasts forward into the lot. The exterior lights are dark, a dull glow coming from inside. The parking lot is at least a square mile wide, an empty smudge filled with painted oil stains.

"Put us by the front doors," says the Prophet without opening his eyes. "And leave it running."

Duane pulls up parallel to the curb in front of a row of sliding glass doors. There is a sign on the window—HALF OFF ALL RADIAL TIRES and another that reads 35 PERCENT DISCOUNT ON ALL FICTION TITLES.

The sliding door beside Simon rolls open, letting in the smell of hot summer asphalt. Then the Texas broil hits him, almost midnight and still ninety-eight degrees. Somewhere a coyote howls. Then Louise is by him, the Prophet close behind.

"Go get 'em, stud," says Duane, winking at Simon, who blushes and stumbles out. He turns, feeling he should say something back, but the van door is already sliding closed.

Louise crosses to the box store's greedy mouth, shut in slumber. "Smile," she says pointing. "You're on camera."

Simon looks up, sees the ominous black dome. A feeling of panic hits him, but he shakes it off. There is a noise behind him. He turns. Flagg is there wearing a Halloween mask; Mr. Rogers, smiling benignly. Katniss crouches behind him, wearing the same mask.

"We came prepared," says Flagg, moving past Simon. He tries the doors, moving methodically down the line, but they're all locked.

"Mr. Rogers," he calls, and Cyclops comes forward, carrying a sledgehammer. He too is wearing a Mr. Rogers mask.

"No," says the Prophet, as Cyclops swings the sledgehammer back, ready to smash in the door glass. Cyclops looks at Flagg, who shakes his placid Mr. Rogers head. The sledgehammer comes to rest on the pavement. The Prophet walks to the door, knocks three times sharply. They wait, peering into the darkness. From close up they can see that there are lights on in the deep interior. Louise puts her ear to the glass.

"Are you hearing that?" she asks.

A shape emerges from the shadows of the

gardening aisle, stops just out of the light and peers at them. It's a small man, possibly Mexican. Next to Simon, the Prophet loosens his collar, pulls out a medallion. He holds it up to the glass.

"Amigos," he calls.

The man edges closer, squinting. Outside the door he sees children, some of them in masks. He comes closer, wary of robbers. His name is Arturo Emilio Diaz III, and he has been in Texas now for six years, three of them spent locked inside the Walmart on the night shift, scrubbing floors with astringents so strong they make his head spin. He was an accountant in Mexico City, and the musical director of his church choir. Every afternoon before he drives his ancient Hyundai to work, he smokes a cigar and listens to Verdi. A few feet away now, he stops by the checkout counters. Louise waves. Simon does the same, feeling foolish. Arturo sees the Prophet's medallion. He crosses himself, comes to the door.

"Soy el cordero de dios," says the Prophet. *I am the lamb of God.*

Arturo puts his forehead to the door. The Prophet places his palm on the glass, blessing him.

"Podemos entrar?"

May we come in?

Arturo steps back, shakes his head. "Ellos nos

encierran," he says. *They lock us in.* He pulls out his pockets to show he has no key.

Simon looks at the Prophet. If he's frustrated, it doesn't show.

"Sledgehammer time," says Flagg. "Or is God gonna send us the key?"

The Prophet takes off his glasses, wipes them. "He already has," he says.

O

They move to the dark side of the building. A half mile of loading bay doors backed up to a cyclone fence. There is a metal security door at the far end of the building. A sign next to it reads PROTECTED BY ALLSAFE ALARMS. Flagg hoists Katniss up so she can black out the security camera with a can of spray paint. Cyclops eyeballs the door.

"Problematic," he says. "See those hinges? That means the door swings *out*. I could maybe knock 'em off with the hammer, but I can't guarantee the door'll fall."

"We could blow it maybe," says Katniss. "I've got some M-80s in my saddlebag."

For the better part of ten minutes, the group debates various methods of breaching the door. Simon sits on the ground. There is a Clif Bar in his pocket. He takes it out, opens the wrapper, but looking at its kitty-litter composite-board texture, he loses his appetite, closes it back up. He stands, walks over to the dumpster, lifts the lid. He is about to toss the bar inside when he sees the glint of something shiny inside. He raises the lid farther, peers in. Overhead, the moon is nearly full.

There is a wooden crate on the ground beside him. Simon steps onto it, leans over. *What is that?* he thinks, peering inside.

Louise wanders up behind him. "Let me guess," she says. "You found a dress that's just your size."

The dumpster is filled with cardboard, plastic, and shredded paper. But in the folds of a box, he sees it again—a silvery gleam. Fighting off his fear—of disease, of roaches and rats—Simon levers himself up and, balancing on his stomach, he leans in and grabs for the flash.

He falls into the dumpster.

"Whoops," says Louise.

But when Simon comes up, there is a chain in his hand. And on the end of the chain is a set of keys. He jumps down on the macadam, hurrying for the back door.

Louise falls in beside him. "Are those keys?" she says.

Simon approaches the door, a skip in his step. "I bet the manager lost them when he took out the trash," he says, passing the bikers, now debating the use of a winch they don't have to pull the door free. The Prophet is kneeling on the threshold, hands clasped. He looks up as Simon approaches, sees the key ring in his hand.

"Amen," he says, and stands.

"I went to throw out my Clif Bar," says Simon. "And I saw them."

There are twenty-five keys on the ring, and Simon thinks he will have to try all of them, but the first key slips into the lock. It turns with a click. And then the door is open. Cold air hits him from the arctic inside.

"Oh, boys?" calls Louise. Flagg, Katniss, and Cyclops turn. They see the open door, the Prophet and Simon already moving inside.

"Try to keep up," says Louise, and sticks out her tongue, then turns and follows them in.

O

Simon has never been inside a Walmart. Sure he's heard talk of them, of the scourge of box stores, places you can buy radial tires, sugar cereal, and gym shorts, but only theoretically—the disdain of NPR commentators and *New York Times* op-eds. And yet inside his first thought goes like this: *It really is the everything store.* Around him are

miles of house and garden supplies, home electronics, books, food, movies, games, automotive
gear, and guns. Lots of guns. Crossbows, long-
bows, deer blinds, varmint traps, salt licks, duck
calls, and camouflage everything (flame retardant
camouflage pajamas only $9.99). He wanders the
store in wonder, as the Prophet talks to Arturo
near the manager's empty office. Six other night
workers have emerged from the shadows and are
gathered around him. They speak in low tones.
Simon knows he should be with them, focusing on
the plan, but the wealth of consumable goods calls
to him, triggering some deeply ingrained instinct
to shop.

I need that, he thinks, passing a pair of bin-
oculars, then again when he sees a cordless drill.
But for what? There are books he wants to read,
movies he's never seen. In the snack aisle, he finds
Louise filling a brand-new backpack with plastic
sacks of salty-sweet.

"You can't—" he tells her. "That's stealing."

But she just shrugs and keeps on stuffing. "We're
getting busted for breaking and entering," she says.
"What's a little light shoplifting thrown in?"

Simon is about to argue more, but then he
sees two Mr. Rogerses pass by, pushing shopping
carts filled with hunting supplies. He catches up
with them.

"Our gear needed an upgrade," Katniss tells him from under her mask.

Simon slows, watches them turn into the electronics aisle. At the other end of the store, he sees another Mr. Rogers eyeballing the gun display. It's Randall Flagg. Simon walks over.

"You ever fired an assault rifle?" Flagg asks him, which is a strange question coming from a man who looks like America's neighbor.

"I'm a little behind on my weapons of death," says Simon.

On the wall across from them are hundreds of long guns, displayed in orderly rows. In the glass case, handguns are arranged by manufacturer, by make and model. Looking at them Simon's anxiety is a throbbing pulse in his neck. He hears Flagg breathing inside his rubber mask.

"What he did, see," says Flagg, "he pulled the fire alarm. So he didn't have to go room to room. He could shoot us when we came out into the hall."

Simon swallows the lump that forms in his throat when he realizes what Flagg is talking about. Parkland.

"My brother knew him. They were older. I was twelve. Tommy used to say how they were weird, Nik and his brother, that they liked to do stuff to animals, especially Nik. Jabbing sticks in rabbit holes to kill the babies, shooting squirrels. I guess he was adopted, and first his dad died and then his mom, and he was living with somebody, a friend. She was old, his mom. Adopted. This was after he got expelled for selling knives out of his lunch box, or maybe it was the bullets in his backpack. Those are just, you know, details."

He points to the wall.

"That's the gun. Smith & Wesson, manufactured by American Outdoor Brands. A .223-caliber that could be modified automatic supereasy. That shit'll punch a dozen bullets through you at thirty-two hundred feet per second. Recoil's real light, standard mag thirty rounds. He probably bought it at a place like this when he was eighteen. No waiting. This was before he put on YouTube that he wanted to become a professional school shooter."

He tilts up his mask, lights a cigarette.

"We all have thoughts, you know," he says. "Who doesn't want revenge for things? But that's, like, hit the guy when he's not looking and run away. Not—I don't know, seventeen dead. Maybe it's Florida. Maybe we're the problem. America's liver."

He reaches under his rubber mask, and Simon gets the feeling he's wiping away tears.

"All I know is, as long as they're packing, I'm gonna be strapped. I'm done hiding in supply closets."

"What happened to Tommy?" Simon asks.

Flagg drops the cigarette on the linoleum, lifts his rubber mask, spits. "What do you think?" he says.

The Prophet comes over. There is a middle-aged woman with him, part native American. She is Wanda Salas Soto, who lives in a double-wide outside Coyanosa.

"Bad news," says the Prophet. "Wanda says the government came for Javier and his father last week."

"Our government?" says Simon, then immediately feels stupid. It has been thirty-six hours since his last Ativan and his brain feels like a box of spiders.

It was 110 degrees in Paris last week.

You Deserve a Break Today.

There are 1,000,000 more guns in America than people.

I Can't Believe I Ate the Whole Thing.

"County sheriff raided last week," Wanda tells them. She is in her midforties, moon-faced with a smoker's cough. Truckers on the dating app she uses describe her as "exotic" when they text her from the road. "Maybe you saw the billboards. Sheriff Roy. He calls himself the real immigration police ever since the ICE purge and that southern border reform bill—which—that shit don't fly in

Texas. So the deputies come in with stun guns and Black Jacks, took fifteen of us. Javier also."

"Where?" says Louise, wandering over.

"Sheriff Roy built a detention center outside Balmorhea," says Wanda. "Cyclone fences and razor wire. A few un-air-conditioned Quonset huts. They keep the kids in cages, away from their parents."

"Wait a minute," says Simon. "How old is Javier?"

"He's eleven," says the Prophet.

"Eleven," says Simon, his mind reeling. "I thought you said he could get us in to see the Wizard."

"Yes."

"An eleven-year-old boy. Did they—"

Simon looks at Wanda. He doesn't want to say what he knows in front of her.

"No," says the Prophet. "Javier's mother worked in the Wizard's kitchens. He knows the secret passageways."

Simon considers asking how he knows this but doesn't. He can guess the answer.

God told me.

"Why not talk to the mother?" asks Louise.

Wanda crosses herself. "Sheriff Roy got her too, but I think she got sent to Brownsville."

Simon looks at Flagg. He is a few feet away, talking to Katniss and Cyclops. "We could visit him. At the detention center. They have to let them have visitors."

"No visitors," says Wanda. "Not even lawyers. Sheriff Roy ain't a big believer in civil rights."

Simon looks at Louise. Neither has any clue what to do next.

"Flagg," calls the Prophet.

"On it," says Flagg. Simon watches Katniss vault the glass gun display case. She tries its sliding doors. Locked. On the wall behind her, the long guns are locked down as well.

"Keys," she calls, looking at Simon.

"What?" he says. Everyone is staring at him.

The last Hawaiian tree snail died in 2019.

Don't be Evil.

Farewell to the giant Yangtze soft-shell turtle.

They're Grrrreat!

Looking down, Simon realizes he still has the manager's key chain in his hand.

"Simon," says the Prophet. "Give her the keys."

Simon lifts his hand, looks at them. His brain feels like it's moving in slow motion. Why does Katniss want to open the gun case? And why is Cyclops coming back with a shopping cart full of fertilizer?

Then Flagg walks over and snatches the keys from Simon's hand. "You're taking too long." He tosses the keys to Katniss, who opens the case and begins pulling out boxes of ammunition and stacking them on the counter.

"We have to find Javier," the Prophet tells Simon.

"I know," says Simon, "but—"

"To *rescue* Javier," he clarifies. "Moses led the Hebrews out of Egypt. He sent the ten plagues. He parted the Red Sea."

Simon's head is spinning. "You want to— we're supposed to what? Break into a federal detention center to rescue an illegal immigrant?"

"Don't call him that," says Wanda. "No person is illegal."

"Sure," says Simon. "Sorry. But—they're—are they stealing those guns?"

No one answers. Simon feels the edges of his vision starting to go black. There's no oxygen in the air he's breathing.

"So, already we've got breaking and entering, and now grand theft arsenal, but that's not—you also want—"

As he lifts it to his face, Simon realizes he's taken the paper bag from his pocket. *In case of emergency...* He holds it over his nose and mouth, huffing into it. Louise helps him slide down onto the floor.

"The kid's day three without meds," she tells the Prophet. "You should probably get him some

Klonopin if you want him to go from state crimes to federal."

Breathing rapidly, Simon feels he will pass out.

The Prophet comes over, kneels beside him. "Do you know what a criminal is?" he asks. "Someone who rejects morality and ethics. Someone who puts their own needs above the needs of society. A cynic. A nihilist. We're fighting for something here, a greater good, this human agreement—balance, community, civilization. Our parents have surrendered. They can't or won't commit to creating a collective system based on sharing, based on the idea that every human life is precious, that we can't sacrifice any of God's children in the name of progress. They can't or won't agree that we are stronger together. That diversity strengthens the species. That power without empathy is a sin."

Through cloudy pupils, Simon watches Flagg and Katniss load weapons and ammunition into an oversize shopping cart with a red plastic steering wheel and a bucket seat.

"This is crazy," he says.

"No," says the Prophet. "Crazy is putting eleven-year-olds in cages. Saving them is the definition of sane."

Simon wants to argue the point, but he can't for the life of him figure out how.

Thirty percent of Americans believe that angels and demons are active in the world.

"But why me?" says Simon.

"Because those who refuse his call are worse than those who never hear it at all."

Simon thinks of his room at Float, the bed he made before he left, his clothes on hangers in the closet, the entrances and exits he committed to memory. A system. He had a system there. Structure. All he has now is chaos. Terrible things could happen if they're not careful, and they are not being careful. They are being the opposite of careful. They are breaking laws. They are arming themselves.

Louise, sitting on the floor next to Simon, puts her head on his shoulder. "Come on, kid," she says. "You're overthinking this thing."

"Overthinking."

"You can't reason your way out of a holy war."

"I'm pretty sure that's the only way out."

Louise rubs his arm. "This is our planet. They had their chance, and what did we get—Mexican babies drowning inside their daddy's shirts. Rising seas and bump stocks. Shit. We got shit, and what's their solution? Conspiracy theories and magical thinking. Well, maybe it's time we got some magic thinking on our side too."

She stands, holds out her hand.

"Let's go get 'em."

Simon stares at her hand for a long moment. The paper bag at his side is forgotten. For as long as he can remember, all he's known is fear. But there's a bigger emotion inside him now. A feeling with no name. He reaches up and takes her hand.

"All right, all right," says Flagg, taking the cigarette from behind his ear and putting it between his lips. "Now let's get this shit loaded up."

Avon DeWitt

It was said there wasn't a jail on Earth that could hold Avon DeWitt. The fact that it was Avon who said it and that he had never once escaped from a lockup of any kind was beside the point. What was important was that every time they sent Avon away, he walked right back out the door—usually six to twenty-four months later (although in 2004 he did a spell of three years, six months for assaulting a police officer with a deadly weapon, i.e., the driver's-side door of his Cutlass). This time he'd been in for four months for tax evasion, a term he disagreed with—as he said while representing himself in Miami-Dade County Municipal Court—*violently.*

If you keep moving, Avon used to tell his son, Samson, they never catch you on the big stuff. Which is why they'd lived in ten states in eleven years. Cowboys of the interstate. American nomads. Samson is grown now, living some-where in the middle of the country. They talk infrequently these days, and unpleasantly when they do. *You teach a boy everything you know,* Avon likes to say, *and then he spits in your face.*

And yet isn't that what Avon did to his father?

He was sixty-one years old when he went in this last time, Avon. He is sixty-two now, having celebrated the date of his birth in a Miami-Dade County holding facility, lying on a mattress so thin it felt like the cheese on a cheeseburger. Food, it turned out, was the main topic of conversation in Miami-Dade County lockup. Each prison has its own particular voice. In Tallahassee, prisoners talked mainly about cars—cars they'd owned, cars they planned on owning, cars that got them laid, the laser-cut speed machines from Fast & Furious 1, 2, 3, 4, 5, 6, 7, 8, 9, 10, 11. In McCreary—where Avon had done eighteen months for passing bad checks in the nineties—the primary subject of conversation was blowjobs. It was there that Avon met Fat Eddy, who was six foot two and weighed a hundred and forty pounds and who swore that he'd gotten head once from Miss America herself, when she was a flat-chested, fifteen-year-old roller skate waitress at the Hula Hut in Boca Raton. He described it as *serviceable,* due mainly to her youth and inexperience, but also to the full set of braces she'd had put on just a few weeks earlier.

It was Fat Eddy who introduced Avon to the idea of sovereignty. Which is a bit like saying it was Jesus who introduced the world to the idea of Christianity. That's the scale of impact the words had on Avon DeWitt, born to Marsha and Dylan DeWitt (sixteen and eighteen respectively) on the Georgia/Florida border in the back of a broken-down Chevy in December 1958. Dylan was driving his fiancée to Jacksonville to take a job on his uncle Dale's car lot, so as to give his firstborn son a stable home and three squares a day. Dale had offered them the use of a trailer on the back forty of a piece of property he owned behind the Tastee Freez. The trailer was where Avon ate his first solid food, took his first steps, and blew off his left pinkie finger with a blackjack firecracker on the fifth of July, 1966.

Sovereignty, Fat Eddy explained to Avon one afternoon while they were standing with their faces to the bars of their cell, waiting for the guards to finish rifling through their shit, is the natural state of all free-born men. "We are all," he told Avon, "creatures of autonomy, masters of our own domain. That's in the Declaration of Independence." The first paragraph of which Fat Eddy had had tattooed on his back by a Oaxacan woman in

Phoenix, Arizona, on a cross-country motorcycle trip in 2001. After the cell search came the cavity search, and while they were pulling up their prison trou, Fat Eddy laid out in minute detail *the truth of our enslavement*.

"The Founding Fathers of American government," he said, "believed that the sole purpose of government was for the benefit of protecting the rights of the citizens, not the right of the rulers. They also believed that the doctrine of the divine right of kings was an oppressive, moral transgression against humanity and that no government, man—or woman, for that matter—had the right to rule over his fellow man without their consent."

Avon was only half listening as he bent to clean his personal items from the floor and reconstruct his tiny corner of human identity.

"How old ye be?" Eddy asked him. He had a way of communicating that was rooted in bygone times.

"Forty-one," said Avon, slipping some nude postcards back between the pages of a Tom Clancy paperback.

"Well, what if I told you the federal government of the United States, Incorporated, owed you half a million bucks?"

This stopped Avon. He laid the potboiler on the sink and turned around. "For real?"

"I shit you negative. See, you're a slave, my friend, and you don't even know it."

And then Eddy proceeded to lay out how at one time there was an American utopia governed by English *common law*. A paradise in which every citizen was a *sovereign*. Back then there were no taxes, no regulations or court orders. In this perfect union, a man was a citizen of the Republic of Ohio or Pennsylvania, or whatever state he claimed as home.

"There was no such thing as a *US Citizen*," Fat Eddy told him. "But then a conspiracy of bankers introduced the Fourteenth Amendment, purportedly to create citizenship for the freed negro. Listen to the fast one they pulled, hidden right there in plain sight. Quote: 'All persons born or naturalized in the United States and subject to the jurisdiction thereof, are citizens of the United States and of the state wherein they reside.'"

Fat Eddy looked at Avon over his readers. He was in his midfifties, still with the metabolism of a seventeen-year-old boy.

"You see what they did there?"

Avon shrugged.

"They used the goddamn slave amendment to define all Americans."

"Okay, but—"

"Keep listening. See, before the Fourteenth we

had what you call *de jure* common law. A man was subject to the rule of nature, the bonds of common sense. But then, a year after the Fourteenth Amendment, these sons a bitches cook up an obscure fucking passage in the United States Code—purportedly to govern the goddamn District of Columbia—that contains the following sentence: *For the purposes of this Code, the phrase 'United States' means a Federal Corporation.*"

He pauses for effect.

"And just like that, Uncle Sam replaces common law and subjects all free-born men of the goddamn American experiment to *commercial law.*"

He paused for effect, taking a pinch of chaw from a tin and tucking it between his lip and gum. Avon offered how maybe Eddy should get to the fucking point on how the government owed him so much dough, because *Who Wants to Be a Millionaire* was about to start. Fat Eddy took off his readers and rubbed his temples.

"Cut to 1933. America decides—out of the fucking blue—to go off the gold standard. Right? Before that every US greenback was guaranteed by a certain weight of precious metal. But then these bankers decide to end all that. Why? And also, if we don't have gold backing our currency anymore, then what the fuck is? See what I'm saying? Otherwise, that shit's just a piece of paper. And what else do we know about 1933? It's the middle of the goddamn Depression, right? The United States of America is going fucking bankrupt. They need money—fast. And how do they get it? They sell us out."

"Us."

"You, me, everybody. See, Uncle Sam goes off the gold standard because he realizes he's got something more valuable than gold. People. So he goes out to all these foreign bigwigs—Jew bankers, et cetera—and he says, *You're gonna give me a loan. And in return, I'm gonna sign over to you the future earnings of all my citizens—* which, whaddya know, that's us. You know what collateral is?"

Avon nods. He says, "Like how when I refinanced my house to put on a new roof, they made me put up my car. It's like a guarantee."

"Abso-fucking-lutely. Except now the collateral is us. You, me, everybody. You follow?"

Avon is beginning to have an itchy feeling at the back of his neck. Like how all the water on the beach goes out first before the tidal wave comes.

"I think so. But how does that get me half a million bucks?"

"Because, my friend, what happens when you're born?"

Avon shrugs.

"The government issues you a birth certificate, right? And when you look at that birth certificate, under name of the baby, you see Avon—you got a middle name?"

"Hamish."

"You see Avon Hamish DeWitt. Except it's written in all caps. This is how the US Government, Incorporated, creates a certificate of debt in your name. And when they do, they open a Treasury Direct Account, a bank account, right? Into which go all the funds you earn them. And that money is just sitting there. Hundreds of thousands of dollars. I heard a guy say once up to twenty goddamn million. And it's just sitting there. But here's the secret. You can get that money for yourself."

"How?"

"Well, not fucking easily. But there's a way. Certain documents filed, forms filled out with the right language. The right punctuation."

"What's that?"

"You know, commas and semicolons and shit. The point is, you are a prisoner."

Avon looks around him at the bars. "No shit, Sherlock."

"I'm saying even after you get out. Unless and until you declare yourself free."

"And how do I do that?"

Fat Eddy smiled. "I'm gonna show you."

O

No one is there to meet Avon when he gets out of the joint this time. Doesn't bother him. He knows how to take a goddamn bus. He stands in the hot Florida sun as the gate slides closed behind him, breathing in the muggy calm. Then goes over and waits in the shade of the portico for the cross-town #6 to arrive. He's been out of pocket for four months, eating soup from a hot plate and jerking off into his socks like a goddamn fifteen-year-old. He wipes his forehead with the back of his arm, thinking about the crisp nirvana of a cold beer (or twelve). The bus, when it comes, connects to a second bus, and then he settles back for the two hours to Jupiter with a packet of salted peanuts and a Coors Light tallboy (snagged from a corner bodega) in a paper bag. All things being equal, he's feeling pretty good about things.

He wedges the sliding bus window open an inch, enjoying the highway breeze. When he was a kid, Avon used to sit on his dad's lap when he drove. Still in his early twenties and rocking a caterpillar mustache, Daddy Dylan had graduated from car sales to roofing and then found a gig at the Honda plant. He was an axle man, soldering metal on metal, and his arms were polka-dotted with burns that would turn a hard white over time. He drove a 1993 Ford Mustang Cobra in reef blue with an opal-gray leather interior, bought third hand from a Black on the assembly line with credit trouble. Avon's dad loved that car, used to wash and wax it every Saturday, parked in the driveway of the faux ranch they rented for $625 a month from Avon's grandpa.

Dylan liked to drive with the windows down, radio going full blast, a Camel Light in his left hand, draped out the window like *la dee da*, sometimes a tallboy between his thighs, sweating its cold into a beer koozie with a cartoon middle finger printed on it. When Avon rode in his lap, Dylan kept the beer in the center console. He drove with the seat belt buckled behind him, to keep the cop in the dashboard from dinging. He'd steer with his right, smoke with his left. Every few minutes he'd ask Avon, six, seven, eight, to take the wheel, and he'd pick up the beer and take a sip.

"Remember this feeling, boy," he told his son once, the wind in their faces, sun setting in the rearview as they drove along the Gulf Coast. "Freedom."

O

It's a ten-minute walk from the bus stop to the house Avon shares with his common-law wife,

Girlie, a fifty-year-old Filipina he met at big Jim Nash's barbecue three years back. She owns a strip mall nail salon, strictly a cash business, most of the girls under her being illegal. Girlie has been a resident of what Avon calls the United States of America, Incorporated, for twelve years. She came over with her sister, Rose, who lives in Los Angeles now, working as a live-in care-taker for an old shut-in. A real witch, is what Avon's heard, which means something different to him than it does to your average Filipino. *Those people still believe in sorcerers, for Chris-sake.*

Avon makes the turn onto his street, feeling a blister coming up on his left heel where the hole sits in the sock. The sun is now midday hot, and he's sweating in rivulets down his back and sides. He lost about ten pounds this time in the joint, and as he steps onto the cracked front walk of the house, the string holding his pants up gives out, so when he reaches the screen door, he's got the sack with his valuables in one hand and the waist-band of his pants in the other. Behind the screen, the front door is open. He can hear the TV going full blast inside, sounds like the Home Shopping Network. He gives the metal frame of the screen door a kick.

"Open the damn door," he shouts. "I gotta piss."

At the end of a short hall he sees Girlie's head pop out from behind the kitchen doorway.

"I thought you were getting out tomorrow," she says in her accented English.

"Well, I got out today. Hurry up, woman, 'fore I piss my trousers."

Girlie comes to the door, drying her hands with a teal dish towel. She thinks blue is the color of luck. So everything in the house is one shade of blue or another.

"You got skinny," she says.

He pushes past her, dropping his sack on the linoleum and hurrying to the john. Girlie *tsks*. She picks up his bag, goes through it, nosy as ever. Down the hall, Avon pisses with the door open, the sound of it—rounded, masculine—fills the small house. She *tsks* again. Men are such animals, really. Even the so-called nice ones.

She rifles through his meager possessions, hair-brush, playing cards, two pairs of worn briefs.

"Get yer nose outta my crap," he tells her, coming down the hall, one hand holding up his pants.

"Yeah, yeah," she says, and drops the sack on a wooden side table with a built-in lamp.

Avon comes up behind her, cups her left breast with his hand, and presses up against her.

"The king has returned from battle," he tells her.

"I got adobo on the stove," she says. "And I didn't

shave a few days. You want special treatment, you gonna have to wait."

He nuzzles her neck, smelling of sweat and beer. "I like you hairy," he says.

She shrugs, leads him to the bedroom. She's not in the mood, but when has that ever mattered? Besides, he's been locked away for months. He'll pop quick. Avon follows, holding her trailing hand, his other hand on his pants, shuffling—scrawny, white-blond hair clipped close to the skin in a flattop—and for a moment he looks like a boy again.

Freedom.

Later, they sit at the kitchen table, drinking Jack Daniel's coolers—they both like the watermelon punch—and eating chicken straight out of the pot.

"You keeping oil in the car?" he asks.

"One time," she tells him, "and now forever we gotta talk about this."

On TV, Fox News is reporting on some kind of Senate committee hearings. Avon doesn't pay much attention to American politics now that he knows what's really going on. But he glances at the screen while he eats. A woman in a suit behind the big table is being grilled by some subcommittee (Justice?). The chyron under her name reads JUDGE MARGOT BARR-NADIR, and she's talking about why she's fit to serve on the Supreme Court.

The chyron changes. The words *Daughter missing 4 weeks* appear where her name used to be.

Avon opens another JD cocktail. He tells Girlie about his cell mates—the dumb one and the stupid one—and how lousy the food was. She half listens, texting her sisters, her friends, her employees all in a constant stream. It's 7:00 a.m. in the Philippines, and everybody's up and writing.

"Of course I'm worried," Judge Nadir says. "I'm her mother. But this isn't a hearing about my daughter. This is a hearing about whether or not I should be a justice on the Supreme Court, and I'd appreciate it if you'd keep your question to that topic."

Avon drops a chicken bone on his plate. "What's she going on about?" he asks.

"The babies," says Girlie, "all everybody's babies. They just kill themselves."

"What babies? They're dying in their cribs?"

"No, stupid. The boys and girls. Teenage. They kill themselves." She makes a gun of her hand and presses it to her temple.

He grits his teeth. She should know better than to call him stupid. "Who? Where?"

"Everyplace, they think. Connie at the shop say her cousin dead this weekend."

Avon scowls. "Sounds like they found another wild-goose chase to keep us from thinking about the real tragedy. Where are the bodies? That's what we should be asking."

"No, it's real. All dead. Babies. So sad."

"Why, 'cause you saw it on TV? 'Cause Connie's got a cousin? How many times I gotta tell you, woman, it's a smokescreen. You can't trust anything that comes over that pipeline. It's all a *diversion*."

Girlie shrugs, her face flushed, poking at her plate. She felt him stiffen when she called him stupid. *Why did I do that?* Thank God he didn't hit her, probably because he got out of prison today, and he's still in a good behavior mindset. But Girlie worries her words will come back on her later, when she's in the bedroom brushing her hair or putting on lotion. She'll feel him behind her, hear the tone shift in his breathing. But by then it'll be too late.

She checks her phone again. In LA, her sister, Rose, is hiding in the bathroom. The Witch is nocturnal, mostly, sleeping the day away in a back bedroom with blackout curtains. The smell of cigarette smoke signals her resuscitation, followed by the sound of deep, hacking coughs, as she brings up balls of brown lung phlegm and spits them into a coffee can she keeps by the bed. Rose brings the missus her coffee then, her eyes adjusting to the slow darkness within. Sometimes after she puts the coffee on the bedside table and turns, the Witch is standing behind her in a sheer nightdress stained brown in places by hacked tobacco spit that dribbles from her lips.

How she laughs at Rose's fear. Laughs and laughs.

She has the black eyes of a succubus.

So these days, when the afternoon turns to evening, Rose tries to make herself scarce. A long trip to the market, an hour in the laundry room.

The Witch is a New York transplant, somewhere between seventy-five and a hundred, thin as a bone. At some point in the last fifteen years, she had lip liner tattooed around her mouth, but as the elasticity has gone out of her skin, the liner has moved farther and farther from her actual lips, until now a dark halo hovers somewhere between her nose and mouth, forcing her either to fill the gap with lipstick or accept the incongruity. She speaks in an old Bronx grind, dressed in black—pants, turtlenecks—her eyes shielded by dark glasses half the size of her face. Whenever she goes out, she perches a NY Yankees baseball cap on top of her head, like a lid on a pot. Rarely does she move in a straight line.

Rose has lived in a tiny bedroom in the Witch's apartment for nine years. She was hired originally to be a nurse, but the boundaries quickly blurred, until now she is on duty twenty-four hours a day, cleaning, cooking, fixing drinks. Her green card status is pending, and whenever she asks for time off, the Witch will pick up the phone and threaten to call ICE, so Rose has stopped asking. She tells Girlie in whispered late-night phone calls that the Witch keeps roots and herbs in a secret trunk. That there are chicken feet in the freezer that Rose can't remember buying. She says sometimes the Witch will give her an eye so evil, it's all Rose can do not to cross herself and weep. Late at night sometimes, she wakes to find the Witch standing by her bed like a shadow, a living ghost. *What is she muttering beneath her breath? Are those growls?*

Girlie has told Rose to run. *Come to Florida. We have room.* But Rose is afraid. She's afraid of the ICE men in their flak jackets and lace-up boots, afraid of the evil eye. She worries the Witch has stolen her soul and keeps it in the trunk with all her spells and potions. She and Girlie were raised in a traditional Filipino village. They know three, five, and nine are unlucky numbers, know that if you break an egg and see two yolks you will become wealthy. They know that when three people pose for a photograph, it is the one in the middle who will die first.

Avon tells Girlie he'll drive to Los Angeles and wack the old bat if she wants him to.

"I ain't afraid of no ancient bitch."

But last Christmas, when Rose sent Girlie a photo of herself, Avon wouldn't let her put it up. They fought about it, long and hard, but of course Avon won. The man always wins. This is the order of the universe. Men talk, women listen. So Girlie kept the photo in her bedside drawer. But as time went by, she realized that she never took it out, never looked at it. When it came in the mail, she was delighted. Here was her older sister, smiling on a sofa, sunlight pouring in through the windows behind her. The photo was a selfie, taken at arm's length. And yet there was something unsettling about the picture that Girlie couldn't articulate. Avon took one look at the thing and said *no fucking way* was that picture going up in his house. Girlie pressed him. What was the problem? It was her sister. Shouldn't she get to put up a picture of her sister? But Avon was adamant. Something about that damn photo gave him the heebie-jeebies.

It wasn't until Avon was in jail again that Girlie *saw* what it was. She had pulled the picture out after dinner, having half a mind to stick it to the fridge. *Avon was gone for months*, she thought. *Why shouldn't she surround herself with her family?* She sat at the kitchen table, smoking a Newport. The sun had just gone down, and the sky was ruby red outside the windows. Down the hall the front door was open, letting in the sounds of kids playing in the cul-de-sac.

Girlie studied her sister's face. Rose had always been the happy one. The optimist. And she was smiling in the photo, but there was strain behind her eyes. Light poured in from the apartment window behind her. The decorations were expensive but old, the drawn curtains a dull green, muting the shadows. Rose looked at her sister and felt a chill. She pulled her cardigan around her, her eyes moving from her sister's face. And then she saw it in the top left corner of the frame—the photo vignetted in darkness by overexposure from the window. The camera had caught a slice of the stone mantelpiece and above it a sliver of mirror. And in that mirror was a face—old, shadowed, staring— barely visible. Once she saw it, Girlie couldn't unsee it. A face, no bigger than a dot, a shaded oval surrounded by darkness. It was the Witch.

She was looking straight into the camera, straight at Girlie.

Girlie dropped the picture, crossed herself. Around her the sunlight had faded, and now the kitchen was dark. Girlie stood, intending to slap on the light switch, but her eyes went to the dark hall and, at the end, the open doorway. Outside the front door, the fading daylight had settled into a low blue glow.

The street was empty, silent.

Where did the children go? Why is it so quiet?

Girlie took a step toward the kitchen doorway, her hand reaching for the light, but her eyes stayed on the open door. A feeling of danger passed through her. She felt *exposed*, like a rabbit in its hovel when the wolves come.

Then someone passed in front of the house. A human shape, shadowy and quick, passing close to the door.

Girlie let out a shriek. She knew she should turn on the lights, but she was frozen in place. Her eyes were fixed on the open door. *Close it,* she thought. *Don't let her in.*

She willed herself to move, slowly at first, then picking up speed. In her heart was a feeling of doom. The door seemed to recede ahead of her, even as her right arm came up. She would push it closed, slam it, and throw the bolt. But why couldn't she reach the door? A low sound of anguish came from her throat. *Why was her house so dark?* She could swear she had turned on the side table lamp in the living room this afternoon.

From the front door came a rumble—ominous, subterranean—and a flash, illuminating everything, the oak tree at the curb throwing a lunging shadow across the walk. *Was that the Witch?*

Hiding behind the tree, only her face visible and one pale hand?

Girlie lunged and slammed the door. She threw the bolt and ran to the downstairs bathroom, windowless, safe, and locked that door as well, slapping on the overhead light. And as the Florida skies opened up and poured down rain, she slid to the floor and wept.

O

After dinner, Avon retires to his library. This is what he calls the room off the kitchen where he keeps his code crackers, his research pamphlets and history books, his gun locker. That $500,000 isn't going to return itself. He lost time in prison with nothing to read but Tarzan and Robinson Crusoe. It is a tough nut to crack, this escape from the clutches of the US Corporation. The first thing one has to do is to opt out of all government contracts, implicit and explicit. So Avon carries no driver's license. His vehicle is unregistered, wears his own printed license plate that reads PRIVATE in bold type. Above that NO DRIVER'S LICENSE OR INSURANCE REQUIRED. Underneath NOT FOR COMMERCIAL USE.

See, license plates are a tool of the straw man, and Avon has long ago surrendered that identity. So too with bank accounts. If you read the fine print on the contract when you deposit your money, it enters you into a contract not just with the bank, but with the US Corporation, in the form of the FDIC. When he works—handyman services—he works cash jobs or for barter. If he had his druthers, he would strictly barter for gold, but Girlie likes to go to Olive Garden sometimes, and she buys her clothes at the mall, so Avon allows himself to remain a conduit for paper currency.

He pays no social security. It kills him that he paid in for so long, a slave without realizing it. Anytime he is forced to sign a federal document—as he was upon his arrest, sentencing, and release from prison—he amends his all-lower-cap signature with the words *Without Prejudice UCC 1-308*, which preserves his common-law rights and privileges, and always makes sure to add *TDC*, for *under threat, duress, and coercion.*

Now he raises the blinds in his library. He can hear Girlie in the kitchen washing dishes. For a moment he relishes the simple value of other rooms, of not being locked in a box twenty-three hours a day. To walk from one room to another, to shit in private with the door closed, these are no small things. They are the simple glories of the free man. Adjusting the thermostat—Avon likes it cold—he sits behind his desk. On the corner, under the lamp, is a framed photo of his kids, Samson and Bathsheba, both born to his first wife—his government legal wife, Jamie, in 2003 and 2005. Both had been home births, delivered without witness, no birth certificate filed, no social security number request filed. In other words, born free. It was the greatest gift Avon could give them, this erasure from the iron eye of the USC.

They were home schooled, of course, taught the real history of America, never brainwashed by the great liberal delusion. Fat Eddy had been their godfather, present for Samson's baptism, but re-incarcerated for Bathsheba's. Not a day went by that Avon DeWitt didn't spare a kind thought for old Fat Eddy, RIP, executed by the pigs in Hot Springs, Arkansas, on the side of the road before he could even get his weapon out. They'd spent two and a half years together in the federal pen, like a master's program in liberation theory. It was Fat Eddy who helped Avon draft his Declaration of Sovereignty, Fat Eddy who'd taught Avon the intricacies of small-case letters, semicolons, and commas. Fat Eddy helped him design his own seals and stamps, taught him to write only in certain colors—he himself communicated mostly in red crayon. All these codes and triggers were employed to baffle and bamboozle the corporate stooges, all in the service of breathing God's air and walking on his Earth once more in complete and total sovereignty.

Uncovering the secret history of America was an awakening for Avon DeWitt, who had never been a good student, had always felt somehow tricked by the teachers at school, judged. *Who do they think they are to call me stupid?* But sitting there in prison, Avon felt the very idea of knowledge was freed from tyranny. A man, a free man, could— upon his own endeavoring, his own initiative— decode the great American trick.

And so it was he sat down, with burning fire and a giddy spirit, to draft his own emancipation.

Margot

The hearings start on a Tuesday. The first day is just speeches from the committee, political statements of party fealty or the airing of grievances. Margot sits calmly, her hands folded on the table, and tries to seem unreadable. She is quick with a smile or a joke when the opportunity arises, quick to offer a humble personal insight or to affirm how her role on the court will be a sacred duty. Margot has always been good with people and comfortable with the spotlight. She knows deep down in her toes that this is a calling, not a career. She was born to be a justice of the Supreme Court. God has granted her wisdom and clarity of thought so that she might stand in judgment over the laws and mores of this complicated and polarized nation.

Her first hard questions come on day two, when Senator Morbach asks her why she is sitting here today and not out searching for her daughter.

He tries to paint her as *ambitious*. A climber with no moral code. But Margot doesn't take the bait.

"Senator," she says, "I am in constant contact with the Austin police and the FBI. My husband and I have put together an international network of friends and family, and we are making calls, sorting through emails, walking the streets, doing everything we can to track her down. Sometimes when I am at my lowest in the middle of the night, I call the hospital—"

Her voice breaks here, but she doesn't cry, just pauses to collect herself and continues.

"I call emergency rooms and morgues across Texas, in New York, anywhere I can think of."

She pulls herself up to her full seated height.

"Now, if you can tell me one other thing I can do to find and protect my daughter—other than working tirelessly to better our judicial system in this country so that if, God forbid, some harm comes to the sons and daughters of Americans everywhere, they have a remedy and a resource—well, if you can tell me that, I will stand up right now and walk out of here."

She leaves it out there as a challenge, and in the silence that follows, she wonders if he will call her bluff, but he knows he has lost the room and anyone watching at home. That he has only made her *more* sympathetic, more noble, so he about-faces to a discussion of precedent.

It is on the third day that Senator Albright asks about her path.

"Judge Burr-Nadir," he says. "Can you tell me how you got here?"

"You sent a town car to my hotel," she says to laughter.

"No, I mean your path. How did you personally come to be a nominee for the highest court in the land?"

So she tells him about her father, about debate club and being first in her class at Yale, about the professors that inspired her at Notre Dame, but then Senator Albright interrupts.

"That's good, thank you," he says. "But I wonder if we could talk about a different process that brought you to us today. A secretive process. A process of dark money and fringe ideology that selects and grooms law students or young lawyers who share a conservative world view."

He pauses for effect.

"I heard you had dinner with Jay Bryant last week. Is he part of the team that's been preparing you for these hearings?"

"Senator," says Margot, "Mr. Bryant and I had dinner with Chuck Malcolm the night I got in. I believe he was also at the Rose Garden reception

the president held for my nomination announcement."

"Would you say he's a friend?"

Margot thinks about that. "More of a colleague."

"Has he ever tried a case in front of you?"

"No, sir. Mr. Bryant doesn't practice law."

"But he is a lawyer."

"That's right."

"In truth, he runs an organization called the
Liberty Society. Is that correct?"

"Yes."

"And what is the Liberty Society?"

"It's a think tank."

"Oh, it's a lot more than that."

Margot doesn't answer. She can tell he isn't looking for information. He has a speech to make.

"What the Liberty Society actually does," he
says, "is work to reshape the entire United States
court system, by manipulating the process by
which judges are chosen and confirmed. And it
does so with the help of tens of millions of dollars
in private donations from a host of unnamed
benefactors. Benefactors with an agenda. I'm sure
you've met many of them."

It's not a question, so Margot doesn't volunteer
that yes, she has in fact met many of the Society's
major donors at retreats and private gatherings.
If she wanted to engage in healthy debate, she

would ask what the problem is with American citizens exercising their free speech through the use of their hard-earned money. She would say the Society exists to give conservative attorneys and judges a home inside an elitist system that considers progressive ideas "normal." A place to engage in study and debate without fear of attack by an establishment trying to turn the Constitution into an unrecognizable proclamation of personal politics. *Why shouldn't we have a clubhouse?* she has asked at safe gatherings. *They get the Soho House.*

Bars and Restaurants.

Drinkers and Cooks.

Apples and oranges.

Senator Albright mistakes her silence for concession. "Now, let's be clear. Jay Bryant has never held a public office. Nobody voted for him, but he has spent the last twenty years working to get control over our courts. He spends millions of dollars of donor money to block confirmation of judges he doesn't like and tens of millions pushing judges who subscribe to his beliefs. Would you say that's accurate, Judge Nadir?"

"It's Burr-Nadir," she says. "Burr is my husband's name, and I hyphenate."

"How progressive of you," says Senator Albright.

For the next fifteen minutes, he tries to paint her

as the acolyte of a dark master trying to destroy America. Margot answers his direct questions patiently. She isn't defensive or combative. She knows that for most people the complicated picture the senator paints of a network of influence and power will go over their heads. Turns out, Cooks like conspiracy theories too. So she maintains her composure and reminds the committee that she is an independent juror, indebted to no one. That she makes her decisions based on precedent and a measured consideration of the law. She has no agenda to push. No ideology.

O

The next morning Hadrian comes to breakfast in a long-sleeve shirt and a hoodie. They are eating in the hotel restaurant downstairs. Margot has gone ahead to prepare for the day's testimony. Remy orders pancakes but doesn't eat. When Hadrian reaches for the syrup, his sleeve slides up, and Remy notices two Band-Aids on his right wrist. Something about the sight snaps him out of his trance.

"What's that?" he says.

"Nothing," says Hadrian, pulling his hand back and lowering his arm under the table.

"Did you get cut?"

"No. It's—I burned myself."

"On what?"

"Dad, just don't—"

Remy sits up taller. He tries to focus. "Wait—in your room? You burned yourself in your room?" He reaches for Hadrian's arm, but the twelve-year-old pulls away.

"Dad," his son hisses, meaning, *Don't do this here.*

Remy looks around. People are looking at them. Remy has a moment of clarity, seeing himself through their eyes, a Black man and his son eating in an otherwise white restaurant at an expensive hotel.

Remy calms himself down, calls the waiter over. "Just put it on room three forty," he says.

The waiter asks if he wants the pancakes to go. Remy shakes his head. Across from him, Hadrian has taken out his phone and is staring at it intently. Remy stands.

"We should get to the capitol," he says. "Let's hit the room and head over."

They ride up in the elevator with an elderly white couple. Hadrian stays glued to his phone. When they reach the room, Remy swipes his card, stepping back to let Hadrian enter first, but when the boy steps into the room, Remy grabs his arm and raises it, pulling back his sleeve before Hadrian can stop him.

The Band-Aids peel back. Underneath is a deep scratch, running across his son's left wrist. It has a slightly downward trajectory, as if something sharp has been drawn across it and in toward the body.

"What did you do?" Remy says, suddenly terrified. His son tries to pull away, but Remy won't let him.

"Stop."

"How did you do this? Did you cut yourself?"

"Dad, stop!" Hadrian pulls his arm away, runs for the bathroom. Remy chases after him, grabs the door just as Hadrian swings it shut. They struggle over it, but Remy has the power of primal fear on his side, and he pulls the door out of his son's hands. It bangs against the wall. Remy puts his heel against it.

"Talk," he shouts.

For a moment it looks like Hadrian will hit him, but then his own fear kicks in. He backs away, a child once more. He looks around wildly for a place to hide, jams himself between the toilet and the wall, knees to his chest.

"I'm sorry," he says. "I'm sorry. I'm sorry."

Seeing him there, cowering, cornered, Remy feels the blood leave his body. The adrenaline that was driving him collapses, and he too goes to his knees, scrambling across the bathroom to reach his son.

"Baby," he says, "what did you do?"

Then he sees the bloody tissue in the trash can and the broken drinking glass and he understands.

"I'm sorry," Hadrian says. "It hurt, and I got scared."

"But why? Why would you?"

Hadrian pulls out his phone, his hands trembling, and holds it up. There in his message app, Remy sees the group chat, a dozen of Hadrian's friends, text bubble stacked upon text bubble, and each one says the same thing.

A11

Simon

Sheriff Roy's Holy Detention Center in Reeves County, Texas, was built in a sandy depression between two buttes. To reach the top of the northern butte from the road, you have to pull off at an unmarked gate and drive a winding deer path through a dry wash and low bramble until you can't drive anymore, then abandon your car and head out on foot, which, on a 104-degree August day, means tying a T-shirt around your head and soaking it with water. It takes Simon and the others just under three hours to reach the crest. Flagg, in his leather duster, is sweating like a waterfall. Tiny lizards scramble in his shadow. Tarantulas creep through the dust, slow-motion-hair hands hungry for meat.

Louise, Duane, and Cyclops have stayed behind with the van, hiding in its growing afternoon shade. Overhead, the sun is swollen, angry, bleaching the bones of the living and the dead. When they reach high ground, Flagg lies on his stomach on the stony ridge. Simon, covered in sticker burrs, lies beside him, his face filthy, fingernails caked with dirt. The Prophet sits cross-legged beside them, his clothes clean, his face sweat free. Picking nettles from his ankles, fingertips stinging, Simon begins to wonder if Paul the Prophet really has been sent by God. He is, as they say, beginning to believe. Maybe, like the Prophet said, he can worship God and reason at the same time. Who says it has to be one or the other? Who says God didn't create the universe *and* science, and so disrespecting science is disrespecting God?

Next to him, Flagg peers through a high-powered rifle scope ($129.99) he stole from Walmart.

"Looks like three Quonset huts and a double-wide," he says. "Ten-foot razor wire all around with a single gated checkpoint. I count two deputies in the booth and four county vehicles."

"How many prisoners?" asks Simon, squinting south. Sweat runs into his eyes, and he wipes them with the back of his dirty hand.

"Unclear," says Flagg. "The internet says three fifty, give or take. About half are kids. We know they keep 'em separated."

"He missed the good old days, I guess," says Simon. "Sheriff Roy. Kids in cages."

He wipes the sweat from his face.

"You really think we can do this?" he asks.

"This is not your crack A team," says Flagg. "Your ICE gestapo slipping down fast ropes. These are local boys in pickup trucks playing soldier."

"So you can get us in?" says the Prophet.

"Definitely."

He pulls a kid's walkie-talkie ($29.99 for a set of four) from his pocket, talks into it.

"Cyclops, put together three action packs, full battle rattle, night-vision goggles, the works. We're going in after midnight."

He looks at Katniss.

"Me and one-eye will go in the front. You circle with Simon and the Prophet and cut your way in from the back."

"Roger Wilco," she says.

On the walk back to the van, Simon falls in next to her. Katniss is six foot one. A high school volleyball star who dropped out senior year.

"So you're rich," she says.

Simon's stomach turns. He hates conversations about money. They make him feel exposed, guilty.

"Not me personally, no. There's a credit card I can use with no limit. But mostly things just get paid for."

"Must be nice," says Katniss. The left half of her

head has been shaved down to stubble. Under the fuzz is a tattoo of a yellow rose.

"Nice?" says Simon, as if that word in this context has never occurred to him. "It's—confusing. Being rich is the same as thinking everything's free. No one ever says *We can't afford that*, so how am I supposed to know that boats or houses or watches cost money? Or that money is a thing that exists in finite supply? My father has so much hidden away in offshore accounts, I can't imagine an object or an experience I could want that I couldn't have without a second thought. That makes everything free. So you grow up defective or, like, handicapped. You look around and see everyone else is fighting, struggling, but you don't understand why. How can they be hungry when everything is free?"

"I grew up in tract housing, washing dishes by hand after taco shell Monday," Katniss tells him. "I found an old bike in a barn once, rode it home, singing *free bike!* Then the kick stand cut my foot, gave me tetanus. So, listen, nothing in this world is ever really free."

They reach the flats by six. Simon feels dizzy from heat that seems to be mummifying him alive. Back at the campsite, Louise is lying on a flat rock by the van, sunning herself, topless.

"You ever eat astronaut ice cream?" she asks

from behind oversize sunglasses. "Those foil packets full of dehydrated dairy? That's what I feel like
right now."

She's so thin he can count her ribs. There's a
mole under her left nipple. From a distance, it
looks like another nipple.

"I don't know about you," she says, "but feeling
like I could die of thirst out here puts all my old
life shit into perspective."

"So this is you achieving nirvana," he says,
squatting under a low cypress tree.

"No. This is me cooking out the toxins. Goodbye, clonazepam. So long, paroxetine."

She lays her arm over her eyes. Simon sits on a
rock. He doesn't know where to put his eyes, given
her nudity. He drinks from his metal water bottle,
water so hot it burns his tongue.

"Hot," he says, spilling down the front of his shirt.

"First time drinking?" she asks.

"Shut up."

He walks over to the van, grabs a plastic water
bottle from the cooler, holds it to his forehead. He
drinks it all at once, the cold a painful cut in his
throat. Louise is right. There is a clarity in him today that feels exaggerated. Four days without pills
after how many years? Five, six? Medication for
anxiety and depression, for ennui, social paralysis,
fear of failure. These days when he thinks about

happiness and contentment, he thinks in terms of milligrams.

Long shadows spill across the calèche, the sun balanced on the lip of the western hills. It will be dark in two hours, the temperature dropping quickly. Not for the first time, Simon wonders if there will be gunfire, if he will be killed. He has gone from liberated to fugitive in less than forty-eight hours. Flagg is kneeling by the action bags, reviewing their gear. Simon watches him pull the clips from an assault rifle, check the action.

Cyclops comes over with a family-size bag of beef jerky.

"Dinner," he says, throwing two ropes of meat to Simon, who catches them reflexively, then says— "I'm a vegetarian." But Cyclops is already gone.

Simon sits on the lip of the open van door, famished suddenly. He sinks his teeth into the jerky. It's spicy, sweet, and tough. He chews, feeling himself crossing another boundary in his migration away from the person he used to be.

"Is that teriyaki flavor?" asks Duane, who's been reclining in the passenger seat, unseen. Simon startles, looks over.

"It's—" he says. "I don't know."

Duane slides out of the seat, takes the jerky from Simon's hand.

He takes a bite.

"Teriyaki," he says, "I like the hickory smoke better."

He hands the uneaten strand back to Simon, who takes it, flushing.

"I haven't—this is my first meat in—I'm a vegetarian."

Duane smiles. "Not anymore."

He stretches his arms out, rolls his neck. Up close Duane smells of sandalwood and Cheetos. His armpit hair is wispy and black.

"You don't dig what we're doing here?" he asks.

"Attacking a federal prison?"

"No. Breaking the cycle."

Simon stares at him.

"Of abuse," says Duane. "Dig it. You heard my haiku. Daddy used to beat me, but also my uncle JimJam taught me to play with his penis when I was six—which, if you think about it, one in every six boys will be molested before eighteen, one in four girls. And it's a cycle, right? Uncle JimJam learned that shit somewhere. But hold on—what about grabby Catholic priests and predatory teachers and varsity date rape? Now the numbers go up and up. One in three rape victims is raped before they're seventeen. High school predators, college roofie artists, faceless men in prowl cars. We're talking about millions of kids. And we know that shit messes you up. So here—look at life with those lenses. Is it so crazy to wonder if all the grown-ups who are acting so nuts now were diddled by *their* uncle JimJam or Father Youknowwho, or Sad Mommy used to beat them, or the quarterback roofied them at the University of Wherever—rich, poor, doesn't matter. It's trauma, right? A nation of victims and victimizers. And what do we know about victims? If we don't deal with our trauma, it deals with us. You carry it like a suitcase forever and ever. And. *And*—it makes an easy mark for other predators. Victims. We become victims for life. So here come the vultures. They seduce us and use us and we don't get mad. No. We blame ourselves until we're so fucked in the head we can't think straight. Dig it. You really think clear-minded, non-traumatized people elected the God King? You think healthy, well-rounded, non-traumatized people made up QAnon or Pizzagate? *Pedophile this and Democratic sex dungeon that.* These people have been fucked over so much they're trapped in a mindset."

"A mindset."

"When you've been used as a nail enough, everywhere you look you see hammers. So fuck authority. Fuck experts. They're all just closet vultures, waiting for us to let down our guard so they can penetrate."

Duane fiddles with a loose bolt in the open door-frame. Simon tries to track what he's saying.

"Your theory is that old people are all victims, and they've ruined the world because they've got, what, PTSD?"

"Not all, but enough, right? Think about it. What's the common denominator? They distrust authority. Divorce, remember? They think people in power are *abusing* their power. Where does that come from? *Experience.*"

He nods knowingly.

"Or maybe," Simon says, "we just go through periods of progress followed by backlash. Maybe what we think is crazy is just normal growing pains. The violent struggle to open closed minds. Think about the Summer of Love followed by Richard Nixon."

"Who?"

Simon takes a bite of jerky. In ten minutes, Randall Flagg will come over to teach Simon how to fire a shotgun. He'll tell him that with a weapon this size, accuracy isn't the point so much as intimidation. He'll force Simon to take it, saying, *I know, I know, you'll hang back by the fence until the shooting starts, but just in case.*

Simon will take the shotgun reluctantly, feeling both excitement and disgust.

"Be firm with it," Flagg will say. "It's not gonna

bite. And don't wet yourself. You'll be firing these Taser rounds, not live ammunition."

He holds up a glass cylinder. Inside is some kind of device.

"When you pull the trigger," Flagg says, "the small charge in the XREP shell activates, propelling the projectile down the barrel of the shotgun. A rip cord connecting the projectile to the shell tightens and snaps. This activates the battery, arming the electric shell."

He will load one into the barrel and ratchet it into the chamber.

"When the projectile hits the target, four electrodes pierce the clothing and skin of the subject. Six Cholla electrodes unfold. Cholla because of the cactus, with barbed spines."

For emphasis, he will take aim at a nearby cactus.

"When shot, most people reach instinctively for the impact site. That's not such a great idea with the XREP. See, when you touch it, the microprocessor in the XREP diverts electricity to your hand, creating a circuit, and—ZAP."

When he says it, he will pull the trigger. The projectile will hit the cactus and stick fast, releasing an arc of blue light.

"So it won't kill anyone?" Simon will ask.

"Just a whole lotta pain."

Simon will take the shotgun. Flagg will show him

how to hold it, with the stock nestled in the meat of his shoulder between collarbone and socket joint. He'll hand Simon a Taser cartridge. It is a feat of modern engineering.

"And they sell these at Walmart?" Simon will ask.

And Flagg will chuckle and adjust Simon's grip on the stock.

"I was like you once," Flagg will tell him. "A child of liberal values, touting the holy scripture. Guns are taboo. But it's a tool. That's all. A tool for a specific task. *A gun task.* Think about it. Recognize your belief system for what it is—*their* bag. Your parents. The media. Now, look around. Do you see any of those people? No. We gotta make up our own minds."

Squinting in the sun, Simon will turn the shotgun in his hands. Flagg will show him how to check the chamber, how to eject a shell.

"You load it here—four shells. Ratchet and aim. When you fire, the gun's gonna kick, and the barrel's gonna wanna come up, but you need to hold it down."

With the sun setting, Simon will practice loading and unloading it. Flagg will watch him, smoking.

"In the libraries of liberal democracy," he'll say, "guns are like unicorns—mythical creatures from a far-off land. But out here they're like rats. Fucking everywhere. They're truck mutts panting in the shiny beds of pickups, or three long guns mounted on the wall in the TV room. If you're classy, the gun case is in the den, all polished wood and glass. Except out here they're not called guns. They're *Just Guns*. Weed whacker, lawn mower, twelve-gauge shotgun, just guns. Check Grandma's purse next to the candies. Look under the Christmas tree when Junior turns twelve. Just guns. A nine-millimeter by the bed for personal defense. Soft cases and hard. Out here gunsmiths cast their own bullets. Melt the lead, set the primer, file the tip. Store-bought can cost you fifty cents a round, and that's real money."

Beside him now in the van, Duane reaches over and touches Simon's cheek. Simon pulls back before he realizes.

"You've got an eyelash," Duane tells him, holding it up for Simon to see. On the other side of the van, the sun has gone behind the hills, and the dull brown scrubland has turned a dusky red. Simon looks at his eyelash resting on the pad of Duane's index finger. A part of him lost, like another day of his life.

"Make a wish," says Duane, holding the lash up to Simon's lips.

So he does.

O

At 12:01 they synchronize the watches they stole from Walmart ($59.99). Cyclops and Flagg set off on foot for the front gate. Katniss takes Simon and the Prophet and flanks to the south. Duane and Louise finish loading up the supplies and take their van back to the main road. They'll head for the detention center, headlamps dark, steering by the light of the moon. When the battle is over and the prison has been liberated, Cyclops will signal them in.

Simon looks at his feet as he walks. He is a city boy, ill prepared for uneven ground. He thinks about copperheads and rattlesnakes. There is a Remington 870 Express Super Mag Synthetic Pump-Action shotgun strapped over his shoulder. It weighs seven and a half pounds, with a black stock and matte-black metalwork. It's loaded with thousands of volts of Taser shells that boast *true knockdown power*, as Flagg described them. Carrying this, Simon feels both more anxious and less anxious at the same time. He knows how to swing it down from his shoulder, to flick off the safety and chamber a shell. It is a practical, tangible task, a visceral, physical response to fear—when you feel threatened, you shoot—not a placebo or a time-release capsule offering mild sedation. It's a poker raise, a defiant *fuck you* to fear itself. The gun as a solution to fear. But also its delivery device.

The sound alone, Katniss tells him, *will make most men piss.*

The Prophet wanders behind them, looking up at the stars. Who knew there were so many? Whole galaxies of milky-white dots, millions of them, scattered across the velvety black. The Prophet's lips move as he walks, but no sound comes forth. Is he praying? They walk in silence for an hour with Katniss in the lead, moving through a narrow arroyo. Coming over a rise, Simon sees the floodlights of the detention center. There are no Hollywood spotlights crisscrossing the landscape, no guard towers, just a rectangle of chain link, bare-bones, industrial. The desert itself serves as a deterrent to escape, of course. The heat. Not to mention, who on earth would be crazy enough to break *into* prison?

Katniss gets them within a hundred feet of the back fence, just outside the range of ambient light. They settle down in a stony ditch to wait. None of them speak. Katniss has warned them that at night in the desert sound travels clear and far. Around them the temperature has dropped below sixty. Simon and the Prophet sit shoulder to shoulder. Simon can feel the taller boy's body heat through their clothes. Earlier, when they stopped for gas, Simon got a glimpse of the front page of *USA Today.*

SUICIDE CRISIS ENTERS SECOND MONTH. 160,000 DEAD.

When Duane went to the counter to pay, Simon picked up the paper. Louise was over in the gum and candy aisle, picking her poisons. There was a color photograph of a funeral on page one. SECRETARY OF STATE BURIES HIS DAUGHTER. Simon looked at the photo. He'd met the secretary of state once, at a dinner party in the Hamptons. *Amy.* That was the daughter's name. She was there too—at the dinner party last year—a pretty blonde in a blue dress fixated on her cell phone. What was she, a year older than Simon?

When he thinks of her now, he sees her face lit blue by the cold light of her phone, as if she were already dead.

For some reason, his mind shifts to a book he used to keep on a shelf in his room. An alphabet book in black-and-white, each page depicting the death of a child.

A is for Adam who drowned in the lake.

B is for Betsy who startled a snake.

He thought of it then, standing at the Gas 'N Go, as he read about a field trip of tenth graders in Tokyo who all jumped off a bridge together. Outside, in the Texas heat, the pumps poured regular, premium, and supreme. The slushy machine churned red and blue ice to be consumed from plastic cups made in China.

Now, sitting in the desert chill next to a holy child from Nebraska and the winner of a fictional Hunger Game, Simon thinks about Amy, the senator's daughter, the cell phone addict. Number 160,001. He'd brought her a piece of cake when the singing was done. Red velvet.

"No, thank you," she said. "I'm watching my weight."

"What are we doing?" Simon whispers.

Katniss hits him on the leg. *Shut up.*

In the distance, Simon sees two figures crouch and run from a stand of low trees.

Flagg.

The figures reach the side fence and, staying low, move their way to the front—weapons up.

Katniss comes up on one knee, flicks the safety off on her Smith & Wesson M&P Sport II AR-15.

The sound of gunshots ricochets off the rocky hills. One crack, then two more.

Simon feels light-headed, his blood pressure up around one twenty. On the other side of the fence, they see two armed county deputies run from the back of a Quonset hut. Simon and Katniss duck low, but the deputies don't even look their way. They run around the side of the corrugated metal building, out of sight.

S is for Simon who panicked to death.

Then Katniss is up and running toward the back fence. Simon feels a sudden wind on his face and realizes that he too is running. Behind him the Prophet moves without effort.

Katniss reaches the razor wire, slides to a stop on her knees.

"Bolt cutters," she says.

Simon runs to her, hands over the heavy tool ($39.95 for a limited time only). Katniss starts clipping.

More gunshots come from the front gate. Three similar shots, then a series of answering shots of a different caliber.

Up front the firefight escalates.

"So much for surprise," says Katniss.

Simon's breathing is loud in his ears. Behind him, the Prophet is definitely praying.

Katniss finishes cutting, kicks the wire loose. And then she is through the fence, weapon up.

"Stay close," she hisses.

And they do.

Overhead scoop lights illuminate circles of earth between the buildings. The doors are all heavy steel. As they round a corner, they see a four-wheel-drive vehicle, headlights on. Two deputies crouch by the tailgate, their backs to Simon, facing the main entrance. Katniss slows, aims.

S is for Simon struck down by regret.

"Don't," says Simon, shoving her arm, instinctually foiling what can only be called murder.

Her rifle goes off, blowing apart the light over their head. Glass and metal rain down.

"Shit," says Katniss, wrestling the gun down, as the deputies turn, their own guns coming up. Then the Prophet is in front of Simon, his arms up.

"Tranquilo," he says. "Tranquilo."

The deputies open fire. They are maybe fifteen feet away. Simon crouches instinctually, Katniss diving to the ground. But the Prophet formerly known as Paul stands without flinching, his hands raised in the universal sign for peace.

Bullets whiz past them, kicking up dirt, ricocheting off the metal structures, and then Katniss is up, squeezing off six responding rounds in contained bursts, and the deputies go down.

The *USA Today* article said that all twenty-five Tokyo schoolchildren climbed onto the rail of the bridge together. There was a cell phone photo of them up there, holding hands, as what must have been their teacher ran to intervene, arms outstretched, his mouth open. Then together they stepped off into the void, plummeting without sound to the raging Sumida River below.

Children no more.

Simon pictures their teacher standing at the rail, shouting, weeping, looking for survivors.

The deputies are down. Gun smoke fills the air. Simon straightens. The Prophet lowers his arms. There isn't a scratch on him. Somehow, at impossibly short range, he has been spared.

"The Lord is my shepherd," he says.

Katniss crouch-runs over, checks the bodies. They are folded together awkwardly, collapsed in the dirt. Behind them, the SUV is full of holes.

S is for Simon somehow still alive.

"Get their keys," Simon hears himself say.

Katniss, beginning to stand, stops and grabs a key ring from the nearest deputy's belt. "Stay behind me," she says, moving toward the nearest Quonset hut door.

Simon grabs the Prophet's hand. Time has stopped making sense. The edges of his vision threaten to close in. People are dead. Riddled with bullets. There is a feeling in his belly that can only be described as *exhilaration*. It feels like he has gone crazy.

"It's okay," the Prophet tells him. "It's all part of God's plan."

Katniss reaches the Quonset hut door. She tosses the key to Simon, motions for him to open it and step back. Dull-witted, in shock, Simon misses the key ring and has to scramble in the dirt to get it. He comes up fumbling, adrenaline shaking his hands. After what feels like an eternity, he finds the right key and slips it into the lock. Only as he turns the key and yanks on the handle does he think about what may wait for them on the other side.

S is for Simon who angered the hive.

The first shot catches Katniss in the arm, spins her sideways.

"Ogres," says the Prophet.

Another shot from inside, the muzzle flash lighting up the night. Still holding the door, Simon sees a hulking figure inside the doorway, weapon high, belly distended, mouth distorted in anger and fear. Overhead, a bloodred emergency bulb colors him in hellish light.

Ogre.

The second bullet whizzes past Simon's ear. He is too stunned to duck. Behind the agent, a hundred cowering children scream through a chain-link fence, their faces painted red.

Ogre.

And then Simon feels himself freeing the shotgun from his shoulder—*am I doing that?*—feels it move into his hands—*stop! don't*—the barrel rising, his right hand clicking off the safety.

Simon—could it be he is an instrument of the Lord?—pulls the trigger.

Boom, says the shotgun. The kick of it is so strong the shotgun rips out of his hands and flies backward out the door, as—in what feels like slow motion—the ogre tilts backward and tumbles into darkness, blown out of his shoes, quivering with electric shock. Blue sparks paint the wall as the ogre convulses, making a series of glottal grunts and shrieks.

In the stillness that follows, the stench of cordite hangs over them. Children whimper and scream.

"It's okay," the Prophet tells them, stepping inside. "Está bien. Somos amigos. Amigos."

Simon turns and throws up in the dirt. Behind him, Katniss has torn off one of her shirtsleeves and tied it around her left arm to stop the bleeding. She pushes Simon inside, her fingers dripping blood. The Prophet goes to the cage door.

"Nosotros tambien somos niños," he says. *We're children too.*

"Juice boxes," he says. "Doritos."

Simon finds a bench, sits down, trying not to look at the deputy he shot. Not an ogre at all in the literal sense, but a man with a family. He can smell the electricity in the air, the smell of burnt flesh.

S is for Simon whose poor heart just stopped.

Katniss flips the guard over, zip-ties his wrists.

"Javier," says the Prophet. "Estoy buscando a Javier."

The children clamor and mill. A hurried meeting is held in the cage. The eldest children take charge.

"Nosotros queremos salir," says one. *We want out.*

"Yes," says the Prophet. "We're here to save you. Simon."

But Simon has gone deep down into himself.

S is for Simon whose body has dropped.

The Prophet calls to Katniss to get the keys and open the cage. She rifles Simon's pocket, swings wide the gate, and then the children are pouring out, surrounding them, pulling at their clothes, clapping them on the back.

We're children too.

A small heavyset boy with a bowl haircut takes Simon's hand. He has the kindest eyes Simon has ever seen.

"Yo soy Javier," he says. "Juice box. Juice box."

O

He was born in a limbo camp on the other side of the border, the youngest of four. His parents had been there for sixteen months already, waiting for an interview. Blue tents and shipping containers, makeshift scoop lights dangling, the ground carpeted in empty plastic water bottles. If you climbed the camp's one tree, you could see America across the Rio Grande. Every day you lined up for water, for food. Every day you lined up to talk to the lady with the clipboard. *How much longer?* Each

child in Javier's family had one outfit they kept in
a ziplock bag. These were their interview clothes,
ready at a moment's notice, in case the lady with
the clipboard said today was the day.

Spring came and went. Javier's sister sickened
and died when dysentery swept through the camp.
Summer became fall. Javier started eating solid
food. His first tooth came in. Finally the lady with
the clipboard called their name. Today would be
their interview for admittance to the United States
of America. The children clamored as Mama
and Poppy opened their ziplock bags, *ooh*ing at
the bright colors of Mama's dress, the sheen of
Poppy's suit. They stayed with their tía Maria as
their parents hurried to the fence line and disappeared. Hot hours passed. The children waited
as the sun crested and started to go down, the
olders running wild.

When Mama and Poppy came back, they were
smiling. Mama and Tía Maria cried and held each
other. The judge had heard their case. Tomorrow
they were going to America.

They settled in El Paso. Javier's father got a job
as an auto mechanic. His mother found work in
an industrial laundry, cleaning hotel uniforms and
gowns from the hospital. Javier's brothers went to
public school, riding the city bus back and forth.
They were happy. Then something went wrong

with their paperwork. A notice got lost in the mail, and they missed a deadline to file for permanent status. His father put on his ziplock suit and went downtown to see a judge, who remanded him to custody and began deportation proceedings. That night, Javier's mother packed the children and took them to their tío Christopher's house. She worried that ICE was looking for them. She quit her job at the laundry and found cash work as a maid in a motel, moving them into a one-bedroom apartment behind a grocery store. Javier turned four. He had a musical laugh and a brain for numbers.

Just before Christmas his father was deported. Sheriff Roy had been elected the month prior, and suddenly you had to be careful walking down the street. Sheriff's deputies would raid the supermarket at random hours, trying to catch mothers shopping for groceries and fathers buying Huggies on their way home from work. After the elementary school on the east side got raided, Javier's mother took the kids out of school. From then on, Javier spent his days at the neighbor's watching *SpongeBob*.

When he turned seven, the neighbor was snatched up at a nail salon. A week later Javier's mother got a new job, working on the estate of a very rich man. She put Javier in the car and drove the ninety minutes to Marfa every morning before dawn. On

the way, she helped him practice his English, singing to songs on the radio. For eight hours, if the
master wasn't in, he would roam the grounds, looking for lizards and climbing the stone walls. His
mother brought him water and beans and tortillas
for lunch. If the master was there, Javier would lie
in the shade under his mother's car and read. He
made stick people, tying the sticks together with
grass and giving them names. His favorite was
always Paolo, which was his father's name. They
spoke on the phone every few days, his father
washing dishes now in a restaurant in Juárez. He
was still appealing his deportation, but a resolution
didn't look good. When Paolo last spoke to a lady
on the phone, she offered a hearing date five years
in the future.

One day the master arrives while Javier is out
by the pool. He is a tall white man with silver hair
and two young women that look like his daughters.
Javier waves. He is a people person, that boy,
always talking. The master frowns and says something to a man in a suit with a pistol on his hip. That
night Javier's mother is fired. A friend gets her a
job at Walmart, working from 10:00 p.m. until 6:00
a.m., but three nights later sheriff's deputies raid
the store and take his mother to jail. At 5:00 a.m.
deputies kick down the door to Javier's apartment.
His eldest brother, Ramon, manages to escape out

a bedroom window, but Javier and Lupo are pulled screaming from their beds.

O

The next thing Simon knows they're in the van. Somehow Flagg has found three bread trucks for the other children. They pull out in a cloud of dust, aware that reinforcements may be on their way. At the interstate they split up, the fantasy van heading west, the bread trucks going east, then splitting further. Flagg and Katniss ride ahead of Simon and the others, dirt bike engines throttled to three thousand RPM. Katniss rides one-handed, her injured arm dangling. They will have to see to her shoulder soon, before she bleeds to death, but if she's weak or struggling, she doesn't show it.

Simon sits in the back of the van, his eyes open but not really seeing. Louise holds a cold compress to his face, dabbing his brow. She sings to him in a low voice, as the Prophet sits on the cooler talking to Javier in Spanish. The words flow over Simon, because he is a submarine sinking down, impervious to the drama of the moment.

Later, Flagg will recount their victory in minute detail, how he flanked the surviving agents at the gate, while Cyclops laid down covering fire. After the men surrendered their weapons, Randall hog-tied them. In the main office he pulled the hard drives from the surveillance system while Cyclops threw open the cage doors. Parents were reunited with children. *Most of you will have to set off on foot,* Flagg told them. *Hoof it.* But if they spread out, slept during the day, and traveled at night, they should be able to avoid ICE patrols. There was no guarantee that they would make it, he said, but it was a shot. But if they trusted their children to him, he would make sure they all got out. That they got somewhere safe. Unbeknownst to Simon, calls had been made over the previous twelve hours. Trucks and drivers rallied. Safe houses arranged.

Outside the detention center, mothers hugged their sons. Fathers hugged their daughters. For better or worse, decisions were made. Crying children were put in vans, reaching for Mommy or Daddy. What impossible choices the people of this Earth are forced to make.

For Simon it was a waking dream.

They drive back roads to Marfa, elevation rising. The old Simon is dead. That coddled, innocent lamb obsessed with his own navel. Blood has been spilled. He has pulled the holy trigger, has shocked the foul ogre. There is no turning back. The war is on, and, as the Prophet tells him over Cracker Jacks and cheese, *No one has ever won a war with words.*

One day when humanity is extinct or reduced to feral tribes living in cave-side retreats, they will sing songs of everything we took for granted. Of mystical signals that flew by wind and burrowed under the ground, lighting up the darkness and cooling the air. Of filthy liquids pumped from the earth, heating the indoors and fueling our metal horses. Of humans traveling at unimaginable speeds over unthinkable distances. How we flew through the troposphere and spoke to people in far-off lands, as if by sorcery. Sweet waters could be chilled and turned into solids and eaten from sticks. *Popsicles*, they called them. Oh, the wonders of the Before Time, in which women on tropical continents sewed clothes that were then loaded on boats and shipped across oceans. So many riches. So much power. And all we had to do was decide.

Would we cleave together or cleave apart?

At a stoplight in Alpine, they wait with the engine idling. Outside the window a red tallboy dances in the breeze. GRAND REOPENING reads the sign. The plastic tube man curtsies and bows, throwing his arms in the air with rabid, Pentecostal fervor. Rationally, Simon knows its movement is driven by an electrical fan based at his feet, but viewed through the window of the van from a prone position, all Simon can see is the miracle of dance. A creature of pure movement, joyous, thin skinned, first ducking from sight, then springing into view.

It is 106 in the shade.

At some point, Louise returns to the front seat. She and Duane are inseparable now, it seems. The new Simon watches them idly, a thousand miles from his emotions. The combat adrenaline has worn off, bringing with it a crash of memories— Katniss shooting, the deputies dropping, and even though he himself used Taser rounds, the blast of the shotgun, the sight of the deputy flying back- ward, the act of shooting him, plays on an endless loop in his head. Somewhere nearby Jesus reveals himself to the faithful in a piece of toast. The sun outside is impossibly bright. Simon feels every rattle of the van in his soul. The wind whistles through him. That's the thing about death that no one ever tells you. How alive it makes you feel when it happens to other people.

"Ogres are creatures of dirt and sin," says the Prophet, settling on an Indian blanket next to Simon. "Venal and small-minded. Brutish and leering. They eat children and torture their mothers and fathers."

Simon looks up. The Prophet is backlit by the rising sun. For the first time in over an hour, Simon speaks.

"So I should feel good about tasing him."

The Prophet frowns. "We didn't ask for this world, friend. Prejudice and intolerance. Sixty million refugees. But we will make it our own. And to do so, those who own it now must die. This will happen naturally or with great violence. Either way, men will become old men and then corpses—handing the world over to the children who come after. Us. But if we wait too long, we'll be stamped into adults who walk the same walk and talk the same talk as those who came before. Who hem and haw and say *it's complicated,* even when talking about the simplest things. Think about the Greatest Generation, raised on sacrifice and patriotism. And of their children, the Me Generation, forged in opposition, obsessed with personal freedom. And of their children, Generation X, raised in comfort and prosperity, a generation of man-children, more consumer than citizen. These arc our barriers to self-definition, to liberation. They raised us with their fantasies of right and wrong, and we bought into it hook, line, and sinker. But that's how they turn us into soldiers in their culture war."

"I know, but I—*shot* a guy. Because of you. What you said."

His voice breaks. The Prophet nods solemnly. Classic rock plays on the Bose sound system up front. *"Wish You Were Here."* Where does Simon wish he was right now? Kansas or Oz? Is what he's doing radical or rational? A frog in a hot pot knows he should jump, but who doesn't like a nice warm bath?

"You said it was a war," he tells the Prophet, "*their* war. And we're being trained to join one side or the other. *Reject the war*, you said. But now you're saying *we're* at war, and I wanna—I know you're trying to help me, but—I'm confused."

The Prophet smiles. He is a teacher at heart, with all the patience in the world.

"Let me quote Saint Greta, who said, 'Our house is on fire. I am here to say, our house is on fire.... You say nothing in life is black or white. But that is a lie. A very dangerous lie. Either we prevent 1.5 degrees [Celsius] of warming or we don't. Either we avoid setting off that irreversible chain reaction beyond human control or we don't. Either we choose to go on as a civilization or we don't. That is as black or white as it gets. There are no grey areas when it comes to survival.'"

He takes a bag of sunflower seeds from his pocket, eats one.

"Are they at war? Yes. With each other, over nonsense. That is not our path. We are at war with nonsense itself. With casual cynicism. With excuses. With politics. We will win the war or we will die, but know this—God doesn't want us to die."

"Then why are so many kids killing themselves? I saw the paper. Hundreds of thousands all over the world."

The Prophet frowns. He licks his chapped lips, thinking.

"Think about it. We weren't made for war. Children. It is abhorrent to our nature. We are, all of us, born hopeful, joyful, and kind. And so we are afraid. We don't want to fight—and worse, fight our own parents. We think maybe it's easier to flee than fight. A one one. God understands. It's not the children's fault. Such impossible choices."

"What does it mean? A one one. I remember them washing it off the hospital walls after OCD Betsy drank bleach. And then I saw it in the paper."

The Prophet finds a red marker, writes on the inside wall of the van.

A11

Then he breaks it out, changing the second number one to the word *one* spelled out.

A1one
A11 Alone.

Simon sits as if paralyzed.
There are no poets named Claire.

He pictures the red Os staring back at him.

Fly, you fools.

"They kill themselves," says the Prophet, "because they can't feel God's hand. All they see is the war they must fight. And wars, in their experience, never end. The War on Terror, the War on Drugs, the so-called Culture War. Our endless human wars. And so they write this—A one one—and they surrender to the night. Because they know what happens to children who go to war."

He gestures to Javier, eleven, asleep on a blanket.

"Look at him. Is that a soldier? In 1986 Ayatollah Khomeini took ten thousand children from their homes and schools. They were driven in buses—through cheering crowds—to the border, where the Iraqi army had buried over a million land mines. The ayatollah's plan was simple. Their children would walk through the minefields detonating mines to clear a path for the Iranian army. Praise the Lord. In Africa, ragged militias capture boys as young as six and train them to kill, feeding them brown-brown, a mixture of cocaine and gunpowder. What do these stories tell us? That adults see children as a tool in their wicked schemes. But no more. We fight for ourselves now. Or we die."

Simon watches Javier sleep. They will be in Marfa in less than an hour.

"You said we have to find Samson and hear his story."

"Yes. And before you ask—I don't know who that is or where we have to look. But I know if he is important to completing our quest, the Lord will put him in front of us."

"So what's the plan?" asks Simon.

The Prophet offers him a sunflower seed. Simon takes one, tasting the sharp saltiness on his tongue.

"Javier says he can get us into the Wizard's compound. That there's a sluiceway leading to a back wall. He says there's a grate on the wall that can be cut away. He drew me a map."

"And there are women there now?" asks Simon. "Girls? We know this for sure."

"God has shown me a single face in a window that will not open."

"Does he have a name? This Wizard. Do the police know about him? Can't we just call them?"

The Prophet shakes his head.

"Calls have been made. Investigations undertaken and dismissed. An absurd plea deal five years back. House Arrest, which—for a man with homes on six continents, a man with his own island—this is just another way of saying *freedom*."

Simon's palms are raw where the shotgun ripped from his grip. His right index finger might be sprained.

"So we break in, what, with weapons hot? What if there are guards?"

"There are definitely guards. Javier calls them *Orcs*."

Orcs, ogres, wizards. Simon feels a laugh catch in his throat, a bitter weed, like the joke you make to the hangman just before he pulls the lever.

"The brothers Orci," says the Prophet. "Sworn protectors of the Wizard."

"Stop calling him that. What's his name?"

"E. L. Mobley, sixth richest man in the world."

For a moment Simon feels faint. His father knows Mobley. Of course his father knows him. Mobley has been to their house. This is how small the world is for those with wealth. They are a small town, a northern island, insular, isolated. Who else can understand the problems of the ultra-rich except those who suffer them too—how expensive it is to service your jets and yachts, how hard it is to find trustworthy money managers who will launder your millions through offshore accounts?

"You know him," says the Prophet.

"I've—met him. All of them. Millionaires, billionaires."

"What was he like?"

"He was—"

Simon thinks back. A New Year's party in

Tudor City. Simon was what? Twelve? The guests came in costume. Mobley and his entourage arrived dressed as characters from a movie Simon had never seen. White shirts and pants with jockstrap worn on the outside. Simon can remember the moment he first saw Mobley—a shadow in a darkened doorway, wearing a black bowler, his left eye ringed in mascara. And with him were six young women, all drinking milk.

"—creepy," finishes Simon. "My sister called him a loser."

"Claire."

"To his face."

Simon smiles. He misses her like she was his own heart.

"In Utah," says the Prophet, "there is a forest of quaking aspen that functions as a single organism. Natives call it the Pando or Trembling Giant. Fifty thousand trees sharing a single root system. It's thought to be more than eight thousand years old."

"I don't understand."

"When a tree gets sick, that sickness can spread to everything around it. The body dies. The mind rots. I'm saying when one of us is spoiled, they infect everyone around them. The myth of our species is that we are individuals first, but that's a lie. I'm saying your sister was right. The Wizard is a loser, in that he cannot be allowed to win. His reign of tears must end."

"Kill him, you're saying?"

The Prophet thinks about that. "Do you know what the Pied Piper did with those children he took?"

Simon shakes his head.

"He led them under a mountain and closed it up over them."

Simon looks out the window. The sun is up now, the hills turning to gold. Styx plays on the radio— *come sail away with me.*

A pickup truck passes them, going ninety. There are three clowns seated in the truck bed, one bald, two with long hair flying in the wind. One holds a sniper rifle, barrel pointed toward the sky. Even at that speed they seem to pass in slow motion.

"Duane," says the Prophet.

Duane slows. The pickup truck passes them, then the two dirt bikes. It swerves right, into their lane, as an Amazon delivery truck closes in the oncoming lane.

Flagg's voice comes over the walkie-talkie, swallowed by the wind.

"Get ready," he says. "This could be it."

"It," says Simon. "This could be what?"

On the floor, Javier stirs, sits up.

"¿Qué hora es?"

The brake lights of the pickup truck flash, a solid red. The pickup slows. Simon comes to his knees, his right hand grabbing a seat belt strap. He looks through the windshield in time to see Flagg jog left and pass the pickup, speeding up. Katniss mirrors him on the right. As the pickup slows, Duane is forced to brake hard. Simon lurches forward as Flagg and Katniss race off toward the horizon.

"They left us," he says, as the van skids to a halt. Ahead of them, the pickup has swung left and stopped across the road. Before Simon can process what's happening, the three clowns are out of the truck bed, coming toward the van, weapons up.

"Calm. Everybody be calm," says the Prophet. He tells Javier to lie down on the floor, covers him with a blanket.

"No te muevas," he says.

Gunshots come from behind the van. Simon turns. Cyclops jumps from his bike and advances, firing. The clowns never flinch. With bullets whipping past, they turn as one and fire. Simon throws himself to the floor. Behind the van, Cyclops goes down like a marionette with its strings cut. And then the side door of the van is sliding open, and the bald clown is there, his shotgun up.

"Ladies and gentlemen," he says, "back by popular demand, it's the one and only get outta the fuckin' van."

He waves them out with his weapon. The two long-haired clowns have taken up spots at the front and rear bumpers.

They pull Louise from the van, chuckling with icy greed at their prize—a Black woman, young and sexy, like a gift from the devil.

This is it, thinks Louise. *Death.* She feels it in her body, for her body is what they want to kill. Her body, which contains the history of all bodies like hers, bodies dragged from cars and strung up from trees, bodies dragged by horses, bodies raped and beaten.

Behind her, Simon steps into the sun, squinting. He looks at Cyclops, lying dead in the road. There is blood pooling under his head, this boy with the stupid code name. This stupid, pimply boy who played with guns and has been filled with holes. A teenager who once drew pictures in crayon and climbed trees. Whose parents named him and held him and cried, and is now

All

Alone

The bald clown marches them to the shoulder, lines them up against a tall fence. He separates the "whites from the coloreds," putting a foot in Duane's back to make his point clear. Muscling Louise in next to him, the youngest clown makes sure to get a handful of ass, because isn't that what these Black girls are all about, shaking that ass? Louise knows better than to complain. Best to become invisible, an absence in the punishing sun.

His hands up, Simon thinks of Javier hiding in the van. The land is barren here, a flat mesa four thousand feet above sea level, devoid of trees. A large jut of rocks fifteen feet behind the fence rises like a wave, throwing a shadow on the road.

At his feet Simon sees dried flowers and a framed photo. In it a young Mexican-American woman smiles shyly.

A shrine. They are standing on a shrine.

The clowns wander over, guns low. They are bedraggled, sunburned, an absurd patrol circling the isolated alpine towns of southwest Texas, looking for (((kikes))) and spies. Their white face paint has melted and run down into the collars of their Hawaiian shirts, leaving streaks of pink and smudges of red on their weathered faces. The youngest is probably thirty-five. The bald clown wears red gas station sunglasses. A hunting knife sticks out of his belt. He was in DC the day they stormed the Capitol, standing under a portrait of LBJ laughing while his buddy J.D. took a shit in a stairwell and wiped it on the wall. As on that day, Bald Clown wears a black tactical vest covered in replacement shells for his shotgun, giving him a jaunty, candy-coated feel. He chews

Big Red gum. Simon can smell the cinnamon bite from here.

"Nice van," says Big Red.

Duane nods, unsure what the etiquette is when being placed against a fence by a band of rabid clowns. The tallest one pulls a pack of Kools from his Kevlar vest, shakes out a butt.

The Prophet steps forward. "We're on a mission from God," he says.

The clowns raise their guns, alarmed by the sudden movement and his lack of fear.

"Back in line, four-eyes," says the shorter long-haired clown. He is full lipped, his face acne scarred.

The Prophet makes no move to retreat. "You will let us pass or face His wrath."

Simon reaches for the Prophet's hand, tries to pull him back in line, but the Prophet shakes him off.

"Looks like we won the Lotto," says Cigarette Clown, nodding toward Duane and Louise. "Couple a cockroaches from the city."

Big Red steps forward, makes a show of sniffing Duane. "What are you, half chink?"

Duane sets his jaw. "I'm half Japanese and half Black."

"Which half?" says Acne Clown. "Top or bottom?"

Louise hikes up her jeans, a tiredness settling into her bones, fueled by jagged adrenaline. She's exhausted by the whole tired cliché of it. For her journey to end this way, her death divorced from her life, her specific life—the girl with the cleaning addiction from San Rafael, whose grandmother used to make flapjacks and bacon every Saturday, the girl with scars on her thighs—that girl isn't here now, the one we call Louise Conklin. Instead, there is a stand-in, a proxy for every African, every Jamaican, every Haitian who has ever had the nerve to draw breath in this land. She will die here anonymously on this spot, thinks Louise, and when they brag of her death, all she will be is her color.

"Are you gonna rape us or kill us or what?" she says, because *just get it over with already*.

The clowns exchange a look.

"Well, that depends," says Big Red. "How come yer man came out shootin'?"

"Seriously?" says Louise. "You forced us off the road. And you're armed."

"You seen those zombie shows?" says Cigarette Clown. "That shit's easy. The apocalypse. See a zombie, kill a zombie. But this shit here—van fulla faggots and race traitors—lotta guesswork and lies."

"Or the Matrix," says Acne Clown.

"Right. The fucking Matrix. This shit's a simulation. Civilization. Democracy. We know what's really going on. Sharia law, secret tribunals, the Frazzeldrip. Deep State election thieves with their Black Lives Matter bullshit. But we know what's coming. Trust the plan. The Great Awakening. Long live the God King."

Beside him, Big Red stands quietly chewing gum, smiling.

"The boogaloo's here, baby," finishes Acne Clown.

Big Red pulls his 9mm.

"Are you glowies?"

"Are we what?" says Louise.

"You know, glowies, spies."

"Spies for who?"

"The three-letter boys—DEA, FBI, ATF."

"Nope," says Louise and starts for the van. "So, can we go?"

Acne Clown steps in front of her. "What's yer hurry, slit?"

He presses his handgun to her temple. Simon sees the fear on her face.

"Make her suck the barrel," says Cigarette Clown.

"Stop," says the Prophet in a voice so commanding it quiets the wind. Acne Clown, who was lowering the gun to her mouth, stops, glances at Big Red, unsure. Big Red spits out his gum, walks over, and puts himself face-to-face with the Prophet, formerly known as Paul.

"Make us," he says.

And now there comes a growl so low and menacing it triggers primordial terror in all who hear it. The bestial snarl of a great predator, as something rises above them and blocks out the sun. Simon jumps, turns. There is a lion standing on the lip of the rock behind them, backlit by the sun, crouched as if to pounce.

An African lion, resplendent, impossible.

"Holy shit," says Cigarette Clown, raising his rifle. Big Red backs away. He's staring at the lion with abject fear. You can see him doing math in his head. *The rock is fifteen feet from the fence. There's no way a lion could jump that far.*

Could he?

Duane grabs Louise, pulls her toward him.

The Prophet stands in the shadow of the lion.

"The Lord has spoken," he says. "We are under His protection. Let us go or die here and now."

Big Red spits on the ground. He is embarrassed by his show of fear, emasculated in front of his men. He pulls the long gun from his shoulder, aims it at the lion.

"Clowns," he says, "let's go on safari."

But then—before he can pull the trigger—a bloom of red jumps from his throat, splashing the asphalt. His eyes widen.

Crack.

The sound of the shot reaches them next, echoing across the mesa. Big Red gurgles, reaches for the wound, but falls dead before his hand can find it. For an endless moment the other clowns stare at him stunned.

"Shooter!" yells Acne Clown, looking around wildly. In the distance Simon sees a quick glint. Then a flash. Acne Clown falls.

Crack.

The pickup truck engine starts, revs. Cigarette Clown looks to his two dead friends, his brain trying to catch up. Hearing the truck shift into gear, he turns and lunges after it. The pickup fishtails, tires searching for traction on the heat-softened asphalt as the driver guns it. Dropping his gun, Cigarette Clown manages to grab the tailgate, one foot hooking the bumper. The wheels grab. The truck races off.

Above Simon the lion roars its primal challenge. Simon, Duane, and Louise duck instinctually, hurrying to put the van between them and it, but the Prophet doesn't move. He looks at the dead men at his feet, the shadow of the lion between them. And it is here, Simon can see, that the righteousness of their cause cements itself in the Prophet's mind.

They're going to win.

Book 3

Half Earth

First of all, your author would like to apologize for the world he has created. He knows it is ridiculous. The fact that the world he lives in is also ridiculous is no excuse. The author's job is to make sense of the senseless. To create coherence from incoherence. But if the author's job is also to reflect reality as he perceives it onto the page, then what is he meant to do when the world he lives in loses all sense? Consider this: as he writes, 34 percent of his neighbors have gone to war against tiny pieces of fabric worn across the nose and mouth. They believe these tiny pieces of fabric are robbing them of their personal freedom. And so they have declared war against these pieces of fabric, even as scientists present evidence that those same tiny pieces of fabric will protect them from a deadly virus sweeping the globe, killing millions. But for the 34 percent, the fabric, not the virus, is the enemy. And so they lie dying in hospitals from a disease they argue *does not exist*.

In simpler times this would have been called *irony*, but your author would like to point out, dear reader, that the times in which he lives stopped being simple long ago. In the new times—the Age of Tribal Thinking, the Age of Inverted Reality— irony has been stripped of its humor.

And irony without humor is violence.

Or in other words—for your author—*ridiculous* has ceased to be a term of derision and has simply become a statement of fact.

Boo phooey.

When the author's son steals a cookie and then says he has not stolen a cookie even though there is chocolate covering 60 percent of his face, well, in the old days this would have been called *a lie*. But in the Age of Inverted Reality, the-stolen-cookie-that-was-never-stolen is now known as *an alternative fact*. Proof is irrelevant. Reality has become a personal choice, denial of reality a weapon. If a man gives a speech in the rain and later insists that the sun was shining the whole time, and if he then wages war against those who show him photos of the rain, calling them liars, branding them as evil, he is not lying so much as asserting power over truth itself. He is the bully who has stolen your coat and is wearing it even as you shiver, telling you that if he sees your coat he'll be sure to give you a call.

It would be funny if your death weren't imminent. The lie is violence. You are its victim. Your injuries are psychological, emotional. Your condition is called *anxiety* and is defined as follows:

1. apprehensive uneasiness or nervousness usually over an impending or anticipated ill : a state of being anxious.
2. *medical* : an abnormal and overwhelming sense of apprehension and fear often marked by physical signs (such as tension, sweating, and increased pulse rate), by doubt concerning the reality and nature of the threat, and by self-doubt about one's capacity to cope with it.

Reality itself appears to break down. And with it the mental health of your author and his neighbors.

O

In the old days there was a form of rhetoric called *satire*. The *Encyclopedia Britannica* defined satire as an "artistic form, chiefly literary and dramatic, in which human or individual vices, follies, abuses, or shortcomings are held up to censure by means of ridicule, derision, burlesque, irony, parody, caricature, or other methods, sometimes with an intent to inspire social reform."

There are many great works of satire in modern literature. Your author has enjoyed several over the years. Cutting works of wit and derision that once had the power to shame. But, in the Age of Inverted Reality, shame has transformed itself into pride, ridicule hijacked by the ridiculous and used to mock other human beings for their empathy and caring. To call someone a bully is no longer an insult. What crimes were once perpetrated in shadow are now committed in the open. What can this mean, if not that criminality is no longer a crime?

You see how irony becomes violence?

Because now the joke's on you.

Your author apologizes if these words seem political. He might point out that the words *politics* or *political* themselves have been rendered meaningless in his lifetime. Words that once described a vital project of civic negotiation have become an accusation of artifice. To be accused of *making something political* is code for *you have chosen a side*. Of this, your author is innocent. He has no side. He just wants words to mean what they were intended to mean. His job is to communicate information and ideas, and how is he supposed to do that when language itself has become meaningless?

Your author would also like to explain that he didn't want to put all those guns in his story, but this is a story about America. At last count there were more than four hundred and twenty million guns in America (population 330,000,000). This makes America a Chekhov play, in which a gun shown in Act One must be fired in Act Two. In other words, if you think the next act of American life is going to unfold without gunfire, you're not paying attention.

In summation, your author would like to apologize for the world he has created. He knows it is ridiculous. He is simply doing his best to re-create reality as he has experienced it.

Boo phooey.

Before

A routine traffic stop. February 2017. A black F-150 outside Blountstown, Florida, with a non-op starboard taillight and a cardboard license plate. The dashboard camera shows the driver's silhouette clearly. A tall man flip-mouthing a lit cigarette. The passenger is harder to make out, like Bigfoot's ghostly image in a dusky wood. There's a red stop sign in the distance, like a blinking jewel. A curving hillock, scrub brush green, rises to the horizon.

The wheel man in the police prowler is Deputy Dave Bullock—though you don't see him until he exits the vehicle and approaches the cab, and then only in profile—born twenty-nine years earlier in Clearwater. The other officers call him Bull, but not for the reason you'd think. He's a little guy, actually, neither ferocious nor stubborn. He describes himself as *verbal*—which in plain English means 60 percent of what comes out of his mouth is bullshit. Thus, the nickname. This may also be why he's separated from his wife, though it could also have something to do with her developing an Oxy addiction after a car accident and leaving their son with a neighbor while she went to score dope. So now Bullock and Nathaniel, six, live at Grandma's house, where they like to eat pancakes for dinner and watch nature shows on the DVR.

Deputy Jimenez, in the passenger position, lugged a .50 cal through Fallujah and the surrounding desert extremes for two tours. He still has shrapnel in his left leg from a roadside IED and likes to joke that, left to his own devices, he would walk in an endless circle. Six foot two and weighing in at two hundred and twenty pounds, he's the *mind over matter* type—in the gym every morning at six, pressing his weight, fighting the wear and tear. He waits to shower until he gets home, though, because his left thigh is like a topographical map of mountainous terrain. After a few drinks sometimes, his girlfriend traces the angry pink scar tissue with her fingers and cries.

Both deputies exit their vehicle together. It's a windy day, and Jimenez reaches unconsciously to secure his hat as he moves to the shoulder. Bullock approaches the driver. He is friendly but direct. The ensuing conversation takes nineteen seconds.

Voices are quickly raised. On camera you can see Deputy Bullock step back onto the road and put his right hand on the butt of his pistol. He orders the driver from the truck. The door opens. A burly white man rolls free, a white T-shirt showing hard fat. His name—we know, but the cops will never learn—is Avon DeWitt, and he is a sovereign citizen. Avon has to shoulder the driver's-side door to get it open, metal protesting at the hinge after a recent accident. Deputy Bullock takes a defensive step back as DeWitt straightens to his full height. DeWitt is smiling without joy, his hands spread wide, like a magician showing you there's nothing up his sleeve.

Shots ring out, a muzzle flashing visibly from inside the cab. On the passenger side, Deputy Jimenez's hat flies off, blood spray evident, and he tumbles backward into a gulley. On the driver's side of the truck, Bullock pulls his service weapon—DeWitt ducking reflexively—as the passenger emerges holding a semiautomatic rifle, later identified as an AR-15. He fires across the bed of the F-150, hitting Bullock three times in the head and chest. As the deputy falls, DeWitt, a mustached man in his forties, jumps back into the truck and yells to the passenger to do the same.

"Let's go. Let's fucking go!" he screams. The passenger lowers the rifle and folds back into the truck, the vehicle fishtailing back onto the road, even as the passenger door remains open.

After the truck is gone, the dashboard camera continues to record everything, except now the painting is a landscape—*Portrait of a Cloudy Florida Day in February*, or *Still Life with Corpses*. The only evidence of the massacre that has just occurred is a single boot visible in the road on the left-hand side of the screen.

And so the viewer is left to ponder how one fact about the shooter stands out over all the others.

He appeared to be a child.

Now

It started with cigarettes, or how to sell people a product that men in Virginia seersucker knew would kill them.

Lucky Strikes. Virginia Slims.

A promise of magic in every puff.

To sell people cancer and lung disease, you have to do more than bury the truth. You have to undermine the idea of truth itself. What is smoking really? Who says it's bad for you? Some Harvard elites who don't understand your suffering? Who would keep from you this sweet relief?

To undermine facts, you can't just question the science. You have to question the expertise of science itself. To create confusion and uncertainty. To reject the notion of consensus.

Or maybe it started with Freud and the discovery of the unconscious. The idea that people are driven by urges and emotions they don't even realize they

have. Sexual impulses, violent desires. Desires
that have been forced out of the conscious mind,
repressed to the unconscious level. Taboo thoughts
and feelings we know we're not supposed to voice.
Secret drives pushing for satisfaction. To marry
our mothers and kill our fathers. Base impulses
that lurk in our dreams. The human mind, Freud
understood, is a denial engine—wanting things it
cannot admit to, all the while pretending that it
does not.

Or maybe it started with Freud's nephew, an
American named Ed Bernays who figured out that
Freud's theory of the unconscious could be used
to sell people products. The key was to appeal
to those unconscious impulses all humans felt
but hid, their latent fears and desires. Manipulate
consumers' unconscious minds, and their rational
minds will follow. He developed an approach he
called *the engineering of consent*, which gave leaders the means to *control and regiment the masses
according to our will without their knowing about
it*. And so was born the devious art of advertising
and a new style of politics.

In the 1920s, Joseph Goebbels, the Nazi minister
of propaganda, sought out Mr. Bernays, hoping for
guidance in building a führer cult around Adolf
Hitler. He envisioned a language of symbols, a
system of manipulation the Nazi party could use to

push the German people toward bigotry and war. At the heart of his challenge was a question: *How do you make people behave in ways they know are immoral?*

The answer he got was this: You undermine the idea of morality itself. You redefine it. What was wrong once becomes right. Imperatively so. Murder becomes self-defense. A moral act, necessary. The Jew isn't human and can therefore be eliminated without guilt or shame. Those who seek to defend the old morality are relabeled as *fiends* and *liars*. They are painted as evil, because once your enemy is evil, then the moral thing to do is destroy them.

The way you sell people cigarettes, it turns out, is the same way you sell them genocide. By undermining the idea of certainty, by rejecting objective reality and traditional morality. By demonizing "experts" who would dare to tell you what is right and what is wrong. *Don't you get it?* they tell us. There is no right. There is only what's right *for you*, and that is for you alone to decide.

Or maybe—yes, of course—it starts with death itself. Or, more precisely, with the denial of death. That human ability to deny death, to live as if the end isn't coming for us all. Our mortality is a locked room we never visit, feeling a shudder and a chill every time we pass by the door—boarded up, walled over—and yet there it remains, waiting, like the devil to whom you sold your soul. We hold our breath when we see it. Our parents die, our friends and colleagues. We attend their funerals, see them lowered into the ground, never once accepting that we will be next.

In the beginning there was denial. And then, thanks to Sigmund Freud and big tobacco and all-politics-is-personal, came *denialism*. The organized rejection of reality in favor of fantasy. That all-consuming industry of denying science, denying experts, denying truth itself. *The world is flat. The holocaust never happened. 911 was an inside job. Vaccines cause autism. COVID-19 is a hoax. The election was stolen*. We don't want to die, so we pretend we won't. And when you get right down to it, if we can deny our own deaths, we can deny anything.

O

Felix Moor, born Samson DeWitt, knows denial intimately. He grew up with a father who rejected the American government's legitimacy. A sovereign citizen, who believed the Fourteenth Amendment had enslaved a formerly free people. A father who manufactured his own license plates, who renounced currency, who filed a Declaration of Non-Consent with the US government, declaring himself exempt from all federal laws and regulations. Who taught his son to shoot using targets labeled ATF and FBI.

Can we really be surprised then that the boy shot two cops before he was fifteen? Heart in his throat, pulse jacked and racing as he clicked off the safety on the AR-15. He heard his dad's voice in his head as he raised the barrel. *They'll be wearing Kevlar, so aim for the head.*

Pop, pop, pop.

And then out of the truck, moving fast.

Pop, pop, pop.

Self-defense. That's what Avon called it. The Feds are coming for all of us, he said. First they take our guns. Next our souls.

You did good, kid. You did all right.

In the truck that day, Avon told Samson, now Felix, that the wisdom he'd given him was a gift, the last in a series of gifts, starting at birth with invisibility. Samson, now Felix, was the boy with no birth certificate, no social security number. As far as the US government was concerned, he was the boy that didn't exist. And yet think that through fifteen, twenty years. What happens when the boy wants to go to school or get a job? What happens if he wants to travel outside the country and needs a passport?

As Samson, now Felix, has discovered, it's easier for an immigrant from a foreign land to prove their identity than it is for a boy born off the grid in central Florida. You are stateless in your own home. Luckily, identities can be faked. A new name chosen, a social security number stolen, someone else's birth certificate unearthed. Which begs the question, when a child who technically doesn't exist disappears, who misses him?

He was the boy raised with a mindset that the black helicopters were coming, that needles were how the one world government implants the microchip. The boy who thought it was normal to run bug-out drills in the middle of the night, who learned to set booby traps and trip wires, who knew to aim for the head.

As far as Avon DeWitt was concerned, God was an American and he was pissed. Pissed that the global elite had undermined his American freedoms, pissed that good-hearted, hardworking, honest citizens had been enslaved, brainwashed, lied to. Avon resolved that he would become a weapon of retribution, and his son would be a soldier of righteousness. So, they drilled. They trained.

A year later the boy chose a new name. He painted his invisible face with face-colored paint. He gave his voice a voice. Samson DeWitt died that day. Felix Moor was born. Or born again, his sins washed clean, his complicity removed. He was a tiger that escaped the zoo. A Manchurian candidate who flew the coop. He moved to Austin, using a dead kid's birth certificate and high school transcripts to get into a state college, met a nice girl. A beauty from New York City.

In this way he became real.

The nightmares still come. The smell of cordite and the sound of the F-150 peeling out, and his daddy's voice—*hot damn, hot damn*. But when he wakes, Felix tells himself those are someone else's dreams. A stranger's. He is a new man now, guiltless and free.

If we can deny our own death, we can deny anything.

Today is his twenty-fifth birthday.

Felix has come to Marfa, Texas, to save his sister from a Wizard.

They are parked outside the Hotel Paisano, he and Story. She of the summertime smile and the Yankee jeer. Story Burr-Nadir, the judge's daughter, who once sang in a clear high voice—*Oh, say can you see.*

A county ambulance loiters on the corner beside them, rear doors ajar. As they watch, paramedics wheel a body on a gurney from the hotel entrance. The body is covered with a sheet. *Hanging*, the girl at the café told them when they got their coffee this morning. *The third one this week.* They nodded and asked for whole milk and sugar. Around the world the global death toll was ramping up. Wanton acts of self-destruction.

Pedestrian and inventive.

Self-immolation.

Suicide by cop.

It started with cigarettes. Where it will end, no one knows.

Beside Felix, Story rattles the ice in her cup. For her coffee is an excuse for chilled vanilla flavoring. She's thinking about her mother again, Felix can tell. Story gets this look in her eye, a slight squint with the left lid, pupils cast down. Remembering. Worrying. Guilt. He's talked her out of calling at least a dozen times in the last three weeks. *It's too risky*, he tells her. *A federal judge, given the connection of money and politics. They don't call him the Wizard 'cause he wears a funny hat. He's got power. The power to make his problems dis-appear. To make* people *disappear.*

"You sound like your father," she tells him. And by father she means the fictional father he has in-vented for her, dead now five years. The Fox News junkie and golf-casual supporter of the God King. Not a white supremacist exactly, but no friend to the Black man. This version of Felix's father falls within acceptable parameters. A gun owner, yes, but not a man who fires explosive rounds at paper targets printed with the image of federal agents. The reality of Felix's youth is too radical, too foreign, like a report from some distant killing field. And so, Felix has kept the truth from her. The truth of his identity. The truth of his lineage. The truth of his crimes.

"You can't call her," he says, reading her mood.

"I'm not—"

She glances over.

"—get out of my head."

He made the mistake of switching on the radio on their drive over from the campsite this morning. *The Supreme Court nomination for Judge Margot Nadir is entering its second week*, the reporter told them. Felix lunged for the dial, but Story slapped his hand. *Supreme Court?* she said, stunned. That's how deep a hole they've been in. No TV, no internet, no news for three weeks. And then the radio talked about the judge's missing daughter, Story. It spoke of their home in Austin, abandoned mid-meal, of the bags packed but left behind. Was Story Burr-Nadir dead? Was foul play suspected?

Felix turned off the radio. He could tell that Story was feeling panicky. For her mother. For herself. She's not used to roughing it. To shitting in the trees. For his part, Felix knows how to stay off the

grid. You pay with cash, avoid places with cameras. No motels. No phone calls. He knows how to
distill fresh drinking water from saltwater, to fashion a tourniquet and compress a bullet wound.

"Do you love me?" he says.

She looks at him, focusing. Behind her the paramedics load another suicide into their rig.

"You know I do."

Felix takes her hand. "Well, I have to do this.
Save her. But you can go. I'll understand. Just
don't tell anyone where I am. Okay?"

Story closes her eyes. They're trying to be
adults here, to make responsible choices, but this
whole thing feels so crazy. Ever since his sister,
Bathsheba, called him that night in Austin and told
Felix she'd been kidnapped and was trapped in the
desert. Ever since Bathsheba told him that they
monitored what she ate, kept her locked in a tower.
Ever since she said she'd been impregnated—
that's the word she used, *impregnated*—and then
told Felix the name—E. L. Mobley, a politically
connected billionaire—and said he couldn't call
the cops. Well, ever since then she's felt like Alice
down the rabbit hole.

"Let me at least tell my mother," Story said
that night. "She's a federal judge. She can call the
attorney general."

But Felix was adamant. No calls. No emails. He

asked Story if she knew how much Mobley had donated to get the current president elected, how connected he was in political circles.

"All you'll do is warn him," Felix told her, "and he'll pack her up and fly out of the country before we can get there."

The whole thing made Story's head spin. They'd abandoned the meal half-eaten—plates on the table, their chairs pulled out. She ran around, trying to get them packed, but in the end they'd left it all behind. It was an eight-hour drive, and Felix was desperate to get started. All they took were some toiletries, a few pairs of underwear.

Travel light. That's what his father taught him. Confuse your trail. And always pack heat. Which is why, after he got Story in the car, he went into the garage and slipped a .32-caliber Ruger from its hiding place behind the furnace. It was tucked into a black Velcro sleeve, which he pocketed, along with a box of bullets.

He came out at a half run, carrying their water bottles.

"Don't worry," Story told him, seeing his face. "We'll find her."

They drove through the night, stopping for gas in Junction. While Story was in the bathroom, Felix swapped license plates with a dented green Ford parked by the air pumps. They were from Georgia now, state motto: *Wisdom, Justice, and Moderation*. Felix had driven through Georgia many times. He doubted Story had ever been below the Mason-Dixon Line before she moved to Austin. Certainly not to the Deep South. Searching the car, he'd found her cell phone in the center console and threw it in the trash. His own he'd smashed at the house, flushing the pieces down the commode.

Leave no trace.

They drove west with the windows down, feeling the wind on their faces. At 1:00 a.m. Story fell asleep, her bare feet perched on the dash. Felix drove the speed limit, keeping his eyes out for cops. It was force of habit for a man who worried his identity wouldn't hold up to real scrutiny. He didn't vote, had never gotten a parking ticket. His high school transcript was real, just not his. True lies, he called them. In this way he'd convinced himself he was safe, hidden, that the truth of what he did will never come out.

This is another form of denial. Wishful thinking.

Felix's anxiety was that of a hunted animal. He woke often in the dead of night convinced that his father was standing by the bed, dressed in camouflage.

They found us, he'd say. *Get dressed.*

For Story, anxiety had come into her life in the form of an eating disorder. A devil that penetrated her brain, telling her not to eat. A demon that stank of bad breath, who refused to let her drink anything, even water. A devil who forced her to exercise all day and pace her room at night until she had burned off each calorie consumed and more. It spoke its devil tongue in her ear, telling lies. *Such a fat, hateful creature,* it said. *No one will love you until you disappear.*

In those days panic kept her awake, an electric terror filling every daylight hour. She was a thirteen-year-old girl, wasting away. For months she hid her condition under oversize sweatshirts. Her mother, busy at work, and her stepfather, preoccupied with her toddler stepbrother, noticed only that she had become more finicky in what she ate. Not that she had become an expert at cutting her food into small pieces and rearranging her plate to make it appear she'd eaten. Not that she had mastered the art of microbiting, outlasting her parents, who wolfed down their meals and hurried to clear their plates.

This is what slow-motion suicide looks like.

When her mother finally realized that Story was a shadow of her former self, when she forced her daughter onto a scale, the number she saw was so small it nearly made her faint.

Oh my God, she said.

And somewhere deep down inside, Story's demon smiled.

She had become a fourteen-year-old skeleton.

What followed were months at an eating disorder clinic, followed by intensive individual and group therapy sessions. Zoloft became Celexa. Slowly she fought her way back. But the demon lives inside her still, in the marrow of her bones, in the whorls of her fingerprints. In high school she joined the track team, hoping to outrun it. She threw herself into her studies, hoping to outsmart it. She loaded up with extracurricular activities, hoping to outlast it. She listened to loud music and books on tape when she ate, trying to drown out its voice.

But deep in the cerebral cortex, she could still hear its demon creak, casting spells.

The spell of starvation.

The spell of regurgitation.

The spell of ex-lax, two fingers down the throat.

She met Felix last year at a bar. He was a skinny, mop-haired boy up from San Marcos with haunted eyes. He wooed her with strange animal facts. *The Texas horned lizard*, he said, *shoots blood out of its eyes when threatened, up to five feet*. He was a fount of facts like these. *Did you know*, he would say, *that when the hairy frog is attacked, it breaks its own toe bones and forces them through its skin to make claws?*

At night he would put his arms around her and hold her for hours, the way animals huddle together for warmth in winter. There were things in his past he glossed over. Did he have any cousins? A favorite uncle? It was clear he was running from something, and yet he was also running *toward* something—a career, adulthood, love. Her boyfriend was no man-child. He seemed obsessed with grown-up things. Savings accounts. Car insurance. On the weekends, he'd help her balance her checkbook. He taught her how to change a tire, where to pour windshield wiper fluid.

The last time Story had been home in New York was for Thanksgiving. Must be two years ago now. She doesn't know for sure, because she doesn't like to think about it, and her family definitely doesn't talk about it. They don't talk about it because just as every family has its myths and legends, so too do families have their taboos, the subjects they won't discuss, the fights they don't revisit. A mother walks in on a child masturbating. A daughter who spent her adolescence trying to eat as little as possible, who was hospitalized, a feeding tube inserted, who went to four residential treatment programs in five years, comes home for Thanksgiving with arms like sticks and eats a sum total of two forkfuls of cranberry sauce, and then—when her mother confronts her about it—

proceeds to scream that she is an adult now and doesn't have to listen to this shit and can make her own decisions, then gets in her car and drives too fast over the yellow line and skids sideways into a set of highway exit barrels, because the truth is she's been dizzy for weeks, light-headed, trapped in what her doctor calls *starvation brain.*

This was between college and law school. What she calls her lost year, before she met Felix. She spent the night in the hospital. When the nurse asked if there was anyone they could call, she said her mother's name, because she was scared, because she was sorry, because back there in the car as it slid toward the off-ramp she thought she was going to die. When her mother arrived, she stood looking down at Story in her short-sleeved hospital gown, her arms like sticks.

"Oh, Story," she said, and the two cried together under the harsh fluorescents in a room that smelled like industrial cleaning products.

They have been camping outside town for three weeks now, Story and Felix, surveying the terrain, tracking the comings and goings from E. L. Mobley's compound. Mobley himself flies in and out of a private airfield just south of town. In his absence security seems to increase, deterring them from making any kind of move to rescue Bathsheba. Felix worries that in the current crisis his sister will kill herself before they can save her. She's always been a dreamer, prone to charmers and snake oil salesmen. Felix can imagine how Mobley hooked her—money, power, the promise to make all her artistic dreams come true.

The Mobley compound is north of town, hidden in the foothills near the McDonald Observatory. From Farm Road 118 there is an unmarked blind driveway leading to an iron gate. Cameras mounted on the adjacent walls monitor your approach. At the Radio Shack in Fort Jackson, Felix bought a drone and a laptop, paying cash. At a rest stop overlooking the state park, he unboxed it while Story found a spot in the shade where she could watch the laptop screen. It took some practice, but over the next hour Felix learned how to fly it well enough to begin. He had the GPS coordinates for the compound, and with Story's help he flew the drone out over the foothills, its camera sending back footage, which Story recorded for later review.

Back at the campsite they cooked beans and tortillas on a cast-iron skillet over the fire and looked at what they'd filmed. It quickly became clear that the blind driveway was the only way in. The house itself—a six-bedroom Spanish-style hacienda with a three-story tower on the south corner—was nestled in a rocky depression. Behind the house were an infinity pool and thirty feet of impossibly green grass, leading to a cliff. From there it was a steep drop to the valley below.

That night Felix dreamed of his sister, locked in that tower, staring out at the rolling emptiness. What else had his father trained him for if not her rescue? All he needed was a plan. And so, the surveillance began.

Three weeks later, Felix sits next to Story, sipping his coffee. They are waiting for the black Suburban. Every morning, an envoy from the compound drives to the Hotel St. George to pick up bagels and pastries. This is the riddle of Marfa, that in the 1970s, a minimalist artist fled New York City and moved to this small West Texas town. He bought an old army base and began filling it with art. Over the next thirty years, the town transformed into an avant-garde performance of a cowboy's retreat. Now vegans shop at the local grocery. Art galleries pepper the one-stoplight town. The tallest building is a four-story minimalist rectangle that sits across the street, directly behind them. The Hotel St. George—Saint George who fought a dragon in the city of Silene in what is now Libya. This was in the third Century AD. The dragon had arrived the previous fall and stayed through winter. Villagers had been offering it two sheep a day to placate the mighty beast. But sheep were not enough. A human sacrifice was demanded. A sacrifice to be chosen by the townspeople. The first, an unpopular young girl, was selected by consensus, then a brutish and stupid boy. A pattern emerged of children fed to the inevitable to save their parents. First the poor, then the gentry. This was the function of children back then, to toss to the wolves so their parents could survive and make more children. But that spring, when all the local children had been consumed, the king's daughter was selected. His only child. So the king sent for George, a Roman soldier of some renown. The rich, you see, have always used wealth to buy solutions to their problems.

Later, in the year 303, George would be tortured and beheaded by the Romans. He would become patron saint of soldiers, scouts, and the syphilitic. Two thousand years later a hotel would be built in his name in Marfa, Texas, inside of which you can buy three-hundred-dollar art monographs and order a fifteen-dollar margarita.

Across the street, Story nudges Felix. Two black Suburbans are inbound from the town square. It's a change from the usual one. Story slips lower in her seat, as both cars turn nose in to the curb in front of the hotel. Two men with earbuds emerge from the lead car and scan the street. The passenger speaks into his wrist, and the back doors of the follow car open. E. L. Mobley steps out. He's wearing a North Face windbreaker over a blue V-neck sweater. His white hair is close cut in the current style, face shaved and moisturized. His sunglasses cost $1,800.

Liam Orci comes around the back of the SUV, eyes scanning for danger. He is a tall man with a crooked smile. Mobley says something to him and laughs. From the car, Felix and Story watch the four men enter the hotel. This is the first time since they arrived in town that Mobley has left the compound to come to town. Low in their seats they have a whispered exchange.

"Shit," says Story. "Should we—I don't know—should we grab him?"

"Four against one," says Felix. "Not without some serious bloodshed."

He checks his watch.

"Could we—it's a thirty-minute drive—maybe we could get to the compound and get in. Three guys here. Three back at the house. Maybe if we—"

But he stops. They're not ready to strike now. They don't have their supplies. It's the middle of the day.

"What if we confront him?" says Story. "Tell him we know he has her. Say *let her go*."

Felix shakes his head. Sometimes he can't believe her naivete. The rich don't do anything unless it makes them richer. He checks his watch again. Three minutes. They've lost three minutes with Mobley inside. Felix makes a decision.

"Come on," he tells Story, already halfway out the door. She slips on her shoes, follows him wincing. Her legs are cramped from sitting for so long. Though she doesn't know it yet, her own face is all over the news—the internet flooded with side-by-side photo comparisons of her college ID photo with the Ghost of the Senate, that girl with oversize sunglasses seen sitting behind Judge Nadir one moment and gone the next, replaced by a bearded man.

Stepping onto the sidewalk, Felix puts his arm around Story, pulls her to him, kisses her cheek. He is playing the role of the good boyfriend, aware that eyes may be on them. They push through the double doors. Ahead of them is the front desk. To their right is a sitting area and bookstore. To their left is the restaurant. Felix glances left, sees Mobley sitting at a round table with Orci and another man. The two body men are at the next table, eyes moving. It's a quick look, enough to place Mobley, and then Felix is eyes front again. He steers Story toward the bookstore.

"Let's see if they have that de Kooning," he tells her.

She nods, mute. Now that they're inside, now

that Mobley is near, everything feels too real. The
insanity of what they're doing—rescuing a girl
from a billionaire—hits her. How alone they are.
How underfunded and unprepared.

The lobby is mostly empty. A family waiting
for the elevators. A woman with a dog talking to
the desk clerk. The bookstore is part of the lobby,
a series of oversize wooden tables covered with
books. Two walls of shelves circle back toward the
front window. There are four customers browsing.
All appear to be teenagers. The nearest boy has
long hair pulled back in a ponytail and wears wire-
rimmed glasses. An older teen in a leather duster
stands next to him chewing gum.

Story glances behind her. She sees Mobley
seated at his table. For a moment, their eyes meet.
At that moment it becomes clear that he noticed
her the moment she entered the hotel. That he's
been following her with his eyes. Checking her
out. Story looks away, feeling burned. The smell
of restaurant food—burgers on the grill, a lamb
Bolognese on the stove—so appealing when they
entered, fuels a sudden wave of nausea.

"I have to—" she says—"the bathroom."

She hurries off, right hand to her mouth. Felix
watches her go, recognizing the green in her skin.
He shrugs theatrically. *Women.* Behind him he can
feel Mobley's eyes burning a hole in his back.

Slowly he circles the nearest table, glancing at the books. He picks up a Ron Mueck monogram, studies the back. To his right, the long-haired kid and the older kid in the duster are having a whispered conversation.

"Now or later," says Duster. "It's your call. All I'm saying is when opportunity knocks…"

The kid takes a toothpick from behind his ear, puts it between his lips. By the window Felix notices a willowy kid, smaller than the others, maybe fifteen. The kid's wearing a down vest, even though it's ninety degrees out. He's looking out at the street, a paperback open in his hand, forgotten. Felix continues circling the table. He lowers the Ron Mueck, picks up a yellow book of poems. *Trustworthy.* He can see the ladies' room door from where he's standing. Around him, the sound system plays Korean trance pop at a whisper. The woman with the dog leaves the front desk, on her way to the elevators. Over the edge of the book, Felix sees Liam Orci wave over the waitress.

"It's not time for that," says Ponytail. "We're here for something else."

"What?" says Duster.

"Answers," says Ponytail.

The bathroom door opens. Story comes out. She's splashed water on her face, brushed her hair with her fingers. Felix raises his hand.

"Story," he calls, not full voiced, but loud enough for her to hear, then thinks, *Shit, why did I use her real name?* She sees him, comes over.

"Sorry," she says. "This is all—a bit—over-whelming."

He hands her the poetry book as if to say, *Isn't this interesting.* She takes it without understanding, puts it down on the table. Behind them Ponytail and Duster are involved in a furious conversation, heads close together. Their eyes are on Felix and Story, whispering excitedly. And by now we know who they are. One is a prophet. The other has given himself the name of a Stephen King villain.

"What are we doing?" Story asks nervously. Every minute they're in the store feels dangerous. Behind her the Prophet takes a step forward.

"Shhh," says Felix.

The Prophet reaches out to touch Story's shoulder. But then a woman is there, hurrying around the front of the table.

"Oh my God," she says to Story. "You look just like her."

The Prophet freezes, hand in midair. Story looks at Felix. *What do I do?*

The woman grimaces a smile.

"The judge's daughter."

She holds up her phone. Story sees a CNN headline—TRICK OF THE TAPE? and below it the side-by-side images of her college ID and some woman seated behind her mother in a Senate chamber.

"You're her, right?" says the young woman, a blonde, maybe twenty-six. She smiles.

Felix grabs Story by the elbow, propels her toward the door.

"Hold on, hold on, lemme get a picture," says the woman, trying to turn her phone around and switch to camera.

Felix race walks toward the door, pushing Story now. From the corner of his eye he can feel Mobley watching them. It was a mistake coming in here. He can see that now. Behind them the woman has her camera on and is hurrying to cut them off.

"Oh, no you don't," she says, taking three fast steps toward the door and turning to face them.

Story freezes as the camera comes up—a second away from becoming the next internet meme—but then the boy in the Duster puts a shoulder into the blonde and she stumbles toward the restaurant. And the boy with the ponytail puts a hand on Felix's back, shoving him and Story out the door.

"Don't turn around," he says.

And then they're out on the street, turning left, passing the window. Glancing inside, the Prophet sees Simon staring out at the street. He raps the glass, gestures—*hurry up*. Simon frowns, confused, looks behind him, sees that his friends are gone. His mind puts the equation together.

"Shit," he says, and hurries to the door, meeting up with Randall Flagg, who has spent the last thirty seconds telling the blonde to watch where the fuck she's going next time. On the street, Randall grabs Simon, steers him in the opposite direction of the Prophet.

"Wait," says Simon. "Where are we—"

But Randall shoves him toward the intersection. Out of the corner of his eye, Simon can see Mobley sitting inside the restaurant. He is talking to his guest, but his eyes are tracking Simon and Flagg as they reach the corner. Mobley has the hint of a smile on his face.

I see you, he says with his eyes. *All of you.*

And something about the smile makes Simon shudder, as Randall pushes him out of the sun and into the shade.

The Wizard

When they write about E. L. Mobley, they often describe him by the things he owns. The private 737, the six-story, fifty-room mansion off Madison Avenue, the five other palatial estates from Florida to Tokyo to Rome. He is a man with his own Caribbean island and possibly a gold mine in West Africa. Journalists list the presidents he befriended, the Russian oligarchs and Chinese party leaders who call him on his cell phone. He made his first billion from the land—specifically from blasting water at high pressure into the shale, forcing oil and natural gas to the surface. The effect of this on the environment was multifaceted, which is why in Oklahoma they called him the Earthquake King and in Louisiana he was the Slurry Man, known for creating a bilious soup of chemicals that leech up into people's groundwater. Since then he has diversified, laundering his money through a cloud storage empire, a packaged food behemoth, and a financial services consortium, until that original billion blasted from the shale is just one one-hundredth of his wealth.

Being rich has made him wealthy, in other words.

He likes women, the younger the better. This part is common knowledge in certain circles and yet remains mostly unreported. He is a lifelong bachelor, after all, a billionaire. Of course he plays the field. What's the point of money if not to buy youth? It's accepted, like an eccentricity, mostly because people assume young means nineteen or eighteen. Perhaps while abroad he flirts with women as young as seventeen.

The truth is, he doesn't like women at all.

He likes girls.

Mobley is a sixty-three-year-old man who prefers the company of children, some as young as four-teen. He has slept with thousands. In New York City they are plentiful and cheap. He used to joke you could pick up a six-pack at the corner store. All you need is some licorice and a smile. A collector of old fairy-tale engravings, he calls the girls his *animal brides*. Mobley has a ranch outside Marfa, Texas, where he flies nineteen and twenty-year-olds on private jets. There, in a special chamber, designed according to the golden mean, he violates them, their cries ringing out inside the perfectly

honed acoustic bowl. E. L. Mobley believes himself to be the most important and original man that
has ever lived. He alone can see the secrets of the
universe. He alone can map the invisible labyrinth
of the human mind. He is a sorcerer.

A wizard.

Everywhere he goes he has enablers, *rabba-
teurs* who corral vulnerable, fertile, helpless young
women for his entertainment, his amusement, his
consumption. And he is hungry all the time, the
Wizard, sometimes seeing three different girls a
day. Massages, that's what he pays them for. *Have
you ever given a massage, sweetie?* And then you
see how far they will go once you're naked on the
table. If you roll over and lower the sheet. If you
put their hand on it, force their heads down.

There is a woman in Los Angeles who keeps a
database of prospects, updated weekly with social
media links—actress and model wannabes mostly,
but also *artists*—tattooed girls with nipple pierc-
ings and daddy issues. The key is to identify girls
with trauma in their past, girls with self-esteem
issues, eating disorders. Victims, in other words.
In San Francisco he has the Troll, a high school
boy he pays handsomely, who charms, seduces,
and bribes young girls to come to the Wizard's
parties. He has invested in a European modeling
agency to feed him girls when he is abroad—Paris,

Denmark, Barcelona. On the island, his handlers recruit poor girls from Barbados to sail over on his yacht. They're curvier than his normal girls—fatter in the *toilet*, which is what the Wizard calls women's bottoms—but you can do just about anything to them if you donate enough money to the local police. This is what wealth buys on Planet Earth in the twenty-first century. Freedom. From accountability, from prosecution, from rules. Freedom from morality, from equality, from justice.

Wheels up from SFO at 4:30 p.m. Pacific Time means a landing time in Marfa, Texas, around 9:00 p.m. Central Time. They eat lobster on the plane, Hunan style, with a tofu lo mein prepared by his West Coast chef. It is Mobley, his majordomo, Astrid Prefontaine—a former It-girl, society-page regular, who was his "girlfriend" for a time and now serves as his *normalizer*, which is how he describes her to rich friends who wonder how E.L. always gets such top-shelf pussy.

"Astrid," he tells them, "normalizes me. She brings the girls in, makes them feel at home. Let's all have dinner, she says, or E.L. wants you to come out to the Hamptons. And then, when we're on the sofa watching a movie, she'll put her hand in the girl's lap or kiss her on the cheek. See, girls know that *men* are predators. We've got that feral glint in the eye. But the doe of the species, their own kind, well, they don't know how to process a woman taking advantage. They freeze up. I could show you six different scientific papers I funded. If a woman does it, it must be okay. And once they get it in their head that what's going on can't be threatening, then Astrid pulls me in—so that even if there's discomfort, it doesn't trump the feeling that yeah, maybe things are weird, but not *dangerous*."

Also on the plane are the Orci brothers—Pete, the pilot; Liam, Mobley's samurai; and Boaz, the fixer who can make any problem disappear. The current *problem* is Mobley's personal assistant, Katie, eighteen, whom Astrid and E.L. have been grooming for weeks now. Katie is a painter wannabe with Big Dreams of New York Celebrity, and a girl with dreams can be overpowered. First you buy a few paintings; then you tell her you want to invest in her future, maybe give her a fellowship, a year painting in peace at one of your properties. Then, isolated, you make things physical. *Have you ever given a massage?* You write her a check if she gets too bent out of shape, or threaten to bury her artistically. Power is a zero-sum game. Nobody has a little. It's all or none. And the Wizard is all powerful, a sorcerer of global renown, a man of supernatural hypnotism and charm, like a shuckling cobra that mesmerizes you with his eyes.

Katie's real name is Bathsheba DeWitt, an appellation that has always felt to her like the call sign of a Florida panhandle stripper. She fits the victim profile perfectly—overbearing father, absent mother. Developed early. Started her period at twelve. She was seduced by her math teacher when she was just fifteen, after a long campaign of notes and calls ending in her deflowering in the back of his Volkswagen. Violent men seem especially attracted to her. Maybe it's her size, five foot one, skinny, and curvy. Or the fact that, despite it all, she still believes in things like love and respect.

It's her first time on a private jet. Mobley watches her study her food, the dry Pinot Grigio he poured her. She seems frozen, overwhelmed by the weightless splendor. He watches her turn and look out the window at the world flying by below, a world she hopes to conquer one day, and *shit*, doesn't it seem like she's off to a rocket start? Across from her, Astrid raises her glass, smiles. Her lipstick is pale, tasteful.

"To Katie," she says.

Mobley smiles, raises his glass.

"To Katie."

He leans forward, clinks his glass against hers. Katie blushes, holding her wine self-consciously. It's clear she can't believe her luck. She clinks glasses with Astrid, then Mobley, then puts down her glass. Astrid frowns.

"It's bad luck if you don't drink," she says. So Katie lifts her glass again and takes a small sip, then a bigger one, a feeling of sophistication swelling inside her, as if this drink, this plane, their attention, has opened the door to a secret world, a world filled with hidden knowledge and access. Somehow Katie has threaded the needle of her shitty childhood and adolescent punching bagocity to land this unbelievable opportunity. For a moment she feels the hot swell of pride. *When life gives you lemons*, she thinks.

If only her father, Avon, could see her now, with his constant belittling, his *you're a piece of shit,* father-of-the-year diatribes. How far she thinks she's come from that backwater purgatory to this moneyed height, a place where she is wanted, where her skills, her worth are valued, where she is seen. Before too long she will learn what a fool she's been, that Katie, born Bathsheba, is still food for a predator, that she has left the frying pan only to land in the fire. The only difference is the *class* of predator has risen, from mangy coyote to great white shark.

To be raised, if not poor, then hardscrabble on the American fringe is to mark time through trauma and scars. The broken finger that healed crooked because Avon taped it himself instead of taking Bathsheba to the emergency room. The dog bite on her leg that should have had stitches. Her brother Samson's missing tooth, knocked out by a fence post. Fevers and infestations, overdoses and car wrecks. This is how she thinks about time. The year her father was knifed in prison, following directly the year her mother lost her hair and took to her bed from stress and worry. The year her great-grandmother drowned in the big flood. The year her best friend was killed on an icy road. Pets that came and went. Her one-eyed cat eviscerated on the porch. The dogs the coyotes didn't eat, the alligators got. In rural Florida, no one lasted long.

The year her flow started, Bathsheba took an Ace bandage from her dad's survival kit and wrapped it around her chest. She knew instinctually that if the boys at school saw her budding breasts they would whisper behind their hands and follow her home, car engines idling as they tried to lure her inside their dark backseats.

In her world you ate what you shot. They hunted deer in the fall, bobcat and otters in the winter. Wild hogs were year-round, raccoons, opossums, rabbit. By the time she was six, Bathsheba knew how to tear the head off a dove, to skin a rabbit and pull out its guts. They used every part of the animal in her house, curing the meat themselves.

Out in the shed were a half dozen storm freezers daisy-chained together with extension cords. At night they made a sound like an elephant's stomach rumbling. Bathsheba would lie in her room and listen, the plywood house shifting around her, snapping and creaking. Somewhere out there were cities where people talked about art, gleaming metropolises filled with stylish independent thinkers. She would go there one day. She would be one of those people, talking about Picasso and Margaret Atwood. She would own indoor shoes, lots of them. But now her days were filled with the acquisition of practical skills, survival drills, and subsistence farming. She longed for abstraction, for the deep human conceptual thinking that separated women from animals.

In her idle hours she experimented with colors you could find in the wild. Onionskins and sunflower petals, huckleberries and charcoal. She mixed her yellows and blues, her rusty browns, and painted pictures on old pieces of drywall she found in the junk pile out back. In autumn she liked to arrange the fallen leaves by color in the field behind her house. The trick was to not mind about the wind, to treat the wind as your partner, when it blew in and upended your designs, because isn't that what the world does always, make a mess of the things you like just so?

The Ace bandage worked for about four months, but then she started getting hips. Her butt filled out and her breasts got heavy. When she ran, parts of her body moved with a mind of their own, pulling her off-balance. Sabotage. That's what it felt like. Her own body was working against her, trying to get her killed. Like clockwork, the boys started circling with their carrion breath, hunting with their eyes, looking for weaknesses, openings. Middle-aged men watched her over the rims of their tallboys, shouting out the things they'd do to her, the places they'd hurt her teenage body. Acts of penetration, age-old demonstrations of ownership. Bathsheba started cutting through the woods on her way home from the store, pickup trucks with inky glass idling in the parking lot behind her. She knew from cop shows on TV that she had become that most endangered animal, a young woman of reproductive age.

At night she lay listening to the groan of the freezers. Her cell phone told her there were places where people wore sheer gowns and tuxedos without socks, where girls dyed their hair pink and wore crop top T-shirts that said #MeToo. If you wore a shirt like that where Bathsheba lived, the boys would take it as an invitation—*like please sir, can I have some rape too, sir, like the kind you gave Melissa Barnes in the backseat of Billy Sanger's car last winter, or what you did to the youngest Haskell girl when her parents were out of town for their anniversary?* These weren't thoughts as much as physical instincts, her survival brain on high alert at all hours of the day and night. If she stayed in Florida, she would be eaten alive. This was her anxiety. They would pick her bones clean and leave her with nothing but babies. At first her body would give her power. She would be the puppet master, Salome on a dais, and they would follow her with their eyes the way dogs will follow the food in your hand. But this power wouldn't last. Five years, ten, and then she would be somebody's mother, drinking too much gin on a Tuesday night. The animals that circled her then would be scavengers, jackals come to pick the leftover meat from her carcass.

If she stayed here she would be smoking by thirteen, drinking by fourteen, pregnant by fifteen. The practical skills she learned would be breast-feeding and changing diapers. One minute she would be the girl with her hands in the wind, driving through the Everglades at night with the radio up too loud and a bottle of tequila between her knees, and the next she would be the woman in the Walmart with the black eye buying frozen peas and carrots in bulk.

So she ran, packing a small bag and hiding it

in the woods. She took all her babysitting money and a fifty-dollar bill from Avon's wallet. By this point Samson was already gone. He'd hitchhiked his way north, telling Avon he was going with his buddy Elvin to Tampa for a boys' weekend. Bathsheba couldn't forgive him for that, for leaving her behind, not just for the sense of abandonment, but for the rise in DEFCON alert that happened in her house in the months and years after.

"Don't you run on me," Avon used to tell her after dark, a pint of whiskey in his belly. He set trip wires on the stairway and hung bells on all the doors and windows. Radar Hunt sold Avon a pit bull bitch that hated other females, especially the human kind, and she would bark every time she saw Bathsheba, her lip curled and murder in her eye. Avon staked her under his daughter's window at night. This is the sad truth of the life of Katie, born Bathsheba. She has been held captive before. In many ways it is the defining factor of her life. And you can say she should have known better, that she should have seen Mobley coming a mile away, but to say that is to betray your own ignorance. Look at your life, the relationships you keep getting into. Can't you see the pattern? The wife who turned out to be just like your mother. The boyfriend who hit you just like your dad. You act like the world is filled with rational choices, that our brains are simple binary systems where if you push the red button and get a shock, you stop pushing the red button. But what if the red button pushes you? What if your father is a red button and he trains you to push him, rewards you for pushing him? What if he teaches you that pushing the red button is called love, a sharp electric shock that leaves behind a dull ache? Doesn't it make sense that when you finally escape into the wild and you see a red button, you would push it, because who doesn't want love?

And here she is, a mile above the earth, eating lobster, drinking champagne, and talking about philosophy, about Mondrian and Kandinsky. As far as she knows, her dream has come true. And this makes her happy, happy, happy.

"Wait till you see the stars," Mobley tells her. "Down near Big Bend there's no light pollution. It's just you in the dark with the universe."

Alone in the dark.

Katie smiles. She can't wait. She takes a forkful of lobster, puts it in her mouth. The taste, sweet and sour, is unlike anything she's ever experienced. She closes her eyes. Across from her Mobley looks at Astrid, who raises her glass once more and smiles.

You see, Katie, born Bathsheba, believes she is going to Texas to become an artist. But the truth is, she is going to be locked away in a tower like a princess, taking Mobley's seed inside her until she becomes pregnant with his miracle child, and then she will be held there under those starry skies until she brings forth his child from her sacred womb. It came to him in a dream one night last year, this vision of fatherhood. An immaculate conception, sired through a surrogate. A vessel. One woman would bear him a son. Then she would vanish, and other women would raise the boy, none outshining his father, the biggest, reddest button of them all. The child would be cared for, pampered, but only Mobley would show him love. In this way would the child's devotion be complete. In this way would he earn the right to be that most sacred of things—E. L. Mobley's heir.

Hallelujah, thought Mobley. *For I am the one true God.*

Simon

Picture a cartoon snowman. He has an orange carrot for a nose.

He sings:

This will all make sense when I am older.
Someday I will see that this makes sense.

His name is Olaf. He lives in a Disney movie. Disney movies are movies for children in which everyone lives happily ever after.

One day, when I'm old and wise
I'll think back and realize
That these were all completely normal events.

The movie is a cartoon, a fantasy. It's set in what they used to call *the land of make-believe*. Olaf is childlike, filled with wonder. He has a child's conviction that growing up will clarify all of life's sordid mysteries.

You know, the way it did for you.

I'll have all the answers when I'm older
Like why we're in this dark enchanted wood.

The adult world, Olaf believes, is a place filled with answers, with certainty, with clarity. Simon Oliver knows better. He knows what all adolescents teetering between childhood and adulthood know: that the bread crumbs are all behind you, and there is a witch waiting in the dark ahead.

I know in a couple years
These will seem like childish fears
So I know this isn't bad, it's good

The world of children *is* the world that makes sense. Freeze tag and four square and I spy. If the floor is lava, it's lava, and the tie always goes to the runner. Simon remembers that feeling, even though he has lost the ability to feel it. A time when everything made sense. When questions had simple answers, because you didn't even know there were hard questions to ask.

Now, crouched in a midnight bush outside the Wizard's compound, all Simon can think of is the complicated questions. Adult questions. Questions of degree. Like how do you get off the ride once it starts? Like what's the difference between a revolutionary and a criminal? Like *how did I get here*, a child about to commit nine federal and local crimes with a group of disgruntled teenagers. There is a sluiceway at his feet, dug into the rock, and a wire grate just big enough for a child to fit through. Simon has pulled tin snips from his pocket, and he is clipping himself an entrance. At fifteen he can be tried as an adult—for murder, for assault or kidnapping or whatever else they choose to charge him with.

How's that for grown-up?

Somewhere a coyote screams.

When I'm more mature
I'll feel totally secure

Javier is sitting on a rock next to Simon, eating a bologna sandwich. He speaks some English, and Simon speaks almost no Spanish, but somehow they've managed to get themselves here, to this blind ravine where in seven minutes Simon will sneak into the Wizard's compound and do his part to rescue a princess.

It's been eleven days since the Hotel St. George, eleven days since Simon, Louise, and the Prophet

met Felix and Story, since they heard their tale—
how the Wizard is holding Felix's sister, Bathsheba,
in a tower, how he brought her here under false pre-
tense and has impregnated her. They came to Marfa
to rescue her, just as Simon has come to rescue—
somebody, anybody. And, oh yeah, *how Felix's
real name is Samson*! He told them in confidence
when his girlfriend was in the bathroom, because
the Prophet kept asking if Felix knew where they
could find Samson. Because Felix was desperate
to help his sister and he thought they would help.
Felix made them swear they wouldn't tell Story—
her name is Story! So *hear his Story* must mean
listen to his girlfriend, to what she has to say—and
they all swore they would keep it quiet, even as
Felix swore he was going to tell her soon.

When Story comes back, he tells them about Bathsheba but says they can't call the cops or the FBI or
the press, because those roads don't lead anywhere
anymore. They end at a river and the bridge is out,
blown from the other side. *Authority* is a runaround
machine now, Felix tells them, designed to create
heat and noise without ever returning a satisfying
result. Justice is no longer the function of the justice
system, in other words, if it ever was.

Flagg agrees. He knows all about sound and
fury. He knows all about solemn funerals and calls
for actions. He knows the talk show circuit. He's

watched his friends testify before Congress. He's worn the red ribbon and the black armband. He's seen performances of outrage and promises for change. He knows the joke—how many grown-ups does it take to change a lightbulb? None, because they don't want the light to change. They like it the way it is.

See, that will all make sense when I am older
So there's no need to be terrified or tense.

It's almost one a.m. before Simon's walkie-talkie buzzes. He's removed the wire mesh, bending back the sharp edges so he doesn't hook himself, trying to remember the last time he had a tetanus shot. Meanwhile, Flagg and Katniss are scaling the drop-off, ready to sneak onto the Wizard's land from the rear. They've been out here every night for the last week planning their ascent, making test climbs, and sinking bolts. It's slow going in the dark, and risky, but Simon gets the sense that, for them, danger is the point.

Felix and the Prophet are waiting outside the main gate, out of sight of the cameras, ready to be let in. Louise and Story are parked in a scenic overlook a quarter mile downhill with Duane, waiting for the signal.

"This is Condor," says a voice on the walkie-talkie. "We're in position."

Simon straightens, the chill in the air making his small bones creak. Javier pulls the top piece of bread off his sandwich. He lays his bologna on the ground, then presses the two pieces of bread together again.

"Hey," says Simon quietly. Javier looks over.

"I'm gonna—it's time."

Javier nods, puts the bread in his pocket. Simon checks the handgun on his hip. *Maybe something with less kick this time,* Flagg said. A .32-caliber Browning, weighing less than a pound. After the shotgun it feels like a toy, but Flagg assured Simon that from close range it'll put a man down. He's had a few days to practice shooting, hearing the echo, the flat crack bouncing off the hills, doubling back. Every shot is an explosion. That's what you forget.

No stun cartridges this time. Now the hunt is real.

Simon keys his walkie-talkie three times to signal he heard the message, that he's going in. Then he lies on his belly, nose filling with the dry loam of the earth, and stares into the dark mouth of the wall. Any second now he's going to slither forward and pull himself through. Any second now he's going to leap into the unknown.

I'll just dream about a time
When I'm in my aged prime

'Cause when you're older
Absolutely everything makes sense.

"Stay here," he tells Javier. "No te muevas."

Javier shrugs, sits again, whistling a tune through his gap tooth. He thinks of his mother, his brothers. As soon as the white boy slips under the wall, Javier will stand and walk back to the road. He is free now and wants only to get home to El Paso, to find Mama and the boys, to restart his life.

Simon exhales, pulls himself through the twelve-inch gap, feeling roots and twigs pull at his pants. And then he's through. He stands, brushes himself off. It's a new moon. The woods around him are dark. But ahead in the distance he can see light in the tower. He puts a hand on the wall behind him. He's not going to the house yet. As quick as he can in the dark, he follows the wall through the trees. He walks low, crouching, for no reason other than it feels smart. He reaches a clearing. Ahead is the main gate. It's on an electric trigger, but Flagg has told him there will be a manual release, in case of a power outage. He pauses at the edge of the driveway. There is a guard post across the asphalt, but it's empty. Simon's breathing is shallow and quick, but he doesn't think about pulling out his paper bag. It's a different kind of nerves, an adrenaline rush, a life-or-death electricity perfectly calibrated to the level of risk he's taking. At that moment Simon realizes there is a difference between anxiety and fear and that he will take fear any day, if the alternative is a generalized dread that never shuts up.

He crouch-runs across the dark road, reaches the guard post, a one-person booth with a space heater and no door. He slips inside, keeping low. On the table ahead of him, small monitors show camera views from the other side of the gate. For a moment, not seeing Felix or the Prophet, Simon panics, but then he remembers they have mapped the range of the cameras and are hiding in a ravine. He casts around for the manual release lever. He has a flashlight in his pocket but has sworn he will only use it in an emergency.

Finally, his fingers find a metal and plastic latch. There is a handle attached to it. Simon hesitates. What if there's an alarm? What if opening the gate triggers the apocalypse? But he shoves those doubts aside, pulls. He hears a solid *clatch,* and the handle goes slack. Simon lets go, crouch-runs back into the trees, and works his way to the gate, staying out of the light. The gate has swung open less than a foot. Simon whistles quietly, then again louder. A beat and then he hears hurried footsteps from the other side of the wall. He strains to make out details in the dark.

Felix's face appears in the gap of the open gate. "Get back," he hisses.

Simon backs quickly into the trees. Felix pushes the gate slightly wider. It gives with an audible creak. Simon covers his ears with his hands, as if blocking the sound can erase it from the world. Felix curses, pushes again. The gate moves, protesting, one foot, two. And then Felix and the Prophet are through, running to join Simon in the trees. They have time only for a whispered *Good job. Are you okay?* And then they are running through the trees toward the main house. They hurry and slow, scanning the darkness for guards. Flagg has reported a security team of six men. Four work the day shift. Two stay up all night, mostly walking the immediate perimeter of the house, but sometimes straying wider, to check the wall.

Felix takes the lead. He is carrying his .38 snub-nosed on his hip, and an AR-15 Flagg offered him.

"You ever held one of these before?" Flagg asked.

Felix stripped the clip, emptied the chamber, checked the barrel and the sight in a way Simon had only ever seen in Michael Bay movies, before slapping the clip back home.

"That's a yes," said Flagg.

Felix lifts the gun to his shoulder with his right hand and raises his left in a fist. They stop. Simon's heart is thundering in his chest. He feels someone take his hand in the dark. *Claire?* he thinks, but when he looks down, it is the Prophet who has grabbed him, who holds him palm to palm. Their eyes meet. The Prophet smiles.

"Then Moses stretched out his hand over the sea," he says, "and the Lord drove the sea back by a strong east wind all night and made the sea dry land, and the waters were divided."

Felix lowers his fist, moves toward the side door of the house, knees bent, his rifle swinging left, then right as he looks for targets. Simon follows, his hand on Felix's back, as he's been taught, feeling the Prophet's hand on his own back. They move in a chain through a pool of exterior light and into shadow. Any second now a siren will sound, floodlights cracking on. Any second now marines will rappel down from helicopters on fast ropes, or a sniper will pick them off one by one from the tower.

S is for Simon blown away from afar.

He thinks about the man he shot. How he literally blew him out of his shoes, like in a cartoon. Except it wasn't a cartoon.

He can feel the Spanish-style stucco rough against his palms. Their backs are to the wall, waiting for the signal from Flagg and Katniss, circumventing the pool with night-vision goggles ($399 marked down at Walmart).

Beside Simon the Prophet whispers:

"Then Samson called out to the Lord: 'O Lord God, please remember me. Strengthen me, O God, just once more, so that with one vengeful blow I may pay back the Philistines for my two eyes.'"

A strong wind kicks up, bowing the trees. Simon can feel the temperature drop. Somewhere a low-pressure system is battling a high-pressure system, a war waged in the clouds.

"And Samson took hold of the two middle pillars which supported the temple, and he braced himself against them, one on his right and the other on his left."

From his hip, Simon hears his walkie-talkie click—once, twice, three times.

"Here we go," whispers Felix. "We breach in three, two, one."

They've surveyed the property, studying Google Earth images and drone footage, deciding that the kitchen door is the weakest. Glass panels line the top half of the door. On zero, Felix uses the butt of his rifle to smash the one closest to the knob, then reaches in and throws the bolt.

"On me," he says, and goes in. Simon follows. He

doesn't pull his pistol. He has decided that he will never pull another trigger. He would rather die.

One day, when I'm old and wise
I'll think back and realize
That these were all completely normal events.

And then they are inside the dark kitchen, but before Simon can get a good look at the room, electricity seems to flash, stuttering the walls blue, and Felix falls, shuddering. Simon stops, the Prophet crashing into him from behind. Around the room the shadows seem to be moving. And then he hears a shot and two thin wires arc over the kitchen island and hit Simon in the chest. Forty thousand volts course through his body. His muscles seize, his knees locking, his jaw snapping shut, taking a piece of his tongue with it, and Simon falls, flopping on the floor like a fish. There are no thoughts in his brain. He is a dancing monkey.

And the walls came down, and the temple fell.

And the last thing he sees before he blacks out is the Prophet falling to the floor beside him, his eyes rolled back, joining Simon in a lunatic pasodoble.

So endeth the Philistines.

On August 15, a Category 4 hurricane hit the Gulf Coast, flooding the lowlands from Galveston to New Orleans. Sea water surged over parking lots and marshes, pushing inland to historic markers. Twenty-two inches of rain fell in sheets so solid it appeared to Alice Holstead in Port Aransas that God had turned on a firehose and was trying to wash all sinners from the Earth. So much rain fell that the city of New Orleans actually sank two inches. Not to be outdone, a Category 5 hurricane hit Florida and the Carolinas two days later, with sustained winds over one hundred and fifty miles per hour. Dave Mertle's tractor ended up in Phil Oxley's barn thirteen miles away, perfectly placed with wheels down on the dirt floor behind locked doors, like a Christmas miracle, until you looked up and saw the tractor-shaped hole in the roof. *Turn around, don't drown* was becoming the unofficial motto of the Southern states.

No one argued the power of wind anymore.

On August 16, in Indiana, all the clouds were said to look like birds. Reports came in later that night from Bailey Island, Maine, that every lobster caught that day was blue. These were one in a million odds, the experts said. Implausible but not impossible. What more evidence do you need, countered the faithful, that God is among us, making plans?

Whatever the answer, disaster preparedness was becoming a billion-dollar business. Sales of home generators and bilge pumps skyrocketed. New guns were sold by the ton. Across the Central Plain states, millions of holes were dug, pockmarking the landscape, the latest in storm cellar design deployed. Some argued we should return to the era of the dugout, cutting homes into hillsides to make use of the natural temperature regulation of packed earth. *Wired* magazine ran a cover story on *The New Troglodytes*, documenting the return to cave living—mostly by technology entrepreneurs and forward (backward?) thinking urbanites. STAY COOL UNDERGROUND! ran the ads in magazines like *Outdoor World*. The planet is heating up, went the argument, *above*ground. Why not dig yourself a hole and cool off?

Outside Pittsburgh, residents reported seeing phantoms at sunset. Smoky figures hovering on the horizon with spectral arms and hooded eyes. They seemed to dance and spin in the final rays of sunlight. Experts blamed exhaust smoke from nearby smelting plants, but their fires had been burning for decades, and no phantoms had ever emerged before.

Somewhere, deep in the electrons of Facebook, a storm was brewing. Posts became memes, became movements. Chat rooms and timeline posts filled with speculation. Follow the clues, we were told. Everything connects. The God King had been stabbed in the back, and now his enemies' children were killing themselves. All those empathetic liberals lost in grief, LOL. How naive to think this was a coincidence. It was a plague, of course, like those that struck Egypt in Pharaoh times. We were returning to the wrath of the Old Testament.

Pundits pointed out that the dead belonged to both parties, but the faithful knew the truth. Anyone who lost a child was a traitor, no matter what allegiance they claimed. No matter how loyal they had been in the past. The death itself was the proof.

We are counting down, went the meme. It showed the image of a clock where all the numbers were fives, taken from a cartoon where a woman at a kitchen table said, *I never drink before five.*

What did it mean? Five what? Five days? Five deaths? By this point the suicide count had reached 210,000.

In Los Angeles, people called 911 claiming to smell smoke and hear the roar of approaching flames, but no fires were burning. Was it prophecy or old trauma? In Nebraska, residents claimed to hear the voices of children calling up from old wells, but when divers descended on ropes, no children were found.

On August 19, millions of Americans woke to the sound of an Amber Alert on their phones. They reached for their devices, groggy, studying the blue glow. They saw the familiar triangle, telling them a child was missing, but instead of a name, the text read *your son, your daughter, your nephew, your niece*, and the description of the suspect's vehicle simply read *pray for their souls*.

Terrified, people took to the streets. Stabbings increased, clashes between police and protesters, but the assemblies had become confusing. Often the protesters' signs were blank. When journalists pointed this out, men and women with angry eyes seemed puzzled. They studied the clear white space where their outrage had once been written. Had they forgotten to pen their grievances, or had the scope of their outrage exceeded the space available? Around the country, men in Hawaiian shirts started showing up at rallies with more guns than they could carry, patriots strapped with six, seven, eight pistols, a stack of rifles weighing down their arms or slung over their backs, like a burden they'd been forced to carry as penance. As if they could solve the world's problems if they could just get the number of guns right, like revolution was some kind of riddle.

Bearded men rolled up in trucks loaded with heavy black metal and formed human chains in parking lots—passing armfuls of rifles from one man to another—to what end?—the trucks so heavy they bottomed out on uneven roads. In Indianapolis, a Ford Fiesta loaded with more than fifty thousand bullets caught fire in a crosswalk. The police evacuated a thirty-block radius, as round after round fired in every direction, pockmarking the buildings and shattering glass. A janitor in a law firm was killed four streets to the south, the windows of a middle school shot out in a cascade of .44-caliber munitions, children diving to the ground screaming in terror.

The next day the number of suicides in America exceeded the number of deaths from every other cause. Cemetery signs began appearing outside apartment buildings. It started in Phoenix but soon became a global phenomenon. Always the same words—*Lost Souls Cemetery*—mounted with brass fasteners on the brick or concrete or wood, as if to say the ten- or thirty- or eighty-story buildings were just a series of drawers in a morgue, as if to say the residents inside were already dead.

In Mumbai, the temperature reached 132 degrees. Coastal residents in Coral Gables, Florida, woke to find the ocean at their doors. Not yet, they thought, but the truth could no longer be denied. The future we dreaded was already here.

Simon

He wakes alone. Hours have passed. It's day going on dusk. Simon's head is throbbing. He hears the sound of engines cycling down. His body is at rest, but he is moving. Darkness pulls him under.

An hour later he wakes again. He is sitting in a soft leather recliner in the cabin of a private jet. A jet he recognizes. Warm running lights and cherry inlays. It smells of Palo Santo and perfume. His mother's perfume. He looks out the window. The jet is parked on a runway in the bright sun. The cockpit is empty.

He hears his father's voice behind him.

"Freud called the baby *his majesty, the baby.*"

Simon turns slowly. His father, Ty Oliver, is sitting across the table from him. His white collar is stiff and open under a gray suit jacket. Every follicle on his face seems to have been shaved individually. His teeth are so white they look new.

"If I said I was disappointed," he says, "would you care?"

"Yes," says Simon.

His father thinks about that. "I'll say it again, God help me, but what exactly is the problem? You have everything a boy could need. You are loved. You are insulated. You literally cannot fail."

"Why me?"

His father forms a sour-milk frown. "Because sometimes you get lucky, kid. And you got lucky. You're my son."

"Was Claire lucky?"

"Claire was stupid. And I know it's hard to hear, but you're fifteen now. It's time for hard truth. Yes, Claire was lucky. She could have been anything, but she chose sabotage instead. This is how it is with some people—you can remove every obstacle to happiness and they're still miserable. Do you know what that makes them? Miserable people. And those people you should run from."

The surge of anger that Simon feels brings him the rest of the way back to consciousness.

"I'm not stupid," he says. "You're stupid. You think things matter that don't matter. Money. Power. Owning shit. Don't you get it? We're all gonna die, and you're focused on the wrong things."

His father sighs. "That's not a conversation we're going to have. About abstraction. About what the world could be if people were different. You are a fifteen-year-old boy with top grades and a brilliant mind and you're running around in the desert with a collection of burnouts and half-wits trying to play revolutionary. Well, congratulations. You had some fun. But playtime's over. It's time to get to work."

"Don't you get it?" Simon says. "It's too much. The house is on fire and you're still pouring yourself a drink."

He rubs his face, too many thoughts in his head. Where is the Prophet? What happened to Louise and Duane? He worries that somewhere Javier is back in a cage.

"Enough," his father says. "Grow up. Your mother and I have indulged this—you—long enough. *Anxiety*. Please. You think you're the first generation to run around shouting the world is ending? The world is always ending. We had the atomic bomb when I was your age, the Soviet Union. Remember duck and cover? And then 9/11 and everything was jihad this and jihad that. You know what the common denominator is? Children. You're all a bunch of hysterics."

Simon slips his hand into his pocket,

unconsciously looking for comfort, for the paper bag placebo, but it's gone. His pockets are empty. His father smiles.

"Fear is for babies, kiddo, helpless blobs, trapped in the moment with no past or future. No way to meet their own needs. You're a man now. It's time to take responsibility, make plans."

"You don't understand," Simon tells him.

"Why? Because I'm old? You ever hear the saying *don't trust anyone over thirty?* My generation invented that saying. And then we grew up. We learned how the world works. We made choices. We succeeded or we failed. But we got in the game."

"It's not a game."

"Oh, please. It's the earnestness. The self-righteousness. My God. Were we like that? So superior, but also paralyzed. Terrified to do the wrong thing, to *offend* someone."

He leans forward. "You know what happens to the anxious animals in the wilderness? Dinnertime."

Simon thinks of Claire, how she loved doing battle with this man, how she thrived on his exasperation, as if having your father's approval meant you were doing it wrong.

"Your friends are monsters," Simon says.

"Which friends?"

"Mobley."

Ty waves a hand dismissively. "Oh, he's okay. Worse than some, better than others."

Ty sips his drink, smiles to himself. "Can I tell you a secret? I don't recycle. I just throw everything in the same damn can. Always have. Sometimes I run the shower for twenty minutes before I get in. Oh, and I keep the heat on in the Hamptons house full blast in winter, even when we're out of town. I actually like eating half my meal and throwing the rest away. I prefer it, seeing all that expensive meat scraped into the trash, mixing with the plastic and metal."

Simon stares at him. His father smiles.

"Does that make you anxious?"

"Where are my friends?"

His father pauses, thinking.

"See, I think that's what's made you so anxious. Nobody tells you the truth. Everyone says what they think you want to hear, or they say what they want, but not the real reason they want it. That's the problem with society. You can't believe anybody. Nothing makes sense. So let me tell you the truth. This Earth was a gift to us from the Lord. He commanded us to use it. He filled the ground with oil for us to burn and filled the sea with fish for us to eat. Every animal living is alive because we allow it to be alive, and if we choose to hunt it to extinction, that is our choice. This planet has seen ice ages and molten eras long before we showed up, and it'll see them again long after we're gone. We don't have to be afraid, because we are doing what we were created to do. To enrich ourselves. And if that heats up the atmosphere and sours the seas, so be it. Do you hear me? We are the dominant species on Earth, which means we get to dominate the Earth. End of story."

"That's—awful."

"It's the truth. My point is, don't be anxious. You're a rich boy, soon to be a wealthy man, in a country where wealth is all that matters. You could have an IQ of eleven and masturbate all day into your mashed potatoes, and you'd still have a better life than ninety-nine percent of the planet. Worried about gun violence or global warming? Build a bunker, buy an island. Solve the problem."

"I want to see my friends."

"You have no friends. You're being used. They're using you."

"No. They like me. I'm part of something."

"They're using you. Because of your money, because of your name. To get to me."

"You don't know anything."

"I know that if E. L. Mobley weren't a friend of mine, you'd be in jail right now, looking at thirty to life for criminal trespass and attempted kidnapping."

A black Porsche pulls up on the tarmac outside. A man gets out of the passenger's seat. It's Gabe Lin. Across from Simon, Ty Oliver stands.

"Now, these next few months are important to me. I need government approval for the Telex merger and after Claire—did you know she reported me to the FDA before she killed herself? That bitch. She even sent documents."

He shakes his head, but respectfully, as if honoring an enemy on the battlefield.

"But now with you and that judge's daughter mixed up in some harebrained kidnapping scheme—well, I can't have you anywhere near that shit show, so I'm gonna put you someplace safe for a while. You and her."

He walks past Simon, stops, turns.

"You won't be happy there, but then, I don't think happiness is really your thing. So, let go of that. Let go of everything. Just—do what you're told and try not to piss her off, your minder. That woman scares the shit out of me, if I'm being honest."

"What does that mean?"

"It means I had you committed this morning. Turns out you're a danger to yourself and others. But don't worry. It's very discreet. Reeducation. Think of it like that—you've been brainwashed and we're rescuing you. Reorienting your priorities.

You'll be out before you turn eighteen, straight to Harvard or Yale as long as you put your head down, focus on your studies."

He steps through the hatch and starts down the steps to the Jetway.

"Your mother sends her love, by the way," he says. "Maybe I should have led with that."

Simon sits stunned. He watches his father cross the runway, slide into the backseat of the Porsche. Gabe Lin closes the door, and the car pulls away.

Cliffs

In the long view of history, mass suicide is not a new phenomena. More than nine hundred Jews are purported to have killed themselves to end the siege of Masada in the first Jewish-Roman War. The men inside knew that if they surrendered, the Romans would kill them and enslave their women and children. And so the men killed their families and then drew lots to see who would kill them in turn.

In 1802 Napoleon's forces surrounded five hundred former slaves in the Battle of Matouba in Haiti. The Haitians chose to ignite their own gunpowder stores when the French troops charged, killing themselves and four hundred French soldiers in a last-ditch act of self-sacrifice. A year later, in Greece, sixty women trapped outside Epirus by Albanian troops chose to leap from the cliff's edge, their children in their arms, rather than be captured and enslaved. They were reported to be dancing and singing when they jumped.

Stories like these can be found from the Punic Wars to the end of World War Two, when, in the face of advancing Russian forces, thousands of German civilians killed themselves rather than face the horrors they had been warned the Russians would force upon them. In the town of Demmin alone, one thousand people are reported to have committed suicide, most by drowning themselves in one of the three rivers that flowed through town. As in Masada, those with children made the grisly decision to kill their young first, weighing them down with stones and tossing them into the deep.

In 2003, in India, 1,707 committed suicide in the face of record crop failure. Three years later, in the province of Vidarbha, 767 farmers are reported to have killed themselves in all the ways that people do: by rope, by fire, by gun. During the same period in Japan, lonely citizens formed assisted-suicide groups online, using anonymous screen names. In sixty reported cases, more than 180 people took sleeping pills and then blocked the exhaust pipes of their cars, turning them into mobile gas chambers. The Japanese, of course, had a long and storied history when it came to organized suicide. At the end of WWII, in addition to the fabled kamikaze pilots, who would crash their fighter planes into enemy ships, the emperor ordered civilians to commit *"sudan jiketsu."* When US troops took Saipan, hundreds of Japanese men, women, and children leaped off a cliff into the ocean. Hundreds more leaped to their death from two high cliffs at Marpi Point, later named Suicide Cliff and Banzai Cliff. Sometimes parents would slit their children's throats before throwing them over the edge and following them.

Perhaps you've noticed a theme in these deaths— a sense of foreboding. The enemy approaches, circling like wolves. Death feels inevitable, but more concerning is the fear of what fresh horrors will come first. Rape and torture. Shame and humiliation.

Then there are the tales of religious leaders and their devoted followers. We know them well by now. Jim Jones and his Kool-Aid massacre, Heaven's Gate's thirty-nine acolytes found poisoned in their beds, wearing thirty-nine pairs of matching Nike sneakers, or perhaps you're familiar with the story of fifty-three members of the Solar Temple blowing themselves to smithereens.

In 1682 Tsar Feodor ordered the leader of a Russian Christian sect known as the Old Believers to be put to death, burning him alive. In response, thousands of Old Believers locked themselves in churches around the country and set themselves on fire.

They too believed the end was near, and rather than wait for the inevitable, they vowed to take control, because dying by your own hand was a choice. A way to wrestle your mortality back from the gods of cruelty and chance.

Was this what our children were doing? Killing themselves before outside forces could erase them? And yet, if so, who was the enemy at the gates, and why couldn't we see them too?

Simon

It's in and out from there. Bits of memory, feelings, smell. Simon's mind is blank. Was there a car ride? An elevator? He remembers a homeless man with his pants down, squatting by the side of the road. Before or after a freeway overpass passing overhead? The memories have the feeling of dream, a story told out of order. The stick of the first needle is lost to time, but there have been countless since. Clear fluids pressed through glass tubes into his veins. And then sleep. Or not sleep precisely, but empty waking. The void. Existence without identity. Fluorescent lighting, meals delivered in soft piles. Bars on the windows. When the dose runs out, clarity seeps in. His name. Simon. And Claire. He remembers Claire.

But then she is there. The face from his dreams, eyes full of teeth.

The Witch.

She comes with the needle, and Simon is under-water. How much times passes this way? A week? A month? He is in a house near a highway in a city. At night he can hear the radial whoosh and rumble. Time is a clock with no hands. This is the mental hospital reality he feared when his parents sent him to Float originally, back when he was having three or four panic attacks a day. Four-teen going on ninety. He envisioned men in white coats administering a Jack Nicholson lobotomy, the big Indian smothering him out. But that was then, before the hugs and the equine therapy of his expensive retreat, before Louise and the Prophet, before soft boundaries for rich kids.

Here he is suppressed. His riches don't matter. His humanity doesn't matter. He is a non-person, reduced to absence. A fifteen-year-old boy alone in a strange house with bars on the windows, locked down in an insane asylum for one. Outside the sun shines hard, baking the concrete, the sky a cloudless desert above. It's a one-story house, surrounded on all sides by bleached stucco, set back off the street. The windows are shrouded with heavy fabric, but from time to time he manages to peer out. The front and back yards are paved, Mexico City style, dusty weeds growing up through ribbons and cracks. Could he be in Mexico? Some-times he hears the oompah of Latin music pumping from bass speakers. Inside, the air-conditioning is set at maximum. He feels refrigerated, his body shivering so hard it feels his bones will break.

F is for frigid, they freeze him to death.

Not to mention, there is a smell in this place. A tenement stew. Cabbage boiled in salty water. The unspeakable parts of a pig. The smell from his dreams. At times he can hear her working in the kitchen, the Witch. The clatter of pots and knives. Cauldron, cauldron boil and bubble. Hands floating in broth. Was that a dream or a premonition? He has seen this woman before—the Witch—in succubus nightmare. She is a pale skeleton covered with a fine downy fur.

In moments when the Witch is absent, he is cared for by a middle-aged Filipina named Rose. It's Rose who rolls him from room to room and wipes the sometimes drool from his chin. Behind her eyes is a human being controlled by fear, a woman who startles when she hears her name shouted from the darkness, who crosses herself when she thinks no one is looking.

He sleeps on a bare mattress in a corner. In moments where he feels capable of rational thought, he wonders if he's being punished or if he's being executed—slowly, deliberately erased. It matters not that erasure this way makes no rational sense, that if his father wants to disown him, there are simpler ways. No. Stuck in here, chemically negated, he remembers that old chestnut: *the cruelty is the point*. But then the needle comes again, erasing every thought. Sometimes in the night he wets himself, the drugs sabotaging control. In the morning, Rose will change his hospital scrubs, sponging him dry, and clucking.

At twilight the Witch sits in the shadows, just out of sight, and speaks to him in low, quavering tones.

"Little boy," she says, "little boy."

He stirs.

"You know who I am," she says, "even if you don't know my name."

He peers into the darkness.

"Your mind has been warped to believe in lies. You need to wake up. Your father is a great man. How do we know? Because he is wealthy. If the poor were so smart, they wouldn't be poor. Your father's success is proof of his destiny, his *superiority*. Who are you to tear him down?"

As Simon drifts in and out of consciousness, she tells him all the old fairy tales from the point of view of the wolf. A lonely witch in a gingerbread house. A wee man enslaved by his own name. The point is not to *see things from their point of view*.

She doesn't try to justify their actions in some reverse moral paradox. Instead, she suggests that empathy itself is a lie. *One is what one is.* Wolves eat pigs. Witches eat children. Poor you, if you're a child, but one can't argue the natural order.

"Bees are born to a hive," says the Witch. "We call them drones, and they do what they're told. Is this the life you want? Where the weak murder the strong? Where those who can't take care of themselves make rules for those who can? To limit us, to tell us what we can be? Like we're children."

Simon wants to answer, but his brain isn't making words. In his mind he is a toddler again, a squirt. Late at night when he couldn't sleep, Claire would lie beside him and stroke his hair. She held his hand in the park. If he could speak, Simon would have said, *Isn't it the job of the strong to protect the weak?* But then what's happening in that room isn't a conversation.

In the bathroom he is sometimes allowed to be alone, but he's usually so out of it he must lean against the wall, even when seated. There is a narrow, frosted window above the sink. Staring at it one day, mind blank, Simon notices a chip missing, a clear indentation in the glass. He leans forward and places his eye to the spot. Across a narrow walkway, he sees an identical window, also frosted. In the grime, someone has written the word *despair* and then drawn a circle around it with a line cutting through. He keeps that picture in his mind when he hears the Witch's fingernails scratching late at night, when he feels the chill of her breath on his neck.

"Fear," she says, "is the first emotion. This is universal. Witness a baby lying on its back in the dark, cold and wet. No sense of place, no knowledge of time. It's terrified no one will save it. So it screams. And when it screams, Mommy comes. So it learns that screaming equals love. This goes on for weeks, months, years. The baby becomes a dictator, screaming for everything."

In those hours between dusk and dawn, she sits in her wicker chair and chain smokes. Her words move through him like sap, the air thick with choking carcinogens. In his dreams he is haunted by explosions of creaking wicker. He pictures her sitting in a chair weaved from human hair.

"Now, you know math. If A equals B and B equals C, then A equals C. Well, let's do the math. If being a baby means living in a state of constant fear, then doesn't it make sense that living in constant fear makes us babies? This state of constant agitation, this fear that the planet is dying, that dark forces are moving against it, this fear has made you powerless. And so you became a dictator— just like all those bleeding hearts bossing honest

God-fearing citizens around—give up your guns, wear a mask."

After a week of eating her soups meal after meal, he is forced to wear a diaper. The edges of his personhood are wavering, turning to liquid, as if he himself is becoming soup.

"Do you know what all your rules kill?" she says. "They kill magic. All those children who were scared of the dark invented a thing called *science* and a word called *truth*, but of course we both know the really important truths defy rational understanding. None of us can know the will of the Almighty or comprehend the mysteries of the supernatural. Scientists can call something an atom and another thing an electron, but that doesn't make it so."

He hears the sound of her cigarette dropping, of her grinding it out, then, just as quickly, lighting another.

"My friends," says Simon, the words blurred.

"Your friends have been corrected. Some of them permanently."

"What does that—"

"Death," she says, "is a permanent correction."

He rolls onto his side to look at her, but when he does, there is nobody there. Just a thin line of smoke wafting from the littered floor.

That night he dreams of Louise dancing in the

desert, so thin she looks like a rib cage with legs. Where are those ribs now? In a soup?

Scientists call our current geological era the *Anthropocene*, meaning the Age of Man. But others have suggested we call it the *Eremocene*, meaning the Age of Loneliness.

In the devil's hour, he stirs. His body is spread across the mattress like a puddle. The room is so dark he's not sure if he's awake or dreaming. His guts are roiling. His face is wet. *Why is his face wet?* Wait. Something is dripping on him. He tries to move, but his muscles are jelly. He hears a voice, low and raspy, chanting. Guttural consonants and glottal stops. A hissing brogue. His eyes adjust to the light. She is standing over him, naked, her thin, flat breasts dangling. There is a wooden bowl in her hands, carved and splintered. She dips her fingers, muttering. What's inside the bowl is more of a paste than a liquid. He feels it hitting his skin like mud, slug trails down his face. She looms over him, her legs a triangle, peaking in a thatch of matted gray hair. She squats down, and he sees her teeth, bared in a wild grimace. There are symbols and runes painted on her face in what may be shit.

The fear he feels is primordial.

The next morning, he is in the living room, watching dust motes shiver in a shaft of light. It has been days since he had a shower or a bath, and the smell of his own body makes his eyes water. He lifts his arm to wipe them but doesn't have the strength to raise the limb higher than parallel to his shoulder, so he turns his head and wipes his face on his sleeve. Through a gap in the curtains, he sees the house next door. It has a concrete walkway and two short stairs. The front door is blood red. As he watches, it opens and Rose emerges, a plastic rain bonnet on her head. She steps down one stair, then turns and locks the door from the outside, one lock, then a second, then a third. She heads up the walkway and out the gate, turning right and disappearing from sight.

Thirty seconds later he hears a key in the lock as she opens one dead bolt, then a second, then a third, and then she is inside, stomping rain from her shoes and muttering to herself in Filipino. He hears the crinkle of the rain bonnet as she slips it from her head and hangs it on a peg, and then she is in the room, smiling her forced smile and clucking.

"Coo-coo," she says. "Coo-coo. How are we this morning? Ready for a little soup?"

Sometime later—days? months?—he is in his wheelchair when the lights go out. Rose is with him, on her knees clipping his toenails. The clippings are collected in a jar along with his hair.

Why? What does she do with them? The bathroom goes dark. Rose curses under her breath, stands. Instead of leaving him alone, she rolls Simon into the kitchen and sets his brake. He has never been in the kitchen before. The back door has three locks on it that must be keyed from the inside. It's even colder in here, vents blowing arctic air onto his ankles. Rose crosses to the wall beside the fridge. There is a gray breaker box on it. She lifts the latch and swings open the cover.

They are in the final minutes before Simon's next shot. This is the morning routine. After breakfast, Rose changes him, grooms him, then gives him his next tranquilizer. Which means that at this moment, Simon is as close to a human being as he will be all day. He studies the kitchen: a four-burner gas stove in the corner near a dirty window (barred), low counters covered in cheap tile. Plywood cupboards, locked. Linoleum floor. He tries to memorize the layout. The drawers have locks too. He sees no knives, nothing he could use as a weapon.

A quote pops into his head. Words he read on a plaque that used to hang on the wall outside the yoga studio in Float. *Anxiety is not fear, being afraid of a definite object, but the uncanny feeling of being afraid of nothing at all.*

He realizes now that his anxiety was a luxury. A

high-priced item, out of reach to most, who have to settle for cheaper fears—fear of hunger, fear of hatred, fear of crime. Anxiety was an abstraction that consumed him when he was younger, because his whole life was abstract—free of challenges, free of debt, free from what most people call reality. What he had was unlimited options, unlimited choices. The paralysis of abundance. But on some level isn't that what being a teenager is all about? Staring into the chasm between where you've been and where you have to go. A future you yourself must define. An endless wasteland of choices he would someday have to make. A self he would have to define. But how? And what if every choice he made was wrong? This is what used to keep him up at night. How much simpler it is to be afraid right now. Afraid of the needle. Afraid of the Witch. Afraid of his father. Of the police. He is a boy in a wheelchair, trapped in an unfamiliar house, trying to memorize the details of a kitchen in hopes it will help him escape. His mind feels like a rusty wheel. *Think*, he tells himself. But then the lights come on and Rose is there, unlocking his wheels and rolling him back into the empty living room. And then the needle goes in and the ocean of forgetting pulls him down. But just before he drowns, he sees it—the missing piece.

And he knows how he will escape.

O

"We are at the center of the cosmos."

Simon stirs. He is lying on his mattress. His mouth tastes like old pennies.

"The sun is barely three dozen miles wide. The world is a plate, not a globe; otherwise you would see the curvature of the Earth every time you rode an airplane. Any fool can see the truth. Did you know that beyond the antarctic ice wall lies thousands of miles of land? Science wants you to think these are lies, but science is just an excuse for people to be stupid."

Simon tries to rub the metal taste from his mouth. "I wanna talk to my father," he slurs.

"Your father has said everything he's going to say to you," says the Witch. "Until you repent."

She lights a cigarette. Her wrists are humming-bird thin. "If you want to find a changeling," she says, "sprinkle eggshells around a lit fireplace. Baking bread inside eggshells can also draw them out. The changeling finds that amusing and will reveal their true selves."

"Who *are* you?" Simon says.

She laughs, a dry sound, like a match strike, exhales a plume of smoke, blue in the moon-light. "People can turn into trolls, or trolls can shape-shift. They take various forms, such as a hollowed-out tree or a ball of yarn. They hunger for the taste of Christian blood."

"What about witches?"

"A witch is what we call a woman who is past her child-bearing years. *What is the point of these women?* people wonder. *Why is their visage, wrinkled and sagging, so offensive?*"

"That's—I can't handle you right now. Comedy routines. You said *magic* before, and the things you do to me at night when you think I'm asleep. The spells you use."

"Once you free your mind of the clutter of non-belief, you start to see what's hidden. Children know this. They build fairy houses. They know what thunder really is. Superstition is just a dirty word for reality we don't understand. When the answer is so simple. You have to believe to make it real."

"Like Santa Claus?"

"You're mocking me because you've already grown up. A big boy with tired eyes. But if you're so smart, why do you rely on pharmaceuticals to flatten the world? Because you're afraid of what's out there."

"You mean like the shit you're putting in my arm?"

Another match strike.

"Oh my dear, you think I'm giving you

some prescription that ends in *ine?* What goes into your arm is a potion first recorded in the Malleus Maleficarum, filled with certain herbs and roots and, of course, a set of intentions."

"Is that what you make in the kitchen?"

"I make soup in the kitchen. What goes into your arm was brewed in the Mojave Desert on a moonless night following the sacrifice of a dozen songbirds and an orgy."

"An—"

"Don't look so offended. When you're my age, all that's left is eating and fucking."

Simon starts to cry. "I wanna go home," he says.

"Good," she says. "That means you're ready."

He wipes his runny nose. "For what?"

"For the restoration."

O

Rose puts warm water in the tub. She helps Simon peel off his hospital scrubs. The smell his body makes forces soup up from between his teeth.

"That's okay, dear," says Rose as he retches. "You express yourself."

She helps him into the bath, uses a yellow washcloth to scrub his skin. He feels like a newborn, helpless, starved for contact, but the soap burns, and the cloth is abrasive. Rose hums "*Nearer*, *My God to Thee*."

"You have to listen to the missus," she whispers. "The missus will fix you right up."

She shampoos his hair. The water turns gray.

"I have a sister in Florida. She marry a man, a not-good man. Criminal man. I tell her this a not-good man, but she love him."

Rose lathers his arms and chest. "You can't save people from themselves. Only God can do that."

She scrubs his stomach, lifts his penis, washes around it.

He grabs her wrist. "Please," he says, "just open the door and let me go. I won't tell."

She pulls her wrist free, smiles without teeth. "Now, now, don't be a silly bird. Let Auntie Rose finish her work. It's almost time for your medicine."

"She's crazy," Simon hisses.

Rose stands up, grabs a thin white towel. "Cluck, cluck," she says. "Don't go name calling. None of us is any better than the other. Jesus say that."

She helps him up out of the bath, dries him off. He stands shakily, his leg muscles quivering. *How much weight has he lost?* Rose lifts a sealed plastic sleeve from the top of the toilet. Inside is a new set of scrubs. She tears the bag, stretching the plastic wide. The pants are scratchy when she puts them on him, stiff. She pulls the shirt over his head, then tosses his hair with her hand.

"As handsome as the president," she says.

She rolls the wheelchair over, but Simon kicks it away.

"I can walk," he says, pushing past her out of the bathroom. He wobbles, almost falls, then catches himself on the doorjamb. He shuffles through the living room toward the kitchen.

"Not that way, sweetie," says Rose.

"I want some water," Simon mumbles, not slowing.

She tries to get in front of him, but the wheelchair gets caught on the card table. He makes it to the kitchen door, fumbles it open.

The Witch is sitting inside, drinking a cup of tea. Simon stops.

"I wanted a glass of water," Simon tells her, feeling his courage drain away. The Witch doesn't answer, just sips her tea. Simon takes a tentative step into the room. The floor creaks. He takes another. There is a cupboard next to the sink, where a glass might live. Simon rattles the handle. Locked.

"I need a glass," he says.

The Witch sips her tea. Rose appears in the doorway.

"I'm sorry, missus. I bathe the boy."

Simon rattles the handle. "I want a glass of water," he demands.

Behind him, he can feel Rose's hesitation. She needs a command from her mistress, but the Witch says nothing. Rose is forced to decide for herself.

"Go stand there," she tells Simon, nodding to the stove. He does, putting his body in the gap between the range and the barred window. Rose takes out her keys, shielding them from Simon's eyes. She looks through them, finds the cupboard key.

Without moving his head, Simon shifts his eyes to the Witch. Her teacup is up at her lips. She is staring at him. Simon looks away, his heart pounding. He feels frozen, rooted in place. She is an iceberg, a white lie, her darkest power hidden below the surface. He shivers.

Then Rose drops her keys. The sound is explosive in the small room. The Witch turns her head. At that moment, Simon does what he came here to do. He lifts his right foot and kicks backward. His heel connects with the rubber coupling, where the gas pipe from the wall connects to the stove. This is what Simon saw without seeing when he sat in his wheelchair, the exposed joint, wrapped in duct tape.

Rose drops her keys. The Witch turns her head. Simon lifts his foot and kicks the coupling, feels it give, then slowly lowers his foot. As far as he knows the kick was silent, but when he turns to look at the Witch, she is staring at him again. Did she see? He meets her eye, keeping his face calm. The drugs they're giving him help. Much of his mind is a thousand miles away. The Witch smiles, and in that smile is the squat of a naked sorceress conjuring all evil spirits. Then Rose has the cupboard open. She takes a plastic cup, fills it at the sink.

"Come on you," she says, coming over, taking his arm. Simon lets her lead him to the wheelchair. He sits, takes the cup, drinks.

"Happy now?" asks the Witch.

Simon lets his eyes pass over the coupling as he turns his head to meet her gaze.

"Yes, thank you."

He smiles.

O

The next shot knocks him out. He wakes in blackness. He has soiled himself through the diaper. Behind him he hears a scratching sound, slow, rhythmic. A *clawing*. Simon turns his head. The Witch is sitting in the wicker chair. She runs her fingernails along the wood.

scrrrtttchh
scrrrtttchh

A pack of cigarettes rests on the arm in front of her right hand. A cheap plastic lighter lies on top.

A year from now that lighter will combine with hot sediment off the coast of Hawaii to form a new kind of rock. A plastiglomerate. This is how your recycling enters the geological record.

The air in the room is so cold Simon can see his breath. He feels death all around him. The Witch scratches her fingernails against the wicker.

"Don't be afraid," she says.

Simon licks his chapped lips and sniffs the air. From science class he knows that methyl mercaptan is added to natural gas to give it a noticeable odor. Otherwise, how would you know if you had a gas leak? So Simon sniffs, digging down beneath the bile of soup, searching for that rotten-egg stink. Evidence that the pipe has busted and the house has filled with gas.

scrrrtttchh

scrrrtttchh

Simon crawls his hands across the bare mattress, reaching out in both directions, looking for the mattress's end. The Witch picks up her lighter, shakes loose a cigarette.

"Don't be afraid," she says again, putting the cigarette to her lips and lifting the lighter.

Simon's hands find the edges of the mattress. He grabs on tight.

"I'm not," he says.

As the Witch's thumb turns the metal wheel of the lighter, Simon throws his body to the left, rolling into the corner and pulling the mattress on top of him. The explosion is like a fist punching him and squeezing him at the same time. He is shoved hard into the wall, the mattress conforming to his body like a blanket. The heat wallops him, smothers his lungs. The sound is beyond sound, a physical roar without pitch. In that endless instant there are no thoughts, other than that the human body isn't designed to absorb all the sensations that are hitting him. Is this death?

And then he is released. He feels heat pressing down and throws the mattress off him. The room is smoky black, flames licking the ceiling. There is a jagged hole where the window used to be. At most ten seconds have passed since the gas that filled the house ignited. Simon scrambles onto his hands and knees, trying to stay under the flames. Then something looms up out of the smoke toward him. A shadowy figure, arm outstretched, hand seized into a terrible claw. It moves toward him and, instinctually, he rolls away. In his heart he knows it is the devil, come to pull him screaming into the molten below. The figure brushes his face and crashes to the floor.

It lies twitching, a black and red skeleton, joints on fire, skin charred stiff. Simon backs away, believing that any moment the charcoal Witch will scramble after him, teeth chattering. He can feel fresh air behind him, mixing with the smoke and flame, and he moves toward it, not wanting to take his eyes off what was once a woman. Her hair is gone. Her clothes have melted into her skin, her head a blackened skull, eyes staring at him from empty sockets. And then he is outside, having propelled himself backward through the gaping hole. Even then, as he stands shaking outside his prison walls, adrenaline races through his veins, and when he runs, he keeps looking back, convinced she is following.

He reaches the street, wild eyed, his feet bare, hospital scrubs singed. Behind him he hears a door open, turns. Rose stands on the top step of the neighboring house, framed by the red door.

"Diyos ko," she says, seeing him. And then a folding chair takes her down, swung from the blackness behind her. It catches Rose in the back of the head and drives her to the cement. One moment she is there, clutching her untied robe. The next she is facedown on the pavement, and Story Nadir is standing on the threshold, dressed in hospital scrubs of her own, holding a broken aluminum chair.

She tosses it aside, then turns and pukes into the bushes.

"Jesus," she says, straightening, "what's the deal with that fucking soup?"

Book 4

The Eremocene

On August 2, Tropical Storm Gilberto muscled its way out of the Gulf of Mexico and into California and Arizona. It was a sluggish beast hundreds of miles wide, driving hot pressurized air ahead of it. The storm hugged the coast as it moved north, forcing dry lightning strikes from San Diego to Marin, and as far east as New Mexico. Forecasters called it a *lightning siege*. Dry atmospheric conditions evaporated the rain before it hit the ground, generating more humidity in the upper atmosphere and more lightning. Wildfires sprang up in the San Bernardino National Forest and Mount San Jacinto State Park, the Angeles National Forest, and Malibu Canyon. By Wednesday San Luis Obispo was on fire, and lightning was setting blazes in Big Sur and Big Basin Redwoods State Park.

It hadn't rained in Northern or Southern California in five months. Within hours reports of fire tornadoes were coming in from residents fleeing towns up and down the coast. The days became choking and surreal. In Los Angeles and San Francisco, the sky turned orange as a thick blanket of smoke blocked blue light from view. On the West Coast, Earth was becoming Mars.

Meanwhile, arguments raged online about the patriotism of athletes in black armbands, outrage over anti-democratic statements made by politicians known for making anti-democratic statements. This is the lesson we had learned: when you don't want to face the consequences of your actions, you focus on the soap opera of public life, with its heroes and villains, its clear narratives. It is always easier to wrestle with our human drama than with the vastness of tectonic shifts on a planet almost four thousand miles in diameter, a planet more than four and a half billion years old, where dinosaurs ruled for one hundred and sixty-five million years, where another sixty-five million years passed before humanity was born, where time is measured in eras. The Cenozoic, the Mesozoic, the Paleozoic. Eras that make up eons. The Phanerozoic, the Proterozoic, the Archean, the Hadean.

Geological time is unconcerned with the life spans of animals, with history. Existence at a scale that defies comprehension, in which our own extinction is not just possible but inevitable.

But we are such short-lived creatures, all we know is now, *this* moment, *these* people—the hyperbolic dramas of our brief window.

And still the fires burned.

That was the week the soldiers began killing themselves. It started with thirteen new recruits at Fort Benning murdering themselves over three nights. On the fourth day six men at a forward operating base in Afghanistan huddled around a live grenade. At the Kelley Barracks in Stuttgart, soldiers awoke the next morning to find five paratroopers hanging from their own parachute ropes. We had given them weapons and taught them to fight the enemy, but it was becoming clear the enemy was us.

The Prophet

They put the Prophet in interview room two. He sits quietly, his hands cuffed to a chain that connects to a ring on the floor. This is in the El Paso offices of Homeland Security, a cement monster of a building, ringed by concrete barriers. His mouth is dry. It's been six hours since Taser wires hit him in the left shoulder and the neck. There is an angry bruise above his collar. His thoughts feel scattered. When the barbs penetrated his skin, the Taser triggered nineteen electric pulses in five seconds with an average current of two milliamps, leading to seizures and intense pain. It created an electric field inside his body that stimulated nerve cells called alpha motor neurons. These neurons then fired their own electrical impulses, which raced to his muscles and caused violent, sustained muscle contractions.

He sits now on a hard plastic chair. Somewhere

during his capture, the Prophet's glasses were lost. The room he sees now is a blur of white and gray. If he's afraid, he doesn't show it. In fact, sitting under the harsh fluorescents, he appears to be meditating, a bass hum rumbling low in his throat.

There are two basic settings available on most Tasers, *pulse mode* and *drive stun*. The first incapacitates. The second uses pain to secure compliance. Human beings invented this device, the way they have invented all weapons meant to incapacitate or kill—without a care in the world.

The door opens. A woman in a pantsuit enters. Behind her there is a man with a sidearm. They smell like smoke. The man closes the door behind them. The woman pulls out her chair and sits. The Prophet's eyes remain closed.

"I want to thank you," he says, "for electrocuting me. It was an extremely clarifying event."

The woman lays a file folder on the table, sits. "I meet a lot of people in my job, Paul. Can I call you Paul?"

"There's no Paul here," says the Prophet. "If you want to talk to that kid, you'll need a time machine."

The woman opens the folder. "Wilson, Wyoming. That's where you're from?"

"I spent some time there."

"That's near Yellowstone, right?"

The Prophet nods. When he was a young boy, he found a copy of a book at a thrift sale. *Handbook for Boys*, it was called, published by the Boy Scouts of America. It was a blue/green paperback with an image on the front of three young Scouts sitting around a campfire. Hovering over them was the apparition of an Indian chief, floating in wispy tendrils, as if created from campfire smoke. Was he their spirit guide or a ghost of America's past come to haunt them? The edition the Prophet bought for fifty cents was published in 1950. In it were lessons about many things: hiking and camping, wildlife and wood lore, but he saw it as a manual of citizenship. On the first page, printed in bold, was the Scout Law.

1. A Scout Is Trustworthy.

"Have you ever heard the word *hyperobject*?" he asks the agent.

"No."

"Picture an iceberg floating in the ocean. You see it ahead of you, bobbing on the surface, and you think you know the size of it, but its true mass below the waterline is beyond your comprehension. A hyperobject is something too huge to fully wrap your mind around. Climate change, for example."

"We're not here to talk about the Fahrenheit in Greenland, kid. We're here to talk about crimes against the state. About terrorism. Because that's what we're calling you and your friends. Terrorists."

Whatever effect she thought these words would have on the Prophet, she sees no sign of it on his face. Instead, he closes his eyes again.

Hummmmm.

"What is that sound you're making?" the woman asks him.

"There is a frequency in this building. Very low. I doubt you can hear it. Most people can't. I find when I match the sound, it opens my mind to possibilities."

The woman opens his folder, looks through it. "You didn't have it easy, did you?" she says. "Abusive home, in and out of foster care, and then there are the arrests."

"It's true," says the Prophet. "I had poor modeling."

She pages through his past. "Now, this is sad. It looks like your dad killed your mom."

2. A Scout Is Loyal.

The Prophet takes a deep breath, holds it.

"Paul's father killed his mother in the kitchen

with a shovel when Paul was six," he says. "Paul went to live with first his grandmother, then his uncle in Nebraska. It was there that God spoke to him for the first time."

"God as in the old man with a white beard?"

"God as in the burning bush, or in Paul's case, a tree stump."

The woman closes the file, looks the Prophet in the eye.

"How do you feel about your father, Paul?"

3. A Scout Is Helpful.

"God is my father," says the Prophet.

"You're a Christian?"

"I'm an originalist."

"What does that mean?"

"It means I understand God's teachings as He intended them, not as the church has interpreted them."

"Which you can do because God speaks to you directly."

"Through the hum."

"Through the hum, right?"

She makes a note.

"Can you tell me," asks the Prophet, "which kingdom are we in?"

"Which what?"

"Main Street, Wall Street?"

Hummmm.

"Paul," says the woman.

"That name doesn't apply to me anymore."

She snaps her fingers in his face. "Wake up, kid. You're in an obscene amount of trouble. You know that, right?"

But the Prophet keeps his eyes on the wall.

"It doesn't really matter, I guess," says the Prophet. "One kingdom or the other. We're almost at the equinox. No one will be able to pretend much longer."

"Pretend what?"

The Prophet opens his eyes. "Have you ever had whiplash, Nancy?"

The woman blinks. "How do you know my name?"

"God told me. See, whiplash isn't so much a physical injury as a form of PTSD."

Nancy rubs her brow. She's been up for close to thirty-six hours.

"How about you answer my questions," she says, "and, otherwise, shut the fuck up?"

Hummmm.

"Cars collide," says the Prophet, "and all the old trauma roars back. You see, all pain is emotional. I think about that sometimes when I travel through this world."

Nancy turns and looks at the agent in the corner. He crosses behind the Prophet, looms over him.

"Where is the judge's daughter, Paul?"

The Prophet thinks about this. "She was with us before my electrocution, but her role in the plan was her own."

"You kidnapped her. You and the guy who calls himself Felix."

4. A Scout Is Friendly.

The Prophet closes his eyes.

Hummmmm.

"Was it God's plan that you kill those deputies in Reeves County?"

"I didn't kill anyone."

"But you were there."

The Prophet thinks about that. "It's interesting you used the word *kidnap* before, as what is the Reeves County Detention Center if not a prison for hostages?"

"So this is political for you?"

"No. Politics don't interest us."

"Us."

"Yes."

"Who is us?"

5. A Scout Is Courteous.

"Your children."

"I don't have children."

"Sorry, I meant *all* children."

"You kidnapped a federal judge's daughter and killed four sheriff's deputies and your accomplices are *all of the children*. Just making sure I have that right."

"When God parted the Red Sea and led his people out of slavery, and then the seas closed on the Egyptians, drowning them, the headline wasn't *God kills slave owners*. It was *God saves Jews.*"

The woman taps the table impatiently. "Who are your literal accomplices? We know about Felix. He's in custody downstairs. And then there were the shooters. The girl was killed by private security forces, and the boy was wounded. But we know there were more. I want names. I want information. What was the plan if your mission failed? Where did they take Story?"

6. A Scout Is Kind.

"Our mission didn't fail," says the Prophet. "Everything is as it must be."

"So God wants you in federal lockup for the rest of your life, or possibly the electric chair?"

"There are no electric chairs anymore. Prisoners in Texas are executed by lethal injection."

The woman slams her hands on the desk. "Where is she?"

The Prophet closes his eyes, hums. When he was a boy, he lived outdoors. His grandfather had a ranch on the edge of a national preserve, and this is where his mother took him when he was four and they were running from his father. His grandfather raised goats. They would roam free during the day and sleep in pens so the wolves didn't get them. On winter nights, his grandfather would make a thermos of coffee and sit on the porch with his Remington and wait for the wolves to make their move. The Prophet, then just a boy named Paul, would sit with him. Even then he didn't sleep. The moon would rise and set as they spoke, often for hours, always on the lookout for night predators. Together they would stand over the steaming corpses of the dead, rifle shot still ringing in their ears. Paul would kneel and run his fingers through their fur.

"Why did he have to die?" he would ask, and his grandfather would spit into the dead grass.

"Him or you," he'd say. "Remember that."

7. A Scout Is Obedient.

"How did we come to be in your custody?" he asks.

"We got a call from the private security team. They handed you over."

"All four of us who were on the property."

"Yes."

"There were five of us. So instead of asking *me* what happened to my friends, maybe you should ask them why they're not telling you the truth."

Nancy blinks at him, processing. "Where is Story Burr-Nadir?"

"Those are the wrong questions," says the Prophet. "The right questions are why are your children killing themselves? How do the pieces fit?"

"Is she still alive?"

"For now."

"Meaning?"

"Meaning none of us live forever. Meaning we're fighting for our lives here, and that can go one of two ways."

"Is she being held against her will?"

The Prophet closes his eyes. He hums to himself for close to three minutes. Then he opens his eyes. "I believe she is."

"I want a list of your accomplices. Where is the judge's daughter, and who has her? Otherwise, you're looking at life in prison without the possibility of parole."

"I told you. I don't know where she is. Only that the Witch has her."

"The Witch?"

The Prophet sits up, straightens his shirt. "I'm sorry I can't look you in the eye," he says. "My glasses seem to have disappeared. In the early days of America, people believed demons were everywhere. The air was thick with them. You couldn't help but breathe them in and sneeze them out. Thus, *God bless you*."

"Paul, you've got, really, a narrow window here to make some kind of deal. To give me something I can bring to the prosecutor to keep him from eating you alive."

The Prophet thinks about that.

Nancy stands, nods to the guard.

"Ticktock," she says and goes to the door, bangs. The door opens.

As she walks out, the Prophet calls after her:

"We have a right to protect ourselves. It's our planet too."

O

One floor down, Felix too is chained to a table. But unlike the Prophet, he is jumping out of his skin. He keeps tugging at his restraints, trying to stand. He shouts at the wall. Somewhere out there his sister is still a prisoner. Somewhere out there his girlfriend could be dead or imprisoned.

Felix struggles to slip from his cuffs. He struggles because Felix is not his real name. Because when he was fifteen he shot two state troopers outside Blountstown, Florida, to keep his daddy safe, and he has been running ever since. He struggles because this room is his worst nightmare, and he has been picturing it for years.

Nancy enters with another agent, who takes up a post by the door. The smoke smell has dissipated some but is still noticeable.

"Where's my sister?" Felix asks, louder than he realizes.

Nancy sits without making eye contact. "Criminal trespass," she says. "Possession of illegal firearms. Attempted kidnapping, or was it murder?"

"Where is she? Does he still have her?"

"You broke into the estate of a high-net-worth individual. Your friends started a shootout with private security forces. The female, Nadine Bolger, is dead. The male is in the hospital. You yourself were arrested carrying an AR-15 that has been tied to the murder of sheriff's deputies at a detention facility in Reeves County."

"I didn't—listen to me," says Felix. "He has my sister. He raped her."

Nancy puts a piece of paper on the table. "We know your name isn't Felix Moor."

Felix looks at the paper. It's a death certificate

for a kid who died in August 2006. A kid whose social security number Samson DeWitt adopted so he could become a new man.

"We're running your prints now," Nancy tells him, "but you could save us all a lot of trouble by coming clean. I won't lie. A lot of people in this building would love to get five minutes alone with you for what you did to those men up north. Good men. Family men."

"That wasn't me."

"It was your gun."

Felix is silent, his mind racing. "Listen to me," he says, "he has her. Mobley. He kidnapped her and put a baby in her, and he's holding her against her will."

"Your sister."

"Yes. Bath—Katie. Her name is Katie. She worked for him in San Francisco. She's a painter, my sister. And Mobley said he would help her. E. L. Mobley. The billionaire. I know you know who I mean. My sister's his prisoner. That's why we were there. To rescue her."

But Nancy doesn't seem to care. "Give me your real name and I'll make a few calls."

Felix thinks about that. The things that would be triggered by his name.

"I don't care what happens to me," he says. "Do you understand? The only thing I care about is getting her out of there."

"What about Story? Do you care about her? Or was that just an act to lure her in?"

"No. Of course I love her."

"Then tell me where she is."

Felix shakes his head. "I don't know."

"But she was with you."

Felix keeps his mouth shut. If they're asking him about Story, it means she escaped.

"I want a lawyer," he says.

"You need a lawyer. But if we do that now, any hope of a plea goes out the window."

Felix sits back. "Could I get a glass of water?"

But Nancy just stares at him.

"Look," he says, "I'm gonna tell you something. Give you something. Something big. But first I wanna talk to my sister. You get her on the phone, and I'll tell you anything you want to know."

After the agents are gone, Felix tries to calm himself. He knows deep in his bones that he will spend the rest of his days in rooms this size or smaller. Rooms with bars. Rooms with thick plexiglass barriers. Rooms with beds *and* toilets. Cells. They are in some ways his birthright. A future gifted to him by a father so oppositional, so repulsed by authority that he raised his son to shoot on sight.

For Samson DeWitt, Planet Earth has shrunk down to four walls.

And they are closing in.

O

Randall Flagg wakes in an El Paso emergency room. He is handcuffed to a bed, tubes running out of his nose, IV line in his arm. The first word out of his mouth is "Fuck."

"Fuckin' what?" he mumbles, reaching for the tube in his nose, his hand stopped short by the cuffs. His brain feels muffled.

"Unh-unh," warns a voice to his right. Randall looks over.

There is a Texas state trooper sitting in a chair by the window, sports pages open in front of him, toothpick between his teeth.

"Be a good sport," he says. "Stay down."

Flagg stops struggling. There is something wrong with his left eye. All he sees through it is black. His chest feels tight. Looking down he sees bandages wrapped around him, stained yellow from an antibacterial wash. Then he realizes what's happened. He's been shot. Probably more than once. In his mind he is fourteen again, trapped in a supply closet at school, hearing the shots, barely breathing. He thinks of his brother, out there somewhere. So many gunshots. So many screams. And then blood trickling under the door.

But he is not fourteen. He is a twenty-year-old man. And his brother is dead.

"Why's the sky orange?" he asks, wondering if he's in a dream.

A nurse enters. She is black, heavyset.

"Careful now," she says. "Don't move around too much. You'll tear your stitches."

Flagg lies back. He can feel it now, like a vise on his torso. His left eye burns.

"What did they hit me with?"

She comes over, checks his vitals. "You got shot," she says.

"I know that. I'm saying large caliber, small caliber?"

"You lost half your liver. You were in surgery for nine hours. Does it matter?"

"What about the eye?"

"You had shards of rock in there. The surgeon cleaned them out, but you'll never see outta that eye again."

Flagg thinks about that. An eye patch, like a pirate.

"I'm hungry," he says.

"We're feeding you through your nose right now. Let your system get back on track."

"How about a beer?"

"Very funny."

She takes his temperature. Flagg turns his head, looks at the trooper.

"Hey, boss. Can I ask you something?"

"No."

"It's just—I gotta admit—I'm worried. I mean, when I make a run for it, how are you not having a heart attack chasing me down the hall?"

The trooper doesn't look up. "Not gonna chase ya," he says. "Just gonna shoot ya."

The nurse glances at him. "No shooting in my hospital."

Flagg stares at the ceiling. He remembers scaling the cliffside with Katniss. It was a beautiful night. So many stars. He was feeling good, because he'd pared his gear down to just twenty-five pounds, including the Remington. There were three clips for it Velcroed to his torso and five on his hip for the Glock. He knew from practice that he could reload both in less than ten seconds. Beside him Katniss looped the rope and pulled herself up, walking the wall like Batman. He'd known her for three years. She was running from something too, but she never said what. They'd both grown up on Marvel movies and Hollywood fables of self-empowerment, where rules and regulations never stopped you on your mission if your heart was pure. But what had they ever known in their lives except powerful people telling them they couldn't do things? Can't go there. Can't fix that. Can't punish your abuser. Can't change the laws. Can't better yourself.

A cool breeze rose from the east as they reached the plateau. This last bit was the tricky part. They'd have to free climb ten feet and pull themselves up and over. They unclipped silently. Katniss went first, dirt from the climb falling on Flagg, who had to duck his head to keep from swallowing it. When she was up, she flashed her Magnum over the edge. He reached up, grabbed a jut of shale. It broke cleanly, and for a second he thought he was dead, but then his other hand grabbed hold and he lunged into the cliff face, stopping himself from going down.

"Goddamn," he said quietly, his heart pounding out of his chest. Then he was up and over. He knew from the walkie that the Prophet and the kid were inside the gate, moving toward the house. From his low position he couldn't see any guards. He and Katniss were lying in the grass on the far side of the pool. Through his scope, Katniss scanned the dark windows of the house. There was a dim light on in the kitchen but no movement. Probably something they left on all night. It was getting on to be two thirty in the morning.

Flagg tapped Katniss's shoulder. Together they rose and low walked toward the house, rifles up. The trick was to avoid the motion sensors. They had identified a rocky outcropping above the port side of the house that would give them high-ground superiority, and they climbed to it now, moving through a terraced garden past cacti and succulents.

Katniss took a knee, and Flagg settled in behind a rock. He saw Felix, Simon, and the Prophet sprint across the driveway and flatten themselves against the house. From his walkie he hears:

"Here we go. We breach in three, two, one."

Flagg and Katniss saw them enter the house, saw the lights flare. And then the night lit up, muzzle flashes popping from the roof, as bullets sprayed the rocks around them. Flagg felt fire in his left eye. He heard Katniss grunt and go down. He ducked, feeling shale rain down on him as what seemed like hundreds of shots raked the rocks above him.

He put a hand on Katniss to drag her to him, but the top of her head was missing and she was bleeding from the chest. Before he could retreat, a ricochet pinged off the wall behind him and punched him in the side, and he fell forward into a stone hammer that knocked him senseless. Only then did it hit him. It was an ambush, and they were fucked.

Margot

The day everything changes starts like any other day. You wake and check the temperature. You pee and scroll through your emails, maybe scan the news. You have coffee and eggs or tea and cereal or milk and toast. But, of course, it's not just any other day. It is the seventh day of your Senate confirmation hearing for a seat on the Supreme Court.

At the witness table, Margot sits up straighter. She has been answering question after question with the precision of a laser-guided missile, always on the lookout for gaffes, terrified she will lose her patience and answer emotionally. Both the Drinkers and the Cooks are suspicious of her motives. Even though Margot did the tour, and Jay called ahead to preach her bona fides, the Drinkers find it confusing that a president from the Party of Lies would nominate a judge from the Party of Truth.

The Cooks, meanwhile, may believe in bipartisan compromise in spirit, but in practice they'd rather have a liberal. They worry she's a Trojan horse, sent to trick them. And yet neither side can find an actual objection to a jurist as qualified and dignified as Margot. And so they agitate, looking for flaws they can sink their teeth into, and what seemed like a slam dunk a month ago has settled into a quagmire of grievances.

Behind her, Remy keeps his eyes focused on the bench. He wears a crisp blue suit with a white pocket square and horn-rimmed glasses. Hadrian is at the hotel with the babysitter, though Hadrian hates it when they call her that, seeing as he is fourteen.

Every day at lunch and dinner Margot and Remy review the day's testimony, along with their lawyers and White House staff. After dinner, Margot washes down two Advil with a finger of whiskey and tells herself she still wants to be a justice on the Supreme Court. That the lifetime appointment is worth the struggle and sacrifice of this gladiatorial contest in which she's engaged. In the years since the God King left office, electoral politics have begun to look more like those of the early days of American legislature, where repre-sentatives would pull guns on one another on the House floor. Margot's instinct is to rise above the fray, to maintain an air of objectivity, to put herself above politics. And yet the definition of politics has changed dramatically since her youth, and now the act of rising above the daily contest for power is no longer considered a virtue. Those who hide their politics are treated with suspicion.

And so she takes her Advil and washes it down with whiskey, and Remy rubs her back and then her feet and tells her she's *almost there.*

One more day.

On Friday she wears her ivory suit with sensible shoes. It's been four weeks since she stood on her daughter's dead lawn in Austin, Texas, waiting for the FBI. She has fended off attacks on her records, endless interrogations into how she will vote on issues from abortion to presidential power. She has remained thoughtful and measured, but strong. It is 3:17 p.m. Lunch was an hour in which she pushed lettuce around on her plate and listened as the deputy communications director and her primary lawyer discussed procedural measures the Cooks could take to derail her nomination. They debated whether she had the votes from the Other Party of Truth to overcome the concerns of more progressive senators hoping for a champion of their own.

Margot tuned them out. She would be approved or she wouldn't. All she had to do was walk back into that hearing room and answer a few more questions, then endure the closing arguments from both sides. She would smile and thank them for the opportunity. She would tell them that her story is America's story. Once again she remembers her daughter standing before a packed assembly, her tiny fists clenched, her eyes closed.

And the rocket's red glare.
The bombs bursting in air.

Her eyes are on her plate, and she's confused to see something drip down onto the ceramic. It's a tear. Then a second. She reaches up and touches her eyes. They're wet. Only then does the feeling hit her, a crushing wave that takes her breath away. She is a mother whose daughter is missing and presumed dead. What the fuck is she doing sitting here eating a beet salad and talking strategy?

Remy looks over, sees her on the brink of collapse. "Babe?"

She stands quickly. "Excuse me."

She hurries to the bathroom, past the DC elite, keeping her back straight, fighting off a sob, and then she is in the bathroom, pushing her way into a stall, the door slapping the flimsy inner wall and bouncing shut. She weeps, her face pressed into her fists, her body jammed into a back corner.

The sobs she can't swallow burst from her lips, an animal sound, as if she is a ragged bagpipe played by invisible hands, unable to control the notes or their volume.

They were young once. All of them. Citizens of Brooklyn Heights wandering idly on a spring evening with laughter in the air. Is this the price of a dream? To lose everything that matters, to trade love for a fancier top line to your obituary? Her breathing is ragged, her legs literally trembling, and she worries she will fall into the toilet, so she puts both hands on the walls and lowers herself like a drunk to sit on the porcelain seat. She has never had a panic attack before. It feels like she's dying.

There is a quiet knock on the stall door. "Hon?"

It's Remy. He has risked the women's room to make sure she's okay.

"I'm fine," she says in a whisper.

"Can I—do you need anything?"

"Go away!" she screams.

For a stunned minute he is silent. Then he turns and leaves. Margot listens to his footfalls recede, to the swoosh of the swinging door as it shuts behind him. She tears toilet paper from the roll, wipes her eyes. The paper comes away stained with mascara. It's the great betrayer of female emotion, mascara, like that chemical they put in the public pool that turns blue where you pee. As her breathing stabilizes, she checks her watch. Five minutes. Five minutes to put her face back together, to get the red from her eyes and find her center.

The children of the world are killing themselves by the thousands, and her daughter is missing. How can any of them be here, acting like the world hasn't fallen off its axis, like they aren't all careening toward extinction?

She stands, drops the wad of stained paper into the bowl, flushes. She can do this. She can win this. For her mother, who worked two jobs. For her father, who was never too busy to help her with her homework. For her sister, who died of ovarian cancer when she was twenty-seven, for Remy, for Hadrian, for Story.

This is what winners do. They win.

She touches her hair, straightens her blouse, and then—taking control of her emotions, dropping them down a deep dark hole—she reaches for the door.

O

The gallery is packed when they reach the Senate hearing room, as if the town can sense that the end is near. All the seats are full, with standing room in the back. They have come to support her, to taunt her, or simply to catch the best drama in town. Margot keeps her eyes light as she enters, lets her lawyer lead the way to her seat. She pulls out her chair, aware of flashbulb pops, aware that her image is going out live. Smoothing her skirt, she becomes aware that Remy is still outside the doors of the hearing room. He is talking to a man in a black suit with an earwig. As they talk, Remy looks in Margot's direction, eyes wide. But Margot doesn't have time to process the look, because the Justice Committee chairman has entered. She stands respectfully as he takes his seat, bangs the gavel.

Behind him, as the inner doors are being closed, another senator enters, Kurt LaRue, junior senator from Idaho. He is wearing a camel hair overcoat on top of his blue suit, despite the heat.

The chairman bangs his gavel, calling the session to order. "Okay, okay," he says, "settle down."

Margot sits. There is something about the scene that sets her teeth on edge, a feeling of wrongness, but before she can unpack it, Remy is at her elbow, whispering in her ear.

"They found him," he says.

"Not now," Margot says, before she can process the words, aware that she is on camera, that the chairman is thanking her for her patience and professionalism throughout this long process. But Remy refuses to take his seat.

"Felix," he says. "The boyfriend. They found Story's boyfriend in Marfa. Arrested him. He's been arrested."

Margot turns. "Where?" she hisses.

"West Texas," he says. "Something about criminal trespass and attempted kidnapping."

"What?"

"Judge Nadir?" says the chairman pointedly, leaning into his microphone.

"Just a minute, sir," says Margot, "please. It's about my daughter."

A wave of intrigue courses through the room, murmuring voices. The chairman bangs his gavel.

"Order," he says. "Judge, do you need a recess?"

Margot looks over at the dais. The chairman is in his seat, surrounded by the other senators on the committee. Their aides sit behind them. Officers from the Capitol Police guard the edges of the dais, wary of protesters.

Senator LaRue is standing behind the chairman. He has a narrow chin and a weak comb-over, and he is sweating in his overcoat.

He mumbles something Margot doesn't hear. Then repeats it louder.

"Mr. Chairman," he says.

The chairman turns, confused. Why is the junior

senator from Idaho standing behind him in a camel hair coat, blinking sweat from his eyes. "What?" the chairman says, the sound of it lost to his microphone.

"I said I have a statement to make," says LaRue loudly, pulling himself to his full height and facing the cameras.

The chairman scowls, turns his back on the junior senator. "Closing statements will be done in order of seniority," the chairman tells him. "Sit down."

Remy squeezes Margot's arm. "Did you hear me?" he says. "The FBI has Margot's boyfriend in custody in El Paso."

Margot's lawyer leans over, the corners of his mouth tight. "Sit down," he hisses.

"No!" comes a voice from the front, and everything stops. Startled, Margot turns to see that Senator LaRue has climbed up onto the dais. His arms are outstretched. He appears to be holding something in his right hand. Is it a pen?

"Enough," he shouts, as the cameras turn. "We are the storm. Look at our majesty and tremble."

He opens his coat with his left hand. Underneath it is some kind of lumpy black vest.

Margot stands without thinking. Behind her there is a scream. She is aware of the Capitol Police moving toward the dais, aware of the other senators stumbling to their feet, confused, only some of them realizing what is happening. That the junior senator from Idaho has used his lunch break to turn himself into a human bomb.

Margot thinks of her son, safe at the hotel, of her daughter, alive or dead. She has time only to grab her husband's hand, to say a one-word prayer, and then—

"Long live the God King," yells Senator LaRue, and everything goes white.

Boogaloo

The Prophet is asleep in his chair when the door bursts open and Homeland Security Nancy comes in with three other agents. They unchain him and hustle him from the room at a dead run, suspending him at the elbows. In the elevator, riding down, the Prophet yawns. He'd been having the most wonderful dream about utopia. Mountain streams and bison, spring snow and summer thaws. Nothing but children as far as the eye could see. They would build houses and grow their own crops. The dream is so vivid, he wakes up crying. But that's tomorrow's promise. He must live in the now, for this is the most dangerous moment of all, what happens in the next twenty-four hours. If Simon is free. If he has found the others. If they are moving north. After all, God can show us the path, but he can't walk it for us.

8. A Scout Is Cheerful

"Are you taking us to Washington DC?" he asks.

"Quiet," says one of the agents.

The elevator descends. The Prophet hums low in his throat. He has the resting heart rate of a man who knows what's going to happen next.

"I told you it was close," he says.

Nancy snaps her head around to look at him. "What did you say?"

"The equinox. We're on the other side of it now. The walls are falling. Your worlds are colliding. This phony civil war you've forced upon yourselves."

They rush him through an underground parking garage and into the back of an unmarked van. Felix is already inside. Two armed agents climb in with the Prophet, and the door slams shut. And then they are peeling out, racing up a steep ramp, scratching pavement as the van pulls out onto the street.

"What's happening?" Felix asks.

"Panic," says the Prophet.

"What do you mean, panic?"

"Do you know what a nervous breakdown is?"

9. A Scout Is Thrifty

"When an animal is unable to flee or fight, it freezes," says the Prophet. "While it's frozen, all the brain chemicals and hormones associated with flight or self-defense kick in—adrenaline, epinephrine. If the animal survives—and we see this in nature—the mouse or rabbit or bird will shake, often for hours. In this way it discharges those toxins from its body."

Felix looks at him. "You can never just answer a question, can you?"

The Prophet thinks about that. "I am answering the question," he says. "People, we freeze too in the face of trauma. But as children we're taught that growing up means being strong. Shaking and trembling are seen as a sign of weakness. So when we freeze in the face of trauma and survive, we bury those toxins deep inside. We act like everything's normal. But everything's not normal. A nervous breakdown is your brain—which has been sending you warnings for days or weeks or years—it's your brain's way of getting your attention. *Ignore this*."

The van turns a corner fast, tires squealing. Felix is thrown into one of the agents, who shoves him away roughly.

10. A Scout Is Brave

"What's happening now," says the Prophet, "is that this land we call America is having a nervous breakdown. Hold on."

The van goes around another turn. Felix slams into the wall.

"I said *hold on*," says the Prophet.

"Where are they taking us?"

"There's been an event in DC. They think we're part of it."

"What kind of event?"

"I don't know. God has told me only that the nervous breakdown has begun. And that Story's mother is dead."

"What?"

But before the Prophet can answer, the van slows, stops. They are blind inside, but outside, Felix can hear words exchanged. Then the van is moving again.

11. A Scout Is Clean

The agent who shoved him leans over to the other agent. "Are we going directly to the plane?" he asks quietly.

The other agent nods. Felix's heart is racing, but the Prophet is calm.

"Prepare yourself," he says.

The van roars forward for sixty seconds, then

slams on its brakes. Almost before it's stopped, the back doors open. Two agents are there with rifles. The Prophet stands, almost in anticipation, and then he and Felix are shoved out the door and onto the tarmac of the Fort Bliss Army Base.

Overhead, the sky is orange.

They are behind the wing of a small jet. The sun is setting. Agent Nancy walks to the plane, confers with the pilot. The other agents hold Felix and the Prophet in place behind the van. The Prophet is watching the horizon. Ash falls on his face. Standing close to him, Felix can hear that he's humming low in his throat. He is stunned by the ochre of the air.

"Why is the sky orange?" he asks, but no one answers.

Could this be the apocalypse?

He has no idea that California, Arizona, and New Mexico are burning. No idea that paramilitary groups have moved on thirty-nine state houses.

He thinks of his sister. How close they were to saving her. *Unless.* Unless she was already gone. *Of course.* It was an ambush. Somehow Mobley and Bathsheba got out. Somehow even though they were watching.

A sound reaches them then. The roar of heavy trucks accelerating and then a crash, followed by gunfire. The agents flinch, ducking instinctually, heads turning. Two panel trucks have broken through the front gate. Soldiers at the gate fire at them, but the back doors of the trucks roll up. There's some kind of heavy machine gun mounted inside. The trucks return fire.

The agents scramble. They shove Felix and the Prophet back into the van, slam the doors. With the engine off, it's dark inside. Felix lies on the floor, facedown, hands cuffed behind his back. The Prophet lies on top of him. There is a feeling in Felix's heart, a profound sense of disorientation, as if the world as he knows it has changed into something unrecognizable. Something foreign. Something insane.

This is it. The day the threads are pulled, and the garment falls apart.

12. A Scout Is Reverent

Gunfire then, close by. It booms through the van as the agents shoot back. And then return fire, a series of metal punches as bullets rip through the van above them.

pop pop pop pop

Felix tries to duck, but he's already on the floor. Above him the Prophet continues to hum. Felix hears the sound of the plane's engines cycling up. Either Agent Nancy is trying to make a break for it, or the pilots are moving the plane out of danger. More bullets hit the van.

pop pop pop pop

Felix hears a grunt from outside and what sounds like a body bounce off the paneling. The return gunfire stops. Above him, the Prophet stops humming.

"It's up to you," he says directly into Felix's ear. "You have to save us now."

Book 5

The Unconformity

Boogaloo II

Randall Flagg wakes to the sound of screams. It's daytime, but the hospital blinds are drawn. The door to the hall is open and Flagg sees an orderly rush by, pushing a gurney. For a moment he wonders if the scream was real or in a dream, but then he hears it again. A wail of anguish. And then a gunshot. *Boom.* Flagg looks for the state trooper, but the trooper is gone, his sports page scattered across the floor.

He knows without knowing that the switch has flipped. The Big Igloo is finally here. The hospital is under siege, the whole state maybe, even the country.

Flagg wastes no time on shock. He has been in this situation before and understands on a fundamental level that unthinkable things happen every day. He struggles to sit up. There is pain in his side, but it's manageable. He is blind in one eye, but that too is manageable. His right hand is cuffed to the plastic rail of the bed. There is an IV line in that arm, rubber tubing running to a saline bag on a stand. EKG monitors dot his chest and belly.

Boom, another shot, getting closer. To Flagg it sounds like the low roar of a shotgun. Because there is no ratchet between shots, he thinks, it must be a high-capacity tactical shotgun. He pulls the IV needle from his arm, but he doesn't discard it. Instead, he tugs hard, tipping the IV stand onto the bed. For ten seconds he considers trying to use the IV needle to pick the lock on the handcuff, but a one-pin lockpick takes time, and from the sound of the shot he has none.

He throws the covers off the bed, examines the rail of the bed, looking for a weak point. It's solid state, maybe four feet wide and two feet tall, made of thick plastic without visible joints. But because it can be raised and lowered it must have a joint somewhere, a weak connection. He gets to his knees, hospital gown open in the back, and lifts the metal IV stand off the floor with his left hand, short sleeved by the handcuff on his right wrist.

Boom.

Adrenaline races through his veins and he thinks: *I am Randall Flagg, the Walking Dude, the Ageless Stranger, who can call beast and fowl alike to my defense, who haunts the dreams of mortal men. Randall Flagg, the Man in Black, Old Creeping Judas, the Grinning Man. Only an atom bomb can kill me.*

He rears up and smashes the IV stand into the plastic arm, once, twice, three times, feeling the cuff bite into his right wrist, feeling his stitches pull in protest. The industrial plastic is tough, but Randall Flagg is a being of pure will. He hits it one more time and it snaps at the base but doesn't fall.

Boom.

Randall drops the IV stand, lies on his back, right arm extended awkwardly, and kicks the wobbly plastic rail, once, twice, until he feels a snap and the weight of the detached rail falls, threatening to snap his cuffed arm at the elbow.

Boom.

He scrambles to his knees, feeling the shooter coming, and has time only to grab the solid-state side rail—which looks like a large plastic tray with a handle—and hold it to his chest, and then he is spinning toward the door as the shooter appears, backlit by the fluorescents, his shotgun smoking from the barrels.

He is a clown in white face paint, tactical vest on over a Hawaiian shirt. Seeing Flagg, he fires. The shot hits the thick plastic tray at Flagg's chest and blows him backward out of bed. He hits the wall, goes down hard, out of sight.

The clown comes into the room, pulling the empty clip from his weapon and sliding in another. He moves quietly around the foot of the bed warily, barrel at low ready. But when he reaches the other side, Flagg is gone. The clown has time for a moment's confusion, and then Flagg rises from the foot of the bed. He has wrapped the IV tubing around his left fist, needle sticking out between his middle and ring finger, and as the clown turns to face him, Flagg punches the needle into his eye. The clown staggers back, blood spurting. Flagg swings the heavy bedrail mace chained to his wrist, cracking the clown in the head so hard, the bedrail (damaged by the shotgun blast) shatters. The clown goes down hard. Old Creeping Judas is free.

He lifts the shotgun from the floor, feeling the AC on his naked butt and legs, and something else, a warm trickle running down his right side onto his leg. He glances down. His stitches are torn, but not too badly, blood soaking into his hospital gown. He takes it off, stands naked in the venetian light from the blinds, shotgun in hands. If he feels self-conscious or vulnerable in this state, he doesn't show it.

His eyes go to the clown's Doc Martens.

The man who emerges from that hospital room

three minutes later is like an apparition, naked except for heavy boots and a tactical vest, side wound weeping like Jesus on the cross. His black hair, shorn at the temples, stands straight up, and there is blood on his face, like war paint. He moves quickly, weapon up, headed for the stairs.

Samson

There are moments in history that defy comprehension. Moments where the world as you know it ends and is replaced by something unrecognizable. Moments where the human mind tries and fails to orient itself. This failure can last for seconds or years. When the Crow Indians were forced from their nomadic existence onto settlements by white generals, they lacked not only a way to orient themselves to their new reality, but the concepts with which to understand who they were now or what the world had become. They literally had no idea what was happening.

This is how Felix feels when the back doors of the van open and the insurgents surround them. Everywhere he looks he sees chaos. The airfield is overrun with revolutionary cosplay warriors. Seditionist frontiersmen, confederate soldiers, and human yetis in tactical ghillie suits. Grown men wander the tarmac wearing animal pelts and flak jackets, wielding primitive blades. In the distance, Felix spots an Uncle Sam dressed in red, white, and blue, standing next to six cowboys with spurs and ten-gallon hats. They take turns posing for selfies with mulleted Aryans in pin-striped uniforms, carrying baseball bats.

Black smoke fills the air, flames from burning vehicles.

A man in an American eagle mask walks past carrying a flamethrower. He's dressed in a red and blue blazer covered with white stars. This is sedition as live-action role-play, a fictionalized version of real events supplanting the events themselves. A cartoon race war, or a *choose your own adventure* game, in which the first step is to design your avatar.

Some patriots didn't get the memo and have dressed for war in basic flannel with red baseball caps or slumped hoodies with neck gators. Others wear homemade costumes that look like they were jerry-rigged at the last minute: ski goggles, bike helmets, and hockey pads, masked men wielding axes with motorcycle gloves. But for each of these there are ten Travis Bickles with black mohawks, camouflage body armor, and grenade launchers, or five *founding fathers* in white wigs and capes, tricorn hats tucked under their arms, firing replica flintlocks. A group of luchadors in thick spandex and leather face masks chant loudly while rocking an army truck back and forth, trying to tip it over. Nearby a clot of Templar knights with metal helmets and broadswords harass a group of military prisoners, men in army uniform forced to kneel with their heads bowed, as the knights take turns anointing them with their swords.

There is blood in the gutters, mixed with the vomit of weekend warriors sickened by their first taste of killing. Dead soldiers lie sprawled on the concrete, limbs folded at unnatural angles, their lifeless faces pointed toward the sky. A Viking prince with a gaping chest wound lies in the rut where the front gate rolls closed, the fence nudging him over and over like a dog that's lost its master. All the while, clouds of Mace and bear spray waft on the wind overhead, until even the strongest man is weeping.

And the beards. So many beards. Chin straps and goatees, Vandykes and Grizzly Adamses, braided beards, ZZ Top beards, beards bleeding out from behind grinning skull balaclavas, neck-bearded warriors with bowl haircuts in homage to a famous spree killer, hirsute, heavyset men straining the confines of T-shirts that read FREE KYLE or VISIT DACHAU! A group of shirtless beards stand by a burning helicopter, modeling CWB tattoos, tattoos so fresh they still bleed.

Over by the barracks a group of "young Republicans," torture prisoners and giggle—clean-shaven, twentysomething white men in suits and ties, who sprint across the tarmac and deliver flying karate kicks to a group of soldiers that have been tied to the perimeter fence with their hands behind them. "USA," they chant, pounding their pocket squares.

Most seem shocked by the speed of their conquest, the way the army base just folded, but of course they had help from the inside, corporals, privates, and captains who knew the hand signs and opened the gates. You see them now, throwing fascist salutes and shedding their old allegiances. They pass out alcohol and smoke electronic cigarettes. Black and brown soldiers have been rounded up and assaulted, first verbally, then with fists and flagpoles. Asian soldiers are forced to strip naked and walk on their knees, begging for forgiveness for *the Chinese flu*.

The battle is over.

The torture has only just begun.

Everywhere Felix looks the symbology is dense and varied—Gaelic runes, tattoos of the Viking tree of life, Pepe the frog T-shirts, the obligatory confederate flags and swastikas, mixed with the three interlocked triangles of the valknut, the number *14*, sometimes written next to the number *88*, the arrow cross and the Aryan fist, the words *blood and honor*, not to be confused with the blood drop cross, fasces symbol interspersed with the black and red *H8*, the Identitarian lambda and the imperial German flag, the Jera rune and the wide-set League of the South X, the life rune and the moon man, the noose and the not-equal sign, the Othala rune and the sonnenrad wheel, ROA and RAHOWA, SS bolts and St. Michael's Cross, the Triskele and the Tyr rune, the Wofsangel, WPWW, and one shirtless dude with a warped belly tattoo of Adolf Hitler, the words *Jew Mad, Bro?* written underneath.

The women tend toward Statues of Liberty and Black Widow from the Avengers. They are no less cruel, taunting their terrified prisoners, questioning their manhood, and Macing their weeping eyes. The men who hold Felix and the Prophet are a mixed bag. A couple of boogaloo bois in Hawaiian shirts, two full-on clowns, and three shirtless bald teenagers, their skin chalk white with ashen eyes.

"We took city hall just now," says a militia Batman sauntering past with a SAW M249 light machine gun pitched over his shoulder, "and I hear in Austin they stormed the Capitol *from the inside.*

The fucking legislators took it themselves, shooting state troopers in the back. This is national, bro."

A man with a patch that read ZOMBIE OUTBREAK RESPONSE TEAM walks down a line of prisoners, spraying them with a fire extinguisher, staining them white, perhaps to make the captives seem less human.

The boogaloo boi in front of Felix spits on the ground, studying his two skinny, handcuffed captives.

"What's this?" he says, confused by the harmless-looking boys trapped in the van.

"More Feds," says a chalk-white teen.

Their guns come up, ready to execute Felix and the Prophet, but then—

"How come their hands are cuffed?" asks a bearded clown.

"We're prisoners," says Felix, struggling to sit up from under the Prophet. "Not with them. We're not with them."

The insurgents stare at their captives, then the tallest lowers his rifle.

"Welcome to the revolution, LOL," he says.

They pull Felix and the Prophet from the back of the van, get them on their feet. Federal bodies lie prone on the runway.

"Prisoners for what?" asks a heavyset clown with a mop of frizzy hair.

"We're on a mission from God," says the Prophet.

"Cool. But crime-wise, what did you do?"

"Nothing," says Felix. "We're innocent."

The revolutionaries laugh. In their eyes no one is innocent anymore. The tall clown lights a cigarette.

"Which side are you on?"

"Which side?" says Felix.

"We have no side," says the Prophet, "in your war."

The tall clown puts his cigarette between his lips, lifts his rifle.

"Wrong answer."

Over by the motor pool, gunshots ring out. The seditionists have started executing prisoners. War whoops can be heard, along with the ringing bicycle bells of the BMX Avengers. What unites this diaspora of grievance warriors? They are primarily white, but not homogeneous. They have come from near and far, running the gambit from teenagers to the elderly. Seventy percent are male, thirty percent female. Are they poor, downtrodden? Some, but among the cosplay soldiers are doctors and teachers, lawyers and police officers, men with 401(k)s and investment portfolios, soccer moms and pharmacists. They are anti-government or pro-authoritarian, or both. Some have high school diplomas. Others advanced degrees.

They carry flags—the green flag of *Kekistan* and the *VDARE*, thin blue line flags and the long-defunct flag of South Vietnam, the Gadsden flag and the flag of the South Carolina Militia, the AF Flag and the *Dues Vult*—or *God's Will* Flag—and everywhere you look is Q.

RELEASE THE KRAKEN, reads one banner, but whether they are the Kraken, or the Kraken is still coming, is hard to parse.

Those that aren't fundamentalist Christians are pagans, a chaotic mix of puritans and hedonists. It is a strange alliance of what once would have been considered fringe thinkers from all walks of life. But they share one essential ideal. All believe that something has been stolen from them, that they are outcasts from the respected majority. All believe that they have suffered a lifetime of hatred at the hands of a powerful elite. They are victims of a vast conspiracy.

More than anything they believe they are acting in self-defense, that if they don't strike now they will be wiped from the face of the Earth tomorrow by military forces of the global pogrom.

Stand your ground.

It is the castle doctrine writ large, the conceit, recognized in twenty-five states and growing, that Americans have a legal right to use deadly force if they feel threatened. Those who view themselves as imminent victims can strike first without legal consequence. And so today blood has been shed, blood that is still warm—unarmed men and women beaten to death in their beds, zip-tied and shot before they can free themselves and finish what these revolutionaries believe others have started.

If you don't fight like hell, you're not going to have a country anymore.

Don't let your eyes fool you, in other words. The civil warriors who took this base are not the aggressor here. They are besieged patriots, defending their country against tyranny.

Can't you see?

Nothing is what it seems.

The tall clown raises his Luger.

"Wait," says Felix. "We're sovereign citizens. Born without documents to right-minded people. Free men."

"Anti-government?"

"Why do you think we're in cuffs?"

The tall clown swings his rifle over to the Prophet.

"What about you?"

The Prophet squints into the last rays of the sunset, the sky scorched and bloody.

"Are you familiar," he says, "with the painting *Saturn Devouring His Son* by Francisco Goya? You've seen it probably. If not in real life, then in a dream. In the painting Saturn, the father, is a giant.

His eyes are wild as he holds his boy's limp, naked body aloft. There's blood on his mouth, the child's torso at his lips. He's already eaten his son's head and his right arm. What he holds in his hand now is a corpse."

Felix puts his hand on the Prophet's arm—*Jesus, stop talking*—but the Prophet continues.

"We're the next children in line, waiting to be devoured."

The tall clown looks at Felix. "So he's the crazy one?"

Felix can barely feel his hands anymore, the cuffs are biting so deep. "Can you get these cuffs off, brother?" he says. "They're killing me."

The tall clown studies him, then nods to the heavyset clown, who goes over to the dead agents, searching their pockets. When he finds the key, he holds it up, as if saying, *Where's my prize?* Then he comes over and sets Felix and the Prophet loose. Felix rubs his bruised wrists, shakes his hands, trying to get the feeling back.

"What's your name, kid?" says the tall clown.

Felix thinks about that. "Samson," he says, "Samson DeWitt."

"No shit?" says an older founding father in the background, who wears his gray hair in pigtail braids like Willie Nelson. He comes forward.

"I did time with Avon DeWitt a few years back. Any relation?"

Felix, now Samson once more, nods. "He's my father."

Willie Nelson turns to the tall clown. "His dad's good people," he says, "solid."

The tall clown takes a drag on his cigarette, looks at the Prophet. "What about *your* dad? Is he good people?"

"My father killed my mother in the kitchen with a shovel," says the Prophet, "and then shot himself in the head."

The tall clown smiles. "Epic," he says.

Felix squints into the falling darkness. "Who are you guys?"

"We are War Boys," shouts the oldest ash-white teen.

"War Boys!" shout the others.

Samson looks at the Prophet. He has heard that shout somewhere before. In the streets? On the news? Or wait, could it be from a movie? It is. It's Mad Max. It's the post-apocalypse. Aqua cola and the blood bag from the bullet farm.

WITNESS ME!

The War Boys take Felix and the Prophet to a low building, where a mix of soldiers and militia carry out the bodies of dead air force officers and lay them on the ground. Inside, they find six air force cadets hanging from the rafters, killed in the night by their own hand. This is what made the base so easy to take. The anarchy of self-sabotage, suicide as the body's way of turning on itself.

The tall clown puts Samson and the Prophet in an office and posts a guard. Samson paces, desperate to get out, but the Prophet finds a corner and sits. He puts his head to the wall, listening to the hum of deep motors, generators, air filtration systems, and other more industrial overtones of war.

"I wanted to join the Boy Scouts when I was little," he says. "I found this handbook at a thrift sale. *A Scout Is Trustworthy. A Scout Is Loyal.* I used to study the badges—*Tenderfoot, Eagle*— and the patches—*Webelos, Senior Patrol Leader, Bugler*—I'd mouth the words out loud at night under the covers, reading with an old metal flashlight. I wanted to be honorable. I wanted to be useful and self-sufficient. But there were no troops in my area. So I taught myself. Trail safety, the names of clouds. Then God spoke to me from a tree stump. I begged my parents to take me to church, but my father had been raised Catholic and he was having no part of it. Good thing, too. The church, the Boy Scouts."

He taps the drywall, looking for hollow sounds. Samson grabs the doorknob, rattles it, earning a throat-cutting gesture from the clown on duty.

"What does it say about a society," says the Prophet, "when it cedes its moral leadership to perverts and pedophiles?"

Samson balls his hands and presses them against his temples. "I can't listen to this right now," he says. "We have to get out of here."

"He will free us in the morning. So, sit. Stop worrying."

Samson looks at him. "Who's gonna free us?"

The Prophet stares at him. "What you have to understand," he says, "is that our captors believe they are right, that they are holy. They too believe they are on a mission from God."

Felix rubs his eyes. His adrenaline levels are finally dropping, and suddenly he feels like he could sleep for a thousand years.

"And all I'm saying," says Felix, "is what if you're both wrong?"

The Prophet leans his head back against the wall, closes his eyes. "Get some rest," he says. "Tomorrow will be very, very difficult."

He is still after that, breathing deeply, seeming to fall asleep immediately. Felix, born Samson, stands at the glass, watching the mayhem of victorious militias. They've erected a bonfire on the tarmac out of office furniture and gasoline, and they set it ablaze with flare guns fired from three sides. It goes up with a *whoosh* that sucks the oxygen from the air. Then the bacchanal begins, death metal played through loudspeakers, insurgents surging in spontaneous mosh pits.

Through it all the Prophet sleeps, lips parted, face relaxed, angelic.

On the tarmac, fistfights break out, then dissolve into drunken celebrations, bottles of vodka and whiskey and gin swallowed and spilled and finally smashed. The boogaloo is here, and it is glorious.

Free at last, they shout, throwing their palms to the sky. *Thank God Almighty, we're free at last.*

Kayfabe

In the hours after Senator LaRue martyred himself in the Senate, flags around the country were lowered to half-mast. Three hundred and forty-seven people had been killed by the junior senator from Idaho, including Judge Margot Nadir, her husband, and fourteen other US senators, including representatives from Maine, Nebraska, and Hawaii. Simultaneously, violence broke out around the country in what appeared to be a coordinated campaign. Police stations and army bases erupted with infighting, as true allegiances were revealed. Was this it? Civil war? And yet in small towns and rural communities around the country, life continued as normal. Farmers rose and milked their cows. Stock-brokers bought low and sold high. Suburban moms dropped their kids at soccer camp and drove to the dry bar, scrolling through Facebook posts telling them that the bombing was a false flag operation, a ploy by the radical left to justify the declaration of martial law.

Whatever question you asked, the answer was chaos. There were two truths now, but in each it was the teller who was the victim. Reality had finally become 100 percent subjective.

Governors from each state quickly named a replacement senator to hold the seat until the next election, in each case choosing a man with more extremist views. In the hours after the bombing, an FBI raid of the junior senator's home uncovered bomb-making materials and booby traps. At the same time, a manifesto was posted on social media by a group calling itself 4Horsemen. Written and signed by Senator LaRue, it claimed the group had four million members nationwide.

"We are everywhere," read the statement. "We are your mailmen, your corrections officers, your mayors and governors. The enemy has infiltrated our world, and now we have infiltrated theirs. We know the secrets they are trying to hide, this liberal swarm. Satan's forces are strong, but we can hide too. Watch your back, demons."

In Montana, the Pick-6 lottery number was 000000. On August 18 the official Internet Suicide Clock reported 31,406 self-murders. For context, two thousand a day is considered "normal." The youngest victim was eleven. The oldest was sixty-three. Off the coast of Oregon on the same day, a pod of 116 blue whales beached themselves. What did it mean? Were these things connected or coincidental?

The next day, 42,108 earthlings killed themselves. The day following that, 55,211 even as men in camouflage vests with Santa Claus beards terrorized boardwalks in Santa Monica and Atlantic City. On each of those days, approximately 360,000 more human beings were born. This is how it is with our species. We just keep coming. But don't worry. The living will never outnumber the dead, for the past is always larger than the present. By 2030 our total dead will outnumber the current living by a factor of fifteen to one. That means those of us alive today represent just 7 percent of all human beings who ever lived.

We are a species of ghosts.

In times of turmoil some people turn to magic, others to math. As death closes in, the line between life and what comes after begins to break down, like a black hole threatening to swallow everything vibrant, everything bright. On the Greyhound route the ghost of Alexander Hamilton begins screaming, hands over his eyes, always at 3:13 a.m. The dead are rising, it seems, clamoring to be recognized.

In the 1980s professional wrestling coined a term—*kayfabe*—which was defined this way: *that thing we all know is fake we agree to call real.* The fights, the rivalries. The chair hits and cage matches. It was never sport. It was always artifice. But people wanted to believe, and the more the audience signed on, the more exaggerated the story lines became, until millions of Americans had trained themselves to accept fantasy as fact.

It's all kayfabe now.

To describe the details of the current American conflict would be impossible. It is both urban and rural. Gun-wielding, country-club wives blasting their way out of the Panera parking lot, determined to protect their sons and daughters from demons that exist only in their minds. Demons with the faces of their neighbors. And yet aren't our neighbors also the product of generations of humanity? Mothers and fathers meeting and consummating back through the ages, as Generation Z becomes Y becomes X becomes Baby Boomers and on and on, the ships sailing in reverse back to England and Spain, Europe and Africa, as the Renaissance becomes the Middle Ages, nomads recross the Siberian land bridge, and Homo sapiens retrace their steps to the African savanna, and on and on to the birthplace of the human race.

One hundred billion people have lived and died on this planet since the dawn of human history, five hundred and eighty-five million of them

Americans, living or dead. One-fifth of us are Muslims. Eighteen point two percent are Chinese. Twelve million are stateless. More than one hundred million live in countries where they hold no citizenship. These numbers can be added or subtracted, divided or multiplied to create the statistics of our existence, numbers that will soon be consumed by other numbers: annual rainfall totals, desertification sprawl, sea-level rise, heat indexes, storm surges, hurricanes per year, tornadoes per month, as we realize that the story of Planet Earth is not the story of the human animal and its victories and defeats, but a story told in geological time, a story without heroes or villains, without progress. A story, simply, of what happened.

On August 26, the FBI raided the homes and offices of sixteen other members of government: congressmen, attorneys general, mayors. Two days later, the deputy director of the FBI himself was questioned. Pundits called it the reverse Deep State, or the Deeper State, or the Counter State. One could be forgiven for wondering if there was anyone working in government today who was actually governing, if half of each department were so-called liberal operatives and the other half were self-proclaimed conservative operatives, all engaged in a hidden battle for control.

People were beginning to forget where their

grievances began, only that they hated everything their opponent stood for, like that old Dr. Seuss story about the Sneetches, those with stars on their bellies and those without. As if a star could make you worthy, as if a star could make you whole.

By August 27, the daily suicide rate had risen to 81,622.

DeWitt

Four weeks after Avon walks out of prison, Girlie's sister calls and says she needs to be rescued. That's the word she uses, *rescued*, like a soldier radioing in from behind enemy lines. Avon has been using his now unstructured days to take care of things around the house, repairing the generator and re-filling the propane. At night, after the whiskey has kicked in, he reads internet printouts from the library. This is how he stays connected to the digital world—anonymously and on paper.

His buddy Arnaud taught him the Google Doc trick: free thinkers from around the country shar-ing ideas by contributing to the draft of an endless document on Google. Invite only, hidden from prying government eyes. Avon hasn't been on since before his recent prison stretch, and to be clear, he never contributes, only lurks. It's impor-tant to stay informed, but you have to find sources of information you trust. The internet is filled with propaganda merchants. Facebook, forget it. It's amateur hour for desperate housewives and back-yard BBQ conspiracy rubes.

It is the day before the Senate bombing and the so-called boogaloo. After the sun goes down, Avon sits at his desk, going through a stack of news-letters. He lets Girlie handle the bills. Seeing those form envelopes with their slim plastic windows enrages him. If it were up to Avon, they'd live in a cabin without electricity, drinking well water. But Girlie, though sympathetic to the sovereign move-ment, is not a full convert. She has too much to lose, being only a green card citizen and subject to censure and deportation. So, she runs her business primarily aboveboard, paying token taxes, deposit-ing funds in an FDIC-insured bank account. When he's not in the joint, he'll often find her seated at the kitchen table, calculator out, running the numbers. In Avon's mind numbers are a problem. If there's one thing he can't abide, it's math—the way all those so-called experts always roll out their data to prove a point, to say they know things to a certainty, where right-minded Americans, like Avon, are only talking their opinion. Statistics. This was the downfall of human civilization.

Everybody knows you can use numbers to prove any damn thing you want, he used to tell his son,

Samson, who had showed a proclivity for math from an early age. *Like how they want us to believe that cow farts are heating the damn planet.* But on the subjects that really mattered, the use of math wasn't just wrong. It was criminal, a tool of oppression. Like how that Covid-19 bullshit killed hundreds of thousands of people, when no one Avon knew died. How it was part of the Deep State master plan to declare martial law, strip away our guns, and rob all citizens of their freedom, once and for all.

Plus, what could math tell you about hugging your kids in the morning, or hitting a perfect fast ball into the bleachers? What did math have to do with watching them raise the flag every morning at the military academy, that lone bugle playing? There's no equation for falling in love. No algorithm for patriotism or loyalty. You knew something because you *knew* it. Because your gut always told you the truth.

His son, Samson, used to nod and chew gum. He'd been collecting baseball cards from a young age and was forever jawing on a powdery stick of pink pointlessness.

"Whatever you say, Pop," he'd say.

"You're damn right, whatever I say."

Bathsheba, by comparison, was a good girl. Did as she was told. Didn't question. Even after her mother got lymphoma and passed, the girl stayed just as sweet and as wholesome as ever, while Samson took to being mouthy and sour. Avon practically wore the strap out keeping that kid in line. And what thanks did he get when the boy reached eighteen without so much as an arrest for general teenagery? None. Nada. Zip. These days he doesn't even know where the boy is. The last letter Samson sent couldn't have been more than a page long, and all it said was that the boy was changing his name, or some other rooster-stupid idea, and moving to Texas.

I don't want you contacting me or trying to find me, his son wrote in his smarmy, perfect penmanship. Talk about judgmental. The swoopy f's alone were enough to make Avon want to swing a belt.

I want a real life, his son wrote, *to be part of this country, this world, not outside of it. But you ruined that for me. Do you know how hard it is to prove I exist without a birth certificate? Without a social security number? It's easier to walk over from Mexico and become a tax-paying American. And yes, I want to pay taxes. I want to vote. I want a marriage certificate and car insurance. I want to be visible, and I know what you'll say—how sticking my head out of the ground is dangerous, how I should hide the rest of my days for what I did. What we did. But I was fifteen, and if that's the price for being real, I will accept it.*

I know you're mad, but don't call Sheba. She's too gentle a spirit for your fits. If you want to yell at somebody, yell at my picture. It won't change anything, but then again none of your yelling or beatings ever did.

Avon read the letter twice, then burned it up in the ashtray with his Bic disposable. As far as he was concerned, the boy was dead now, laid out by the side of the road with a state trooper's bullet between his eyes.

Which, maybe that's how it shoulda gone.

He puts his feet up on his desk, thinking how over time this country takes everything from a man. It grinds him down, separates him from the people that matter, but then being a man of principle has always been a recipe for isolation. That's why the Bible is full of prophets and martyrs. Consequences. That's how they trap you. If you stick to your principles, vote your conscience with words and bullets, well—there aren't many who will stay by your side, the human animal being driven by a need for safety, comfort.

Avon holds no illusion that if the shit hit the fan, Girlie would be gone in a New York minute. Love is a lie, just like all the other lies, or what's the name of that Al Gore movie, the made-up one they call a documentary, *A Convenient Truth?*

All Avon knows is that one day he'll be looking down the barrel of somebody's gun and he's gonna have to answer the celestial question—*did I live true to my principles? Was I a man?* What else matters? Some woman you got used to? A child born from some Wednesday fuck? They were all bricks stacked in the tower you called your life. And Avon's tower was going to reach all the way to heaven.

The conditions of Avon's parole state that he is to avoid all contact with other convicted felons and is not allowed to possess a firearm, plus all the standard bullshit about not leaving the state, et cetera. Before he went in this last time, Avon buried all his weapons in the backyard in an insulated steel box he'd welded himself. It took a winch to get it in the four-foot hole he dug with the John Deere parked behind the garage. It takes most of his second night home to dig it out. He drops it in the back of his pickup and pulls into the garage. By dawn the hole has been refilled and the John Deere's engine is ticking behind the garage once more.

Avon is in the kitchen making coffee and eggs when Girlie gets up.

"Aie, my floors," she says, seeing him standing

on the linoleum in his filthy work boots. He ignores her and takes his breakfast into the garage. In prison the best he could do on his hot plate was Spam on toast. At home he's been living it up, milk, butter, hamburger every night. He sets his plate on the worktable, climbs up into the pickup bed. The steel box has three combination locks on it, each set to the birthdate of a founding father. He cleans the box thoroughly before opening it, oiling the hinges.

Inside the guns have been set into foam cutouts. Nothing extreme. Working guns for a working man. A compact semiautomatic rifle, a shotgun, and three pistols, two semiautomatic and a revolver. He has enough ammunition to hold off federal agents for a few hours, but Avon has always been practical. He knows that when the shock troops arrive, he won't be walking out of here. He just wants to make it as painful for them as possible, so that when they say his name it's with a scar on their souls.

He empties the crate, storing the guns behind a panel in the wall. He fills the crate with tools from his workshop and puts it under the worktable. Thomas Jefferson himself said "the tree of liberty must be refreshed from time to time with the blood of patriots and tyrants. It is its natural manure." When you read your history, Avon thinks, there's no excuse for surprise. It was always going to end in blood.

The path of the righteous man is beset on all sides by the inequities of the selfish and the tyranny of evil men, right? Isn't that the *Pulp Fiction* quote? This shit isn't complicated. Someone has to shepherd the weak through the valley of darkness, to protect them from politicians who use them, insurance companies who exploit them, landlords who evict them, elites who seek to oppress them. This is why the sheriff is so fundamental to the heart of America. A western figure, a county father, supreme in his authority, an American Solomon able to consider facts and render judgment. A simpler figure from a simpler time.

He sits on the tailgate of his pickup truck and eats his egg sandwich and drinks his coffee. He doesn't care that they're cold. He is a free man, free to eat what he wants, when he wants. When he's done, he hoses out his truck bed and coils the hose on the wall.

Girlie comes out at nine thirty to say she's going to work. She tells him she's sorry what she said about the floors. All that matters is he's home. He can see from her eyes that she doesn't mean it, but what matters is she shows him respect. That she respects the natural order, man over woman, white over colored.

An hour later she calls him in a panic. Rose is in trouble in California. They have to rescue her. Avon tells her California is on fire, and besides, he can't leave the state. Girlie tells him she's serious. This old Witch is holding her sister hostage. A real *bruha*. Girlie talks a mile a minute about bad juju, about old-world evil sorcery. *Mangkukulam*, she calls it. She says they don't just have to save her sister's life. They have to save her soul, and *if you love me, you have to do this*. Otherwise, Girlie says, she's going herself.

They fly Southwest from Orlando to Long Beach. Girlie pays for everything from her rainy-day fund. They ride in the back of the plane. Girlie does sudoku. There is a 9mm disassembled in her suitcase in the cargo hold, packed by Avon. The stewardess comes around with the snack basket. Avon has some chips and asks for a Coke. When the plane hits turbulence, he grips the armrests. He likes an enemy he can fight. Rose gave her sister an address in Van Nuys. Avon figures it's a walk-in, walk-out situation. Bang on the door, *get your shit*, maybe pull the gun for show, and then they're on their way.

They see the smoke as far away as New Mexico, the clouds below them darkening, as if in storm. The seat belt light chimes on. Over Arizona they begin their descent. The smoke billows up toward them, not like mist, but like wool. It is an oil painting of grays, browns, and swirling white, lunging toward the plane in sudden waves. Fear moves through the plane, passengers craning toward the windows. Darkness rises to meet them. They enter it with great reluctance. A collective gasp arises. Near the front of the plane a baby starts to cry. People start to question the intelligence of the captain with increasing volume.

The plane continues to descend. There is no floor to the smoke it seems, and they begin to worry they are falling into the fire itself. That their whole lives have been a series of seductions by silver-tongued devils, personal and professional, leading to this moment outside the gates of hell. They wonder if somewhere in the fine print of all those digital terms and conditions they signed—new apps, new media, new phones—they forfeited their rights to eternal peace.

They are over Joshua Tree when an orange glow rises. The mountains ahead of them are on fire. Avon orders a Jack Daniel's. The captain comes on the radio to say the plane is rerouting. They will head for San Diego and approach the airport from the south. Through his starboard window, Avon watches as an ocean of flames devours everything in sight.

Have you ever spilled water on a table and

watched it run in all directions at once? Before your brain has even finished processing that the glass has tipped, the water is everywhere. That is how the wildfire looks from ten thousand feet. A liquid heat spilling across the mountain range, uninhibited by obstacles or friction. It races through the trees the way a tidal wave consumes a city, forcing its way through walls, through buildings, through everything. It is a force beyond rational thought, primordial, dwarfing human civilization, an insatiable god devouring the world.

At this moment, watching an entire mountain range burn, it is possible to see the end of all life on Earth. Not their individual lives, but life in its entirety. For Girlie it inspires the monsoon terror of her youth, the acute dread of the island dweller surrounded by endless sea. *What chance do we have?* she thinks. The plane they're on seems tiny in comparison, as do their cities, their lives. She pictures the flames racing east, consuming deserts, mountains, cities, and savannas until the whole planet is burning. Next to her, Avon feels a testosterone thrill, the unhinged panic of a boy who wants to see what happens when he lights a match and finds himself trapped inside his burning house, flames blocking every door.

For a moment, every person on that plane understands with piercing clarity that they have lost control of the future. They know that whatever creature comforts they have accustomed themselves to are an illusion, a violin to be played as the *Titanic* sinks. Except here there are no lifeboats, no rescue ships.

Here they are all going to drown.

The rental is a yellow Kia, covered in ash. Girlie drives. Avon sits in the backseat with his wife's valise open in front of him. He reassembles the 9mm methodically, tests the slide, loads a clip. He puts two more clips in the patch pockets of his cargo pants. Up front, Girlie listens to religious radio, dedicated FM stations of the California prosperity gospel.

"The Bible is the greatest book in the world in terms of money management," says a sonorous male voice. "The secrets locked inside will lead you to staggering prosperity. Proverbs 28, Psalm 119, Joshua 1:7. Did you know that the Bible says that God takes pleasure in the prosperity of his servants? He wants you to revel in unfathomable wealth."

The sky above them is blood red, a low ceiling of filth cutting off the city skyline. Girlie takes the 5 north, switches to the 134. She has the AC on recirculating, but even so the smell of smoke is thick inside the car. At the airport she looked up the address Rose gave her on Google Maps.

It's in a residential neighborhood near the highway. She thinks of the *mambabarang* and the tropical darkness of her childhood. In her country there has always been a war between good and bad magic, between faith healers and the aswang, shape-shifters. The werebeasts and viscera suckers. *Silagan*, with its hatred of white clothes, and *magtatangal*, who wandered the woods without head or entrails. Her grandmother would scold her when she was bad that the magtatangal was coming for her, with its bat-like wings and its endless tongue used to suck the hearts from the fetuses of sleeping women.

When Rose called, she said that a mangkukulam had her. That she had been tricked by the woman's words and was now her slave. Girlie had never heard fear like that, so thick it was like honey coating her sister's tongue. They had always been close, but when they got to America they were sent to live with different aunts, Girlie in Florida and Rose in California. They stayed in touch by phone, hugging at family reunions, the words flooding out of them. And then they were adults and the urgency softened. Rose married for a green card, but her husband beat her. She went to school to become a home health aide. *Come to Florida*, Girlie begged her. *You can work in the shop*. But Rose never chose the path that was good for her. She chose wife beaters and con men, internet scams and shaggy dog stories.

And now she had been seduced by black magic. Girlie knew that freeing her would not be as simple as walking her out of the building. They would need strong *sumbalik* to shake this curse.

"For the husband is the head of the wife," says the radio, "even as Christ is the head of the church; and he is the Savior of the body."

She thinks of the photo Rose sent, of the reflection in the mirror. Does she know they're coming, the Witch? Girlie was sure she felt her presence on the plane, black eyes watching her, hot breath on her neck in line for the rental car. She checks the rearview mirror, finds Avon staring out the window.

"If this takes longer than a day," he says, watching the eastern mountains burn, "there might not be a California left to get out of."

He asks her to put on some music, and she scans the dial. It's then they hear the news of a bombing at the US Senate, how a senator from Idaho wore a suicide vest in the hearing room. Girlie wants to know what it means. Avon tells her to shut up. He's thinking about the Google Doc, how Arnaud wrote that something big was coming. That the boogaloo was finally here. Avon thought it was more zealous posturing. He'd gone through a revolutionary phase as a younger man. It peaked with a traffic stop and two dead state troopers. Now all he wants is to be left alone. But fourteen dead senators and a government building in flames? That's not the end of a story. It's the beginning.

"We need to get home," he tells Girlie, thinking of his bunker, the stand that they could make—insulated, secure.

"We get Rose," she says, "then home."

"Turn the car around."

She ignores him, nudges the gas pedal. She doesn't care if the entire world blows up. She's getting her sister back.

O

At first, when they turn onto the 1600 block of Auster, Girlie thinks the smoke is from the mountains, but the mountains are behind them and the smoke is too thick, and then she sees flames. When they pull up to the address, it's on fire. Not just on fire, but the roof is missing and half the front wall. And there is a teenage boy walking between it and the house next door. Girlie pulls over to the curb. The heat of the fire reaches her through the passenger window. She turns in her seat and sees the boy go up the steps of the neighboring house. And then the front door opens and Rose is there.

Girlie feels a wave of euphoria. Her sister is alive! And then something hits Rose in the back of the head and she falls forward into the front yard. A young woman steps out behind her, tosses the chair. Girlie screams. Avon clicks off the safety on the 9mm and throws open the back door.

"Stay put," he says, approaching the house, gun at high ready, safety off. The woman crouches next to Rose.

"Don't touch her," says Avon firmly. The man and woman turn, startled to see him. He watches their eyes as they register the gun, then realizes that the youngest, the man, is just a kid. They are, we know, Simon Oliver and Story Burr-Nadir.

"Wait," says Simon. "She was—we're hostages. Were hostages. She was—the Witch kidnapped us, or not a literal Witch, though maybe. But I'm—I was at an anxiety center in—"

"Stop talking," says Avon, but Simon can't.

"—and wait, she's—"

He points to Story.

"—she's that judge's daughter. The one on TV. There's probably a—there could be a reward."

Avon looks at Story. "That judge is dead."

Story goes white. "What?"

"There was an explosion. At the—whatdyoucallit—the Capitol. A bombing. It's on the news."

"The—I'm sorry?" says Story, her knees going

weak, her mind going cloudy as she slips into shock. "What?"

Then Girlie is there, kneeling next to Rose, shouting in Filipino.

"Shut up, woman," says Avon, as Rose stirs. He looks at Simon.

"Where's the other—the Witch?"

Simon points to the building.

"I think she's dead. We had a—gas leak. She lit a match."

Avon walks toward the wreckage of the neighboring house, still burning. He wonders for a moment what's taking the fire department so long to respond, but then he realizes they're probably all in the mountains trying to keep the world from ending.

He goes around back, finds that most of the first-floor siding has been blown off. Inside, he surveys the charred wreckage gun up. He figures if he finds her, this Witch, and she's still alive he'll put two bullets in her head and call it mercy. Either way, problem solved. He steps through the hole in the wall into the room where Simon slept. The mattress is a smoldering stain now, the wicker chair consumed in its entirety.

There is no sign of the Witch. Avon kicks open a burning door, peers into the next room— a living room from the look of it—still actively on fire. Where the kitchen used to be, there's just a hole.

"Lady?" he calls, but quietly, the way you lure a frightened animal. There are no lights on in the house except the dancing orange flicker of the flames. Shadows move across the walls. Avon walks through the living room toward an open door. Closer, he sees it is a bathroom, white tile unmarred. He toes the door open the rest of the way.

"Lady?" he says again, "are you in here? Need me to call the hospital?"

He ducks inside, gun up, sweeping. Despite the flames, the bathroom is humid, condensation running down the walls, the floor slippery. It feels like a hothouse inside or some kind of sweat lodge. The mirror over the sink has cracked from the heat. In it, his own face is fractured, lit from behind by the burning living room.

Then he becomes aware of the sound of running water and his eyes go to the tub. The faucet is on, the bath filled to overflow, water running down the porcelain onto the floor. Avon steps closer. The water is murky, blackened by soot and ash, but there is the suggestion of a figure inside. *Is that*—he leans closer—*a body?* He lowers the gun, squints at what, it becomes clear, is a charred figure submerged beneath the surface. As he peers under the water, it seems to clear, the body becoming easier to see. Male, female? He can't tell anymore, any discernible features burned away. The head is a charred lightbulb on a thin black neck. Could it be her? The Witch?

And then the eyes open, and Avon falls back, hitting the sink with his hip, the impact spinning him around.

"Jesus," he says, as he slips on the wet tile and falls hard, the air going out of him. His gun skitters across the floor and out the door. He lies stunned, as behind him he hears the sound of falling water and realizes that the charred corpse is rising out of the tub. He scrambles onto his back in time to see her rise, impossibly black, water raining from her seared skeleton.

She is looking at him.

He propels himself backward, some instinct in his basal ganglia telling him to keep his eyes on her, what now in his soul he realizes is the Witch, an actual witch, tool of Satan. He bumps his head on the doorjamb, corrects, feeling the heat of the flames on his back. Under his hands the wooden floorboards are crumbling, but he doesn't stop. All the while the Witch walks after him, slowly, like a death you can't outrun.

In his heart, Avon knows that when she catches him she will consume him, and his life will become her own, putting skin back on her bones, putting hair back on her head, and he will burn forever in the devil's playground.

His hand finds his gun, the metal so hot it burns him, but he doesn't hesitate, just grabs it, pulls the slide, chambering a round, and fires. The first two shots knock her back, and then he is on one knee in a shooter's crouch, emptying his clip into her as she flies back into the bathroom, bounces off the wall, and disappears from sight.

Avon rises, ejecting the empty clip. Reflex has another one out of his cargo pants pocket and into the gun in under three seconds, and he chambers the first round, ready to go again if that bitch comes back for seconds. But then he hears a cracking sound, like a tree snapping in two, and half the roof comes down. Avon, by sheer instinct, dives out of the way. Feeling the rest of the house coming down, he scrambles toward the kitchen's absence, blinded by smoke, racing on his hands and knees toward the smell of fresh air, and then the floor disappears from under him, and he tumbles out of the house and onto the concrete outside.

He gets to his feet and runs, still blind, crashes into a fence, the burning house listing toward him, ready to topple over. He rears back and hits the fence again, then again, driven by the heat and by this core certainty: the Witch isn't dead and she is coming for him.

He hears the wood splinter, smashes the fence again, and then he is through, tumbling forward onto dirt. He scrambles up, moving away from the feet, away from the inevitability of death. And then Girlie grabs him, stops him, her voice in his ear. But the fear is still in him, so he pushes her away, brings up the gun, steps back off the curb, trying to find some tactical distance. As he does, he blinks away the soot and smoke, his eyes clearing. He sees them there, Girlie and Rose, the boy and the judge's daughter. And something else, a shadow figure in the flames, standing impossibly still in the heart of the fire.

"We need to go," he tells Girlie. "Now."

Keeping the gun up, he nods toward the car. "Get in the car now."

"But," says Girlie.

"Now!"

Simon sees the fear on Avon's face. He knows what it means. She isn't dead. He grabs Story's arm.

"Move," he says.

"With them?" Story asks, but Simon shoves her and keeps shoving her until they are in the backseat of the Kia, folded in next to Rose, and Avon jumps in the passenger seat, gun pointed back out the open door.

"Go," he says, and the fear in his voice makes Girlie stomp the gas pedal all the way to the floor, and the car leaps forward, tires eating asphalt, until they are at the corner, running the red light, flying toward the freeway. Only then does Avon holster his pistol and slam his door.

O

They drive till they run out of gas, mostly in silence. In the backseat, Rose starts to cry, big broad tears, her bosom quivering.

"I'm sorry," she tells Story and Simon, over and over. "So, so sorry."

Story has her feet under her and her face buried in her knees. They have listened to the reports on the radio. The world has gone crazy. Margot and Remy are dead, along with fourteen senators and more than a hundred bystanders. And around the country there have been attacks on military bases and state houses. Story knows she should cry, but her heart feels like a glass ball stored in Bubble Wrap. Once upon a time she was a baby who couldn't sit or stand, who needed everything, and isn't that what a mother is? Everything? Food and warmth, safety and love. Once upon a time Story was a toddler stumbling through the world, heading for every sharp corner, an engine of grievances and demands. And still her mother was there, patient, nurturing. Once upon a time her father left, and a new father came, and she stopped eating. But still the mother was there.

Once upon a time, she stood on a stage and sang the national anthem, but where is her anthem now? That human anthem, nationless and true, with all its sorrow and yearning, all its hope and grief. The music of existence. Everyone you love will die. Everyone you need will pass from this world without warning or reason. Where is their song, the anthem of their lives, soaring to the rafters, celebrating all their sweet, pathetic attempts at permanence? Where is their anthem of fury, their anthem of love?

When the people who fill your heart die, Story thinks, all that's left is emptiness and regret. Nothingness. And a heart filled with nothing feels nothing. So she doesn't cry. She just rocks back and forth and stares into the void.

Sitting next to her, Simon watches the sun rise through smoky haze. The Santa Ana winds are blowing hot and dry from the east and in places the sky is clear, pockets of morning blue. Not for the first time he thinks about the others: Louise and the Prophet, Duane and Felix and Randall Flagg. Are they alive? In prison? They were on a mission together, a quest, but it all seems meaningless now in the face of catastrophe, in the face of revolution.

"Can I borrow your phone?" Simon asks quietly, leaning into the front. Avon is putting first aid cream on his burned right hand, the skin blistering where he gripped the gun. Girlie reaches into her pocket, hands him back her Samsung.

"No log ins," grunts Avon, wrapping a light bandage around his hand.

Simon opens the phone, finds Instagram. He is looking for a specific account, unconnected to any of them. In Marfa they devised this plan, that if any of them were separated they should post a photo on @bassethoundsrule. He searches for the account, finds it, scrolls through the filler images—Basset hounds at the beach! Basset hounds in the woods! Basset hounds in clothes!—until he finds a photo of a walled estate. A teenage Black girl stands in front of it with a handwritten sign. The sign is blocking her face. The girl is rail thin, wearing a sleeveless T-shirt, her arms like twigs.

The sign reads BASSET HOUNDS LOVE PALM SPRINGS!

Simon backs out of the page, erases the browser history, then turns off the phone.

"I have to go to Palm Springs," he says.

They are headed east toward Interstate 5. Racing

back to the Long Beach airport, Girlie sees a Shell station, puts on her blinker.

"What are you doing?" Avon asks.

"We need gas," she says, pulling onto the off-ramp.

At the pump, Simon and Story get out. Rose is asleep in the backseat. Avon goes inside to buy some supplies. Story stands on a strip of grass, staring at the sky. The smell of smoke from the east is overpowering.

"Are you okay?" Simon asks.

"You really want me to answer that?" says Story.

"No, sorry. That was—I'm an idiot."

They stand together, watching traffic race by on the highway. Like everything else in the LA sprawl, the gas station has the air of urban decay. It is what happens when you take a beautiful valley and pave it, cementing even the river, then fill it with people without rhyme or reason, and finally neglect it all for decades, investing neither time nor money in its health or beauty.

"I had a sister," Simon tells Story, "Claire. And she—died."

Story nods.

"And then my parents just pretended she never existed. We didn't talk about her. They put away her pictures, redecorated her room."

Simon is still wearing hospital scrubs. He has

no shoes on. Neither does she. He takes Story's hand.

"I'm saying, I'm here if you want to talk."

She nods, tears in her eyes.

"What do you want to do?" Simon asks her. "I could call someone, get you home?"

She doesn't answer.

"I think Louise is in Palm Springs," Simon tells her. "I don't know about Felix or the Prophet. They were with me when I was—"

He pauses.

"You were with Louise and Duane though," he says. "Did they—how did they get away?"

Story sighs.

"They had to pee, and I said I'd stay in the van near the radio. And then these cars pulled in, and this man grabbed me out of the car. They called themselves *goblins*."

Simon nods. "It was an ambush," he says. "The Wizard saw us. They were waiting."

Story wipes her eyes as Avon exits the Q-Mart carrying two plastic bags.

"Why are they in Palm Springs?" she asks. "Louise."

"I think maybe they found Bathsheba," he says.

Avon, walking toward the car, stops. "What did you say?" he asks.

Simon turns. "No, nothing."

Avon drops the bags. A can of Coke inside pops a hole, hisses soda onto the parking lot. Avon walks to them. "Did you say Bathsheba?"

Simon nods, looks at Story.

"We were—she's our friend, *her* boyfriend's sister," he says, nodding to Story. "And we were—rescuing her when we were—kidnapped."

"And her name is Bathsheba," says Avon.

They nod. Avon thinks about that. *What are the odds?* And yet how many Bathsheba's can there be in America?

"You said he's your boyfriend's sister?" he asks Story. "Who's your boyfriend?"

"His name is Felix, uh, Moor with no *e*."

Avon frowns. "Describe him."

"He's, uh, six foot, brown hair."

Avon digs through his pocket, pulls out his wallet. Inside he finds a worn, folded photograph. He shows it to her. In it, Avon stands with two teenagers, a boy and a girl. The girl is barely twelve. The boy is probably sixteen.

It's Felix.

Story's eyes widen. "That's—"

Avon blows air through his nose, marveling at the miracle of the universe. "His name is Samson," he says. "Samson DeWitt."

"No," she says. "He's—that's Felix."

"Listen to me, honey. Felix is a made-up name.

He's my son. His name is Samson, and Bathsheba is his sister."

"But why would he—" she says.

"Well, for one, to get away from me. But two, he was raised outside the law, you feel me? A sovereign. And there are—issues in his past. Things he's running from."

Story starts to laugh. In the space of an hour she has lost her entire family and learned that her boyfriend is an entirely different person. It's so absurd, so outside the boundaries of human comprehension, that her mind decides to treat it like a joke. And so she laughs, and then she starts to shake, because the truth is, if this is a joke, then she's the punch line.

Simon puts his arms around her. "I'm sorry," he says. "It's been a long day."

Avon spits on the ground. His right hand is throbbing now. There's Tylenol in the bag on the ground, but he doesn't reach for it.

"Where are my kids?"

Simon glances at Girlie, topping off the tank. She's on her phone, talking to someone. Avon takes a step forward.

"The world's on fire, boys and girls, and I'm three thousand miles from the bunker. You got thirty seconds to tell me where my children are, or I'm gonna put a big hole in your heads."

"We don't know," Simon tells him. "We got sep-arated. I was with Felix—Samson. We were—the Wizard took her, your daughter. E. L. Mobley."

"The billionaire?"

Simon nods.

"In Marfa. We went there to save her, but when we broke in, it was an ambush, and we—we never saw her. I'm not even sure she was there."

"But she's in Palm Springs."

"Maybe. That's—before we split up, we figured out how to send a signal. At least one of my friends is in Palm Springs. I don't know where the Prophet is, but he says we have to save her, so that's what we're gonna do."

"The Prophet and the Wizard."

Simon rubs his eyes. "It's a long story."

Avon thinks about the Witch in the flames.

"Take me to them," he says.

"Look," says Simon. "Thanks for the ride, but I think we're gonna—we need to find our friends. Hitch a ride, I guess. Maybe, if we find Bathsheba, we can call you."

Avon stares at them. He feels that same dawn-ing flood that came over him when Fat Eddy started telling him about all that money locked in a hidden government account. Purpose. He feels purpose.

"Wait here," he tells them.

Girlie is screwing the gas cap back on the Kia.
Avon comes over.

"Babe, I need you to call one of those Uber
things, take your sister back to the airport. Take
her home. Call Charlie One-Eye. Tell him it's the
D-Day scenario. He'll make sure you're safe."

"Why?" she says. "We have the car."

"I need the car. The kids know where Sheba is,
they say, and maybe Samson. I gotta find them.
That's why I'm here, I think."

"You're here to get Rose, and we got her and it's
on fire and we have to go home. You have to take
us home."

He ignores her, goes to the back door, opens it.
He shakes Rose by the shoulder.

"Rose," he says, "time to wake up."

He turns back to Girlie, who is standing there,
her mouth open.

"Get on your damn slave device and call yourself
another car," he says. "I'm taking this one."

He pulls Rose out of the car. She blinks groggily
under the yellow fluorescents.

"Kids," calls Avon. Simon and Story look over.
Avon beckons. "Time to go."

They exchange a look.

"Haul ass," he says. "We're gonna find your
friends."

Simon grabs Story's hand, leads her to the car.

Avon opens the trunk, takes out Girlie's suitcase, rolls it toward her.

"I'll call you when it's safe," he says, then gets in, slams the door. Simon puts Story in back, opens the passenger door. He sees Girlie and Rose staring at him, offers a halfhearted wave.

"Stay safe," he says, then squints. In the orange glow of the new day, he sees something in the shadows behind a dumpster. A black figure, crouched down, watching. It smiles with bone-white teeth.

Time

Chaos descends. Information and disinformation collide. The only common language people speak now is violence. Emergency rooms all over the country are flooded with gunshot victims, beating victims, stabbing victims. After the Senate bombing, cars and trucks become weapons, bats, boards, frozen water bottles launched from T-shirt guns. Individuals aggregate, become crowds, human mobs drawn outdoors by outrage and fear. The time for talking has passed. Reports from the street echo reports from other streets. Face-offs between men and women screaming into one another's open mouths under a summer swelter to *accept reality*. But what is reality, if not conflict?

Heads are broken, bodies blown apart, injuries rarely seen outside of war zones. Ambulances fight the crowds, racing toward emergency rooms, but the hospitals are already filled with failed suicides, jumpers with broken bones, drug overdoses, and self-asphyxiators forever muffled by brain damage. And now we are forced to ask, did they know what was coming, these first movers? Is that why they jumped? Is that why they swallowed the pills and fired all those guns into their own minds? Did they see the fall before it happened? Some animals are more attuned to disaster, after all, like birds startling from the trees before the earthquake hits.

And all the while the fires grow.

This wasn't how it was supposed to work. They told us we had more time, that the fossil fuels we burned would cause damage *in the future*. But there are ice squalls in Texas now and heat waves in Siberia. Time itself is breaking down, our linear concept of a warmer future, of the storms to come, because the storms are here now. The heat is here now, making it simultaneously the present moment but also the hothouse future. Models of prediction teeter on the verge of pointless, for the Chaozoic era has arrived. The end of history. Not humanity's demise, but the end of the chronological story of a human species carving civilization from its animal past.

Down on the streets the words *law enforcement* lose their meaning, as badges surrender their power to convince and dominance becomes a matter of ballistic superiority. Soldiers turn on soldiers.

Children throw punches in schoolyards across the continent. The Manichean battle between good and evil has arrived, with no clarity regarding who is good and who is evil.

Behold the war of pure noise.

For a while the world made sense. What was good or bad was quantifiable. We could look to the past and see our mistakes, the places we could excel. The quality of life overall improved year by year, decade by decade. For a while the goals were clear, but then the ground began to shake and all the savvy birds took flight.

Louise

Louise is bored, but then waiting has never been her strong suit, the patience it takes to save your pennies and bide your time. It's August 17, and she and Duane are in a Motel 6 outside San Bernardino. *A shithole*, Louise calls it, filled with methheads and crack whores. They have driven west from Texas, moving only at night, subsisting on a diet of Cheez-Its and Sprite. They don't talk about what happened, about Story's face in the Valkyrie's window as the black SUVs roared in, and how she met Louise's eyes, while Louise—who had gone off for a private pee—was hiding in the trees. They don't talk about the surgical precision of the strike team that pulled Story from the van and had her in the back of an SUV disappearing down the road in a cloud of dust thirty seconds later, or how the last one to leave put two shotgun slugs into the van's engine block and left it for smoking dead.

For the first day they didn't talk about anything, moving cross-country on foot, staying away from roads and houses. As far as they knew, there was an all-points bulletin out for their arrest. At a gas station in Alpine, they stole a pickup truck with its keys tucked in the driver's-side visor. Duane drove in silence, radio off. He felt what Louise felt, the guilt of those who have survived when others have not.

They switched vehicles in Arizona, hot-wiring an ancient Buick LeSabre outside a Walmart. During the day they slept in the shade under the car, pulling off the road and down into a gulley or ravine. They had no plan. This wasn't the fail-safe. It was flight. When they reached California, the storms moved in, ominous clouds crackling with lightning, scissoring the sky. The scale of it jolted them from their reverie, the cloud ceiling dropping, high pressure pushing down, making their teeth itch. They headed south at Victorville, dropped down through the San Gabriel Mountains, as fires ignited the hills around them—emergency vehicles racing by in the other direction—and then the sun was rising and Duane couldn't drive anymore, so they pulled into the Shithole 6.

They eat Doritos from the vending machine, sitting on the industrial carpet.

"Are you in love with Simon?" Duane asks her.

She searches for the darkest nacho cheese Dorito, the one coated with the most powder, and presses it to her tongue. A sensation moves through her, not exactly taste, but an intense mouth experience that makes her salivate in the chemical simulation of flavor.

She closes her eyes. "Are you?" she says.

He drinks his Diet Coke. Through the wall they can hear the throb of death metal.

"He's fifteen," he says.

"So? What are you?"

"Nineteen."

She makes a *whatever* face.

"You think he likes you?" she says.

Duane shrugs, then sniffs the air.

"Do you smell smoke?" he says.

"The world is on fire."

He nods. She finishes the bag, crumples it up, throws it over the bed.

"You think he's dead?" she asks.

Duane shakes his head.

"I think they're all dead," says Louise. "Or tortured somewhere in a dungeon."

"He has a dungeon?"

"He's a wizard. Of course he has a dungeon. Or maybe just a dungeon room with, like, whips and chains and a dildo iron maiden."

"Is that where he took you?"

"No, with me he liked the schoolgirl act."

In the next room what sounds like a mosh pit has started up. It's 10:30 in the morning. Duane finishes his Coke, crumples the can, shoots for the trash can.

"Nice shot," she says, as it rattles off the rim.

Duane rubs his eyes. Sleep is coming for him. "You really think he's dead?"

Louise gets up, goes to the bathroom. She strips off her shirt. "I'm gonna take a shower," she says, then turns suggestively. "Coming?"

He shakes his head.

"Wow," she says. "You really are in love."

She kicks the door closed. Ten minutes later, when she comes out wrapped in a towel that smells like bleach, he is fast asleep on the carpet.

O

They buy a burner phone the next day at the 7-Eleven. Louise has a plan. It came to her in the night. She was in the woods and a woodchuck told her to *seek the Troll*.

"Really?" Duane asks when she tells him.

Louise laughs, peels off the packaging, slips a sim card into the phone.

"No," she says. "It came to me on the shitter, but that's not how these stories are supposed to go, is it, Bilbo? We're supposed to get a sword from some bitch in a lake, so whatever, a woodchuck whispered the secrets of the universe in my ear, and then we made mad love under a blanket of stars."

Duane sighs. It's not that Louise isn't his absolute favorite person on Earth. It's just she can be a bit *much* sometimes, especially after four solid days.

"So who's the Troll again?" he asks her. "That's not his real name, is it?"

"Evan? No. He's just this whatever, rent boy, upturned-collar, pimp motherfucker who deals in high school girls, pills, blah, blah, blah."

She turns on the phone.

"And you have his number?"

She nods.

"Get this," she says. "Homeboy calls himself a *rabatteur*, which is, like, a French word for the guy who leads a fox hunt and beats the bushes and stuff."

"For what?"

"To drive your prey into the open, Jim. That's what we were. The prey."

She enters Evan's number from memory, all those nights texting back and forth. Part One: the prey is seduced into the open. Part Two: predator eats the prey.

She types.

—You still like it in the ass?

They smoke cigarettes in the parking lot while they wait for a response. The mosh pit boys stumble out around three and pile into a silver Honda.

Her phone beeps.

—Who dis?

She writes back.

—It's Louise, Romeo.

—Are you in town?

She looks at Duane. He shakes his head.

—Not far.

—What you need? A little DP from a BBC?

—I need some sugar, daddy.

Overhead the sky turns from gray to orange. They can smell the flames surging through the mountains. A police car races by, chased by a pickup truck with a machine gun mounted in the bed, in an inversion of cause and effect. Louise wonders if she played the wrong hand, then—

—Sugar daddy is lying low right now, butterfly. Maybe next year.

—baby needs $. baby do anything for $

Duane throws rocks at a dead rat while they wait for him to reply, then—

—You still look young? he writes. You know what He likes.

So Louise goes inside and takes a photo of

herself in panties, making her most innocent sex-pout, and sends it to him. She knows there's no universe in which the Wizard is lying low. He is a bottomless pit of sexual debauchery, a ravenous monster, never satisfied. *I mean, shit, he fills his veins with the blood of younger men, and has six personal trainers, four chefs, and, like, a cryo chamber in every house.* He doesn't know how to restrain himself. Restraint is for human beings.

She puts her clothes back on, waiting for the chime. Her phone rings instead. She looks at Duane, who raises his eyebrows. Louise answers.

"Meow," says the Troll.

"Baby," says Louise breathlessly. "Did you miss me?"

"Like a hooker misses herpes. You look like shit."

"Liar. I'm premium number one all time."

"Where you been, prison?"

"Grandma put me in the looney bin, but I'm one hundred percent cured now and ready for love."

From the sounds on the other end of the phone, the Troll is eating a bowl of cereal.

"Listen, lady bird," he says, "maybe we can help each other out. Sugar Daddy needs his three meals a day, but in case you haven't noticed, California is on fire right now, and it's not the usual easy peasy to find food."

"In San Francisco?"

"I wish. Sounds like he had a close call in Texas, so he went to ground. Where are you?"

"Riverside."

"What the fuck for?"

"What do you care?"

"You're right. I could give a shit."

He takes another mouthful, slurping milk. "That's perfect actually. Fucking Riverside. Genius. Meet me tomorrow outside the art museum at four."

"There's an art museum in Riverside?"

"Ha ha. Don't be late, bitch."

He hangs up. She throws the phone on the bed.

"Can we get a real meal tonight?" she asks Duane. "I can't eat another fucking bag of chips."

Duane grabs her by the shoulder, fakes slapping her.

"What did he say?!"

"We're in. Riverside art museum tomorrow at four."

"Wait. There's an art museum in Riverside?"

"That's what I said."

She puts on her shoes, dreaming of burgers and fries. They've got $35 between them. That should get them fed and a little drunk while they figure out a plan.

O

The next day when they check out, the LeSabre won't start. Duane and Louise hoof it through the urban sprawl, looking for a new set of wheels. Louise's plan is to kidnap the Troll and make him take them to see the Wizard. Duane says, *"It sounds like we don't need force,"* and, *"Didn't he say he's taking you there already?"* But Louise says they're on a payback tour, and this preppy motherfucker deserves some payback like nobody's business.

Duane thinks about arguing, but he's still angry about the ambush, so he says, *"Fuck it. I'm in. Let's go get this cocksucker."* And Louise says, *"Careful, some of my best friends suck cock."* And then, 'cause they're in such a good mood, they decide to steal an Amazon delivery truck, because it's funny and because there's one idling driverless at the curb when they turn the corner. And so they jump in and Duane hauls ass, and they're laughing and the radio is way up and Soundgarden is playing, and the sky is fucking orange overhead, and the mountains are on fire, and there are clowns in the streets with chain saws, but they're young and alive and, for a few minutes, it feels like they're in control.

And then Louise gets the idea that they should kidnap Evan using only items boxed up in the back of the truck.

"What does that mean?" Duane wants to know.

"It means we're on a mission from God, right?" she says. "So you gotta figure he put this truck here for us and filled it with everything a girl might need to get some bloody revenge."

"You mean to rescue Felix's sister."

"Right. What did I say?"

So while Duane drives to the art museum, Louise climbs in back and stares at the hundreds of boxes inside. She feels like a kid on Christmas, but she can't open them all in the next thirty minutes. What's a girl to do?

Louise decides she will open only four boxes. Whatever she finds inside will be what they use to grab the Troll.

Yes comes on the radio. "I've Seen All Good People."

"Knife," she yells, and Duane slips a folding knife from his pocket and tosses it back. Louise catches it, flips open the blade. She studies the boxes. So many shapes and sizes. Heavy boxes, light boxes. Short boxes, tall boxes. How is a girl supposed to choose?

She closes her eyes and grabs a light rectangle. She shakes it, and something solid moves inside. Slice goes the knife. Pop goes the box. And then she's looking at a package of C batteries and some Velcro straps.

"This is gonna be interesting," she says to the front seat.

The next box has a fanny pack in it that looks like a beer belly. She puts it around her waist, clips the clasp. "How do I look?"

Duane eyes her in the rearview mirror. "Gross," he says.

Louise puts the batteries in the fanny pack, strips the packaging from the Velcro straps and drops those in too. She grabs another box, a bigger cube.

"Come on, snake eyes," she says, and cuts the packing tape.

"Just take the knife," says Duane.

"You're no fun."

She unfolds the flap. Inside is another box. The label reads PORTABLE PERSONAL SAUNA, 2L, FOLDING INDOOR SAUNA SPA, WEIGHT LOSS, DE-TOX, WITH REMOTE CONTROL, TIMER, FOLDABLE CHAIR.

Louise squeals.

"What are you gonna do with that?" asks Duane.

"Something memorable. That's for sure."

She puts down the box, straightens, brushing the hair from her eyes. If she's going to keep her vow, she can open only one more box. So far, she has straps, Velcro, a fanny pack, and some kind of foil spa. She spins in a circle. There must be two hundred boxes in the panel van with her.

"So many choices," she says, waggling her fingers.

Duane is keeping watch in the parking lot. "Better make it quick," he says. "There's a car coming."

Louise crosses herself, grabs a box. She tears open the tape. Inside is a Nerf gun, a bottle of hot sauce, and a copy of *Room to Dream* by David Lynch.

"Is it him?" she calls, her mind working.

"I don't know. Does he drive a red Mercedes convertible?"

Louise stuffs the hot sauce in her fanny pack, zips it up, sticks the Nerf gun into the strap at her waist. "He sure does."

She straightens. "I'm going in. How do I look?"

Duane looks her up and down. "Psychotic," he says. "Want me to come with?"

"No," says Louise. "Keep it running."

She opens the back doors, jumps down. The asphalt is sticky under her feet. The temperature in the parking lot must be 115 degrees. Louise puts on her sunglasses, walks toward the entrance.

She can see the Troll behind the wheel of his douche-mobile. He's listening to yacht rock, because he knows it will annoy her. She sits on the front steps and waits. He pulls up, gliding to a stop.

"What are you wearing?" he asks.

She stands, twirls. "You like it?"

"Tell me your panties have some old guy's dick printed on them."

"Come on over and find out," she says.

He taps the steering wheel.

"Seriously," he says, "we've gotta jet. I told the Wizard we're coming, and he said *hurry*."

"Come here for a second first," she says.

Evan makes his annoyed face. "Kid, I'm gonna leave your ass at the fucking art museum of Riverside, if you don't get a move on."

She pulls the Nerf gun from her belt, unzips her fanny pack. "Come on," she says. "I wanna show you something."

"What? I can see your whole retarded outfit from here."

Louise takes a C battery from the fanny pack, slides it into the Nerf gun.

"Dude," she says, "you're such a fucking drag. Come and see something hysterical."

He sighs, puts the car in park, climbs out. He makes a big show of slow walking the steps. "Fine," he says, "but this better be grade A, supermodel-pussy good."

Louise pulls back the plastic hammer. "You tell me," she says, and lifts the Nerf gun at his head and fires.

The battery comes out fast, catches him under the

right eye, turning his head and throwing his body off-balance. Stunned, he falls backward down the stairs, hitting his head on the concrete. He lies in a jumble, unconscious.

Louise claps her hands, delighted.

"Did you see that?" she calls, as Duane gets out of the Amazon van and runs her way, looking around to make sure no one else saw. "It was like the fucking Matrix."

O

She wakes him with the hot sauce. One drop under each eye. Evan thrashes around, but his hands are Velcroed together behind his back, his legs at the ankles. There's an ugly bruise forming on his right cheekbone. For a long time, he can't figure out where he is or what's happening—a windowless van surrounded by stacks of Amazon boxes. And then there's the fact that he is kneeling inside some kind of giant foil bag, with his head sticking out the top through some kind of rubber seal. It is the portable sauna. Louise has plugged it into the AC jack in the center console of the van and set the remote on high.

"What the fuck?" says the Troll.

Louise sits cross-legged on a box across from him, the David Lynch book open in her lap. She reads. "So we were down at the end of this street at night, and out of the darkness—it was so incredible—came this nude woman with white skin. Maybe it was something about the light and the way she came out of the darkness, but it seemed to me that her skin was the color of milk and she had a bloodied mouth."

The Troll struggles, aware now of the impossible heat. Sweat is starting to pour down his face.

"Seriously, retard. You got ten seconds to cut me loose."

Louise turns the page. "She couldn't walk very well and she was in bad shape, and she was completely naked. I'd never seen that, and she was coming toward us but not really seeing us. My brother started to cry—"

She closes the book. "Welcome to Duane's House of Torture," she says.

Duane, sitting on the center console watching this spectacle, frowns. "Leave me out of this. I'm a pacifist."

Louise jumps down off the stack, grabs another box. "Let's see what America's consumers have chosen for your punishment today," she says. The Troll struggles. He's an eighteen-year-old high school dropout named Evan who lives in the town house his parents bought him in Santa Monica. In his mind he's always been a victim of persecution.

Don't say cunt. Don't say wetback. Don't say kike.

"If this is your, whatever, hurt feelings about having to suck a few dicks," he says, "why don't you go shout about it in some butch dyke drum circle. I'm innocent."

Louise snorts, opens the box. Her eyes light up. "Yahtzee," she says, and pulls a spray bottle out of the box. She displays it like a product model, turning at the waist to show Duane, then Evan.

"What the fuck is that?" says Evan.

Louise uses her open right hand to underline the words *Coyote Urine*, written in cursive on the plastic bottle. "Looks like some poor Riverside resident has got himself a marmot problem." She holds the bottle up like a gun, nozzle pointed at Evan's face.

"Don't you fucking dare," he says.

"Where," says Louise, "is he?"

"Who?"

She sprays Evan in the face. A musky stink fills the van.

"Jesus," says Duane.

Evan screams and thrashes his head from side to side. There is urine in his eyes and mouth.

"Round two," says Louise. "Where is he?"

"You fucking bitch," yells Evan. "You fucking cunt."

She sprays him again. He thrashes, retches, a wave of nausea hitting him.

"Unh-unh," she says. "If you're gonna barf, do it in a box."

She throws the spray bottle behind her, grabs another box. Inside her is a simmering rage older than her body. She would hurt them all if she could, all the white boys with their tiki torches and backward baseball caps chanting *Jews will not replace us*, all the muscle car drivers plowing through crowds of peaceful protesters, all the minivan drivers with their Blue Lives Matter bumper stickers, all the cops they worship with their choke holds and high-capacity magazines. But she can't, so she takes it out on the Troll.

"You're crazy," says Evan, then spits, "I was taking you there."

Louise picks up a smaller box, thinking about the journey each one of these packages took to get here, the fossil fuels burned, plastics extruded. Items manufactured and flown hundreds, maybe thousands of miles, to a sorting facility, staffed by freelance contractors working long hours for low wages. Boxes sent by God so that she could be his righteous hand.

"You've got no right," Evan sputters, "assaulting an honest white man in broad daylight just because you got your snowflake feelings hurt. That's the fucking world."

Inside this new box is a smaller black box with flames on it. The words MEAT CLAWS are printed on the side in yellow all caps.

"Inshallah," says Louise, and shows the box to Evan.

He spits coyote piss. "What is that?" he asks.

She tears open the box. "Ever have a pulled pork sandwich?" she asks him, taking the black metal claws from the box. They have metal loops for her hands to slide through, the claws settling onto her knuckles. They are made of polished, sharpened iron.

Evan realizes he may be fucked.

"He's in Palm Springs," he says. "The Wizard. He's been going crazy. Four days without pussy. I told him I could bring him some girls, but it's loony tunes out there, kitty-cat, end of the world and all that, so bitches are hiding in their storm cellars."

"Don't call me that. Kitty-cat."

"Fuck you. Your name is whatever I decide to call you."

She holds up her clawed hands. "I'm the Wolverine, bitch," she says. "Say my name."

Duane stands. "Louise."

But she steps toward Evan, already picturing the blood.

Duane puts a hand on her arm. "Louise. He told you where he is."

She shrugs him off. "Address," she says. "Number of guards. Exits and entrances. We're nowhere near done."

She clacks the claws together, causing sparks. "I wanna see what his guts look like on the *outside*," she says, and smiles.

Evan thrashes against his restraints. Inside the foil bag it's 122 degrees.

"It's in my phone. He sent a photo. I don't know about security. He just texts me, asks me for girls or drugs. I swear."

She scrapes the claws together, making an awful screech.

"Evan, baby," she says. "I wanna help you. I really do. But God has other plans."

Bathsheba

The Orcs put Bathsheba in the wine cellar. It has been three days since they left Marfa, fleeing in the middle of the night in a rush. Katie remembers the lights going on in her tower room, then hands on her shoulders and a sharp pain in her arm, and then nothing. She woke in a helicopter flying over mountains. Was this still Texas? Were there mountains in Texas? They landed in a clearing, black SUVs waiting. Ahead of her she saw the Wizard and Astrid climb into the lead car with Liam Orci, and then the other Orci brothers pulled her out of the chopper and carried her by the elbows to the follow car.

"Where are we going?" she asked, but neither answered. They drove for twenty-five minutes, pulling through the gates of another impossible estate at high speed. Before the SUV had even stopped, armed guards were moving toward them, car doors opening. They pulled Katie from the car and hustled her into the house—a Cape Cod–style mansion—through an elaborate kitchen and down a flight of stairs into a windowless basement. A cot had been set up next to a stone wall. Boaz Orci put her suitcase on the floor and told her she'd be *safe here*, then retreated with the other guards. Katie heard the door lock behind them. She had no sense of time. How long had it been since they left San Francisco? Since that first night with Mobley, since he held her down with Astrid stroking her hair, telling her *everything would be fine*, to just *lie back and enjoy it*.

She put her hand on her belly, once flat, now a noticeable slope. The morning sickness had started a few weeks ago—months? She had thrown up everything they tried to feed her, meal after meal, until they'd had a doctor come in and put an IV in her arm. Bathsheba pleaded with him to help her, to call the police, but the doctor never faltered from his task, taking her temperature, measuring her blood pressure. She had turned nineteen that morning, but no one noticed. No one knew. It took three Orcs to hold her so he could get the needle in for her intravenous fluids. They had to strap her down so she didn't pull it out.

Time passed. The nausea faded. The tube came out. Then came the middle-of-the-night panic, the helicopter ride, and the windowless basement. She sat on the floor, listening to movement on the floorboards overhead. Eventually, she dozed. The sound of footsteps wakes her, the clip-clop of heels on the basement stairs. Astrid steps into the light, carrying a tray.

"Hey there, sleepyhead," she says. "I've got that quinoa salad you like and some soup."

She puts the tray on top of a plastic folding table. The plate and bowl are metal, as is the cup. The cutlery is biodegradable, no knife, only a spoon. As rosy a picture as they paint, her captors are clearly aware that a woman in her position might consider suicide as a means of escape.

"Welcome to California," Astrid says in a breezy voice. "Sorry about all the drama."

She takes a tube of lip balm from her pocket, rolls it on.

"Come on," she says, "eat up. You don't want to go back on the feeding tube, do you?"

Katie climbs to her feet, goes to the table, sits on a folding chair. "We're in the mountains," she says.

The quinoa has cherries and almond slivers in it. She pokes it with her fork.

Astrid pulls out the other folding chair, sits. "Your résumè says you're from Georgia originally."

"Why? Does Master wanna meet his in-laws?"

"Cheeky little thing," says Astrid with a sour face.

Katie pushes her plate away. "I'm from Florida, actually. My real name is Bathsheba DeWitt."

Astrid smiles, as if to say, *Yeah, right.*

Bathsheba sips her water. "There are thousands of us, actually, born off the grid, no birth certificate, no social security number. When we escape into the wild, we have to forge fake documents, driver's licenses, school transcripts. So that's what I did."

Astrid's face falls. "Wait," she says. "You lied to us?"

"Seems only fair," says Bathsheba, "since you lied to me."

Astrid looks away, doing the math, the investment that they've made, her worth to them as the mother of his child.

"So you're what?" she says. "Some Tallahassee mall rat?"

"I'm from Lake Mystic," says Bathsheba, "and we weren't allowed to go to the mall, because of the police state, surveillance cameras, facial recognition software. We had a generator and a septic tank. Our water came from a well."

Astrid smiles. "How novel," she says. "You're one of those *survivalists*. And here we thought you were just another artist wannabe."

"Oh no. I can live in the woods for weeks, eating

berries, collecting rainwater. I know how to build a lean-to and make weapons."

She holds up her biodegradable spoon.

"Like how, with a dull tool, you wanna scoop out the eyes first, blind your opponent. Then, while they're screaming, you crush their windpipe with your fist."

Astrid blinks at her, all the color draining from her face.

"Well then," she says. She slides her chair back, stands. "That's—I'll leave you to it." She takes a step toward the stairs.

Bathsheba grabs her hand. "You made a mistake," she tells Astrid. "When you picked me."

Astrid pulls her hand away, eyes wide. "Boaz will be down shortly to collect your tray," she says, hurrying to the stairs. "Try to get some rest. You must be exhausted after all that travel."

She runs up the stairs, slams the door behind her.

Bathsheba, now Katie, reaches for her tray, and this time the meal tastes good. She eats every bite, even the vegan brownie, licking her fingers when she finishes. In hindsight, she shouldn't be surprised to find herself here. Just look at her mother, who rose before dawn, making breakfast, chopping wood, folding laundry until long after her kids had gone to bed. What was she if not a captive? Avon wouldn't let the children go to school—

government schools, he called them, *where kids are programmed to be a cog in the machine—* so their mother taught them how to spell, how to add and subtract. When she was tired, which was always, their mother sometimes lost the ability to watch her tone of voice. Her reward was the back of her husband's hand or a blow from a rolled-up newspaper, the way one might discipline a dog.

Samson was the firstborn, named for the strongest man in the Bible, a favorite of God's, betrayed by a woman. Bathsheba came second, named for a biblical object of lust, wife of David, mother of Solomon. A woman whose sole value was in her service to men. Bathsheba, now Katie, was a girl in a family that valued boys, that viewed the female sex as duplicitous. This presented her with a choice, either act like a boy or be owned by one. So she learned, first to wrestle, then to fight, then to shoot. She learned that there is power in a woman's voice, but only if she is willing to take a beating to be heard.

At night she would lie in her bed reading old *National Geographic*s with a flashlight, dreaming of faraway places. She would climb the Himalayas, sail the Mediterranean Sea. Her friends would be great apes and snow leopards.

During the day her father taught her to survive in the wilderness, how to build a lean-to and set an animal trap. He taught her how to hide and stay hidden. When she was twelve, she spent two weeks living in a ravine, drinking rainwater and eating squirrels she shot with an air rifle. Even then she was practicing, planning her escape. Except this time it wouldn't be government men hunting her; it would be her own father, scouring the ground for footprints, sniffing the winter air. But she would beat him at his own game, vanishing like a snow-flake in a storm.

Bathsheba cleans her plate, turning it upside down on the table. To fight off leg cramps, she walks around the empty basement, memorizing the terrain, looking for weak points.

She has been a fool, lured into a trap by the promise of a better life. But she has been trapped before. She escaped once. She will do it again. And then she will burn this place to the ground.

O

The storm comes in the middle hours of the night. A hot wind slams the shutters closed. The pressure drops. Lightning ignites the ridgeline. Bathsheba wakes to the sound of running feet upstairs. Her door opens, three men come down, bundle up her suitcase. Boaz Orci throws her clothes at her.

"The mountain's on fire," he says. "We're moving again."

They hustle her out to an SUV and blow through the open gates, spraying gravel. The air is heavy with smoke. Bathsheba sits in back between two guards. *Did I do this?* she wonders, still only half-awake, *set fire to the world?* Boaz is up front in the passenger seat, chewing Nicorette gum. He speaks into his wrist, listening to inaudible patter through an earpiece.

"Go around it," he says. "We need to get to the highway."

They're in a convoy of three SUVs, piloted by men with tactical combat experience. Together, they race down winding mountain roads, the fire so close sometimes they can feel the heat.

In the center car, Astrid sits with Mobley. His mood is toxic, body emanating clouds of medieval wrath. Even he can't spin this recent turn of events as positive. He has been chased from two homes in two weeks, once by infidels and now by weather. This is not the story of a god.

They are headed for Palm Springs, where it's 104 in the shade, and then maybe out of the country, if this persecution continues. E. L. Mobley holds no allegiance to anything as petty as a nation. He is a citizen of the world, or rather a member of its ruling class. He has billions in banks all over the globe, real estate owned by trusts he controls, and a fleet of planes to take him wherever he wants to go. Customs and Immigration are barely a formality. There are concierge services he uses, fixers he employs on every continent. People don't say no to him. Governments cater to him. The biggest law firms in the world bill him thousands of hours a year for civil, criminal, and tax work. They have protected him from police investigations in Germany, Bermuda, and France and negotiated a slap on the wrist from the American Justice Department for that incident with the Calloway girl.

What force on Earth could stop a man like this?

Astrid has learned to anticipate his fickle needs, which is how she knows before Mobley snaps his fingers that he wants to make a call and what number he wants her to dial. Gabe Lin answers on the first ring.

"How soon can you have a team in Palm Spring?" Mobley asks.

"I can have men on the ground in ninety minutes," Gabe says.

"We're being chased out of the mountains by these ridiculous fires," says Mobley. "Insult to injury after the events in Marfa, which—thank you again for the warning. I assume you dealt with the men you caught."

"Yes, sir. My client had instructions for all of them."

"Good. Can you send a team of six?"

"I'd recommend two teams of eight, Mr. Mobley. We're hearing chatter that the domestic situation could turn violent in the next few days. Politics and all that. I'd want to make sure you don't get any on you, if you know what I mean."

"Two teams of eight it is. Contact Ms. Prefontaine to set up the details."

He hangs up, hands the phone back. Astrid puts it in her jacket pocket. Sometimes when she wakes in the morning, there are bite marks on her stomach. She has the feeling of cold eyes watching her in the bathroom. She tells herself they're spider bites, that the feeling of being watched is just that, a feeling. But Astrid has always felt that Mobley is something more than human. For her the feeling is secular—this is a man with the genetic superiority of a billionaire. Money and power coat him in a blanket of invulnerability. They cloak him with power in its purest form, the power to make anyone do anything, to influence governments, to bring corporations to their knees. She has heard others refer to him as *a wizard* in reverential tones. This is just their supernatural brains, she thinks, trying to deify something beyond their comprehension. What does the word even mean anymore? Who are the wizards of modern life? Technology nerds. Boys with pocket protectors you call when you can't print.

Mobley is an emperor, a centibillionaire, worth one hundred billion dollars—$100,000,000,000. A man with more personal wealth than the annual GDP of Cuba or Ethiopia or Guatemala, Oman or Kenya or Luxembourg. A man worth twice the GDP of Slovenia and Lithuania, three times the GDP of Yemen and Latvia and Cameroon. Each of his billions = 100 x $100,000,000—itself a sum so large as to be achieved by only five thousand Americans. Each hundred million is in turn made up of individual millions, more money than most human beings on Planet Earth earn in a lifetime. Astrid looks over. Mobley is on her phone, reviewing photos of young women on an app he's had designed—photos fed into the system by recruiters all over the country.

He has more money than 7,800,000,000 people. What does that make her boss, if not a god?

O

They reach the Palm Springs estate at 2:00 a.m., their SUVs covered in thick black soot. It is a thirty-acre compound on the edge of a suburban neighborhood, walled on all sides, with a main gate and one for deliveries behind the guest house. There is a tennis court, a stable, and a palatial pool, as well as a putting green and a helipad. The main house is over ten thousand square feet. There are two guard houses, one on the north side, the other on the south.

A six-thousand-square-foot pink adobe guest house sits near the western wall, surrounded by palm trees and cacti. In addition to Mobley's advance security team, there are sixteen security goblins from Gabe's firm. Legolas and Aragorn have seniority. They meet Mobley's SUV as it pulls in.

"Orci the senior gave us the lay of the land," Legolas tells Mobley. "We've mounted additional security cameras around the neighborhood and set up a mobile command center behind the stables. I took the initiative to bring on a drone team at no additional cost."

Mobley doesn't answer, just walks across the Italian paving stones and into the main house, taking a glass of cucumber water from his Korean majordomo. Astrid puts herself in front of Legolas, insulating her boss from the details.

"I'll expect hourly updates," she says, "night and day."

In the distance, she sees Boaz Orci pull Bathsheba out of the rear SUV and walk her to the guest house.

"We'll need a dedicated security team for our guest," Astrid tells the goblins. "They've already come for her once."

"Yes, ma'am," says Aragorn. He'll be the day commander. Legolas will run the night shift. And both will coordinate with Liam Orci, who leads the Orc security detail.

The estate is surrounded on three sides by desert, giving them good visibility, but the shared wall with the gated community could be a problem. Mobley built the estate fifteen years ago, before this neighborhood of McMansions—envy-green multi-millionaires with their air of superiority. What do they know about true wealth? He has been to this estate twice in fifteen years. Despite that, there is a full staff working daily to keep the grounds and facilities in top condition, should the billionaire ever choose to fly in on a whim, but the truth is, most of the employees have never seen his face.

O

This time Bathsheba gets a whole house to herself. Before she arrived, the staff removed the cutlery and glass. They took down the curtain rods. There is a suicide epidemic in America, they reasoned. Who knew how it spread? So all the furniture has been removed except for one bed and a table in the dining room with a single chair. Orci lays out the rules as he shows her around.

"The kitchen's off-limits," he says. "Meals will be prepared and brought to you from the main house. You'll notice all the doors have been removed. This is to ensure a clean line of sight for the cameras. If you need anything, just say it out loud. Someone will be listening."

He leads her into the bedroom, puts her suitcase on the floor.

"You like this job?" she asks him.

He looks around. The closet is empty and doorless. The toilet seat has been removed from the bathroom, as has the mirrored door to the medicine cabinet.

"I'm a fan of clarity," he says.

"Meaning?"

"Meaning tell me what you need and I'll do it. Meaning, pay me X amount for Y scenario."

"And you don't care that he's evil? That Y scenario is you kidnapping a pregnant woman?"

Orci sits on her suitcase. "Did you know that air pollution protects the Earth? Keeps it from getting hotter? I mean, it's getting hotter, that's just—go outside. The state's on fire. But I'm saying aerosol pollution, what they call aerosol pollution, is keeping our planet cool by reflecting sunlight back into outer space."

"You're making that up."

"No. I heard it on Joe Rogan. So, you tell me—all the terrible things in the world, are they really that bad?"

"He fucks children."

"Half of India is fucking children. Haven't you ever heard of arranged marriages and child brides? The age of consent is a construct, like voting. You think it's science? You think an eighteen-year-old is really more qualified to vote than a seventeen-year-old? Show me the science."

"I feel like I'm sitting here and watching you masturbate."

"Sorry. That's not in the cards for us, sweetheart. I've got boundaries."

Bathsheba goes to the window, looks out. Smoke from the fires is blowing west, so the sky is blue and clear, with tiny perfect clouds. The lawn is thick and perfect. She can see the pool from here, a perfect rectangle, tiled in orange and white. There is an armed guard standing beside it, wearing mirrored sunglasses. Bathsheba feels certain that no one has ever swum in that water, the same way she knows there are whole cities in China filled with empty apartments. Just another place the rich store their wealth.

She remembers her brother's voice on the phone, how for the first thirty seconds he thought it was a social call. They have a system, a way to stay in touch without their dad finding out. He asked her how she liked San Francisco. She told him she made a mistake, that she'd trusted the wrong person and now she was a prisoner. She could hear his brain trying to process the information, could hear the stammer in his voice. *Who, what, where?*

Marfa, she said, *E. L. Mobley.*

But someone was coming and she had to hang up.

She thinks of him now, her brother. Was he the reason they had to leave Texas? Did he come for her? While she thinks about this, she does what her father taught her. She catalogs the exits. She searches for defendable positions.

"The vine is really beautiful," she tells Orci. "On the wall. What is it, wisteria?"

"How the fuck should I know?"

"You don't see those in the desert. So much water."

Orci stands. "He can afford it."

Bathsheba says nothing.

Orci taps the doorjamb three times. "Get cleaned up. Dinner's in half an hour."

She hears him leave, hears the front door open and close. She knows that somewhere, someone is watching her on a screen. That they will watch her sleep, watch her bathe, watch her pee.

It's been weeks since she saw Mobley. He used

to visit her every night before she was pregnant, but once she started to show, she could tell he found her disgusting. So now she only sees Astrid, the fixer, and a rotating array of muscle. This is her life now. The old her feels like a different species, Homo Originus, a creature of the placid savanna, an herbivore targeted and tracked. And yet isn't she the girl who survived two weeks alone in the Everglades on one of her daddy's *missions*? Who beat up Bobby Spencer in grade school when he made fun of her dress? Wasn't she the one who put the animals down when they were sick or lame, because Samson was too soft?

Bathsheba DeWitt is not the damsel in distress. She is the dragon. They just don't know it yet.

The Prophet

Let's be honest. We have always been a nation at war. Or not always, but for twenty-plus years now, since the planes hit the towers. Since the then-president stood on the rubble and bullhorned his words to the world—"I can hear you. The rest of the world hears you. And the people who knocked these buildings down will hear all of us soon!" Twenty-plus years of bombs and bullets, of improvised explosive devices and traumatic brain injuries, before Enduring Freedom and the Patriot Act, before *yes we can* and Obama, before Beyoncé married Jay-Z, before smartphones and tablets, before the euro, before GPS, before Occupy Wall Street, before Facebook and Twitter, before YouTube, before Hurricane Katrina, before Black Lives Matter, before oxycodone, before Tesla, before *Avatar*, before *The Lord of the Rings*, before *Bourne*, before *Twilight*, before

Harry Potter, before the swine flu, before political correctness and its backlash, before *NCIS* and *Game of Thrones* and *The Walking Dead*, before low-rise jeans and high-rise thongs, before twerking, before "WAP," before premium cable and the birth of streaming, before mortgage-backed securities, the housing bubble, and the Great Recession, before seven Super Bowl rings for Tom Brady, before #MeToo, before *Stranger Things*, before the God King and the pandemic that stopped the world.

Before your children were born.

That's how long we have been at war in Afghanistan and Iraq. A forever war with 3,000,000 soldiers serving 5,400,000 tours of duty. They were under thirty, on average. Fifty percent were married. Fifty percent had children. Three hundred and fifty-nine thousand marines, 18,000,846 army soldiers, 464,554 navy sailors, and so on.

More than seven thousand of them have been killed and 52,671 wounded—had body parts amputated, been intubated or concussed. But the actual human toll is much, much higher. Some studies estimate that more than 480,000 people have been killed in these wars, directly or indirectly, more than 250,000 of them civilians.

Twenty-three years ÷ 480,000 = 20,869 per year, at the time of this writing. Fifty-seven per day. Each human death brought about by a fellow human being pulling a trigger or dropping a bomb.

That age-old equation of killer and killed.

Nietzsche once wrote, "In times of peace, the warlike man attacks himself."

Everyone has a theory.

The Pew Research Center places the start of Generation Z as 1997, which means our youngest adult generation has never known a time in which their country was not at war. It is their permanent reality. For them, combat is normal, and—in the same way a bee can see only flowers—a country at war comes to accept war as its natural state of being.

So we strap on our guns and fight.

O

All through the first night there is infighting. Now that they've taken the air force base, this loose coalition of militias understand they must hold it and somehow plan their next move. To do this they realize, almost as an afterthought, they will need leaders. And so the bosses of each faction brawl through the night—mostly verbally, but sometimes physically—until the question is settled.

Three-tour marine veterans battle weekend warriors. Neo-Nazis and fascist-anarchists fight

Jesus-patriots, paintball champions, and evangelists of the God King. Though they disagree on most things, they all ascribe to what can best be described as *hyperfreedom*. The old way of eliminating obstacles to individual choice has become unsatisfactory, because one is always stopped from achieving true independence by the constraints of reality—that is, we live in a nation of laws and taxes, where the few make rules for the many. With *hyperfreedom,* the movement realized they could expand personal freedom ad infinitum, releasing all Americans to do, say, or believe anything they choose, individually.

The men on this airfield, and they are mostly men, would rather die than live another second in what they call Illegitimate America, ruled illegally by a false king, a king dedicated to controlling their thoughts and actions, to telling them what to believe, a king who demands they teach their children that all police are racists, that whites should apologize for some four-hundred-year-old bygone.

And so, when the Prophet and Samson look around, they see flat-earthers and debt-hawk libertarians, anti-Semites and Orthodox Jews, anti-vaxxers, incels, and enlisted men. Their captors either hate cops or they *are* cops, shooting their guns in the air like Mexican revolutionaries in an old John Ford movie. The Legalize Marijuana Coalition is smoking skunk weed in the motor pool. The Tyler Durdens are punching corpses. There are Green Berets and Klan knights in the guard towers. They know the war isn't over yet because wars never end. Now is not the time to relax. They know the enemy is out there—that vile opposition— and that the enemy is more powerful than they are, even though their enemy is mostly unarmed, because believing they are facing an evil empire causes fear, and facing their fear makes them feel righteous and heroic. These are the things men do to feel real.

The next morning, the Prophet and Samson are woken from their cement floor slumber and dragged onto the tarmac. The sun is a fiery red ball igniting the sky. Soot blizzards down around them, covering everything in fine ash. Shirtless muscle boys lift weights near the refueling station, music blaring from inside an M1150 Assault Breacher vehicle, Nine Inch Nails on autorepeat.

I wanna fuck you like an animal.
I wanna feel you from the inside.

The Tyler Durdens have been put in charge of base security. They stand shirtless under an orange sky, chemical lip burns scarring their hands. Some have black skull bandannas tied over their noses and mouths. Their leader wears a bandolier around his bare chest. He is a deity of sit-ups and Alex Jones vitamin supplements.

"Boys, boys," he says, grinning. "Project Mayhem es aqui. Can you feel the burn?"

The Prophet gets to his feet. He has found a pair of glasses with a somewhat similar prescription, but the left lens is cracked. He adjusts them now on his face.

"We want to thank you," he says, "for aiding us in our time of need. But we're on a mission from God, and we must leave."

Boss Durden steps toward the Prophet. The sky above him is apocalypse orange.

You tear down my reason
(Help me) it's your sex I can smell.

"You are not special," he says. "You're not a beautiful and unique snowflake. You're the same decaying organic matter as everything else."

Samson runs a hand through his matted hair. He has been awake all night, trying to plan their escape.

"Brothers," he says, "what a glorious day. Can you believe it? The revolution is finally here. What can we do to help?"

"You can clean the shitter," says one of the masked Durdens. The others laugh.

The Prophet takes a deep breath. When he exhales, smoke comes from between his teeth. This is how choked the air is from wildfires burning uphill.

"You're afraid," he says. "We understand."

The Durdens stop laughing.

"In moments of existential angst," says the Prophet, "beings as a whole slip away, so that just the nothing crowds round. That's Heidegger. You should like him. He was a Nazi, too. *Das Nichts selbst nichtet*."

One of the Durdens pulls a large hunting knife.

"Dude," says Samson, putting a hand on the Prophet's arm. "Cut it out."

But the Prophet is done being a prisoner. He has someplace to be, a holy mission, and no shirt-less poser with a five-dollar philosophy of macho nihilism is going to stop him.

"God talked to me all night," he tells them, "all night lying on a concrete floor. His voice was the hum of cables deep underground. You will let us go, or face His wrath."

"Tyler," shouts the Durden with the knife.

"Yes, Tyler," shouts the boss, drill sergeant-like.

"Can I cut him now?"

"Please."

Knife Durden dances forward, slashing the air.

"This is your life, kid," he says, "and it's ending one minute at a time."

Samson sighs. Like a one-eared pit bull, he was raised by his father to fight. Part of him always knew it would come to this. He unbuckles his belt, pulls it through the loops.

"God," says the Prophet, raising his voice, "is unhappy."

Samson steps in front of the Prophet, snaps his belt between his hands.

Knife Durden feints a lunge.

You let me violate you
You let me desecrate you.

"With Noah it was the flood," shouts the Prophet. "In Sodom and Gomorrah, He turned the sinners to stone. Look around you. The sky is burning. What did He tell us—no more flood, the fire next time."

Knife Durden spins, slashing. Samson steps back. He flicks his wrist, and the belt buckle catches Knife Durden just below the left ear, drawing blood. Two other Durdens step forward. The Prophet moves into the center, his hands raised.

"You will let us go or feel His wrath."

The Durdens stare at him, losing interest in the circus. Some of them are hungover. The rest are still drunk. The sooner they filet these boys, the sooner they can find some Marla Singers to violate. Samson tightens the belt around his right hand, ready for the next wave.

Boss Durden steps forward, pulling a revolver from his belt. He aims it at the Prophet's face. "There is no God," he says.

An explosion rocks the hangar behind them, blowing hot debris ahead of it like a shove. Simultaneously, they hear the scream of an incoming missile, and the M1150 Assault Breacher explodes, blowing the Durdens off their feet.

The army is here to take back the base.

Samson ducks instinctually, but the Prophet doesn't flinch. God is here. In his might and majesty He has parted the seas and torn down the Jericho walls. The Prophet lowers his gaze to find Boss Durden lying in a pool of his own blood. Half his jaw is missing, and he gurgles his confusion to the sky, left arm outstretched.

Somewhere, a .50-caliber machine gun starts up, and then everywhere they look they see muzzle flashes. Samson grabs the Prophet's hand, pulls him toward the fence line. A tank crashes through the barbed wire ahead of them, firing a depleted uranium shell with a deafening *thoom*. Samson and the Prophet duck behind a jeep, wait for it to pass. Smoke from the incoming gas grenades mixes with the smut in the air, turning the day into a blur of light and dark shapes.

The apocalypse becomes an impressionist painting. In a patch of clear air they see an anarchist in a giraffe costume stumble across the runway on fire, his arms and legs windmilling. Overhead they hear the heavy rotors of army helicopters, Special Forces operatives in midnight black descending on unseen fast ropes, here to mop up the strays. Samson and the Prophet climb an embankment and squeeze through a hole in the cyclone fence, and then they are free.

O

The apocalypse, it turns out, is easy. There is no confusion, no uncertainty about stakes. The world is in chaos. You must survive. End of story. It is the Time Before that tests your strength, your mind. The years of not knowing—is the world ending? Are we descending into some new dark age? Before is the era of great anxiety. You live in a state of heightened awareness, of constant adrenaline, looking, always looking for the straw that will break the camel's back. The smallest sounds wake you in the night. You reach for your phone, checking the news, wondering if the zombies have risen while you've been asleep. For clarity, we shall call this period the pre-apocalypse. The Age of Unknowing. And it is over now.

Samson and the Prophet run through the urban sprawl. They are on the low desert streets of Morningside Heights in El Paso. Sounds of gunfire from the base reach them like distant fireworks, fierce at first, then sporadic. There are tanks in the street, transports filled with National Guard soldiers, but also pickup trucks on kamikaze missions, jumping the center divide. Pockets of discord arise ahead of them and must be avoided, militia clusters laying down covering fire wearing makeshift gas masks and firing armor-penetrating rounds.

They move west down Nations Avenue, past the high school and the library. From inside they hear the sound of chain saws and do not slow. The Prophet appears to be praying under his breath.

"We need to check Instagram," says Samson, thinking now of Story, of his sister. He could give a shit about God's mission. He wants the people he loves to be safe. Wind blows in hot gusts from the west, swirling dust and ash from the fuselages of cars. They cover their mouths and noses with their hands and run, crouching low for no good reason other than it feels like the right thing to do. Three hundred miles away, in the mountains, catastrophic wildfires surge, firebrands leap miles ahead of each conflagration, starting new fires, like a lie you can't control. Twisters of pure flame cyclone up into the clouds. Those who can, flee, but for many the fire moves too fast. Later firefighters will find the corpses of desperate people boiled alive in their swimming pools, others huddled together in grim embrace, like the victims of an atomic bomb. The mountain air fills with the sound of car tires exploding, their aluminum wheels melting in rivers that flow down sloping driveways, plastic garbage toters reduced to colored stains on the bubbling asphalt.

In Morningside Heights, the residential streets are empty now. Residents have fled or gone to ground. They pass house after house with the blinds drawn.

"Here," says the Prophet, turning up the front walk of a single-story home. The front door is open. Samson hurries to keep up, blinded momentarily by the darkness of the interior. It is a modest house with a big-screen TV. On-screen, QVC is selling its wares—cubic zirconium necklaces, agate bracelets now at reduced prices. There is a laptop open on the kitchen table. Samson sits, turns it on.

"It's password protected," he tells the Prophet.

The Prophet opens the fridge, takes out a carton of orange juice, finds a glass. He fills it, drinks, gulping it down with singular focus. Samson tries 1234, then 4321. The Prophet puts down the glass.

"PraiseHim," he says.

"What?"

"The password is PraiseHim. Capital H."

Samson tries it. "No go," he says.

The Prophet thinks about that. "PraiseHim exclamation point," he says.

Samson types it in. The screen unlocks. He is looking at a desktop jigsaw filled with cats. He opens a browser, but it won't connect.

"There's no internet," he says. "The internet's down. Probably the government hit the kill switch." He stands.

"Look for a phone or a tablet. Something with a cellular signal."

They search the house. In a back bedroom, Samson finds a Samsung tablet. He wakes it up. There are three bars. On the wall above the bed are eleven crosses laid out in a diamond pattern. Samson finds the Instagram app, opens it. He searches for @bassethoundsrule. The Prophet wanders in and studies the crosses.

"I know you don't believe," he says. "And I'm not asking you to have faith. But can we agree they've been doing it wrong? Humanity. Two thousand years of burning bushes, of sermons on the Mount, and what do they have to show for it? The prosperity gospel? Hassidim refusing to vaccinate? Muslim honor killings? Jihadis in suicide vests? This is God's will?"

Samson scrolls through photos of basset hounds, with their sad eyes and droopy cheeks. His heart is beating a mile a minute. The apocalypse his father warned him about is here, and he is hundreds of miles away from everyone that matters.

"These aren't mistakes," says the Prophet. "This isn't *Oh, I must have heard God wrong.* This is opportunism. This is twisting His will to corrupt ends. Because people are corrupt. Adults. They live in a world of hypocrisy. They will do anything to be rich, to get laid, to have power."

"And you don't want any of that."

"I want to disappear. I want to be forgotten. I want a little house with no electricity hidden in a dell. But what I want doesn't matter. This isn't about me. He's giving us one more chance, one more chance to do His will, to get things right. A do-over. Find a new Garden and start again. Utopia."

Samson holds up the tablet. On it is a picture of a teenage girl with a handwritten sign in front of her face. Samson recognizes the T-shirt. It's Louise.

"They're in Palm Springs."

The Prophet holds up his hands, smiles. "Praise be," he says.

Simon

Utopia is a made-up word, coined by Thomas More in 1516. It is a pun, meaning both "a good" place and "nowhere." So even in its conception, the impossibility of finding a land free from the imperfections of human society was evident. And yet, throughout history, human beings have set out to build their perfect communities. Failure after failure, it matters not. Dreamers will always dream.

A purer future. A better way.

America itself was seen as utopia at first, the New World, filled with natural beauty and infinite resources, uncultivated by "civilized" hands. Like most utopian ideals, the New World rose from discontent. It was the idyllic fantasy of Europeans fed up with the world they had. They saw this new Garden of Eden as a gift from God. One that offered escape from the problems that plagued them—hopelessness, debt, religious oppression. Escape too from the responsibility of rebuilding a system that was fundamentally flawed. Flee, don't fix. And here, just a boat ride away, was a turn-key solution, where life would be peaceful and beautiful and good.

The natives who populated the New World were a problem, but they could be killed or "civilized." To avoid staining their utopia with the scourge of backbreaking labor, the settlers turned to slavery, bringing millions of men, women, and children over from Africa in chains. They realized that this utopia offered something that no other utopian society had ever offered before—profit. In America, one could live in the kingdom of heaven and get rich at the same time. Truly, this was the land of plenty. The trick was to revise the idea of utopia to include slaves. To do this, they amended the teachings of Christ. He had created Africans to free his followers from endless toil. Immoral became moral.

In this way, an act of hope became an act of fantasy. And when the pressure of living this lie became too great, some disillusioned Americans packed their belongings and fled their original settlements. (Flee, don't fix, remember.) They headed west, determined this time to find the *real* utopia.

As the sociologist Ralf Dahrendorf once wrote: "All utopias from Plato's Republic to George Orwell's brave new world of 1984 have had one element of construction in common: they are all societies from which change is absent."

And yet isn't it our right as human beings to dream? And so, a new set of utopians built towns named New Harmony, Oberlin Colony, and Oneida. Here life would be fertile and ideal. Here humanity would escape the shackles of the old ways, would build a more perfect union with liberty and justice for all.

And yet, in the words of Immanuel Kant:

Out of the crooked timber of humanity, no straight thing was ever made.

O

They drive through the night, taking back roads when the highway is closed due to the fires. Avon avoids the roadblocks and fire engines, like a man who has spent his whole life sneaking around the law. They are heading east toward the fires, passing armadas of fleeing cars, some so hot their paint has bubbled. Ahead, the roads empty. At the 243 junction, they find themselves alone in a blizzard of ash. They take off their socks and stuff them into the AC vents to block the smoke. It is 1:00 a.m. Avon peers into the murk, the car's headlights reflecting back into his eyes, swallowed whole by a fog of incineration.

On the radio they hear Mexican tubas.

Avon sees a roadblock ahead, slows. There is an army jeep and a Bradley tank blocking the highway. He stops the car. No soldiers are visible. Story, asleep in the backseat, startles awake.

"What's going on?" she says.

Around them, the road is still. No one approaches. Outside, the midnight sky glows bloody.

Avon takes out his 9mm, checks the chamber.

"Wait here," he says, and climbs out of the car.

They watch as he approaches the truck, then circles to the Bradley, disappearing from sight.

"Are we close to the fires?" Story asks, rubbing her eyes.

Simon leans forward and squints through the dusty windscreen.

"We're in the fires," he says.

Story slides across the backseat to the passenger side. She peers into the underbrush, coughs.

If we stay here much longer, she thinks, *we're going to run out of air.*

There is a leg sticking out of a ditch on the shoulder.

"Simon," she says.

He looks over. The ditch is full of bodies.

Simon opens his door.

"Don't," says Story, but without energy.

Simon gets to his feet. His eyes start to water immediately. He takes a shallow breath, coughs. The ash under his feet is like Utah powder, the driest snow. But unlike snow, it doesn't crunch when he walks. It is an absence, the feeling of walking through nothing. He takes three slow steps to the shoulder. The ditch is filled with soldiers. Their bodies are perforated, their uniforms saturated red.

He hears movement, turns. A figure emerges from the shadows, moving toward them. Simon's pulse quickens.

Story calls from the car. "Simon."

He moves back to the car. The smoke clears. The figure is Avon, coming back toward them.

"Nobody," he says, and tucks his gun into his belt.

Then Simon hears something whistle past his ear, followed by a crack. Avon grunts, falls to one knee. Another crack, and the side-view mirror of the rental car explodes. Story scrambles into the driver's seat.

A third shot. Simon dives into the ditch. It is soft with corpses, their blood already dry from the wildfire scorch. In the distance, he sees three figures emerge from the darkness.

"I got one of 'em," calls a voice.

More shots ring out, these from behind him. Simon turns. Avon is leaning against the front bumper, his arms resting on the hood. Blood is weeping from his side, just above his belt line.

He squeezes off ten shots, drops the clip, grabs for another.

To the west, one of the shadows says *oof* and tumbles backward. The others dive for cover. Simon can see them now. Two men wearing red firefighter helmets, like trophies, and carrying AR-15s. Avon reloads.

"Kid," he calls. "Help me to the damn car."

Simon thinks about that, about going out there, exposing himself. But there is no time for anxiety, only fear, and fear he can handle. He crawls out of the ditch, crouch-runs to Avon.

"Quick now," says the older man, pushing himself up with his left hand, keeping his gun trained out over the car. Simon gets his shoulder into Avon's armpit and lifts. Together they slide along the car to the open passenger door. Avon gets a grip on it.

"I got it," he says. "Go."

Simon moves toward the back passenger door. He grabs the handle and pulls the door toward him, but then bullets punch into the doorframe and shatter the glass. One of the shots takes Avon's left ear off.

"Son of a bitch," he says and drops into the car, firing wildly.

Simon tumbles onto his back, the wind knocked out of him by the road.

A dozen bullets punch into the trunk and shatter the back windshield. Simon crawls around the front of the car, scrambling to the driver's side. He has visions of Story panicking and running him over. For some reason the idea of this is more terrifying than the firing squad, so he gets up and runs, staying low. He is barely inside the back door, before Story floors the car and tears off, the two back doors slamming shut from centrifugal force.

Gunfire tears up the car, spiderwebs the windshield. Story ducks low, peering over the dash. Beside her, Avon has his hand to his bloody head.

"Motherfucker," he says. "Son of a goddamn cunt fucking Jew."

Simon is in the rear footwell, hearing the hard thwacking sounds of bullets zippering the car. Story steers onto the left shoulder, scraping the guardrail as she veers around the parked truck. The nose of the Bradley tank clips the passenger door, tearing a gash, but then they're past and racing into the night.

And it is here that the levy breaks for Story. Tears pour from her eyes. Her breathing stops, chest tightening. They're going ninety miles per hour, and suddenly everything gets blurry. A wave of grief hits her. No, forget wave, a crushing tsunami of grief, because, of course, her heart isn't empty. It's weak-walled and swollen bigger than her body, and when it bursts, the feeling that floods through her is animal and uncontrollable. It explodes out of her, a ragged caterwaul. Her parents are dead and she is alive. Her brother is out there somewhere alone and scared in the middle of a civil war. Her boyfriend is either dead or a different person than he said he was, or both. The world is on fire, and she is on fire with it, and when the fire stops there will be nothing left.

O

The two shooters get to their feet, rifles smoking in their hands. They can't see the car anymore, but they can hear the engine.

"Shit," says the heavyset one. His heartbeat is jacked, on account of he worked in a battery and lightbulb store until this morning. Now he's a full-on warrior.

"Shiiiit," he repeats, "that was all the way epic."

The pimply one looks down at Leroy, their corpse friend. Or corpse acquaintance is probably more accurate, seeing as how they just met him this morning. When Avon shot him, Leroy fell straight back with both legs bent under him, like a gymnast stretching.

"Look at Leroy," says Pimply. Two hours ago, he slid out of the hills like a ninja and shot the living fuck out of six army boys, watching them dance, just like in the movies.

Fortnite Megadeath, he calls himself now.

Heavyset peers down at Leroy—who, ten minutes ago, wouldn't shut up about how he sold ladies' shoes and sometimes got to look up women's skirts when he was fitting them.

Pimply crouches down, holds out his phone.

"Get my picture," he says, throwing a peace sign, his AR-15 in his other hand.

Heavyset takes the phone, snaps the picture. Pimply's face is streaked with soot like an Indian in war paint.

"Sick," says Pimply, checking himself out on the screen.

Then they hear a low rumble, getting closer. Another sucker headed for the spider's web. They see a muffle of light pinprick the highway to the west. Together they run back toward the army truck, Heavyset holding his pants up by the waist. Pimply is giddy. He doesn't even mind coughing so much. They set up behind the truck's real bumper, swapping in fresh clips.

A single headlight approaches, slows.

"Dude," says Pimply. "Motorcycle. Think I can shoot him off?"

He raises his barrel, but Heavyset pushes it down.

"No, no," he says. "Hold up. Let's—"

He lies down on the ground, points toward the shoulder. "You go—and I'll—" He moans. "Ohhhh. Help. I'm—I'm hurt."

Pimply gets it, cracks up. He grabs both AR-15s, crouch-walks over to the ditch, slides in sloppy, getting a mouthful of soot, but he doesn't care because this is how rock stars fuck.

Down the road the headlight slows, stops. They can hear the engine idling.

"Ohhhh," moans Heavyset. "Please. I'm hurt real bad."

Pimply puts his elbows in the dirt, raises the rifle. He wipes the soot from his eyes, weeping, wishing they'd found some night-vision goggles in the truck. The smoke is so thick he can't see shit. Then he hears the sound of the bike's kickstand going down.

"Ohhhhh," moans Heavyset, and Pimply has to stifle a giggle.

Footsteps approach at a slow, deliberate gait. Pimply flicks off the safety. He hears a snap behind him, turns. A deer stumbles out of the bushes, eyes wild, its horns on fire. Pimply ducks, the buck jumping over him and running across the road.

"Fuckin' hell," he says, as on the road, the footsteps stop.

"Ohhh," moans Heavyset. "Mister, please. I'm hurt real bad."

Shaken, Pimply gets back in position. He can make out the figure now. A young man with shoulder-length hair, wearing some kind of eye patch. He stands twelve feet from Heavyset, who is rolling on the ground, moaning, making it look real.

Pimply tightens his grip on the gun.

On the road the young man turns his head toward him.

"I wouldn't do that if I were you," he says.

Pimply feels a chill go through him. How the fuck does this guy know he's there? Pimply panics, pulls the trigger. The gun clicks. *Shit.* Pimply bangs it with his fist.

"Steve," he shouts. "It's fucking jammed."

On the road, Heavyset rolls onto his stomach, pushing himself up. There is a 9mm in his waistband. He reaches for it. The young man doesn't move.

In the ditch, Pimply pulls out the clip, jams it back in, tries to clear the breach. He hears movement behind him again. Another fucking deer. He doesn't turn, working the rifle until the jammed round pops from the breech.

"Yes," he hisses, raising the rifle. But then there is a growl behind him, impossibly low, so low he feels it in his bones. Pimply has time only to turn his head, and then the bear is on top of him. Half of its fur has been burned off, its left flank bubbling red. The bear thunders out of the brush and pounces on him, sinking its teeth into Pimply's throat. He screams briefly, but then his head is off and bouncing in the road.

Heavyset has his gun halfway out when the bear strikes. He freezes at the sound of it, a nine-hundred-pound predator, half-mad with pain and fear, launching from the underbrush. And then Pimply's head is rolling in the road, and the bear is turning toward him.

Heavyset tugs at the gun, but now it hooks on his pants. He yanks on it as the bear rises out of the ditch and onto the asphalt. It paws at the ground, bellowing in pain, then explodes up onto its back legs, towering twelve feet in the air. The crotch of Heavyset's jeans go dark. He looks to the young man, who stares back at him with a bemused smile, like, *What are you gonna do?*

Heavyset starts to cry. Gun forgotten, he turns and runs toward the center guardrail, hearing the bear drop to its front paws, hearing it chase after him. He grabs for the rail, tries to vault over it, but his foot catches and he tumbles over into the oncoming lane. His gun clatters away, skidding onto the far shoulder. And then the bear is on him. Its teeth sink into his spine. He screams. Behind him, the hillside ignites, flames racing down toward the road.

Randall Flagg gets back on his bike and drives on.

O

They move Avon into the backseat so he can stretch out, clearing the mountains near Bonnie Bell. Story pushes the needle to ninety-five mph. In back, Simon tears the sleeves from his hospital scrubs and fashions a bandage for Avon's ear. He crouches in the footwell, applying pressure. Avon pulls up his shirt. There is a .40-caliber entrance wound above his left hip and a larger exit wound in the small of his back. Inside his body cavity, Avon's kidney and spleen are a kind of toxic soup, mixing with his blood and viscera.

"It didn't used to be like this," he mutters, feverish now, his voice growly from years of smoking unfiltered Camels. "It used to be open and wild, and he'd let me sit in his lap and drive."

"Who?" says Simon, then rings the bloody rag out onto the footwell.

"Daddy," says Avon. He grabs Simon's wrist. "Don't you get it," he says. "It used to be better. We used to be free."

The farther east they drive, the more the air clears, until outside Whitewater they are able to roll down the windows and let in the first fresh air any of them have breathed in three days. The sun is rising when they stop for gas in Palm Springs. The back windshield is gone, the teal four-door exterior perforated with fifty-five holes. While the car is filling, Story goes into the shop and buys Simon a new outfit, yellow sweatpants, a thin white T-shirt with the blue and red Valvoline logo on it, and a pair of flip-flops. She also buys three rolls of paper towels and some duct tape.

"We're taking him to the hospital, right?" says Simon, pulling the T-shirt on over his head, as Story changes Avon's bandages, wrapping the gray tape around his waist.

"No hospitals," mutters Avon, seemingly from sleep.

An Amazon delivery truck drives by, beginning its daily rounds, despite the melee.

The backseats are fabric and have absorbed most of the blood. A red Mercedes pulls into the next pump. A balding man in a pink polo shirt and cargo shorts gets out. There is a sidearm strapped to his waist.

"What the fuck are you looking at?" he asks them, swiping his card. He sets the nozzle, then goes inside. In his mind, the equation is clear.

He's the one with the gun and they're the ones with the car full of bullet holes. Losers, in other words.

Story screws the Kia's gas cap back on. She goes over and peers into the Mercedes.

"Story," warns Simon, but Story leans in through the open window and grabs the preppy asshole's cell phone. Then she is sliding into the Kia's driver's seat as the bald avenger comes out of the shop, carrying a blue Slurpee.

She hands Simon the phone, puts the car in gear. They pull out onto the road.

Story changes lanes, driving the speed limit. They pass a supermarket where all the windows have been smashed. Looters run out carrying frozen meat and ice cream, charcoal briquettes and box cereals.

Simon scrolls through the stolen phone. He finds Instagram, sees the original photo of Louise holding her sign. Under that are a series of images of basset hound puppies shaking their flappy lips. Then he finds a photo of an aquarium in the window display of a store. He shows Story.

"Look it up," she says.

He finds three pet stores in Palm Springs. Only one sells aquariums. It's in the north part of town. The phone relays directions, a left, a right, straight for two miles. They pass six police cars along the way, blue and reds flashing, and a dozen private security vehicles, some of them tactical. The corpses of weekend warriors litter the road. Here in moneyed Palm Springs, the wealthy are leaving nothing to chance. Story turns into a strip mall parking lot. Ulysses Pet Emporium is straight ahead, next to Angel's Sporting Goods on the left and a nail salon on the right. At 2:00 a.m. everything is shuttered and dark.

"Go around back," says Simon.

They park in the loading bay, in front of a rolling garage door.

Simon opens his door.

"Here," says Avon from the backseat. He had been asleep until now, moaning and talking to long-dead relatives. Simon looks back. Avon is up on one elbow, offering Simon his pistol. Simon thinks about arguing but doesn't. He knows the journey they're on. He takes the gun, approaches the back door. In the distance, to the west, he can see the mountains burning, a red zipper drawn across the horizon.

He raps on the back door quietly with his knuckles, waits. Story is outside the car, standing by the driver's door, engine still running, ready to make a quick getaway if it turns out to be a trap.

Simon is about to knock again when he hears the sound of a bolt being thrown back, and the door opens a crack. It's dark inside the store, but he can see eyes looking out at him.

"Cual es la contraseña?" comes a female voice.

"What?" says Simon, thrown.

"The password, Chuck. What's the password?"

He peers into the dark, recognizing the voice. "Louise?"

"Call me Peppermint Patty, and this is my buddy, Marcy."

She opens the door. Simon sees Louise wearing a brown Ulysses vest over a bathing suit top and checked trousers. Duane stands behind her, waving gently. They hug as a trio, a puppy pile of relief and joy, which ends with Louise humping Simon's leg and Duane kissing him on the mouth.

"Hi," he says.

"Hi," says Simon, breathless. And then Story is there with the reality check.

"He's bleeding again," she says. "Burning up."

The four of them walk out to the Kia.

"Let me guess," says Louise, studying the bullet holes and smashed glass. "It was like this when you found it."

Simon opens the back door, leans over Avon. His forehead is hot.

"Who's the geriatric, Chuck old boy?" says Louise.

"Felix's dad," says Story. She grabs Duane's

hand, consumed suddenly by hope and worry. "Have you heard from him?"

Duane shakes his head.

"Just us so far," he says, "and the Troll."

"The what?"

Duane shrugs. "This boy Louise used to know. He told us where the Wizard is."

Duane squeezes Story's hands.

"I'm really sorry you got caught," he says. "We just didn't know how to save you."

She nods.

"Was it cops?" he asks.

She shakes her head. The truth is far stranger and more unsettling.

"Some kind of private security. They took me to LA and had these two women watching us. At least I think they were women. They might have been witches. Simon was next door, it turned out. He blew up the house and we escaped, and then Felix's dad was there."

She rubs her eyes, worn out by grief. "It all feels like a dream."

They carry Avon inside, lay him on a long Formica counter, leaving a blood trail on the concrete. The old man is unconscious again, lips pale. Duane finds some scissors, cuts his shirt open. Around them, a dozen liberated dogs bark and jump. The walls of the store are lined with cages, doors open, and it's clear from the smell that in the last few hours the pet shop has become a bathroom for a host of animals, exotic and domestic. Duane gets a first aid kit from the office. He tells them his dad drove an ambulance for a year, the night shift, and when there were no babysitters available, Duane would ride with him.

"We used to practice stitching up pieces of pork," he says, "mostly the tenderloin. We'd sew them together and then cook them for dinner."

He studies the entrance and exit wounds. "Louise," he says, "I'm going to need antiseptic, a needle and thread, and some antibiotics."

"On it," she says, and walks to the Amazon delivery van parked in the loading bay. Simon follows her.

"This is your ride?" he says.

"God sent us a mystery box," she says, opening the back doors and climbing up.

"I thought the cops caught you," Simon tells her, his voice shaking from relief and worry. "Back in Texas."

Louise picks up a box, holds it to her forehead, as if divining the contents. "They got Story. I was taking a piss."

Simon finds a padded envelope with AMAZON PHARMACY printed on it. He shows it to Louise.

"Open it," she says. "I haven't got a dud yet,

though sometimes you gotta interpret the use. This is how God talks to us, I guess. In, like, riddles."

He rips it open. Inside is a prescription bottle for doxycycline. He shows it to her.

"And then sometimes," she says, "no interpretation required."

She paws through a pile, chooses a small box. Inside is what looks like a lifetime supply of dental floss, unflavored.

"Any word from the Prophet?" Simon asks her.

She shakes her head.

"Nobody calls, nobody writes," she says. "But he's coming."

"How do you—"

"The boxes told me," she says, then chooses a heavy box the size of a large suitcase. Inside is a professional sewing machine with a foot pedal, scissors, and needles.

She smiles.

"If Moses had had this truck," she tells him, "the Jews woulda been outta the desert in three days tops."

They carry their haul into the back room. Story says she'll stay with Duane and help him sew the old man up. Louise grabs a can of Alpo and some kibble. She tells Simon he should help her feed the Troll. Inside the office, Simon sees what was once a teen aesthete now bungied to an office chair, his face scratched, some of his hair missing. An elastic hair band has been used to fasten what looks like a tube sock over his mouth.

"Like I said," Louise says, flipping on the lights, "you gotta get creative sometimes with what he gives you, but it does the trick."

The Troll's eyes open. Seeing them, he starts thrashing in the chair. Louise puts the dog food on the desk, takes a spray bottle out of her vest pocket, and approaches him. She holds up the bottle.

"I'm gonna ungag you," she says, "if you try to bite me again, I'm gonna empty the whole bottle in your eyes. Understand?"

He nods.

Simon reads the label. "Coyote urine?"

She pulls the hair band from the Troll's face. He spits the tube sock on the floor.

"Help me," he says to Simon. "She's crazy."

Louise steps back, shows him the dog food.

"Which do you want? Wet or dry?"

"Please," says the Troll. "I told you everything. Can't you just let me go?"

"No," says Louise. "You'll call him."

"I won't. I swear."

Louise uses a screwdriver to open the Alpo can. The label reads LONDON GRILL.

"You'll be fine," she says. "It's just a few more hours."

Simon sees a water cooler. He takes a paper cone, fills it, brings it to the Troll.

"Watch him," says Louise. "He spits."

Simon lifts the cup to the Troll's lips. He drinks, bottom lip trembling.

"Please," he says, "my name is Evan. I just wanna go home."

"Save your shit," says Louise, coming over with the Alpo. Simon steps back.

"Did you know," she says, "young master Evan sold me to the Wizard for ice money?"

Evan starts to object, but Louise shoves a spoonful of dog food into his mouth.

"Louise," says Simon, worried.

Evan half chokes on the brown meal, then forces a swallow as another spoonful knocks against his teeth.

"Can we talk outside?" Simon asks.

Louise frowns, drops the can on the floor.

"Whatever," she says, turning and walking to the door.

"Not a sound," she tells Evan, turning off the lights.

Simon closes the door behind them. "What are you doing?" he says.

"No," says Louise. "You don't get to—"

"Louise. You're torturing him."

"I'm *punishing* him, so he'll change."

"You think he's gonna change? Because you scratched his face up and fed him dog food?"

"I'm expressing my anger, as instructed by my psychiatrist."

"You want revenge."

"You're fucking right I want revenge. I *deserve* revenge."

"It's not moral. What you're doing."

"It's justice. Isn't justice moral?"

"It's payback. Justice is he goes to jail if he committed a crime. There's a difference."

She takes off her employee vest, throws it across the room.

"Oh, Simon," she says. "It's exhausting, really. How sweet you are."

"Me?"

"Justice failed. The whole thing, the idea of it. Some impartial system weighing the pros and cons. It doesn't work. There's just power— who has it and who doesn't. And when *they* have it, they abuse us. So when *we* have it, we have to abuse them. That's how we find balance."

He stares at her.

"So, justice," he says, "is you've got the power, you can do whatever you want?"

"Bingo. He hurt me and now I'm hurting him back. That's called morality. And, hey, if God didn't want me to hurt him, he wouldn't have sent me the tools in his magical van."

"So you're like, what, the Spanish Inquisition?"

"Look around, kid. There's a civil war going on, because what we called justice didn't work for any fucking body. We're back to basic principles. An eye for an eye. I don't care if you're a bum or a billionaire. If you hurt me. If you rape me. I'm coming for you. Can I get an amen?"

She walks away.

Simon stands looking at his reflection in the plate-glass window. What was clear in the day becomes mirrored at night. At that moment it hits him. He is 100 percent certain that God has no plan for Simon Oliver. That this whole adventure has been a desperate farce, an excuse for him to focus on anything except the fact that his sister killed herself, his parents are monsters, and the world is ending. It's fucking ending. And there's nothing he can do about it.

What a fool he was for believing. But who can blame him? Who doesn't want to be saved?

He stares at his reflection, lit from behind by the blue lamps of glass aquariums, and then a face appears inside his own face. Another man's kind eyes. A stranger's long hair. *Jesus?* he wonders. But then the image clarifies. The Prophet, his prophet, puts a hand on the glass and smiles, seeing Simon within. One lens of his glasses is missing. He presses his lips to the window, like a pilgrim kisses the ground. And then the front door is opening, and the Prophet is hugging Simon, and everyone is rallying together, and the dogs are barking and jumping. It feels like the impossible is happening. How certain they've been in the last few days that death had come for them all, that their friends were dead or in jail, that they had been left alone.

Coming in behind the Prophet, Samson looks for Story, terrified Simon will tell her she's dead or in jail. He has no idea her parents have been killed. No idea that she has learned the truth about him, that she knows his real name. Finally, he sees her at the back of the pack, lurking in the shadows. His heart leaps and he moves to take her in his arms, but she steps back, her hands coming up to block him.

"Hey," he says, flustered. "I was—you're okay?"

But she won't meet his eye. She is thinking instead of how much disdain it takes to lie to the person you claim to love about something as fundamental as your name. She can't believe she chose him. Her mother is dead and she chose him. She went into hiding for him. She allowed her parents to worry, to think God knows what—that she'd been kidnapped, killed?—when she could have called, could have flown to DC and been with them in the days and weeks before they died. Could have saved them, maybe, or at least could have been there for her brother when they died. Could be with him now, instead of here on some farkakte mission to save the sister of the man who lied to her about his fucking name.

"I love you," says Samson, reaching for her again.

"Your dad's here," Story tells him, turning away.

"What?"

Story points over toward Duane, who has finished sewing up the old man and is now wrapping him with duct tape and hand towels.

For Samson there is a moment of vertigo. His first thought is his dad has tracked him down, has come to punish him for his disloyalty, but then he sees the blood-soaked towels and his father's pale face, and a different feeling hits him.

"Dad?" says Samson, feeling his eyes start to water. He touches his father to make sure he's real—and yet how can this be?

Avon opens his eyes and grabs his wrist. *How are you here? How is this possible?*

"Your sister," he says weakly.

"We're getting her."

And then it hits him. *His father is here.* Story said *Your father is here.* She wouldn't hug him, wouldn't look him in the eye, which means the unthinkable inevitable has happened. The past and the present have collided. Every lie he has ever told has burst. The man he pretended to be, the man she loved, has blown away with the wind. What's left is a scarecrow, a straw man in human clothes. And nobody loves a scarecrow.

He turns to look for her, desperate suddenly, but she's gone.

Avon squeezes his wrist. "Don't go," he says.

Samson stands paralyzed by doubt, filled with self-loathing.

"How?" he says. "How did you get here?"

"Everything's connected," says Avon.

At the door, Louise gives the Prophet a kiss on the mouth, embarrassing him.

"You old softy," she says. "Wait till you see what God sent us."

The Prophet grabs Simon's hand. "You," he says.

"Me what?" says Simon.

The Prophet takes off his glasses, wipes his remaining lens on his shirt, puts them on.

"You must lead us now," he says. "God told me. Your time has come."

Simon feels the blood leave his body. A coldness washes over him. He has just finished renouncing his faith. He is a fraud. How can he lead them when the world is on fire and he has no way to put it out?

"Palm Springs, huh?" says a voice from behind him.

Simon turns.

Randall Flagg leans in the open doorway, smoking a Newport. He is dressed in all black, with a shotgun slung around his body. There is a red bandanna tied over his left eye.

Simon can't help himself. He throws himself into Randall's arms, hugs him.

"Jesus, kid," says the Walking Dude. "Ease up."

Simon retreats, crying now, as much from confusion as from relief. The world has become a missile, moving too fast to steer. All you can do is hold on and pray. For the first time he wishes he were an adult, clear in himself, a man with experience and perspective, who has already made all his mistakes and learned from them. Instead, he is a beginning skier poised at the top of a mountain. He doesn't know the terrain ahead, let alone how to turn, how to slalom, how to stop.

This will all make sense when I am older, he thinks, but even as he thinks it, he knows that no one in the history of humanity has ever been that old.

Randall comes in and closes the door.

"Which one of you motherfuckers has a plan?" he says.

O

They find a band saw in the Amazon truck and use it to cut a hole in the drywall that connects the pet store to the sporting goods store. Busting through the cinder block takes more effort, but they're young and motivated, and Flagg finds some steel pipes in the back room, and they go to town, smashing, smashing, smashing. It feels good after everything they've been through. To whirl and swing, to jab and kick. On snack breaks they compare their wounds—physical, emotional. Everyone agrees that Flagg, with half a liver and a missing eye is the winner, although when Simon describes his and Story's ordeal with the Witch, the room gets quiet.

Louise starts to shiver.

Avon is touch and go, they figure, and Samson sits with him while the others work, not sure what to feel. He has lost so much already, has renounced his father and changed his name, and yet here he is, the old man, like a thought you don't want but have to face. The Prophet would say that God brought Avon to him so they could heal their old wounds, but Samson isn't so sure. Sometimes, he thinks, the world is just a fucked-up, random place, where everything happens and nothing makes sense.

We make our own meaning.

Simon is the first through the wall. The sporting goods store has been ransacked pretty well in the last few days—not looted, just shopped out. The gun racks are empty, bullets sold, but not all the shelves are empty, and they stock up on what they think they might need, or what seems funny in the moment. At first Louise refuses to make the pilgrimage to Angel's Sporting Goods. Her logic is that God gave them everything they could need when he delivered them the truck. But then the Prophet suggests that maybe it was God who put a sporting goods store next to the pet store in the first place, and *who are we to reject such a blessing*, and Louise shrugs and climbs on through.

Later, Samson finds Story sitting by herself on the floor of the pet shop, her back to the wall. She has her hands pressed to the cold cement, needing to feel something physical, something real. He slides down beside her, careful not to get too close. In the back room, Simon told him what happened. The explosion at the Capitol. How her family is dead. His lies seem pathetic now in comparison to the magnitude of her grief.

They sit for a minute in silence.

"I don't even know what I'm doing here," she says, not looking at him. "I have to find Hadrian. But who do I call? The FBI? Social Services? Not that—I mean, the phone lines are down. He's a twelve-year-old boy and the satellites, whatever, are screwed, because, I don't know, the world is ending."

He nods. "Whatever I can do," he says. "I want to help."

"No," she says, "I think you've done enough."

He thinks about that. The last thing she needs right now is for him to explain himself, to shift the focus, to say, *I know your parents are dead, but let's talk about my rough childhood. Let me tell you how hard I had it, so you'll forgive me, and we can what—go back to the way it used to be?*

"I'm sorry," he says.

She nods.

"Do you want me to drive you to DC?"

She looks at him for the first time.

"Drive three thousand miles in the middle of a civil war?"

"If you want."

"What about your sister?"

He thinks about that. "I'm trying to make things right," he says.

"There is no right. Right is a fantasy."

"Help me save my sister and then I'll help you find your brother."

"Help you?"

He nods.

"Because," he says, "she's a kid too, and she's all alone, and the monster has her, and she's here.

And it's something to do that's not sitting on the floor feeling terrible."

"My parents died."

"I know, and I'm sorry, but nothing's gonna get fixed staying here. And I don't know if the kid is right, the—whaddaya—Prophet, that God talks to him and we have to do this so that we can start over, humanity, but what if he is? What if this is the moment? What if this is history? Aren't you tired of talking about everything? Always saying something's wrong, but nobody ever does anything. All they do is tell you there are rules, systems? Well, fuck it. I'm done talking. We save her, we save your brother, and then we find this utopia he keeps talking about and start over."

For a long time she says nothing, and he worries he's lost her for good. But then she closes her eyes and nods. "Okay."

They spend the next three hours planning their assault on the Wizard's compound—scouring the fuzzy map on Google Earth for entry points, blind spots, et cetera. The compound has been smudged in the satellite image, but they find old photos online and study them for details. Who knew there was a price you could pay to literally erase your home from the map?

"Is that a helipad?" asks Louise, pointing at the blurred image. They gather around, squinting.

None of them know how to ground a helicopter without shooting it from the sky. For a moment they're silent. The only way they can think to rescue Bathsheba is to die trying, which—Flagg says, *fine with him.* He knows what the rest of them aren't willing to say out loud, that blood is about to be shed, and nobody goes to war hoping for a tie. In the middle hours of the night, they map out their options—Samson attacks from here, Simon vaults the wall there—but every scenario ends in death. They are a ragtag group of kids, planning an assault on a fortress defended by special forces. The best they can hope for is chaos and luck.

And then Simon has an idea so simple, so foolproof, it leaves them all light-headed. He sees past the battlefield, past the objective, to the heart of human nature itself. As soon as he says the words out loud, the room realizes that this is what they must do. The Prophet kneels before Simon and kisses his feet.

"I told you," he says, and Simon blushes.

With renewed vigor, they fortify themselves for the attack to come. They pack their vehicles with stolen loot and load their weapons. Their plan is to leave at dawn. Everyone has a job, even Avon, who wakes around 4:00 a.m., and offers advice on their plan. He's the one who tells them that if they soak tennis balls in gasoline and fire them through the windows of the house, they can create what he calls "a hell of a diversion." He shows them how to turn the small camping stove propane tanks into bombs. To Samson's surprise, he doesn't shit all over their strategy, doesn't try to force his own adult plan on them. Avon seems to understand something fundamental in his vulnerable state, which is that his time deciding things is over. It's their turn now. All that's left for him is to defend the decisions he's made, the ones worth saving. And the only ones that seem to matter right now are his children.

Do they overpack? Maybe. But they know that the key to victory is to make themselves look like an army, an overwhelming force. Only in this way can they force the Wizard to make a mistake.

At 5:13 a.m. they're ready. They will take separate cars, will rally at the rallying point. Before they leave, they set all the animals in the pet store free, dogs and cats, snakes and hamsters. The Prophet blesses them with water from the plastic cooler before throwing open the doors.

"There will be no pets in the new world," he says. "No supremacy of human beings. The Anthropocene era is over."

Out they go, two by two, cats and mice, rabbits and beagles, trailed by a single lonely iguana.

Simon's plan has him riding with the Prophet and Flagg. They will be the endgame, the final line of defense. Together they load up the Kia. Flagg finds a tin of chewing tobacco in the sporting goods store, and he chews a wad now, spitting watery brown chaw onto the asphalt. Simon goes to find Duane.

"Hey," he tells the older boy, trying to sound casual. "I've gotta go do this crazy rescue thing now."

"Which was your idea," says Duane.

"I know, I just—I like you, okay, and I don't know if you—but seeing as how I'm probably gonna get killed, I thought I should say the words out loud, and see."

He looks the taller boy in the eyes.

"Don't die."

Duane nods. "Thank you," he says. "I know that wasn't easy."

"Uh," says Simon, his stomach sinking, "you're, uh, welcome."

He turns to go, face burning, but Duane grabs his hand.

"And as soon as you turn seventeen, you and me are gonna talk again, okay?"

Simon flushes. "Okay."

Duane smiles. "Just—listen," he tells Simon. "You make me want a future?"

"Uh-huh," says Simon, his eyes watering.

Duane kisses his hand. "Now go be a leader."

Simon crosses the empty store, avoiding piles of scat. He finds Louise exiting the back office, a black Sharpie in her hand.

"Did you set him free?" Simon asks her.

"I left a box cutter on the desk," she says. "It won't be easy, but he can reach it."

"What's the Sharpie for?" Simon asks.

She throws it across the room.

"It's so every time he looks in the mirror he'll understand what he is."

"Which is?"

"All."

Simon gives her a quick hug. There is too much to say. Louise reaches down and squeezes his ass. He smiles.

"You were right," she says when they separate.

"About what?"

"Trusting you."

Louise

She pulls up to the front gate in the Troll's Mercedes. Her lipstick color is to die for. It's 5:23 a.m., and the sky is just starting to brighten. There are several unique types of anxiety in the DSMIV. Louise Conklin is suffering from none of them. The fear of death has liberated her from the grip of anonymous dread. Instead, she has the top down and she's playing "Rock Steady" by Aretha Franklin. On her body are tight camouflage pants and a bathing suit top.

A guard in a black T-shirt and tactical cargo pants waves to her as she pulls in.

"Special delivery," she says, the bass pumping.

Louise is the first wave. Her goal is simple, get inside, get close to the Wizard, and put her eyes on the princess in the tower. Fully expecting to be shot to death in the car, she smiles at the guard, who steps closer, tells her to turn down the music.

She does but not all the way. The music is what's giving her courage.

"Evan sent me," she says. "I hear our Wizard is a lonely, lonely boy."

She puts out her boo-boo lip, knowing that this big man with his big gun is going to underestimate her. Not only is she Black and female, but she is fifteen years old and weighs all of ninety-eight pounds. She doesn't even have a driver's license. Before she drove over, she had to practice in the parking lot of the pet store.

"Tell him it's his kitty-cat, Louise, here with some sweet chocolate milk."

The guard talks into his wrist, listens.

"Look at the camera," he tells her, pointing.

She looks up, smiles. Though the wind is blowing east from the desert, she can smell smoke from the wildfires out west. Somewhere in the distance there is the sound of insurgent gunfire.

The guard puts his hand to his ear, nods. There is an electronic buzz, and the gate swings open. It is a paradise inside. The pool is enormous, with a blooming fountain. The driveway is surrounded by impossibly green grass and towering palm trees. Louise follows the driveway to the main house—a cross between a Turkish mosque and a Spanish hacienda—past a dozen men in black T-shirts, all carrying assault rifles. For a moment,

the impossibility of what they have to do overwhelms her, but she muscles it down. Would
Beyoncé quit? A guard with a tactical headset
waves her in, pointing to where she should park.
She pushes the brake too hard, jerks to a stop,
then glides in, acting like driving is no big deal
for her. As she puts the car in park, it occurs
to her she hasn't felt the urge to clean anything
in weeks.

She climbs out, slams the door, smiles at the
eight hundred pounds of muscle between her and
the door. The sky is fully blue now, and it is a
testament to how orange it's been for the last few
days that for a moment Louise wonders if this is
normal.

Astrid comes out onto the verandah. Boaz Orci
is behind her, wearing a sidearm on his hip.

"Well, look at you," says Astrid, smiling.

Louise twirls.

"Evan said it was nine one one," she says, lifting
her hand to shield her eyes from the low sun.

"Arms out," says Orci.

Louise puts her arms out, juts a hip fetchingly.
The bathing suit top doesn't cover much. Orci puts
his hands on her hips, pats her down.

"Whoops," she says, when he runs his right hand
over her crotch.

He stands, nods to Astrid.

"Master's upstairs," says Astrid. "He's, well, he's worked up. You know how he gets."

"Evan said it's been a few days with no massage, poor baby."

Astrid studies Louise for a moment, a smile frozen on her face.

"Where is Evan?" she says.

Louise shrugs.

"What can I say? The streets are full of clowns with AK-47s, literally. And our Evan isn't, you know, brave, so he's holed up someplace with the dead bolt thrown."

"But not you?"

"Astrid, sweetie. Who's gonna hurt little ol' me?" She fluffs her hair for effect.

"A Black girl in a bikini top," says Astrid, "driving a hundred-thousand-dollar Mercedes during a race war, you mean?"

Louise gives the blond bitch her most innocent smile.

Astrid looks at Orci. He chews his lower lip. If it were up to him, he wouldn't let this girl within a mile of the principal, but the way Mobley's been raging around the house for the last three days, the best thing is to get her in and out fast.

"He's in the spa," says Astrid. "Come on, I'll show you."

They enter the house together. A crystal

chandelier hangs in the atrium. The tile work is stunning.

"I love your pants," Astrid tells Louise as they go up the stairs. "Very of the moment."

The upstairs hall is carpeted. Two guards stand on the landing. Astrid leads Louise to a set of double doors.

"Just be aware," she says, "it's been a few days, so he may ask for—special treatment."

They stop in front of the doors. Louise studies the older woman, with her perfect hair and makeup, her pursed lips and tapered pantsuit.

"You know I'm fifteen, right?" she says.

Astrid flushes. "My love," she says, "we don't talk about those things."

She opens the double doors. "Darling," she says, "look who I found."

The room Mobley sits in is palatial, tiled white. There is a sauna and a steam room, a massage table and a shower. In the center is a leather couch. This is where Mobley sits in chinos and a cardigan, reading the *New York Times*. On the wall, three televisions play silently—one showing Newsmax, the other Bloomberg, and the third CNN.

Each screen shows footage of troops in American streets, battling armed groups.

Mobley sighs. Without looking up, he says:

"Tell Orci to gas the jet."

"Bahamas?" says Astrid.

"Paris."

He folds the paper, rests it on the sofa. Only then does he look at Louise, who feels an icicle of fear pass through her in places she doesn't like to acknowledge. There is a power to this man that only grows with time. A man worth so much money that the interest on his wealth alone earns him $68,000,000 a day. A man who could buy every NFL and Major League Baseball team combined and still be worth billions. This man, this physical entity in front of her, who was once a baby and will one day be a corpse, has all the benefits of being a king with none of the burdens. He does not have to feed his kingdom or keep his citizens safe. He does not have to worry about the disfavor of the church or infighting in his court. He has no court, no successors. He is a king with no subjects, only servants, a king who controls a vast army and yet has no country. In fact, he is the king of every country, as worshipped in France as he is in Hong Kong. As powerful in Brazil as he is in Moscow. That's the power of the almighty dollar. And when he looks at you, you feel like what you are—disposable, insignificant.

Louise forces a smile.

"Hey, Daddy," she says. "Strange day, huh?"

Mobley pats the sofa next to him. Behind him

the sauna is on, its cedar door hanging open, and the temperature in the spa room is close to 110 degrees. Louise lifts her arms and dances over to him. Any minute now the assault will begin. All she has to do is keep it together.

"I'll go see about the flight," says Astrid, and she closes the doors behind her, taking Orci with her.

Louise swings her hips, looking around for a weapon she could use. Being alone with Mobley is like being alone with a dragon—there is a hunger to him, a cold-blooded enormity—and here she is, Bilbo Baggins without a ring. But then, this isn't a fairy tale. There will be no invisibility, no magical escape. Just an ugly struggle of bodies fighting for survival. Next to the sink she sees a small pair of scissors, shiny and sharp. She slides herself over in front of the mirror, dancing to her own music, arms in the air, hips twisting. She turns seductively, putting her back to the counter, then does a little stripper dip, bounces on her heels. When she comes back up, she puts her hands behind her on the counter.

The Wizard slides the newspaper off the sofa, pats the seat next to him. It's been days since he was serviced, and the feeling that pulses in his groin is urgent and animalistic. For a moment his brain is all verbs. His eyes drop. Louise slides the scissors into her back pocket, then pushes herself off the counter and crosses the room to him, slipping down onto the sofa, her skin slick with sweat. Up close, the Wizard smells like wood smoke and rosemary. In his lifetime he has spent more money on clothing than he has on sex, and yet there is nothing he thinks about more. Hand jobs and blowjobs, boobs and butts. His mind is a Kama Sutra of sexual domination. His needs are insatiable. When Louise was in his regular rotation back in San Francisco, Evan told her that the Wizard was being served up to five times a day, young girls recruited to give him "massages" for cash. Some he would coerce into a wank or suck, some he would rape, some he would force to watch him jerk off. It all depended on what he thought he could get away with—what vibe the girl gave off—victim or Victim.

If he was feeling generous, Mobley would throw $1,000 at a girl, but that was rare. Usually, it was a few hundred dollars, but if you saw him three days a week it added up, especially for high school and middle school girls, who had no rent to pay, no taxes or student loans.

But let's say for the sake of argument he spent $500 a fuck, averaging three fucks a day. That's $1,500 a day x 365 days or $547,500 a year.

Now multiply that by twenty years and you get $10,950,000.

Think about that. Mobley has paid eleven million

dollars to underage girls over the last twenty years, under the auspices of buying a "massage." (Not including a few million in payouts to girls who went to the cops, plus bribes paid to the cops themselves.) If each fuck on a given day was with a different girl, that means Mobley saw three different girls per day. Now, assume that the most a single girl would come to give Mobley a "massage" was three times a week—3 fucks x 3 girls = 9 fucks per week, subtracted from the total 21 required fucks per week.

This meant Mobley would need at least one additional set of three girls, or probably two sets to be safe to cover the remaining twelve fucks.

So nine different girls a week. But hold on. Let's not forget that Mobley was always on the move—meaning from week to week he might be in a different city or country, and therefore would require an all-new set of girls, and that those girls would have to be recruited and available at a moment's notice. So, assume nine girls on call each week in six locations, or fifty-four girls available to Mobley somewhere on Planet Earth each week.

Three girls a day x 365 days = 1,095 fucks per year. Fucks requiring a small army of scouts and recruiters, all trolling for girls in the Bahamas, in France, New York, California, or wherever he chose to fly—girls between the age of fourteen and twenty who could be manipulated, intimidated, or coerced into becoming his sexual servants.

From here the statistical analysis begins to randomize. One must factor in his travel schedule in any specific month, which was always changing, plus a shifting rate of return among the girls. Some came once. The more brainwashed or desperate came for years. Mobley himself has lost count of the number of girls he has forced himself on in his lifetime, but it's safe to assume there have been thousands.

Thousands of girls coerced and/or raped a grand total of 21,900 times in twenty years, all at a cost of just .01 percent of Mobley's total net worth ($100,000,000,000).

For perspective, the median family income for 2019 was $68,703.

.01% of that is $6.87.

Six dollars and eighty-seven cents. That's what the lives of these girls meant to him, the regard he had for their value. They're sofa change. They're a pack of cigarettes—not individually, but together—thousands of daughters and sisters smoked and crushed under his heel for less than the cost of a six-pack of Budweiser.

I defy you to find a dragon in Middle Earth who has ruined more lives.

Louise crosses her legs. She has never told anyone what happened in rooms like this with Mobley over a period of six months. She was a fourteen-year-old girl with a deadbeat mother and a cleaning obsession, who was still trying to figure out adolescence. Yes, she had had a few drinks and taken a few pills, but she had no idea the monsters who were out there in the world, lurking, watching, waiting to devour her whole. She had no idea the things men wanted to do to women's bodies. The debasement, the violence. To be choked and spit upon. To be bound and penetrated.

Isn't that the definition of evil?

Mobley picks up a remote, turns off the televisions. He smiles at her, but not in recognition. It is a shark's smile, the smirk of a crocodile. Louise is not a human being to him, not a face worth remembering. She is a Kleenex to be sneezed in and thrown away.

"Tell me your name again, kitty-cat?" he says, hooking a finger under her bikini string.

"Death," she says.

"Beth?" he says, frowning.

Louise slides her right hand down her hip until she can feel the scissors in her back pocket.

"No," she says. "Don't you remember? I'm Death. Destroyer of worlds."

That's when the gunfire starts.

O

Legolas is walking the perimeter when the Amazon truck pulls up to the service gate. There are three guards on duty. They watch it come up the drive, pull into the circle, and back up to the gate, beeping jauntily. The driver is mixed race, Black and Asian. He has his arm out the driver's window, radio on, playing Sinatra.

Fly Me to the Moon.

The gate is a barrier of welded metal bars. Through it, Duane can see the main house down a short driveway. There are two more guards visible on the roof. Duane opens his door, steps down. He is wearing a blue Amazon shirt and white cargo shorts. He gives the guards a wave, walks to the back doors, whistling.

"It's exciting, right?" he says to the guards. "When the present fairy arrives."

He pats the back doors, Sinatra swinging, then pulls them open. Inside is a wall of boxes. Duane takes a scanner off his hip, scans a couple. The scanner beeps—*wrong box*. In the gap, two of the guards move toward him.

Duane speaks without turning.

"Lemme guess. The anticipation is killing you."

He turns, smiles. "Must be up front." He walks back to the driver's seat. "Just be a sec," he says.

The guards stand behind the van, waiting. The sun rises in front of them, and to keep it out of their eyes, the two guards take a step closer to the van, into the shade. To their light-flooded eyes, the inside of the truck is a black box.

And then, inside, something glints.

The first two shots hit them above the Kevlar. The closest, Dean, is killed instantly. Next to him the other, Morgan, is shot in the neck and falls to the ground, flopping, blood jetting. There is nothing clean or cool about the violence. It is brutish and messy. And fast. So fast. Inside the panel truck, Avon DeWitt takes aim at the guards on the roof and starts shooting.

O

A complex of tennis courts sits on the far side of the Wizard's north wall. There are five in total, abutting the suburban subdivision that developers named Desert Glen. The courts are flanked by large cypress trees, watered at enormous expense.

This is a desert, after all. At dawn, most of the houses are locked up tight, curtains pulled. Blond heads peer out from time to time to check if the apocalypse has arrived at their door in the shape of unruly mobs of black-clad Antifa come to destroy their American freedoms, or at this point who knows—maybe spaceships from above, or the rise of hidden lizard overlords. It's August. Everything seems possible.

As the sun rises, a young woman in tennis whites pushes a Lobster Elite Liberty Ball Machine up the middle of the quiet main street. The Lobster Elite is loaded to capacity, with one hundred and fifty balls. It can fire them at adjustable speeds to a distance of up to one hundred feet. The young woman, Story Burr-Nadir, pushes it ahead of her on a set of rear wheels like a hand truck. In her right hand she carries a can of gasoline.

It is 5:25 a.m. and the temperature in Palm Springs is already 104 degrees. Ahead she can see Mobley's fortress. Its perimeter wall stands ten feet tall, but from up the street Story can tell that the roof of Mobley's guest house is maybe thirty-five feet away, the main house farther on a southwestern trajectory. She pictures the rain of tennis balls she is about to launch.

A pickup truck passes her on oversize tires, slows to a stop. The cab rides some six feet above the ground. There is a gun rack in the back window. The driver's window slides down. Inside is a man in a baseball cap.

"Need a ride?"

Story looks up. Samson DeWitt sits behind the wheel. He found the truck in the parking lot of an IHOP. All the diner's windows had been shot out, the bodies of diners mixed with fallen patriots, police officers, soldiers.

The engine was still running, keys inside.

God or luck?

"Stop fucking around," Story tells him. "We're late."

"Yeah, yeah," says Samson, pulling forward. He flips a bitch in the cul-de-sac, aiming his back bumper toward the chain-link fence that separates the center court from the street. He puts the truck in reverse, steps on the gas. The impact throws him back against the seat, but the chain link gives, the fence toppling. Samson parks the truck next to the net, tailgate aimed at the Wizard's back wall. He jumps out of the truck, carrying a large plastic Super Soaker—the Soakzooka ($20.99 at Amazon)—which can hold ten gallons of water and fires a deluge up to thirty feet. It is designed to be shot from the hip, like some kind of pool toy weapon of mass destruction. Samson goes around back and lays it in the truck bed. He wears a Smith & Wesson 9mm on his hip for when the real bang bang begins.

Last night, Samson sat with his father in the dark pet shop. Together they fed the store's thirteen dogs with treats taken off the rack, throwing them across the room and watching the dogs run.

"Promise me you'll get her back," Avon said, not looking at his grown son. The bandages patching him up were already soaked with blood.

Samson threw a handful of treats. "We'll get her together," he said.

Avon thought about this. They sat in silence as the others loaded the vehicles. Neither father nor son had shaved in six days. Samson remembered standing on the toilet when he was small, watching his dad run the disposable razor over his face. It was still so surreal for him, having his father here in this place at this time. And yet of course this was how the story had to end.

"Dad," he said.

Avon looked at him. It had been over a decade since Samson called him by anything other than his Christian name, or motherfucker.

"Do you ever—" the boy asked, for in this moment he looked like a boy again, small and scared. "Do you ever feel bad—about what we did."

Avon turned back to the dogs, who were crowding

around them in a frenzy. He threw another handful of treats.

"No," he said.

Samson nodded. Not a day had passed since Blountstown when he didn't relive the moment, didn't see the troopers' faces as he fired, didn't feel the flush of adrenaline and the wave of shame and despair.

"I do," he said. "I think we made a mistake. Me."

"You protected your father," said Avon, "as God intended."

Samson sighed, not wanting to descend into another rabbit-hole conversation with the old man about Bible codes and Constitutional cabals.

"They were just doing their jobs," he said.

"They were agents of oppression."

"Dad." Samson put his hand on his father's arm. "They were somebody's sons, too."

Avon stiffened, pulled his arms away. He threw the bag of treats itself, hurling it away from him, as if renouncing the whole facade.

"All that matters now is your sister. Understand?"

Samson nodded. He thought about arguing, but there was no point. He scratched a golden retriever between the ears, got to his feet. Some divides are too big to cross.

"I'll get her back," he said.

Now, on the tennis court, he and Story lift the

ball machine into the truck bed. Story removes the lid, and Samson pours gasoline over the pile of balls. The smell of it hits them—that semi-sweet toxic waft. Story coughs as Samson uses a plastic funnel to fill the Soakzooka.

"Surf's up," he says.

They settle on a forty-five-degree arc, dialing in the angle on the ball launcher. They've agreed that Story will stay up here for the first ten balls, to make sure nothing goes wrong, and then head for the rendezvous point. Samson has a different journey to take. He jumps from the tailgate, takes a gas lighter with a telescoping nose from his pocket. He sets it under the mouth of the ball launcher, rigging it with duct tape to ignite the balls as they fire.

They stand for a moment, staring at the tiny blue flame. It dances in the low morning breeze.

"I'll see you soon," he tells her.

She nods, thinking of her mother and stepfather, now dead, who used to make chocolate chip pancakes with smiley faces on them. And somewhere out there her half brother, the orphan. If she lives, she will find him and never let him go.

"Nobody else," she says. "We don't lose anyone else."

He nods, then grabs the Soakzooka and runs to the cypress tree that's closest to the compound wall. The water cannon came with a nylon strap, and he hooks it now over his neck, starts to climb. Ten feet up, he hugs a fat branch, peers over the lip of the wall.

The guest house is a two-story building, about one hundred feet wide, that sits a stone's throw from the wall. It has a tiled, Spanish-style roof and a balcony on the second floor, where the master bedroom must be. The sliding door to the master is open, and there is a guard sitting in a recliner on the balcony, his assault rifle leaning against a glass table. He appears to be dozing. In the distance, Samson can see other guards walking the property. He counts to five on the roof and balconies of the main house, another dozen on the grounds.

Samson looks down at Story and gives a thumbs-up. He works his knee into a depression in the tree, securing himself in place, and raises the Soak-zooka. The smell of gasoline is overwhelming. Were someone to light a match near him, Samson would go up in a whoosh of flame, taking the whole tree with him.

He aims for the guest house roof and pulls back on the trigger. A plume of gasoline arcs from the mouth of the gun and sprays over the wall. About half of it splashes down on the ground, but the rest traces a line up the back wall of the guest house and onto the roof.

The process is not silent.

Samson hugs the tree as the guard on the balcony stirs but doesn't wake. It's clear that stealth will be impossible, so Samson settles for shock and awe. He straightens, hugging the branch with his thighs, and begins firing arc after arc of gasoline at the house, hosing it down as quickly as he can.

Gas rains down on the roof, the walls, the balcony. The balcony guard wakes as gasoline sprays him from above. He looks around, disoriented, face wet, grabbing for his gun.

Samson looks down at Story, mouths, *Now.*

She flips the switch on the ball launcher. The first tennis ball comes out like a shot, passing through the stove lighter's flame and igniting. It arcs above the wall and fires clean over the roof of the guest house, landing in the pool.

"Lower," yells Samson, as the guard gets to his feet, his rifle coming up, scanning for the source of the assault.

Story drops to her knees in the pickup truck, finds the angle dial and twists it, lowering the nozzle. A second tennis ball flies out, but she's set it too low now, and it bounces off the top of the wall, shooting back over the pickup truck into the street.

"Shit, shit, shit," she says, dialing it up again, trying to find the mid-point.

In the distance, shots ring out. Samson ducks reflexively, but it's only Avon in the Amazon truck.

The assault has begun for real. There's no turning back now. On the balcony, the guard's eyes go to the cypress tree. He sees Samson, lifts his rifle, as Samson fires another torrent of gasoline directly at him, splashing his clothes and spraying in his eyes.

The guard curses, finger tightening reflexively on the trigger, as he turns away from the deluge. The rifle fires, igniting the cartridge and heating the barrel. The gasoline coating the gun erupts. The guard and the balcony go up in flame. At the same moment, the next tennis ball fires, flying a perfect arc onto the guest house roof. Flames race across the building's exterior and onto the ground below.

Hearing the balcony guard's screams, Samson drops the Soakzooka. He vaults onto the lip of the wall and drops into the bushes inside the compound. Behind him a roar goes up as flames consume the building. Samson feels the heat. Aware that he himself is now eight percent gasoline, he pulls his pistol and runs for the side of the house, careful to stay away from the inferno.

O

Bathsheba is in the bathroom when she hears the first shot, and then the world outside her window turns orange, and flames shatter the glass. She manages to get her pants up and stumble into the hall, hearing more gunfire now, and then the sound of shouting voices. *Is this it?* she wonders. *Rescue or death?*

The front door of the guest house opens and Boaz Orci is there with Aragorn and two other guards. They pick her up by the elbows and rush her out the door, running for the main house. Behind her, the guest house burns. A gun battle is raging at the service gate. Then one of the guards stumbles as a shot rings out, and he goes down. Liam and Aragorn speed up, each with a hand under her arm, as the other two guards stop and return fire at a shooter who has appeared from around the side of the house.

It's her brother.

O

The door to the spa room flies open. Liam Orci is there with the guards. This is the scene he finds—Louise half rising from the sofa, a pair of scissors in her right hand, as she lunges for Mobley—but the men bursting into the room distract her, and her first stab slices Mobley across the cheek. He curses, grabs her wrist, and they struggle as Liam pulls his pistol. He moves into the room, trying to get a clear shot.

Slick with sweat, Louise doesn't hear gunfire from outside or the explosion as the guest house goes up. All her mind lets in is the sound of her breathing and the Wizard's breath as he rolls on top of her. The smell of it changes as they struggle, to something feral and sharp, a predatory musk. She tries to force the scissors into his body, but his weight is on her, shoving her down, and as they struggle, Louise realizes she's sinking into the sofa, disappearing between the seat and the back cushions, like a woman being swallowed alive. Part of Mobley—elbow? shoulder?—comes close to her face, and she bites hard. He grunts and twists her wrist. Louise hears a snap, and then the scissors are gone from her hand, and before the reality of this reaches her brain, she feels a sharp pain in her left side under her rib cage as the Wizard plunges the scissors in—once, twice, three times. Her screams are muffled by the sofa cushions, leather cushions smothering her, and then everything goes black.

The Wizard rears up, placing his palm on her face and driving her down. He roars like a lion who has escaped death, before Liam Orci and the guards grab him physically and run him out of the room, leaving Louise for dead, like somebody's daughter rolled up in a carpet and left by the side of the road.

For a minute there is silence in the room, Louise

buried completely in the gap between the seat and rear cushions. Only her left knee juts out, part of her arm. Her face is just a slash of color. Then the cushions begin to move, and she struggles up out of her leather coffin, like a hope that just won't die.

Her side is on fire, blood pouring from a wound below her ribs. She gets a hand over it, wheezing when she breathes. The fastest way off the sofa is to fall, and that's what she does, getting to her hands and knees and crawling over toward a stack of towels, leaving a bloody trail behind her. Breathing in the heat from the sauna, Louise realizes she doesn't want to die. This surprises her. She always assumed she was pretty fifty-fifty on this whole life experience, with its endless trials and tribulations, but now that she feels her own blood pouring through her fingers, she realizes she didn't make it this far just to bleed out in the Wizard's bathroom, like some discarded condom.

Louise makes it to the towels, presses one to her side. Outside she can hear the sound of multiple assault rifles firing in concentrated bursts, and something else—the sound of a helicopter powering up.

Everything is going according to plan.

The Plane

The helicopter comes in low, moving fast over the treetops. From a hundred feet up they can see wild-fire consume the mountains to the west. Mobley sits in back with Bathsheba and Liam Orci. The cut on his cheek is bleeding, but his adrenaline is still too high to feel it. Legolas sits up front with Boaz. Aragorn rides point, standing in the open doorway, scouring the approach with his AR-15, like this is Fallujah, not Palm Springs. When Astrid tried to squeeze aboard—face panicked, gunfire pinging off the paving stones—Bathsheba kicked her physically out the door with her right foot. She can still hear the scream as Astrid toppled to the ground, the helicopter already five feet high and rising.

One down, she thought. *Three to go.*

They've radioed ahead to the plane—*wheels up in five*—and Legolas can see it now, parked on the tarmac ahead, nose stairs down. He signals to Orci to bring it in close, fuck FCC regulations. Liam leans forward, shouting into his headset.

"When we touch down, I want the *Lord of the Rings* twins on the tarmac setting up a perimeter. My brother and me are gonna get the principals onboard. Shoot anything that moves until we're in the air. Clear?"

Legolas and Aragorn *hoo-ah*. Boaz Orci pushes the stick and sets the chopper down, powering off before the bird is even settled, and then they're out of the helicopter and running for the plane. The jet engines are on, cycling at a deafening whine. Liam supports Mobley under the arm, while Boaz has Bathsheba by the back of the neck, pistol out. The temperature has hit 107 in the shade. Aragorn and Legolas break off, sweeping the perimeter, but the airfield is clear.

And then Mobley, Bathsheba, and the Orci brothers are on the plane.

Aragorn signals Legolas to move to the tail. He slow-walks to the nose, sweeping for movement. On the far side of the plane, out of sight, a shadow descends from the wing, a figure dropping silently to the ground. It is a young man in black with long hair and wearing cowboy boots, a shadow wraith with one eye. He slides under the plane, moving in a low crouch. There is a 9mm on his hip and a bowie knife in his right hand. Lying flat, he watches his quarry's legs. Then he makes a choice.

On the plane, Boaz shoves Bathsheba toward the back. The plane is a 737, customized to indulge the most discerning billionaire. Mid-century modern furniture, a full bar, arcade games for the kids, and a fully soundproofed bedroom in back. Liam guides Mobley to a chair, sits him down.

"Stay here," he tells the billionaire, handing him a handkerchief for his bleeding face. "I'll get us off the ground."

He turns and nods to Boaz, who walks to the closed cockpit door, tries the handle. It's locked. Boaz frowns, bangs on it, as Liam moves to the nose stairs, reaches for the lever to raise them and close the plane's outer door.

He has his hand on it when four things happen simultaneously.

1) The bedroom door opens and Simon steps out. In a loud, clear voice, he says, "I figured it out."

2) The Orcs turn toward him.

3) The cockpit door opens, revealing the Prophet, standing alone with a spray bottle of coyote urine.

4) Randall Flagg vaults the air stairs and lands in the open passenger door, gun out and up, the bodies of his enemies splayed out on the tarmac behind him. He shoots Liam under the right arm, the bullet passing through his heart and lodging

in his left biceps, as the Prophet sprays predator piss into Boaz's eyes, blinding him. The surviving Orci brother screams, stumbles back, bouncing off the sixty-inch wall-mounted television, as his brother falls. Flagg shoots him twice in the back, the bullets exiting through his chest and passing through the TV into the lavatory.

Sparks fly. The Orcs lie together, arms entwined.

In that moment, Bathsheba launches herself onto Mobley from the sofa, her hands going to his throat. Her knee drives itself into his crotch. Then she rears back and hits him again. His screams are choked and hysterical. Agony paralyzes his rational mind. Bathsheba knows the key to killing him is not to cut off his airway but to stop blood flow to his brain. She squeezes with all her strength, seeing the pain and fear in his eyes. She watches as he starts to lose consciousness. Then the Prophet and Simon are on her, pulling her free. Bathsheba, now Katie, shouts and kicks as they carry her back to the sofa.

"Get off me," she screams. "I had him. I had him."

Mobley sucks air, his hands on his crotch. It's a miracle he doesn't vomit. For the first time in decades he's found a feeling his billions can't numb or erase.

The Prophet crouches before Bathsheba, gazing at her with just the kindest eyes.

"You're safe now," he says. "We're with Samson."

"I had him," Katie repeats, but the fight is leaving her, relief setting in.

Across from her, E. L. Mobley struggles to sit up.

For the first time in his life he has no idea what to say or do.

Simon sits across from him.

"I figured it out," he repeats. "It's grief. The five stages of death, right? Denial, anger, bargaining, depression, acceptance, but we're all trapped in the first two stages. The whole country, or maybe the Earth. We're in denial and we're pissed, because something we love is dead, except, for half the country, what they're grieving is the past they think they've lost, and the other half is mourning the progress they thought they'd made, but everyone feels the same way. Like someone they love is dead. And I get it. I'm grieving too. I miss her and I don't want her to be dead, and I'm pissed."

He leans toward the Wizard.

"But we can't move on," he says, "none of us, because you're preying on us, you and the others, turning our grief into cash, keeping us angry, keeping us fighting, keeping us divided so you can take our children and bleed us dry."

The Wizard drops the handkerchief in his lap.

"Are you finished?" he says, making no attempt to disguise the contempt he feels for them.

"No," says Simon. "Because I'm not in denial. I'm pissed, sure, but I know what's real. And what's real is that you're killing us. With your greed and your doublespeak. You're killing our planet. And the only ones who can see it are the children. And that's why we're killing ourselves. Because the death we're really grieving is our own."

Bathsheba stands from the sofa and comes over. She's trembling. "Kill him," she says.

Simon looks at the Prophet.

"No," says the holy man who once was a baby named Paul. "We need him for one last thing."

Epilogue

The Legend of Yes and No

My daughter asked me how I'm going to end this book. I told her I wasn't sure. Actually, what I said was—*you got me.*

I explained to her that her father is a romantic, which means he wants life to work out for people in the end. He wants good things to happen to those who do good and bad things happen to those who do ill. This is how we are, humanity. We want relationships to last. We want families to stay together. We like it when the good guy wins.

Fairy tales. I'm describing fairy tales.

My daughter said, *Yeah, but how do you end a story when nothing ever really ends?*

We'd been talking about World War One, which she's been studying in history class, and I'd just finished telling her how you can't really tell the story of World War One without telling the story of World War Two.

That's how it goes. One thing leads to another.

The best you can hope for, I told her, *is a feeling of catharsis. That something meaningful has changed. That growth has occurred.*

And has it? she asked.

Stop asking so many questions, I told her. But of course that's her job. She's thirteen, and I'm handing her the keys to a car called Earth. *What's this dent?* she's asking. *Why is this broken? Is it safe?*

O

She's on two different kinds of anxiety medication, my daughter. She wasn't on them when I started the book. She was an eleven-year-old girl still missing a tooth, who chewed her tongue to help her concentrate. But when childhood gave way to adolescence, something happened. That beast called anxiety crept in.

Last year I asked her, *What's going on? What are you so afraid of?*

This is what she told me: she didn't want to grow up. She didn't want to think about the future. I tried to convince her that planning for the future is the only way she'll have any control over it, but she was skeptical. We were in the middle of a global pandemic, after all.

Control, she had learned, is an illusion.

O

Stop me if you've heard this one before.

In the beginning was the land and the sea, the trees and fields and mountains. There was the sun and the moon, the flowers and the bees, the fish and the bears, and all of life's wondrous gifts.

In the beginning there was Alaska, the Yukon Delta, and the Bering Sea. On the first Thursday in September, a private plane lands on a secluded runway just north of Allakaket. The land surrounding it—two hundred thousand acres—has been purchased the month prior by a reclusive billionaire who has since disappeared.

The nose stairs lower. Eight teenagers descend. It is a foggy morning. The temperature outside is sixty-five degrees. There are two sets of siblings, the rest of the kids are friends.

Two hundred thousand acres = 312.5 square miles. Walking at three miles per hour, it would take one hundred and four hours to leave what is now their property. The prefab housing will be delivered in a week, along with a rainwater collection system, a seed bank, and livestock. This is what a billionaire's money can buy. A planned community for a few hundred people that will grow in time.

A prophecy has led them here. A quest, if you

will. First they had to overcome their anxiety. Then they freed the kid in the cage. They rescued the dragon from the tower and vanquished the Witch and the Wizard. Now this land is their reward. Heaven on Earth.

Utopia.

Simon Oliver steps onto the grass. It has been sixty days since his last pill. His sixteenth birthday is tomorrow. He feels like Noah leaving his ark. Two by two they come. Left behind is a burning world, roiling with hatred.

For Claire, he thinks when he sees the aspen trees waving in the breeze.

O

Recently, I've been asking myself—are we as a species suffering from an empathy problem? And if so, is our dilemma that we aren't feeling *enough* empathy? Or is empathy itself the problem?

Hear me out.

In 2019, the former first lady, Michelle Obama, gave a speech at the Democratic National Convention. She spoke about polarization and a surge of aggression in America.

"Empathy," she said. "That's something I've been thinking a lot about lately. The ability to walk in someone else's shoes; the recognition that someone else's experience has value, too. Most of us practice this without a second thought. If we see someone suffering or struggling, we don't stand in judgment. We reach out because, '*There, but for the grace of God, go I.*' It is not a hard concept to grasp. It's what we teach our children…

"But right now, kids in this country are seeing what happens when we stop requiring empathy of one another. They're looking around wondering if we've been lying to them this whole time about who we are and what we truly value."

In her estimation, our biggest problem is a lack of empathy. Me for you and you for me. Her solution is to create more.

Paul Bloom, on the other hand, a moral philosopher, argues that empathy itself is a problem in human interaction, not a solution. He says empathy, "however well-intentioned, is a poor guide for moral reasoning. Worse, to the extent that individuals and societies make ethical judgments on the basis of empathy, they become less sensitive to the suffering of greater and greater numbers of people."

Paul Slovic, another moral philosopher, agrees. He says empathy is a poor tool for improving the lives of others, because the human mind is bad at thinking about, and empathizing with, millions or billions of individuals.

"An individual life," he says, "is very valued. We all go to great lengths to protect a single individual or to rescue someone in distress, but then as the numbers increase, we don't respond proportionally to that."

He describes a phenomenon called *psychic numbing*, loosely defined as the larger the number of suffering people, the more apathy.

So is the problem not enough empathy, or empathy itself?

O

Samson DeWitt (now Felix) descends the stairs behind Simon, with his sister, Bathsheba (now Katie). In front of them, Randall Flagg stands weaponless in bare feet, blinking at the snowy peak of Mount Denali. He will bury his rifles in the dirt, he decides. Starting today he will fight no more.

Nearby, Story Burr-Nadir holds her brother's hand. Hadrian, too, looks up at the mountains, but in his mind are different words. He thinks, *This is a place we can heal.* He spent six days locked in a hotel room in Washington DC eating energy bars and watching the world end on TV, before his sister and her friends came to rescue him. He looks over at her now, squinting at the wildflowers, and smiles.

"You and me," she tells him, and he nods, because what else is there?

Duane Yamamoto comes up behind Simon and takes his hand. They are pioneers, who will sleep on the plane until their homes arrive. They will eat the food they've brought until they can lay in provisions. There is one phone between them, which they've agreed to use only in case of emergencies.

Last out, the Prophet Paul descends the nose stairs and kneels in the loam. He bends forward and kisses the mossy ground, thanking God for delivering them here to the new promised land.

Is that what happened? Simon wonders. *Or did we deliver ourselves?*

As with everything else about God, where you come down on the issue revolves around faith.

O

As a writer, your author has long believed that fiction is an empathy delivery device. He believes that if, on the page or the screen, a writer can make you, the reader, care about someone who is not you, you will go out into the world with a broadened empathy for others. And that this will make the world a better place.

Consider this, however.

Empathy, like any emotion, can be manipulated. Isn't that what I've just described? An author writing a story to produce feelings? Empathy, therefore, is a tool that can be used for good, or for ill. As Adam Smith once wrote, to feel empathy for someone who has been wronged is to feel anger or hatred toward those who've wronged them. So if I want to make you angry, I just paint you a picture of a poor victim and the person or people who abused or manipulated them.

Help the victim, I might say, but also punish the victimizer.

Say I told a large group of people a story that they themselves are victims—of manipulation by dark forces, of disdain by people they've never met, of being left behind like a dog on the side of the road—what would those people do to help themselves and punish those they believed had abused them? For who among us doesn't empathize first and foremost with themself?

O

There were 3,478,769,962 people alive on Planet Earth the year I was born. There are 7,794,798,739 today. In my lifetime, 4.3 billion extra people have come to live with us here on this shimmering blue-green ball. Babies with parents. Human beings who need food and water, homes, and schools, who generate waste and drive cars and have babies of their own.

It's possible we haven't thought this thing through all the way. There's no denying that an individual person, after millions of years of evolution, is a very efficient problem solver. But what he or she can reliably solve is their own *individual* problem, perhaps—for a select few—the problems of a community bigger than a city, but smaller than a country. And yet, at some point, our ability to solve a problem breaks down when the size of the problem grows too big.

This inability is made worse by the fact that, as discussed, our motivation to solve each other's problems drops when their numbers grow too big. And yet, the dilemma, in this case, is not the babies. Babies are wonderful. The problem is that there is a scale differential between the number of people on Earth and our ability (and desire) to solve their problems.

Think about it like this: When two parents give birth to a third child, they start using sports analogies. They say, *Now we have to play zone defense,* by which they mean they're outnumbered and can no longer maintain a one-on-one approach to their children.

So what if a family had ten children, or thirty

children, or a hundred children? At a certain point, their ability to solve their problems would break down. The best they could hope for would be survival.

Which, as we know, is the lowest standard of living.

O

How is the book going to end? my daughter asked me again yesterday. It's important to her that everything turns out okay. It's important to me, too.

I still don't know, I told her.

Later that night I lay in bed, worrying.

Are they going to make it? I wondered. *Simon and Duane, Paul and Louise.*

Her wounds were healing, I decided—our Louise—she ate the soup they heated for her in the plane's galley, but in the aftermath of her attack, Louise had yet to speak.

This too is a form of healing.

Look what they've survived so far, I told myself that night, trying to be reassuring.

If they made it through a war, they can make it through this—starting their own community, surviving the harsh winters, the soaring summer temperatures.

Bear attacks.

Other people.
But I'm worried.

I'm worried because, for these children—like my own children—the future is unclear. What will they do to feed themselves? What if they get sick? What if there's a natural disaster or bad men visit in the night with hate in their hearts? What happens when the oceans rise and the ice caps melt? Will they be able to fix what we have broken? Will they be able to save the world?

O

Here's another question.

What if empathy doesn't lead to anything?

What if—like happiness or misery—feelings of empathy hit you intensely in the moment but then wane over time? For example, when we see a homeless child, we feel a swell of empathy. The feeling brings with it a bloom of moral righteousness—*I feel empathy, therefore I am a moral being.* This, in turn, increases our conviction that we are good people. We carry that feeling of moral goodness with us through the rest of our day, and yet the child is still homeless. What have we done to help her, other than feel her pain?

O

How's it going to end? she asks.
   You tell me, I say.

O

Once upon a time there was a boy who would only say *no* and a boy who would only say *yes*. And they fought the endless war, leading their endless armies.

No! screamed one side.

Yes! screamed the other.

On and on it went, year after year.

And then one day a new generation was born. And they saw the world for what it was. The beautiful things were beautiful. The problems could be fixed. But not with *no* and not with *yes*.

Look, they said, the solution is simple.

Those with more should share with those with less.

Those who are sick should be made well.

Those who pollute the air and the sea, the forests and plains should stop.

Give, they told the world, don't take.

They knew what we didn't.

That it is impossible to be useful and sad.

How lucky we are, they said, to have so much wealth in the world, for all that wealth can be used to end the endless war and create an endless peace.

We can stop fighting.
We can clean up this mess.
We can forgive each other.
We don't have to die.
Don't you see? they cried. All we have to do is change.

O

That's it.
My story is finished. The rest is up to you.
Boo phooey.

Acknowledgments

This is my sixth published novel. The first three ended up in a drawer, then a box, and finally a wastepaper basket. I can't look at this book without seeing all of them, sentence after sentence, word after word, without seeing my mother and my grandmother, both writers, without seeing my father, who taught me not to say all my words out loud, without seeing New York City, where I learned how to be tough and funny and how to read and snake through a crowd, without seeing Sarah Lawrence College, where I studied to be a philosopher-king because I thought that was a real job, without seeing the Juvenile Rights Division of the Legal Aid Society, which was a real job, maybe the most important one, without seeing the Writers Grotto in San Francisco, where I found a community of artistic friends, without seeing Bob DeLaurentis or Warren Littlefield, my Hollywood mentors, who taught me that you can succeed beyond your wildest dreams and still be your best self. I can't look at this book without seeing my agent, Susan Golomb, who—after three novels—judged me by my work and not my sales history, without seeing Michael Pietsch, my editor and publisher, who still believes that literature should be a meritocracy, where you publish the books you love. I write books because I read books. Because books can save us. I would not be a writer without those early inspirations, without Don DeLillo or Milan Kundera or Toni Morrison or Kurt Vonnegut or Gabriel García Márquez or Haruki Murakami. I want to acknowledge them and all the other writers who continue to inspire and challenge me. And to my Kyle, my daily inspiration—don't worry, these kids are going to grow up and they're going to thrive, even though it might not seem like it all the time. I'll be honest. I never liked the acknowledgments page of a novel. It always felt too personal to me, authors sharing their earnest intimacies, but now that I'm older I feel like it matters. We must say our gratitude out loud. Résumés should have an acknowledgments page, where job applicants thank everyone in their lives who helped them. A little humility never hurt anyone. So I encourage you all to sit down and make a list, like the one above, of everyone and everything that made you who you are. I promise, it will be the most rewarding thing you do today. That's it. Thanks for reading my book.

About the Author

Award-winning **Noah Hawley** is one of the most accomplished auteurs and versatile storytellers working in television, film, and literature. Over the course of his more than twenty-year career, Hawley's work as a novelist, screenwriter, series creator, showrunner, and director has garnered acclaim—winning an Emmy®, Golden Globe®, Edgar, PEN, Critics Choice, and Peabody Award. As a bestselling author, Hawley has published five previous novels: *A Conspiracy of Tall Men*, *Other People's Weddings*, *The Punch*, *The Good Father*, and *Before the Fall*.